PRAISE FOR STEPHANIE BOND

"Stephanie Bond's latest is an entertaining tale with an interesting mix of secondary characters and character development."
—*Romantic Times* on *Seeking Single Male*

"…a sassy, ultra-sexy tone not often found in category romance."
—*Romantic Times* on *Cover Me*

"Stephanie Bond (aka Stephanie Bancroft) dishes up a tasty treat sparkling with yummy sensual tension and pure fun."
—*Romantic Times* on *Manhunting in Mississippi*

STEPHANIE BOND

Stephanie Bond was reading Harlequin novels long before she began to write them. College and a career in systems engineering briefly distracted her from her love of romance novels, but her obsession would not be denied. The writing bug bit her, and in 1997 her first Harlequin novel was released. Since that time, Stephanie has left the corporate world to write full-time, and has written numerous romantic comedies for Harlequin. She hopes that the books bring much love and laughter to her readers' lives! Visit Stephanie at www.stephaniebond.com.

Stephanie Bond

Tempt Me Twice

HARLEQUIN®

TORONTO • NEW YORK • LONDON
AMSTERDAM • PARIS • SYDNEY • HAMBURG
STOCKHOLM • ATHENS • TOKYO • MILAN • MADRID
PRAGUE • WARSAW • BUDAPEST • AUCKLAND

ISBN 0-373-83660-0

TEMPT ME TWICE

Copyright © 2004 by Harlequin Books S.A.

The publisher acknowledges the copyright holder
of the individual works as follows:

ABOUT LAST NIGHT...
Copyright © 1999 by Stephanie Bond Hauck.

SEEKING SINGLE MALE
Copyright © 2001 by Stephanie Bond Hauck.

ABOUT LAST NIGHT…

This book is dedicated to romance booksellers everywhere, who do their part to ensure that readers find a happy ending. Thanks so much for your ongoing support.

1

"PINEAPPLE JUICE," Janine Murphy said, holding back her sister's light brown hair to scrutinize the two hickeys on her neck. Or was it one? She blinked, trying to focus through the effects of a half bottle of wine on an empty stomach—the piece of her own bachelorette party cake didn't really count. Two hours ago she'd eaten the exclamation points at the end of GOOD LUCK, JANINE!! But after reflecting on her and Steve's relationship most of the evening, she was beginning to think question marks would have been more appropriate.

"Drinking pineapple juice will make hickeys go away?" Marie met her gaze in the dresser mirror, her eyebrows high.

Janine nodded and the movement sent showers of sparks behind her eyes. She wet her lips and spoke carefully around her thickened tongue. "The vitamin D helps the broken blood vessels heal."

Marie screwed up her face. "When you put it that way, it's kind of gross."

"Good," Janine said, letting Marie's hair fall back in place. "Because it *looks* kind of gross. You're not in high school anymore. Besides, hickeys can be dangerous."

Her sister laughed. "What can I say? Greg's an animal."

Envy surged in Janine's chest. She'd been living vicariously through Marie's sensual escapades for years, listening to her adventures in between offering homeopathic treatments for bladder infections from too much friction, skin rashes from flavored body potions and strained muscles from unnatural positions. "Well, you better tell Greg to stay away from your jugular with those Mick Jagger lips of his."

"Always the doctor," Marie said with a wry smile.

"Physician's ass..." She stopped and they giggled at her words. "Physician's assistant," she corrected primly, then fell back on her bed where they were sitting amidst stacks of gifts. Marie fell back too, toppling boxes, and they broke into gales of laughter.

Janine sighed and toyed with her empty wineglass. "Thanks for arranging the party, sis. It was fun."

"You're welcome," Marie said. "But don't lie. These kinds of things are always a roaring bore for the guest of honor."

She laughed—her older sister was nothing if not honest. Instead of basking in the glow of the spotlight, Janine had spent the evening nursing a bottle of zinfandel, listening to a roomful of women talk about their fabulous sex lives. Someone had started a round robin of, "What was your most memorable encounter?" and when her turn came, she'd recounted a fantasy as if it had actually happened. She'd felt a little guilty about lying, but somehow, the middle of a raucous bachelorette party didn't strike her as the best place to divulge the fact that she was a virgin. Not even Marie knew.

Janine sipped her wine and reflected on her chaste history. Her virginity certainly wasn't a source of personal embarrassment. On the other hand, she didn't deserve to be pinned with the good-girl-of-the-year ribbon—given the right man and the right circumstances, she imagined she would have indulged as enthusiastically as the next person. She'd simply…never gotten around to having sex. In high school she'd been too shy to attract a boyfriend. In her ten grueling years of part-time college and med school, she'd been too busy working and studying to be a social butterfly. And afterward…well, afterward, she'd met Steve.

"I just wish you had let me hire some live entertainment," her sister said, breaking into her thoughts.

Janine flushed, relenting silently that her sense of modesty *was* perhaps above average. "You know that's not my style."

Marie scoffed. "After that story about doing it on a penthouse balcony?"

"Oh, that." Janine smiled sheepishly. "I, um, might have stretched the truth a tad."

"How much?"

"Like a piece of warm taffy."

Her sister laughed. "You have a great imagination—that part about you dropping a shoe really had me going."

The details were specific because she'd relived the hot summer-night scene in her head so many times. She suspected her claustrophobia made her fantasize about open spaces, and she suspected her celibacy made her fantasize, period.

"And I thought your penis was pretty impressive," Marie continued, her lips pursed.

"Thanks," Janine said a bit wistfully. "I didn't think it was half-bad myself." Marie's brainchild of seeing who could sculpt the best penis out of a Popsicle before it melted had been a big hit, especially after the wine had started flowing.

"I guess Steve was your inspiration."

Janine pushed her long hair behind her ears to avoid eye contact. "I got an A in anatomy."

Marie's eyes lit with curiosity. "Oh? Is the infamous plastic surgeon's operating equipment lacking?"

For all she knew, Steve's equipment could be as blue as her Popsicle prizewinner, but she decided to cover. "Marie, I'm not going to discuss my future husband's physical assets."

Marie pouted, then assumed a dreamy look, already distracted. "Can you believe that in less than forty-eight hours you'll be a married woman?"

She stared at the ring on her left hand, the cluster of huge diamonds perched atop a wide platinum band—a priceless heirloom that once belonged to Steve's grandmother. "Yeah, married." She wished the light-headed anticipation and breathless impatience she'd read about in *Bride* magazine would sweep down and roll away the stone of anguish in her stomach. Wasn't cold feet a malady for the groom?

Marie held up a troll doll wearing a bridal gown. "Ugh. Who gave you this?"

"Lisa. It's kind of scary, don't you think?"

"Well, she's still bitter over her divorce. She told me she ran her husband's Armani suits through the wood shredder and mulched her azalea bushes. Cold, huh?"

"Brrr."

"Heeeey, what about this sexy little number?"

She had to hold her temple when she turned her head. Upon seeing the pink and black bustier and garter belt, she frowned. "Sandy."

Marie pushed herself to her feet, holding the outfit in front of her curvaceous figure, and posed in the mirror. "Why the attitude? I think it's hot."

Propping herself up on her elbow, Janine twirled a strand of honey-colored hair around her finger. Her split ends needed to be trimmed before the rehearsal dinner tomorrow—how would she be able to fit in an appointment? "It might have something to do with the fact that she assured me pink was Steve's favorite color on a woman."

Marie's mouth formed a silent O. "Well, she's his receptionist. She should know, I suppose."

"*I* didn't know," Janine murmured, feeling ridiculously close to tears.

"Oh, come on. You don't think there's anything going on between Steve and that bimbo, do you?"

She shook her head. "Honestly, I don't think he has enough sex drive to have an affair." Her fingers flew to her mouth. Had she actually said that?

Marie's eyes flew wide. "Oh? You should get drunk more often." She bounced on the corner of the bed, scattering more boxes. "Do tell."

Janine hesitated, wondering how much of her musings could be attributed to last-minute jitters.

"Come on," Marie urged. "I gathered that you and Steve don't exactly set the sheets on fire, but I figured it wasn't all that important to you."

"Should it be?"

"What?"

"Important to me. Sex, I mean."

Marie's eyes widened. "You're asking *me*?"

She smirked. "Try to be objective, sis. Haven't you ever had a good relationship without great sex?"

"Let me think—no."

"You're a big help."

"Okay, I'm sorry." She crossed her arms and donned a serious expression. "What seems to be the problem? Foreplay? Duration? Frequency?"

"Frequency would cover it, I think."

"Hey, lots of couples abstain for several weeks before the wedding to, you know—" she pedaled the air with her fists "—shake things up a little."

"We've abstained for longer than a few weeks."

"How long?"

"A year."

Marie's eyes bulged and she guffawed. "No, really."

"*Really.*"

"But you've only known the man for a year!"

"Precisely."

Her sister's head jutted forward. "You've *never* had sex with Steve?"

"Bingo."

"Unbelievable!" Jumping to her feet, Marie began pacing and waving her arms. "How come you never said anything?"

At the moment she was wishing she *still* hadn't said anything, and now she darn sure wasn't going to admit she was a virgin on top of everything else. "I started to mention it several times, but I was just too…I don't know—embarrassed, I guess."

"So have you two ever talked about it?"

"I've brought up the subject lots of times, but he only said that he wanted to wait until we're married."

"Which explains why he proposed so quickly."

Janine frowned.

"And the fact that he loves you, of course," Marie added hastily. "Maybe you need to be more aggressive. You know, take the bull by the horns, so to speak."

She reflected on the few awkward episodes when she'd tried to make her physical needs known to Steve. "I've tried everything short of throwing myself at him."

"Hmm. Maybe he's truly trying to be chivalrous."

She pursed her lips and nodded. "And I'm glad he respects me. But it's more than not having sex. He gets angry when I bring it up, and he shuts me out. Sometimes he doesn't call for days afterward."

Marie let out a low whistle. "Sounds like he might have some hang-ups. Maybe he's burnt out from fixing all those breasts and butts and lips and chins."

"Maybe," she agreed.

"Well, you know he's a full-fledged hetero—Steve's other girlfriends weren't known for their, ahem, virtuous restraint."

Janine closed her eyes, suddenly sick to her stomach. "That's what worries me. I've heard him say there are two kinds of women—the ones you sleep with and the ones you marry."

Marie winced. "Uh-oh. Therapy alert."

Janine nodded, blinking back tears.

"So if you're worried, why did you say yes?"

She inhaled, then sat cross-legged. "Good question. I think I need another glass of wine."

Marie obliged, filling her lipstick-smudged glass from the bottle sitting on the dresser. "No more for me, I'm going over to Greg's later."

Janine swallowed a mouthful of the sweet liquid, savoring the slight tingle as it slid down her throat. "Why did I say yes? Because Steve is great-looking and he has a terrific future, and he's charming and he likes the same things I do."

"Harvesting herbs and practicing yoga?" Marie looked dubious.

"Okay, not *every thing* I like to do, but we're good to-gether—you said so yourself."

"Uh-uh," her sister denied with a finger wag. "I said you *look* good together—blond and blue-eyed, you the flower child, he the Valley guy. But that doesn't mean you're *good* together."

This conversation was not making her feel better. No one at the clinic was more surprised than she when Steve Larsen, the hunky surgeon who had every woman in white shoes worked into a lather, had asked her out. Frankly, she'd antic-

ipated losing her virginity rather quickly to the ladies' man
with the notorious reputation, but instead, he had scrupulously avoided intimate contact.

"Steve's a gentleman," she murmured.

"Janine!" Marie said, exasperated. "You shouldn't marry
the guy just because you think he's nice. Are you sure you
want to spend the rest of your life with Steve Larsen?"

She'd lain awake last night asking herself the same question, wallowing in her concerns, trying to sort through her
overblown fantasies of passionate love and what appeared to
be a less interesting reality. "His life and his family are just
so…fascinating."

"You're fascinating," Marie insisted.

"I thought I was the one drinking. Sis, I have the most boring life of any person I know."

Marie lifted her hands. "I'm sure there are exciting things
going on at the clinic all the time."

"Oh, yeah, flu season gives me goose bumps."

Marie crossed her arms. "Okay, I'll bite—what would you
consider exciting?"

Janine studied the ceiling, smiling in lazy wishful thinking.
"I'd like to be caught up in a passionate relationship with
Steve—you know, where we can't keep our hands off each
other. I want…something irrational. Illogical. And highly irregular."

Her sister sighed. "Don't we all? If you're having second
thoughts, you need to be proactive. Look in the mirror, Janine. In case no one's told you, you don't have to settle."

"Spoken like a true sister," she teased, but panic swirled in
her stomach. She gripped her glass tighter. "And I don't feel
like I'm settling…most of the time. I love Steve, and I know
sex isn't everything, but what if he and I aren't physically
compatible?"

Marie angled her head. "Couples can work through those
things, although Steve doesn't strike me as the kind of guy
who would agree to see a counselor."

"You got that right." Steve prided himself on having his

life together, from his thriving cosmetic surgery practice to his low golf handicap.

Marie quirked her mouth from side to side. "You're not married yet. There's still time."

Janine laughed miserably. "Right, I can just see telling Mother I'm canceling the wedding because Steve won't have sex with me."

"No, I mean you still have time to find out if the two of you are sexually compatible." Her mouth curved into a mischievous smile. "Where is Steve tonight?"

"The groomsmen gave him a bachelor party at the resort. He's spending the night there."

"Perfect! You said you'd tried everything short of throwing yourself at him, right?"

"Yeah," Janine offered, wary.

Marie held up the pink bustier and grinned. "I can't think of a better outfit to wear while throwing yourself at the man you're about to marry."

"But—" Her mind spun for a good reason to object, except she couldn't think of one.

"Try it on and see how it looks."

Janine stood and considered the outrageous getup while she sipped her wine. "I don't know if I can figure out all those hooks."

Her sister scoffed. "I have one of these things, although it's not nearly as nice." She glanced at the label and whistled. "Darn, Sandy must have dropped a pretty penny on this outfit."

"Steve obviously overpays her," Janine said, then immediately felt petty. Steve's receptionist wasn't to blame for the holes in their relationship. Maybe Marie was right—maybe she hadn't been vocal enough about her...needs.

"A little big," Marie observed, handing over the various pieces of the naughty ensemble, "but probably more comfortable this way."

Janine held up the lingerie, incongruous against her long, shapeless navy dress. A woman of twenty-nine had needs, after all.

"You're going to rock his world," Marie said over her shoulder.

She took her vitamins every day, she stayed fit, she read *Cosmo*...she could do this. Besides, she was a summer—pink was on her palette. "Okay, I'll do it."

Marie clapped her hands. "What a story for me to tell your daughter."

"Not until she's fifty, or I'm dead, whichever comes first."

MINUTES LATER, they were still struggling to get all the pieces in place. Marie grunted behind her and jerked the bustier tighter. "Inhale and hold it."

"I thought you said this was a little big," Janine gasped, afraid to exhale. "I think you detached a rib."

"For Steve's sake, I hope this thing is easier to remove than it is to get on." With a final yank, Marie straightened and backed away. "Where are those black heels you bought when we were at the mall a few months ago?" She walked to the closet.

"You mean those shoes you made me buy because they were such a great deal but they weren't such a great deal because I've never worn them?"

"Yeah."

"On the bottom shelf in the orange box."

Marie went to the closet, and emerged, triumphant. After Janine stepped into the shoes, she stared in the full-length mirror at the pink-and-black creation: the boned pink satin bustier pushed her breasts to incredible heights and left her shoulders bare above black ruffly trim. Black laces criss-crossed her back, and Marie had tied them off with a large bow at the top. The matching panties were cut high on the legs, veeing below her navel, and trimmed with more scratchy lace. The black garter belts connecting the bottom of the bustier with the top of her thigh-high black hose were drawn so tight, she was sure if they popped, she'd be maimed for life. "If I had a feather boa, I could walk onto the set of *Gunsmoke*."

Behind her, Marie laughed. "You look awesome! You hide

that fab figure of yours. Believe me, Steve won't know what hit him. You two will be so exhausted after tonight, you'll have to postpone the wedding."

Maybe it was the effects of the wine, but she had to admit she was feeling pretty sexy, albeit a little shaky, in her stiletto heels. "But what will I do?"

"I'll drop you off at the resort, and you can surprise him."

She looked down. "I'll be arrested if I walk into the hotel like this."

Her sister went back to the closet and returned carrying a black all-weather coat. "Here."

Janine shrugged into the coat and belted it.

"See—perfectly innocent," Marie said. "No one will ever know that beneath the coat is a red-hot siren getting ready to sound."

"But what will I do for clothes tomorrow?"

"Are you serious? You two won't leave that room. Don't worry, I'll come early and bring your outfit for the rehearsal dinner. Now let's get going before you lose your nerve."

Janine grabbed Marie's arm. "I think I'd better call him first."

"But this is supposed to be a surprise!"

"But what if he isn't there? I mean, what if the guys stay out late?" She fished a thick phone book from a deep drawer in the nightstand.

Marie checked her watch. "It's after midnight, and it'll take us thirty minutes to get to the resort."

"But if they went out, the bars are still open."

Her sister sighed. "Okay, but no talking—if he answers, just hang up."

"Agreed," she said, dialing. An operator answered after a few rings and transferred her to Steve's room. When the phone started ringing, for the briefest second she hoped he wouldn't answer, to let her off the hook. She *was* a little tipsy, after all, and things would most likely make sense again in the morning. Their relationship was strong and their sex life would probably be great after they were married.

But on the third ring, he picked up the phone. "Hello?" he mumbled, obviously roused from sleep.

A thrill skittered through her at the sound of his smoky voice. He wasn't out at the strip clubs with the guys after all—not that she'd been worried.

"Hello?" he repeated.

She smiled into the phone, then hung up quietly, considerably cheered and suddenly anticipating her little adventure. They would make love all night, and in the morning she would laugh at her fears. She stood and swung her purse over her shoulder, then grinned at Marie. "Let's go."

But while climbing into her sister's car—she practically had to lie down to keep the boned bustier from piercing her—she did have one last thought. "Marie, what if this stunt doesn't work?"

Her sister started the engine and flashed her a smile in the dark. "Whatever happens, Janine, this night could determine the direction of the rest of your life."

DEREK STILLMAN MUMBLED a curse and rolled over to replace the handset. He missed the receiver and the phone thudded to the floor, but his head ached so much he didn't move to replace it. Just his luck that he'd finally gotten to sleep and someone had called to wake him and breathe into the receiver. He lay staring at the ceiling, wishing, not for the first time, he were still in Kentucky. There was something about feeling like hell that made a person homesick, especially when he hadn't wanted to make the trip to Atlanta in the first place.

The caller had probably been Steve, he thought. Maybe checking in to see how he was feeling. A second later he changed his mind—his buddy was too wrapped up in enjoying a last night of freedom to be concerned about him. He sneezed, then fisted his hands against the mattress. Confound his brother, Jack! In college Jack had been closer to Steve than he, but since Jack had dropped out of sight for the past couple of months, Derek had felt obligated to stand in as best man when Steve had asked him. Once again, he was left to pick up his younger brother's slack.

He inhaled cautiously because his head felt close to bursting. He'd obviously picked up a bug while traveling, which only added insult to injury. On top of everything else, the timing to be away from the advertising firm couldn't be worse—he was vying for the business of a client large enough to swing the company well into the black, but he needed an innovative campaign for their product, and soon. If ever he could use Jack, it was now, since he'd always been the more creative one. Derek was certain their father had established the Stillman & Sons Agency with the thought in mind to try to keep Jack busy and out of trouble, but so far, the plan had failed.

Hot and irritable, Derek swung his legs over the side of the bed and felt his way toward the bathroom for a glass of water. His throat was so parched, he could barely swallow. He banged his shin on a hard suitcase, either his or Steve's, he wasn't sure which. If his trip hadn't been enough of an ordeal, he'd arrived late at the hotel and they'd already given away his room. Since Steve was planning to be out all night partying, he'd offered Derek his room, and since Derek had felt too ill to join the rowdy group for the bachelor party, he'd accepted.

The tap water was tepid, but it was wet and gave his throat momentary relief. He drank deeply, then stumbled back to bed, knowing he wouldn't be sleeping again soon.

Too bad he hadn't come down with something at home. Then he would've had a legitimate excuse to skip the ceremony. He thought of Steve and grunted in sympathy. *Marriage.* Why on earth would anyone want to get married these days anyway? What kind of fool would stake his freedom on a bet where the odds were two failures out of every three? Wasn't life complicated enough without throwing something else into the mix?

They were all confirmed bachelors—he, Jack and Steve. Steve was the womanizer; Jack, the scoundrel; and he, the loner. He couldn't imagine what kind of woman had managed to catch Steve Larsen's eye and keep it. The only comment his buddy had made about his fiancée was that she was sweet, but anyone who could convince Steve to set aside his philandering ways had to be a veritable angel.

Achy and scratchy, he lay awake for several more minutes before he started to doze off. Oddly, his head was full of visions of angels—blond and white-robed, pure and innocent. A side effect of the over-the-counter medication, he reasoned drowsily.

2

"I'M SORRY, ma'am, but I can't give you a key to Mr. Larsen's room without his permission." The young male clerk gave Janine an apologetic look, but shook his head.

Janine bit down on her lower lip to assuage her growing panic. What had she gotten herself into? Marie was long gone and said she was going to stop by Greg's on the way home. Janine would have to call a cab to get a ride back to the apartment they shared. Which would be fine except she'd left her purse in Marie's car, and she had no money or apartment key on her person.

And beneath the raincoat, had very little *clothing* on her person.

"Okay, call him," she relented. It would still be a surprise, just not as dramatic.

The clerk obliged, then looked up from the phone. "The line's busy, ma'am."

She frowned. Who could Steve be talking to at one in the morning? A sliver of concern skittered up her spine, but she manufactured a persuasive smile. "He's probably trying to call *me*. If you'll give me his room number, I'll just walk on up."

"I'm afraid that's against hotel policy, ma'am." The teenager ran a finger around his collar, and he looked flushed.

Sizing up her options, she leaned forward on the counter, making sure the coat gaped just enough for a glimpse of the pink bustier. She looked at his name tag. "Um, Ben—may I call you Ben?"

He nodded, his gaze riveted on the opening in her coat.

"Ben, Mr. Larsen is my fiancé, and we're getting married here on Saturday. I dropped by to, um, surprise him, and I'd hate to tell him that you're the one who wouldn't let me up to his room."

Ben swallowed. "I'll call his room a-g-gain." He picked up the phone and dialed, then gave her a weak smile. "Still busy."

She assumed a wounded expression, and leaned closer. "Ben, can't you make an exception, just this one teensy-weensy time?"

"Is there a problem here, Ben?"

Janine turned her head to see a tall blond man wearing a hotel sport coat standing a few steps away.

The young man straightened. "No, Mr. Oliver. This lady needs to see a guest, but the line is busy."

The blond man's clear blue eyes seemed to miss nothing as his gaze flitted over her, then he turned to Ben, obviously his employee. "Ben, there seems to be a bug going around and you look a little feverish. Why don't you take a break and I'll help our guest."

Ben scooted away and Mr. Oliver took his place behind the counter. "Good evening, ma'am. I'm Manny Oliver, the general manager. How can I help you?" His smile was genuine, and his voice friendly. She immediately liked him and her first thought was that he was as sharp as a tack. She hoped she didn't look drunk.

"I'm Janine Murphy and I came to visit my fiancé, Steve Larsen. We're having our rehearsal dinner here tomorrow— I mean, tonight, and our wedding in your gazebo on Saturday."

He nodded. "Congratulations. I'm familiar with the arrangements. Now, let me see what I can do for you." He consulted a computer, then picked up the phone and dialed. A few seconds later, he returned the handset. "Mr. Larsen's phone is still busy, but I'd be glad to walk up and knock on his door to let him know you're here."

The best she could manage was a half smile.

Mr. Oliver leaned on the counter, an amused expression on his smooth face. "Why do I have the feeling there's more to this story?" He nodded to her gapped coat.

Janine pulled her coat lapels closed. "I...I thought I would surprise him. He's staying here tonight because his house is full of relatives and his groomsmen were taking him out for his bachelor party."

He checked his watch. "And he's back already?"

She nodded. "I called before I left, and he answered the phone."

"So he *does* know you're coming?"

"No, I hung up. This is supposed to be a surprise."

He pursed his lips and mirth lit his eyes. "You've never done anything like this before, have you?"

Janine winced. "No, but after a half bottle of wine, it seemed like a good idea when my sister suggested it."

Suddenly he laughed and shook his head. "You remind me of some friends of mine."

"Is that good?"

Pure affection shone on his face. "Very."

"So you'll give me his room key?"

He stroked his chin as he studied her. "Ms. Murphy, even though it's none of my business, I have to ask because you seem like a nice woman." He lowered his chin and his voice. "Don't you think it's a little risky to surprise a man on the night of his bachelor party?"

"But he was asleep when I called," she said.

He pressed his lips together and lifted his eyebrows, then stared at her until realization dawned on her.

"Oh, Steve wouldn't," she said, shaking her head.

"Alcohol can make a person do things they wouldn't ordinarily do," he said, giving her a pointed look. Then he patted her hand. "My advice would be to save it for the honeymoon, doll."

She wasn't sure where the tears came from, but suddenly a box of tissues materialized and the man was dabbing at her face.

"You'd better switch to waterproof mascara before the ceremony," he chided gently, and she had the feeling he'd wiped away many a tear. "Did I say something wrong?"

"N-no," she said, sniffling. "It's just that...well, I don't want to wait for the honeymoon—that's sort of why I came here."

His eyes widened slightly. "Oh. Well, now I understand your persistence."

"So you'll give me a key?"

Mr. Oliver chewed on his lower lip for a few seconds. "What will you do if you walk in and find him in bed with someone else?"

She blew her nose, marveling she could be so frank with a stranger. "I'd thank my lucky stars and you that I found out before it's too late."

"No bloodshed?"

Janine laughed. "I'm not armed."

"Not true, I saw those stilettos." He reached under the counter and slid an electronic key across the counter. "Top floor, room 855. Good luck."

"Thank you, Mr. Oliver." She smiled, then turned on her heel, somewhat unsteadily, and headed toward the stairs. With her claustrophobia, she avoided elevators, and the long climb upward gave her time to anticipate Steve's reaction. Maybe she should simply open the door and slide into bed with him. After all, this was her chance to let it all hang out, and to find out if Steve would continue to draw sexual boundaries for their marriage.

By the time she reached the eighth floor, her heart was pounding from nervousness and exertion. A blister was raising on her left heel, and her breasts were chafed. Being sexually assertive was hard work, and darned uncomfortable. She stopped to refresh her pink lipstick under the harsh light of a hallway fixture, and didn't recognize herself in the compact mirror. Her angular face was a little blurry around the edges, a lingering effect of her wine buzz, she assumed. Blatant desire softened her blue eyes, intense apprehension colored her cheeks and rapid respiration flared her nostrils. One look at her face—plus the fact that she was trussed up like a pink bird—and even a fence post couldn't mistake her intention.

Janine drew color onto her mouth with a shaky hand, then gave herself a pep talk while she located his room. Her knees were knocking as she inserted the electronic key, but the flashing green light seemed to say "go": Go after what you want, go for the gusto, go for an all-nighter.

So, with a deep breath—as much as she could muster in the binding bustier—Janine pushed open the door, limped inside and closed the door behind her.

THE SQUEAK OF HINGES stirred Derek from his angelic musings, and the click of the door closing garnered one open eye. Steve's conscience must have kicked in; apparently he was back earlier than he'd planned. Derek faced the wall opposite the door, and he didn't feel inclined to move. Steve could take the floor. He felt grumpily entitled to a half night's rest in an actual bed for making the darned trip south.

Suddenly the mattress moved, as if his buddy had sat down on the other side. Removing his shoes, Derek guessed. Indeed, he heard the rustle of him undressing. But then the weight of the body rolled close to him.

"Hey, honey," a woman whispered a split second before a slim arm snaked around his waist. "Tonight's the night."

Whoever she was, she had burrowed under the covers with him. Shock and confusion paralyzed him and, for a moment, he convinced himself that he was still dreaming.

"I just can't wait any longer," the woman said, suddenly shifting her body weight on top of him. "I need to know now if we're good together."

Through his medicated fog, he realized the woman was straddling him. In the darkened room, he could make out only a brief silhouette. He opened his mouth to protest, but mere grunts emerged from his constricted throat. Small, cool hands ran over his chest and his next realization was that he was being kissed—soundly. Moist lips moved upon his while a wine-dipped tongue plundered his unsuspecting mouth. A curtain of fragrant hair swept down to brush both his cheeks. His body responded instantly, even as he strained to raise himself.

Everywhere he touched, a tempting curve fit his hand. Curiosity finally won out, and he skimmed his hands over the mystery woman's body, letting the kiss happen. He'd nearly forgotten the rapture of warm, soft flesh pressed against him. He was midstroke into arching his erection against her when sanity and wakefulness returned. Extending his left hand to the side, he fumbled for the lamp switch. With a click, light flooded the room, blinding him.

He caught a glimpse of long, long blond hair and something pink before the woman drew away and screamed like a banshee. Derek caught her by the arms, strictly for self-defense, and as she tried to wrench from his grip, his vision cleared, if not his brain.

The woman was slender and dark-complexioned with wide eyes and so much hair it had to be a wig. And she was practically bursting out of some sexy getup he'd seen only in magazines that came in his brother's mail. She floundered against him, flaming the fire of his straining arousal. It appeared the woman liked to struggle, but since that was a scene he did not get into, he released her to take the wind out of her sails.

She scrambled off the bed in one motion, and ran for the farthest corner, where she hovered like a spooked animal, arms laughingly crossed over her privates. Derek's skin tingled from the scrape of her fingernails, but at least she had stopped screaming.

They stared at each other for several seconds, giving Derek time to size her up. She was around five-eight or -nine, although her black spike heels accounted for some of her height. Despite her stature, the first thing that came to mind was that she was elfin—petite, chiseled features and lean limbs, with stick-straight blond hair parted in the middle. The naughty outfit accentuated her amazing figure—her breasts were high, her waist slight, her hips rounded. Between the wig and the getup, she had to be a hooker the guys had bought for Steve.

"I thought this was Steve Larsen's room," she gasped, inching her way along the wall in the direction of the door, her gaze on a black raincoat draped over the foot of the bed.

She was a hooker who knew Steve well enough to recognize him, which didn't surprise him. "This *is* Steve's room," he said, and she stopped. Pressing a finger against the pressure in his sinuses, he pushed himself to his feet. As silly as standing around in his boxers in front of the woman seemed, having a conversation with her while lying in bed seemed even more absurd, especially since she herself was in her skivvies.

"Stay right there!" She pointed a finger at him as if a laser beam might emerge from her fingernail at will. "Who are you?"

Derek put his hands on his hips, irritated to be awakened and not amused by the idea that the woman had come to Steve's room for an eleventh-hour fling before his wedding. "Since Steve gave me his room for the night," he asserted, "maybe you should tell me who *you* are."

She shoved her hair out of her eyes, and her chest moved up and down in the pink thing that resembled a corset. She seemed very close to spilling over the underwire cups, and he felt his body start to respond again. The woman was one incredibly sexy female.

"I'm J-Janine Murphy, Steve's fiancée. "

Derek swallowed and abruptly reined in his libido. He realized he'd been cynical in his assumption about the reason for this woman's presence in Steve's room—blame it on years of witnessing his brother's shenanigans. Not many things surprised him these days, but her declaration shook him. *This* was the woman who'd snared Steve? So much for his theory of her being a missionary type. But he had to hand it to her—the woman's costume made it clear she knew how to communicate on Steve's level. Guilt zigzagged through his chest when he acknowledged he'd been affected by her himself—he, the man of steel, who prided himself on discretion and restraint.

He stared at his friend's bride-to-be and realized this was about the most awkward predicament he'd ever landed himself in. And, he thought wryly, par for the course of his life lately—in a hotel room with a gorgeous half-naked woman, and she was totally, utterly and indubitably off-limits.

Derek's dry laugh was meant to express his frustration at the accumulation of injustices of the past few months, but the woman was clearly offended.

"What's so funny?"

He pursed his mouth. "Well, now...Janine...this *is* a bit awkward." Picking up her coat, he slowly walked toward her, using the gesture of courtesy to help shield his appallingly determined arousal. "I'm Derek Stillman. Your best man."

3

JANINE FROZE, although her insides heaved upward. "My b-best man?" *Oh, please dear God, take me now—no wait, let me change clothes first.* The stranger's smug expression mortified her, but at least he'd carried her coat to her, which she snatched and held over herself.

"Technically speaking," he said, curling his fingers around one wrist and holding his hands low over his crotch, "I guess I'm *Steve's* best man."

She snapped her gaze back to his and squinted at him in the low lighting. She was certain she'd never met him before, although granted, people looked different with their clothes off. He was a big man—even in her preposterous shoes, he towered over her. His dark hair was cropped close at the sides and back, with the top just long enough to stick up after sleeping. His face was broad and pleasing, with a strong jaw, distinct cheekbones and an athletically altered nose which now appeared red and irritated. On his mouth was the telltale stain of her pink lipstick and she cringed, recalling the way she'd kissed the perfect stranger. But on the list of kissing transgressions, surely kissing your fiancé's best man was worse than kissing a perfect stranger... Her brain was too fuzzy to work it all out—she'd have to ask Marie.

But one realization did strike her with jarring clarity: she hadn't even realized she wasn't kissing Steve.

With that sobering thought, Janine refused to look lower than Derek's wide shoulders, although she vividly remembered the mat of hair she'd run her fingers through while straddling the man. She wasn't even sure Steve *had* hair on his chest. A wave of dizziness hit her and she realized the bustier was probably limiting her oxygen supply. "You..."

Are the most physically appealing man I've ever laid eyes on. "You must be Jack's brother."

The man's mouth tightened almost imperceptibly. "Yes."

"You went to college with Steve?"

He nodded, and she noticed his eyes were the deepest brown—quite intense with his dark coloring.

"Um…" She glanced around, spying Steve's suitcase sitting next to a writing desk. "Where *is* Steve?"

"At his bachelor party."

Not a man of many words, this one. "Why aren't you with him?"

"I wasn't—that is, I'm not—feeling well."

She peered closer, taking in his drooping eyes. "Do you have a cold?"

"I suppose."

"What are you taking for it?"

His eyebrows knitted in question.

"I'm a physician's assistant."

He looked thoroughly unimpressed. "I'm taking some stuff I picked up in the gift shop."

He reached for a handkerchief on the nightstand next to the bed, then sneezed twice, each time causing his flat abdominal muscles to contract above the waistband of his pale blue boxers—strictly a medical observation of his general fitness level, she noted, which was important when prescribing treatment. "Bless you. You really should get some rest."

He turned watery eyes her way and smirked. "I was trying."

Her cheeks flamed. As if the mix-up were *her* mistake, as if she'd planned this fiasco. Flustered, she flung out her arm to indicate the dark walls of the room, but somehow ended up pointing to the bed where the covers lay as contorted as her thoughts. "What…when…" She jerked back her offending hand. "Why did Steve give you his room?"

"My flight was late, and I didn't have a room when I arrived. Steve said he wouldn't need—" He broke off and averted his gaze.

"Wouldn't need what, Mr. Stillman?"

Glancing back, he massaged the bridge of his nose and winced. "Don't you think we can drop the formalities since we're both in our underwear?"

At his sarcastic tone, anger drove out any vestiges of fear that lingered, since she didn't appear to be in imminent danger of anything other than dying of humiliation. Still, she forced herself to speak in a calm tone to Steve's best man. "Okay. *Derek*, Steve wouldn't need what?"

He wiped his mouth with the back of his hand, then frowned at the streak of pink lipstick. Janine squirmed when he looked to her. "He said he wouldn't be needing the room—I suppose the guys were going to party all night." His gaze fell to her shoes and one corner of his mouth drew back. "I take it he wasn't expecting you."

She summoned the dredges of her pride and lifted her chin. "It was supposed to be a surprise."

"Trust me, it was," he said, then retrieved a pair of wrinkled jeans from the arm of a chair.

Distracted by the fluid motion of his body performing the simple act of getting dressed, she almost lost her own opportunity to don her coat in relative privacy. But she quickly recovered, and by the time he'd pulled on the jeans and a gray University of Kentucky sweatshirt, she had buttoned the coat up to her chin and knotted the belt twice. With his back to her, he used the palm of his hand and pushed his chin first right, then left, to the tune of two loud pops of his neck bones.

"You really shouldn't do that," she admonished. "It could... be...danger...ous..." She trailed off when he looked up, his lips pursed, his expression perturbed. Janine swallowed. "M-maybe I should call Steve on his cell phone."

He nodded curtly and walked past her into the bathroom without making eye contact. A few seconds later the muffled sound of the sink water splashing on floated out from behind the closed door.

With her heart in her throat, Janine trotted to the nightstand, then followed the phone cord to the handset that lay under the bed. Now she knew why the line had been busy, and with shock realized that smoky voice on the other end when she'd called from home had been none other than Derek Stillman's. She bit the inside of her cheek. What a fine mess she'd gotten herself into. Steve's surprise was ruined, and she'd never live down this scene. She sat on the floor, her finger hovering over the buttons. Maybe she should just call a cab and vamoose, after swearing Derek to secrecy. Assuming she could trust the man. He seemed pretty surly for someone who was supposed to be a friend of Steve's.

Her fingers shook as she punched in the number of her sister's boyfriend's place, but no one answered and Greg didn't believe in answering machines. She called twice more, allowing the phone to ring several times, to no avail. Next she called her and her sister's apartment, but Marie was either in transit, or still at Greg's—probably indulging in something wonderfully wicked. When the machine picked up, she left a quick message for Marie to stay put until she called again.

Janine hung up and glanced over her shoulder at the closed bathroom door, still tingling over the accidental encounter with the unsettling stranger. Talk about crawling into the wrong bed—Goldilocks had officially been unseated. To top it off, Derek had shrugged off the sexualized situation with a laugh, while she'd been shaken to her spleen, not just by her unbelievable gaff, but by her base response to the man's physique.

To curtail her line of thinking, she punched in Steve's cell-phone number, willing words to her mouth to explain the awkward situation in the best possible light. Steve might get a big kick out of the mix-up and return to the hotel right away. She brightened, thinking the night had a chance to be salvaged, if they could shuffle the best man to another room, that is. After Steve's phone rang three times, he answered over a buzz of background noise. "Hello?"

"Hi, this is Janine," she said, fighting a twinge of jealousy that Steve was probably out ogling naked women. The fact that she'd been ogling his friend didn't count because she hadn't gone looking for it, and besides, Derek hadn't been naked. Completely. And she hadn't tipped him.

The background noise cleared suddenly, then he said, "Janine, look over your shoulder."

Perplexed, she did, and scowled when she saw Derek standing in the room, talking into a cellular phone.

"Steve left his phone in the bathroom," he said, his voice sounding in her ear. His mouth was pulled back in a sham of a smile.

She replaced the handset with a bang. "That's not funny."

He pressed a button on the phone and pushed down the antenna. "No. Not as funny as the fact that you can't recognize the voice of the man you're going to marry."

Annoyed, she flailed to her feet and was rewarded with a head rush, plus a stabbing pain in her heel that indicated she had burst the blister there. "You sound like him," she insisted. Only to tell the truth, Derek's voice was deeper and his speech slower, more relaxed.

Derek's jaw tightened, but when he spoke, his voice was casual. "I'm nothing like Steve."

An odd thing to say for someone who was supposed to be Steve's friend, but he was right. Steve was gregarious, carefree. Derek carried himself as if the weight of the world yoked those wide shoulders, and she wondered fleetingly if he had a wife, children, pets.

He held up a pager. "This was in the bathroom too."

Her shoulders fell in defeat. It was obvious Steve hadn't wanted to be bothered tonight. "Do you know where he went?"

He shook his head and shoved his feet into tan-colored loafers. "Sorry."

She frowned as he strapped on his watch, then stuffed a wallet into the pocket of his jeans. When he picked up a small suitcase and a computer bag, then headed toward the door, her stomach lurched. "Where are you going?"

He nodded toward the door with nonchalance. "To get another room."

Humiliated or not, she couldn't help feeling panicky at the thought of Derek leaving. What must he think of her? What would he tell Steve? "But I...I thought you said the hotel was out of rooms."

Derek shrugged. "There has to be an empty bed somewhere in this place, and no offense, but I feel lousy and I need to get some sleep."

"*I'll* leave," she said quickly, walking toward the door. "I'll call my ride from the lobby."

He held out a hand like a stop sign and laughed without mirth. "Oh, no. Steve would never forgive me. The place is all yours." He put his hand on the doorknob and turned it.

"But—"

"It was, um—" he swept her figure head to toe, and for the first time, genuine amusement lit his dark eyes "—*interesting* meeting you." Then he opened the door and strode out.

4

DEREK MARVELED at the turn of events as he stumbled toward the elevator. Whew! Steve had one kinky nut of a fiancée on his hands, that much was certain. His buddy's and his brother's escapades with women never ceased to amaze him, and every time he felt the least bit jealous of their ability to attract the most outrageous litter of sex kittens, he reminded himself that their lives were roller coasters and his life was a...a...

He frowned and rubbed his temple to focus his train of thought. Searching for a metaphor to symbolize his solid, responsible position in the amusement park of life, the best he could come up with was...a chaperone. God, he felt older than his thirty-five years.

Thankfully the elevator arrived, rousing him from his unsettling contemplation. On the ride to the lobby he snorted at the memory of Janine Murphy straddling him, thinking he was Steve. Tomorrow when he felt better, he was sure he'd have a belly laugh over the case of mistaken identity, but for now he knew he desperately needed sleep. He glanced at his watch and groaned. Almost two in the morning, which meant he'd been awake for nearly forty-eight hours, thanks to Donald Phillips. And Steve Larsen. Oh, and Pinky Tuscadero.

Back in Lexington, Donald Phillips was one of the largest producers of honey in the Southeast. Dissatisfied with his product sales, Phillips had decided to shop around for a new advertising firm, and Stillman & Sons, which at the moment consisted solely of himself, was being given the opportunity to swipe the account from a larger competitor. But Derek was having one little problem: inventing a campaign designed to entice consumers to buy more honey. *Honey*, for crissake—a sweet condiment best known in the South for spreading on toast and biscuits; consequently, market growth was not projected to be explosive.

Computers and wireless phones and home stereo systems were flying off the shelves. Branded sportswear and gourmet appliances and exercise-equipment sales were booming. Large vehicles and exotic vacations and swimming pools were experiencing a huge resurgence. With all the sexy, progressive products in the world, he was chasing a darned *honey* account to save the family business.

When the elevator dinged and the door slid open, his exhaustion nearly immobilized him, but he managed to drag himself and his bags across the red thick-piled carpet to the empty reservations counter. Just his luck that everyone was taking a break. He looked for a bell to ring, but he guessed the hotel was a little too classy for ringers. Live flower arrangements the size of a person graced the enormous mahogany counter shiny enough to reflect his image—in his opinion, just another overdone element of the posh resort whose decorating philosophy seemed to be "Size *does* matter."

He wondered briefly how much green the bride and groom were dropping for the wedding. Between the rehearsal dinner, the ceremony and the reception, all of which were supposed to take place at the resort, he suspected his buddy would have to perform an extra face-lift or two to foot the bill. Derek scoffed, shaking his head. Marriage—bah. He gave his pal and the Murphy woman six months, tops.

"Hello?" he called, trying to tamp down his impatience. He was not above stretching out behind the counter to sleep if he had to.

A door opened on the other side of the elevators, and his mood plunged when Pinky herself emerged from the stairwell, pale and limping, hair everywhere, coat flapping. "Oh, brother," he muttered. The last thing he needed was to spend one more minute with the leggy siren.

Stepping up next to him, she said, "Derek, I insist you take the room."

One look into her blue eyes gave him a glimpse of Steve's

future—the woman would be a handful, even for Steve. He might have felt sorry for his pal, but, he reasoned perversely, the man who had led such a charmed life to date probably deserved a little grief. "Janine, go back upstairs."

She frowned and planted her hands on her hips. "I thought people from the country were supposed to be polite."

His ire climbed, then he drawled, "I get testy when I run out of hayseed to chaw on."

Her eyebrows came together and she crossed her arms, sending a waft of her citrusy perfume to tickle his nose. "What's that smart remark supposed to mean?"

He did not need this, this, this...aggravation, not when his body hummed of fatigue, stress and lingering lust. Derek felt his patience snap like a dry twig. He leaned forward and spoke quietly through clenched teeth. "I'll tell you what it means, Pinky. It means I left my firm in the middle of a very important project to fly here and stand in for my runaway brother in a ceremony I don't even believe in, only to catch some kind of plague and have my reservation canceled and have my sleep interrupted by a stranger crawling into my bed!"

She blinked. "Do you have blood pressure problems?"

Heat suffused his face and he felt precariously close to blowing a gasket. She and Steve deserved each other, and they'd never miss him. So after one calming breath, he saluted her. "I'm going home. Please give Steve my regrets." He turned, then added over his shoulder, "And my condolences."

He picked up his suitcase, then headed toward the main lobby, not a bit surprised to hear her trotting two steps behind him. "Wait, you can't go!"

"Watch me," he growled.

"I'm sorry—you can have the room."

Derek lengthened his stride.

"After all, you made the trip down here..."

As he approached the lobby area, a buzz of voices rose above the saxophone Muzak, reminding him of bees. But then again, he did have honey on the brain. Good grief, he needed sleep.

"And you're not feeling well," she rattled on. "Blah, blah, blah…"

The buzz increased as he rounded the corner. He stopped abruptly at the sight before him, and she slammed into him from behind, jarring his aching head.

"Oh, I'm sorry," she gasped. "I didn't realize—"

"Can you be quiet?" He pulled her by the arm to stand alongside him, too distracted by the scene to worry about her tender feelings.

The step-down lobby of the hotel was swarming with people, some in their pajamas sitting in chairs or lying on couches, others in lab coats, tending to the guests, others in security uniforms, hovering.

"What the hell?" he murmured.

"They're medics," Janine said. "Something's wrong." She walked over and knelt in front of a young man in a hotel uniform sitting in a chair looking feverish and limp. While her lips moved, Janine put a hand on the youth's forehead and took his pulse. The coat she wore fell open below the last button, revealing splendid legs encased in those black hose, and bringing to mind other vivid details about what lay hidden beneath the coat. She tossed the mane of blond hair he'd come to suspect was real over one shoulder, evoking memories of its silkiness sliding over his chest and face.

Recognizing the dead-end street he was traveling, Derek shook himself mentally and strained to remember what she said she did for a living. A nurse? A nurse's aide? No, a physician's assistant. Except the woman seemed way too flaky to oversee someone else's welfare.

She rose and patted the young man on the arm, then returned.

"What's wrong?" he asked.

Janine shrugged. "No one knows. Several employees and guests have come down with flulike symptoms, so they called for medical assistance."

The remains of pink color shimmered on her full mouth…

a mouth that had been kissing him not too long ago. His groin tightened. "Is it serious?"

She shook her head. "It doesn't seem to be. My guess is a bad white sauce served in the restaurant, or something like that." Then she stopped and angled her head at him. "Wait a minute—when did *you* start feeling bad?"

He shrugged. "When I got here, there was a mix-up on my reservation, so I hung around the lobby for a while until Steve arrived. I remember asking the clerk for directions to the gift shop to buy some cold medicine before I walked up to Steve's room."

She stepped closer and tiptoed to place her small hand on his forehead. He flinched in surprise, but relented. Her eyes were the same deep color of blue as his mother's favorite pansies. The best part of winter, she always said. His pulse kicked higher. He had to get out of here, fast.

"You're a little warm," she announced, her forehead slightly creased. "But not anything alarming."

He stepped around her, his eye on the revolving exit door on the far side of the lobby. Outside sat a yellow taxi, his escape hatch. "Listen, I'm going to grab that cab to the airport. I'll see ya, Pinky. Have a happy marriage and all that jazz." *And good riddance.*

"But wait, don't you want to see a doctor?"

He shook his head as he turned to go. "Nope."

She grabbed his arm. "Derek, what are you going to tell Steve...about tonight?"

He took in her wide eyes and her parted lips and for a minute he wondered if she knew what kind of man she was marrying. She seemed so innocent. Then he laughed at himself—dressing up in naughty lingerie and coming to the hotel to please Steve was not the act of an innocent. Besides, for all he knew, Steve *had* changed and would be a faithful husband. On the other hand, sometimes women knew their boyfriends were philanderers and didn't care, or liked the freedom it afforded them. Steve was probably well on his way to becoming a wealthy man, and money could make people overlook a variety of indiscretions. Either way, it was none of his business. He wet his parched lips. "What do you want me to tell him?"

She averted her eyes, and he could see the wheels turning in her pretty head. When she glanced back, she looked hopeful. "Nothing?"

He smirked. Nothing like honesty to get a marriage started off on the right foot. "You got it, Pinkie. Nothing happened. We ran into each other in the lobby as I was leaving."

"Okay." Her smile was tentative as he increased the distance between them. "Well, goodbye," she said, then waved awkwardly.

He nodded. "I'll leave Steve a message when I get to the airport and I'll touch base with him next week."

"We'll be in Paris for two weeks," she called.

"Better him than me," he said, knowing she couldn't hear him. He waved and smiled as if he'd said something inanely nice, then turned and strode toward the exit, his steps hurried. He couldn't wait to feel bluegrass under his feet again. Steve and Jack could have the high life and the high-maintenance women. Right now he'd settle for a honey of a good advertising idea.

And a good night's sleep to banish the memory of Steve's bride in his bed.

WITH MIXED FEELINGS swirling in her chest, Janine watched Derek's broad-shouldered frame walk out the door. She was off the hook. She could leave now and Steve would never know she'd been there. Derek had said he wouldn't mention the incident, and for some odd reason, she believed him. His seriousness had struck her—he was a man with a lot of responsibility. What had he said? That he'd left at a busy time to attend a ceremony he didn't believe in?

Actually, she should be feeling nothing but giddy relief. Instead, she had the most unsettling sensation that something...important...had just slipped through her fingers...

Janine shook herself back to the present. She still had tomorrow night—technically, tonight—after the rehearsal dinner to broach the issue of having sex with Steve. Leaning over to massage her heel, she acknowledged she might have to regroup and come up with a different outfit, but Marie would think of something.

She headed toward the pay phones, threading her way through the people in the lobby. She was tempted to offer assistance to the medics, but they seemed to have everything under control, and she was still feeling the effects of the wine. Tomorrow morning—correction, in a few hours—she'd call that nice Mr. Oliver to make certain the problem had been resolved. The last thing she needed was to have the entire wedding party food-poisoned at the rehearsal dinner. Her mother was already on the verge of a nervous breakdown.

She picked up the phone and redialed the apartment using her memorized calling-card number. Her sister answered on the first ring.

"Marie, thank God you're home."

"I just walked in the door. I stopped on the way home to pick up pineapple juice. Why aren't you, um, *busy?*"

"Because Steve's not here."

"What? But he answered the phone when you called."

"No, his *best man* answered the phone. Steve gave the guy his room because the man was sick and didn't feel like going out with everyone else." She waited for the revelation to sink in and was rewarded with a gasp.

"You mean, you greeted the best man wearing that pink getup?"

Janine relived her humiliation yet again. "Noooooo. I mean, I crawled into bed with the best man wearing this pink getup."

For once, she had achieved the impossible—Marie was struck speechless.

"Marie, are you there?"

"Are you saying—" her sister make a strangled noise "—that you put a stroke on the best man?"

"No!" she snapped. "We sort of realized the mistake, Marie."

"At what point?"

Janine remembered the kiss and experienced her first all-body blush—not completely unpleasant—then leaned against the enclosure. "My virtue is intact."

"Unbelievable! See, exciting things do happen to you."

"Really? *Humiliating* was the first word that came to my mind."

"Isn't your best man that dreamy Jack Stillman?"

"He was. But Jack disappeared, so Steve asked Jack's brother, Derek, to stand in."

"Is he gorgeous too? And single?"

Her head had started to throb again. "Marie, I didn't call to discuss the Stillman gene pool. I called to see if you would come to pick me up. I left my purse under the front seat of your car and I have no money and no key."

"Well, sure I'll come back, but don't you want to wait for Steve?"

"I don't think so." She wasn't sure she could go through with her plan to seduce Steve with the memory of another man's mouth on hers so fresh in her mind.

"You lost your buzz, ergo your nerve."

"Well—"

"Janine, if you come home, you won't be any closer to the answer you went for."

The sick feeling of anguish settled in her stomach again, but she appreciated her sister's objectivity, quirky as it was. "You're right, but Derek said the guys are supposed to be out all night."

"Okay, so you wait in Steve's room until morning." Marie laughed. "That is, unless you think he won't do it in the daylight."

Janine tried to smile, but she felt too disjointed to respond.

"Oh, wait," her sister said. "You said that the best man is staying in Steve's room."

"No," Janine said morosely. "He left."

"Left to go to another hotel?"

"No," she said, swinging her gaze toward the revolving door. Flashing lights outside the front entrance caught her attention. Two ambulances and several police cars had arrived, along with a van that bore a familiar insignia: the Centers for

Disease Control. A knot of people stood outside, as if in conference, and she recognized the general manager she'd been talking to earlier as one them. The revolving door turned and, to her amazement, Derek walked back in, his expression as dark as a thundercloud.

"He's back," she said into the phone.

"Steve?"

"No, Derek. Hang on a minute, sis. Something is happening in the lobby." With every turn of the door, more and more suited and uniformed personnel filtered into the lobby of the hotel. Mr. Oliver walked in, and his smooth face seemed especially serious.

A terrible sense of foreboding enveloped her. Janine waved at Derek and motioned him toward her. He seemed none too pleased to see her again, but he did walk toward where she stood, his gait long and agitated.

"What's going on?" she whispered.

Derek gestured in the air above his head. "I don't know. A deputy said I couldn't leave and asked me to come back inside."

A man in a dark suit and no tie lifted a small bullhorn to his mouth. "Could I have your attention, please?"

The lobby quieted, and for the first time, Janine realized just how crowded the expansive space had become. Her lungs squeezed and she breathed as steadily as she could, trying to hedge the feeling of claustrophobia. Standing next to Derek didn't help because his big body crowded her personal space. She stepped as far away from him as the metal phone cord would allow, which garnered her a sharp look from his brown eyes. With much effort, she resisted the urge to explain and gave the doctor her full attention.

The man had paused for effect, sweeping his gaze over the room. "My name is Dr. Marco Pedro, and I'm with the Centers for Disease Control here in Atlanta. As you can see, several dozen people have been stricken with an illness we are still trying to identify. With a recent outbreak of E. coli contagion on the west side of town, we can't be too careful."

Janine's knees weakened with dread. Because of her medical training, she knew what the man's next words would be.

"So, until further notice," Dr. Pedro continued, "guests cannot leave the premises. Every individual in this facility is officially under quarantine."

5

JANINE'S HEART dropped to her stomach. "A quarantine?" she whispered. *This can't be happening.* Next to her, Derek muttered a healthy oath that corresponded with the collective groan that went up throughout the lobby.

"Janine," Marie said in her ear. "What's going on?"

"The CDC just put the place under quarantine," she croaked. "I'll call you back." Then she hung up the phone unceremoniously.

"Was that Steve?" Derek asked.

"No, my sister," she replied, distracted by the uproar.

Angry guests were on their feet, firing questions at the doctor:

"For how long?"

"But I have to leave tomorrow!"

"Am I dying?"

Dr. Pedro held up his hands. "One at a time. We will answer your questions as soon as possible. The symptoms at this time don't appear to be life-threatening. For obvious reasons, we don't know how long the quarantine will last, but I estimate you'll be detained for at least forty-eight hours."

"Oh no," Janine murmured, and the lobby erupted into more chaos. A few people tried to make a run for the exits, but security guards had already been posted. Her heart tripped faster when she realized she was confined to the building, and might be for some time—a claustrophobe's nightmare.

"There is no need to panic," the doctor continued in a raised, but soothing voice. "Believe me, ladies and gentle-man, the quarantine is for your own protection and for the protection of the people outside these walls with whom you would otherwise come into contact."

As a health professional, Janine knew her first concern should be her own welfare and the safety of those around her, but as a bride-to-be, her thoughts turned to wedding invitations, ceremony programs and honeymoon reservations, all with a big red Cancel stamped on them. She swayed and reached for something to steady herself, meeting soft cotton and solid muscle.

"Easy," Derek said, righting her. "Are you okay?"

"Yes." She swallowed. "But my mother is going to have a stroke. We'll have to postpone the wedding."

One corner of his mouth slid back. "Gee, and the rest of us only have to worry about a slow, painful death from a mysterious disease."

Remorseful, she opened her mouth to recant, but the doctor spoke again.

"Please, everyone return to your rooms immediately. If you need assistance, ask anyone who is wearing a white coat or a yellow armband. If you develop symptoms, call the front desk and leave a message, a doctor or nurse will be with you soon. Medical personnel will be canvassing the hotel room by room to ensure no potential case is overlooked. We'll keep everyone updated as the situation progresses. We'd like to have this area cleared. After that, do not leave your room unless you are given permission by a person wearing a yellow armband."

Now she knew what it felt like to be hit by a truck and live, Janine decided. So many emotions bombarded her, she didn't know what to feel first—outrage that her life would have to be rescheduled, fear that she'd been exposed to a dangerous contaminant, or panic that she was expected to spend at least the next forty-eight hours in close quarters with a virtual stranger. A virtual stranger who had been vocal about the fact that he didn't want to be here at all.

A sentiment now reinforced by his brooding expression. His jaw was dark from the shadow of his beard, his eyes bloodshot and his nose irritated.

"You look terrible," she said without thinking.

The sarcastic glance he shot her way made even her creeping panties seem comfortable by comparison. In a dismissive move, he picked up his suitcase and joined the throng moving toward the elevator and the stairs.

"I'll be right behind you," she said. "I'm going to leave my name with the doctors just in case they can use my help." She was trying desperately not to think about the fact that she and Derek might be sharing a room for the rest of the night. Or the little issue of having no money, no ID, no toiletries, no makeup, no clothes, no shoes and no underwear save the costume beneath her coat.

His only acknowledgment that he'd heard her was the barest of nods. Janine frowned at his back, then turned to approach Dr. Pedro.

A crowd of guests had gathered around him, some angry, some concerned, all asking questions. The doctor spoke succinctly in a calming voice, assuring the knot of people that quarantine procedures would be distributed to every room, then asked them to clear the lobby as soon as possible. She touched the arm of a woman who appeared to be the doctor's assistant and asked if she could have a word with the doctor about a professional matter. The woman nodded and made her way toward him.

"Ms. Murphy, our paths cross again."

She swung around to see the general manager approaching her, a hint of a smile hiding the worry she knew lingered under his calm surface. "I trust you found room 855?"

"Um, yes."

He looked as if he was curious about the outcome, but was too much of a gentleman to ask.

She cleared her throat. "Mr. Oliver, I was hoping you would speak to the doctor on my behalf."

"On your behalf?"

"Well, since you can verify I arrived at the resort less than an hour ago—" she splayed her hands "—I was hoping you could arrange for me to leave."

He poked his tongue into his cheek. "Leave? If I remember correctly, when I first saw you, you were having a nose-to-nose conversation with Ben, who is now quite ill."

She leaned forward and whispered, "I'm also extremely claustrophobic."

A slight frown creased his forehead. "I suppose I could consult the doctor about your situation, Ms. Murphy, but what about your fiancé?"

"He, um, wasn't in the room after all."

He pulled a notebook from his pocket. "We have to account for all guests—I'll make a note that the room is empty."

She told herself she should keep her mouth shut, but Derek *was* ill and, therefore, probably needed to be kept under surveillance. Her medical ethics kicked in, and she sighed. "Actually, there was another gentleman in the room."

Mr. Oliver's blue eyes widened. "Oh?"

At that moment, the doctor walked up, nodding to Mr. Oliver, then to Janine. "My assistant said you wished to speak to me."

She tried on her professional face, wondering how disheveled she appeared. "Dr. Pedro, my name is Janine Murphy. I'm a P.A. here in Atlanta, and I wanted to offer my services in case you find yourself short of personnel."

He was a pleasant-looking man who seemed unruffled in the midst of the pandemonium. "It's kind of you to offer, Ms. Murphy, but we're fully staffed. Are you feeling well?"

She was sick to her stomach with worry, not to mention a little hungover, but she nodded. "Yes, and Mr. Oliver can verify I haven't been at the resort very long, so if you don't think you'll need my help, I was wondering if you might see your way to release me from the quarantine."

Dr. Pedro gave her a regretful smile. "Ms. Murphy, because of your medical training, you understand why I can't release you, but if you don't fall ill and a lot of other guests do, indeed we might need your help. I assume you have your license with you?"

Too late, she remembered she didn't have her purse, in which she kept a card-size copy of her license. "Um, no, I'm sorry, I don't have my license with me."

"If you have other ID on you, my assistant can verify your credentials over the phone."

Her shoulders fell. "Actually, I don't have ID with me, either." She conjured up a laugh. "You see, my sister dropped me off to visit my fiancé. I, um, hadn't planned an extended visit." Her temperature raised with every mortifying word that seemed determined to spill out of her mouth for both men to hear.

The dark-haired man's gaze dropped to her black high heels for a split second, then he lifted one bushy eyebrow. "I see. And how are both of you feeling?"

She squirmed and manufactured a you're-not-going-to-believe-this laugh. "Well, it turned out that my fiancé isn't here after all. He let another man have his room for the night. His best man. Our best man, that is. For the wedding."

Mr. Oliver pursed his mouth, and put pen to paper. "The man's name?"

"D-Derek Stillman."

An amused smile crossed his face. "Is that with two D's?"

The doctor looked completely lost. "Forgive me, but I'm a very busy man—"

"Wait, Dr. Pedro." Janine looked behind her, relieved to see Derek was definitely out of earshot, then turned back and encompassed both men with the smile she'd been practicing for her wedding photos. "Perhaps I could at least get a separate room." When the doctor hesitated, she added, "I barely know the man, and he's exhibiting symptoms." *Two of many reasons for separate quarters.*

Dr. Pedro made a sympathetic sound, then looked to Mr. Oliver. "Do you have any empty rooms?"

The general manager shook his head.

The doctor shrugged. "I'm sorry, Ms. Murphy."

"Perhaps I can stay with the medics," she urged, grasping.

Her face must have reflected her distress because his face softened into an indulgent smile. "No, but maybe we can arrange to place you with a female guest who isn't exhibiting symptoms and who hasn't been exposed to someone who is."

She smiled, enormously cheered.

"Unless you've already spent time in the man's room."

Her smile dropped while Mr. Oliver's eyebrows climbed. She considered lying, then glanced back to the doctor and nodded miserably.

"For how long?"

"About thirty minutes, total."

He pursed his lips. "That's not so bad."

Hope resurrected, she smiled.

"But how close was your contact?"

Her smile dropped again. "Fairly close. I checked to see if he had a fever." *Among other things.*

The manager must have read her wicked mind, because his lips twitched with suppressed mirth.

"Well, if that's all—" the doctor began.

"No," she broke in, exasperated with herself, but knowing she had to tell the truth. "Actually, I k-kissed him."

Both men blinked.

"Completely by accident," she assured them hastily. "I thought he was my fiancé." She sounded like a raving idiot, but she couldn't seem to stop, as if she needed to purge herself.

Dr. Pedro's eyes widened. "Are the men identical twins?"

"N-no, but it was very dark."

Looking completely baffled, he cleared his throat. "Ms. Murphy, if you've already been exposed, you simply must stay in the room." He turned to the general manager. "Moving guests would make it impossible to identify whether the problem is isolated to certain areas of the hotel."

Mr. Oliver nodded solemnly. "I'll make certain my staff is aware."

The man turned back to Janine. "I hope you understand, Ms. Murphy, why I cannot compromise the quarantine. I'm sorry if these circumstances put you in a delicate situation."

She nodded, backing away, wishing a tornado would rise up behind her and spirit her away to Kansas. "Thank you for your time, Dr. Pedro. And please let me know if I can be of service somehow." As if he would ask her now. He probably thought she was an escapee from the state loony bin. *She* certainly would if she were in his shoes. And right now she'd trade shoes with just about anyone in the building.

He nodded, his expression wary. "I'll examine your, um, *friend* myself as soon as possible."

"Thanks," she said, then felt compelled to add, "But he's not a friend, he's just my best man."

He stared at her as if she might be dangerous.

Janine managed a tight smile for Mr. Oliver and turned to join the exiting crowd. Maybe she had already contracted the mysterious disease and didn't realize it. How else could she explain her leaking brain cells and runaway mouth? Of course, exhaustion could have something to do with her state of mind, she reasoned as she waited at the end of the line to climb the stairs to the eighth floor. Stairwells were confining even without the swell of bodies to deal with, so she hung back.

When she leaned against the wall, she spotted a curtained door at the end of the perpendicular hallway. There had to be a way out of this place, she decided suddenly, then squared her shoulders. It was dark, she was wearing black…she could walk the half mile to the convenience store on the main road and call Marie.

After making sure no one was watching, she slipped down the hallway and opened the curtain an inch. The solitary office was neat and whimsical, but the best part was that the neat, whimsical person had left open one of the three high windows. The cool night air beckoned. She could climb up and over the windowsill, then drop the eight feet or so to the ground and be gone in a matter of minutes.

Stacking a sturdy stool on a chair beneath the window gave her enough height to reach freedom. Cursing her bulky coat, she carefully climbed up and steadied herself on the stool, then reached up and grasped the sill. While propelling herself up on her elbows, she kicked over the stool, which crashed to the floor, taking the chair with it. Janine looked down and made a face. Nowhere to go now but up unless she wanted to drop back to the marble floor. *Ouch.*

But going up wasn't as easy as she'd thought, because she'd overestimated her upper-body strength. After a few seconds, she'd managed to chin herself up to the sill, only to drop back and hang by her hands when her arms gave out. Then both high heels dropped to the floor, leaving her hanging shoeless, suspended between the window and the floor, too weak to go up, and too fond of her anklebones to go down. On hindsight, maybe trying to escape hadn't been one of her brighter ideas.

"Well, if it isn't Ms. Murphy," a man said behind her. She craned around, hanging on for dear life, to see Mr. Oliver standing in the middle of the room, his arms crossed.

She gave him her most dazzling smile. "Hi."

"You neglected to tell me and the good doctor that you were also Bat Girl."

"Um, it slipped my mind."

"Do you need a hand back to earth?"

She nodded, her chin rubbing against the wall. "That would be good."

He was tall, and had no problem assuming her weight from below. When he set her back on her feet, he gave her the tolerant look of an older, wiser brother. "Have we learned our lesson?"

Rubbing her arms, she nodded, then picked up her high heels. "I think I'll be going back to my room now."

He nodded. "Sweet dreams."

She found her way back to the stairwell, stinging from her failed jailbreak, and dragged herself up the flights of stairs. At last she reached the eighth floor and retraced her steps to room 855, surprised to see Derek waiting in the hall, his face a mask of concern. "Where did you go?"

Janine frowned at his impatient tone, not about to admit she'd been caught trying to escape. "I told you I was going to talk to the doctor."

"Oh, right," he said, his voice contrite. He pushed his hand through his hair. "Sorry, I'm a little punchy, I think." Then he turned and extended his right hand to her. A peace offering, she thought, absurdly pleased. She smiled and put her small hand in his for a friendly squeeze, and her heart pitched to the side. "I hope we can be friends when this is over, Derek."

But his smile seemed a bit dim. "That seems highly unlikely, Pinky." He extracted his hand and wriggled his fingers. "The room key?"

"Oh." Her cheeks flamed at mistaking his gesture. Was she destined to forever embarrass herself in front of this man? She shoved her hands into her pockets, hoping she might also find money she'd left the last time she'd worn the coat. One pocket produced a quarter and two pennies and a half a pack of chewing gum. From the other she pulled an ancient tube of lipstick and—she stared, incredulous—a brand-new strip of lubricated condoms. *Marie.* She groaned inwardly and slid her gaze sideways to see if Derek had noticed. He had.

"All the necessities, I see."

"But these aren't mine," she began.

"Okay, okay—whatever. Just...give me...the key." His smile was pleading and his hands were shaking. "Please, can you do that? No talking, just the key."

She swallowed and fished deeper in her pocket to remove a parking ticket, a lone glove, and finally, the room key, which he plucked from her hand.

"Where's *your* key?" she asked tartly as she returned the trinkets to her pockets. Then, remembering she sometimes stuffed cash in the inner pockets, she turned away, unbuttoned her coat and reached inside. Dammit—nothing.

"I didn't think I would need a key, so Steve took it with him."

Which made Janine wish she hadn't even asked, because Steve's name triggered another avalanche of emotions—dread, shame, remorse. She closed her eyes and moaned. Not in her wildest dreams could she imagine what else could go wrong.

"Janine Murphy, isn't it?"

She whirled and stared blankly at the attractive woman walking by in designer pajamas.

"Maureen Jiles, sales rep for Xcita Pharmaceuticals," the woman said.

Her memory clicked in, and she pulled a smile from somewhere, realizing she knew the woman from the clinic. Maureen Jiles was the buzz of the doctors' lounge—with her exotic looks and plunging necklines, she couldn't have been more suited to peddling one of the industry's new impotence drugs. And judging by the way she was eyeing Derek and licking her chops, her reputation as a man-eater had been well earned.

Janine bristled, not because the woman was ogling Derek, of course, but because she apparently ogled every man. "Maureen. Sure I remember."

"You were going to marry that yummy plastic surgeon, weren't you?" As she spoke, the woman perused Janine's outfit beneath the gaping coat, from her shiny bustier to her black-stockinged feet.

Janine nodded and jerked her coat closed, then leaned over to slip on her shoes despite her aching, raw heel. "The day after tomorrow here at the resort," she said, smiling wide. "Well, isn't this quarantine the most crazy turn of events?"

But Maureen had eyes only for Derek. "Oh, I don't mind being confined…with the right person. Janine, aren't you going to introduce me to your friend?"

"Derek Stillman," he said, stepping forward.

"And we're not friends," they said in unison.

Maureen looked back and forth between them.

"He's my best man," Janine offered.

Maureen's eyebrows drew together.

"And if you ladies don't mind," Derek said in a tired voice, "I'd like to go to bed now." He nodded to Maureen, then picked up his bags and disappeared inside the room.

"He's ill," Janine offered in the ensuing silence, then lowered her voice to add, "and probably very contagious."

The woman made a sympathetic sound. "Too bad. So why are *you* at the resort?"

"Oh, you know, taking care of last-minute wedding details," she sang. "Are you staying on this floor?"

"I'm right here," the woman said, gesturing to the door directly across from theirs.

Her empty stomach lurched. "Oh. That's…lovely."

"Where is your room?"

The door behind Janine opened and Derek appeared. He was naked to the waist, and barefoot. Splendidly so. "Here's the key," he said. "I'm going to take a shower."

Janine took the key he shoved into her hand and stood rooted to the floor after the door closed again. Interminable seconds later, she lifted her gaze to find Maureen's eyebrows up to her hairline. Everyone she worked with, including Steve's associates, would know about the sleeping arrangements in a matter of hours unless she thought of something fast.

"It's n-not what you think," she said hurriedly. "I came to see my fiancé, b-but he planned to be out all night for his bachelor party, and he'd given his room to Derek b-because he wasn't feeling well, and now there aren't any rooms available, and, well…" She swallowed, desperate. "Derek is gay."

Maureen's smile fell and she grunted in frustration. "All the cute ones are!"

Janine sighed and shook her head. "I know."

Dejected, the woman turned and unlocked her door. "Well, good night, I guess."

She gave her neighbor a fluttery little wave. When Maureen's door closed, Janine leaned heavily against the wall, mulling over the events of the past—she checked her watch—*three* hours? Geez, it seemed a lifetime had passed since she and Marie were in her bedroom, joking, planning her sexy adventure.

Whatever happens, Janine, this night could determine the direction of the rest of your life.

Janine sighed again. She'd always had a terrible sense of direction.

Numbly, she turned and faced the door, her mind reeling. She couldn't bring herself to go in because even after everything that had happened, she had the strangest feeling that things would only get worse before they got better. She wasn't sure how long she'd stood there before a security guard came by and asked that she return to her room to keep the hallways clear.

She nodded and inserted the key, then opened the door and walked inside. Derek stood by the phone with a towel around his hips, his skin glistening, his hair wet and smoothed back. Her pulse kicked up in appreciation, but she acknowledged that her body was so shell-shocked, it no longer knew how to respond appropriately. She was suddenly so tired, she wanted to drop on the spot and curl into a fetal position.

Derek looked up and held the phone out to her. "It's for you."

"At three o'clock in the morning? Who is it?" she asked wearily, taking the handset, thinking Marie had tracked her down for more details.

He shrugged and stretched out on the bed, still wearing the towel. "She says she's your mother."

6

DEREK HAD HEARD of being too tired to sleep, but he thought he might have reached the point where he was too tired even to breathe. He lay still on the bed, eyes closed, waiting for a burst of energy that would allow his lungs to expand. Meanwhile, he listened to the perpetually frazzled Janine murmur and moan and otherwise fret up her nerve to speak to her mother. Unfortunately for him, hearing was the only one of five senses that required no energy whatsoever.

"Mom?" Her voice squeaked like a cartoon character's. "I'm fine—yes, I'm sure. I just walked back into the room. Uh-huh."

She must have a decent relationship with her mother, he noted, else she wouldn't be so eager to reassure her.

"How did you know I was here? Oh, I forgot about your police scanner. You called Marie? And she told you I was here. Ah. Hmm? Yes, we're definitely under a quarantine." She cleared her throat. "Yes, we might have to consider p-postponing the wedding."

A staticy screech sounded through the phone. He opened one eye to find her holding the handset away from her ear. When the noise subsided, she pulled it closer. "Mom, I said 'might.' I'll know more in a few hours. Right now I really need to go to bed."

An unfocused thrill rumbled through his beleaguered body at her words—a base reaction to a woman's voice, he reasoned. Any woman's voice.

Her gaze lowered to meet his, and she blanched. "I m-mean, I really need to get some rest, Mom. Not necessarily in bed. A person doesn't have to be *in bed* in order to rest. Hmm?" Her eyes darted around. "The man who answered?"

He might have laughed at her predicament if he'd had the

energy. As it was, he was having trouble keeping the one eyelid half-open.

She was staring at him, chewing on her lower lip. "That was, um, the, um..."

"Best man?" he prompted, barely moving his lips.

She scowled and turned her back. "That was the...be—ll man. Yes, the bellman."

He wondered briefly what the bellman's job paid and how it compared to advertising.

"Why am I here?" Another fake laugh, except this one sounded a tad hysterical. "I'll tell you all about it later, okay?" She bent over, still talking as she moved the handset closer to the receiver. "Good night, Mom. Okay...okay... okay...bye." She jammed the phone home with a sigh, now the only sound in the room the faint whir of the air conditioner, which he'd turned up. He closed his one eye. Man, was it hot down here in Atlanta.

"I assume you requested a cot."

His eyes flew open at the accusing tone in her voice. She still wore that black raincoat, rendered even more ridiculous because he knew what lay beneath it. Her arms were crossed, and with her blond hair falling in her eyes, she looked like a cross between Rapunzel and Columbo.

He closed his eyes again to summon enough strength to speak. "Yes."

He'd nearly drifted off to sleep when she broke in again. "And are they sending one up?"

Sigh. "No."

"Why not?"

She was like a pesky fly, and he was too tired to flick his tail. "They were out," he mumbled.

The haze of sleep was claiming him again.

"Okay, you can get up."

He jerked awake and cast his weary gaze in her direction. "Excuse me?"

"I said you can get up."

He scoffed—a tremendous feat—and shook his head.

"I'm not about to share this bed with you," she said, her voice laced with indignation.

"Relax, Pinky," he muttered, then yawned. "Even if you were my type, which you're not, I'm too tired to take advantage of you."

"If…think…sleeping…you…another think coming."

He squinted at her because her voice faded in and out. "Suit yourself." It was her fault he was in this worsening mess, her fault he was in Atlanta, period. Hers and his brother's, dammit. At the moment, he wasn't sure which of them he resented more. He would sleep on it, Derek decided.

JANINE WASN'T CERTAIN he'd fallen asleep until one of his pectoral muscles twitched, causing her to jump. She pressed her lips together in anger. Surely the man didn't expect her to crawl into bed with him. She swallowed. Again.

As if he'd sensed her thoughts, he groaned in his sleep and rolled on his side to face her, hugging the pillow under his head with a bent arm. The cream-colored towel around his waist parted slightly, revealing corded thighs covered with dark hair and the faintest almost-maybe-could-be glimpse of his sex. A pang of desire struck her low—or had her corset simply ruptured? Feeling like the most naughty of little girls, she strained for a better look, but when he shifted again and the towel fell away completely, she squeezed her eyes shut and whirled to face the wall.

Yesterday she was a yearning bride-to-be, and today she was peeping at sleeping naked men. She was going to hell, she just knew it.

Bone-deep weariness claimed her and she scanned the room for another place to lie down. She hadn't realized how opulent the room was, and now she crinkled her nose at the decor, designed more for southern aesthetics than functionality. Being on the top floor, the room boasted a cathedral ceiling and a garish chandelier with fringed minishades over the lights. Several bouquets of flowers were situated around the room, emitting a cloying sweetness. The walls were a deep burgundy with a nondescript tone-on-tone design, broken up with a jutting off-white chair rail. To her left, a large pale-painted writing desk with curlicued legs and gilded accents sat at an angle. She walked over and tested it for strength, but didn't like the looks of the distance to the hard parquet floor, at least not the way her luck had been running.

A bulky armoire in the same gaudy style contained a television and colorful tourist guides. A wooden valet sat next to it, draped with Derek's jeans and sweatshirt, white socks balled on the floor. Janine stared, struck by the innocent intimacy of those socks.

Past the door, a padded straight-back chair sat mocking her with its stiffness. Next came a fat, curvy dresser with a mirror, which, to her chagrin, reflected Derek's partially nude figure reclining in the comfy-looking bed. Sprawled amongst the sheets, he seemed even larger than when standing. He looked absurdly out of place, broad shoulders and long limbs against the ornate headboard, his feet practically hanging over the end of the mattress.

Despite his massive form, the other side of the bed appeared plenty large enough for her. Perhaps if she slept on top of the covers and put some kind of divider between them—

What was she thinking? She'd be better off bedding down on the loopy cotton rug situated outside the bathroom door, a small island against the dark parquet floor. Wanting to wash her face, Janine kicked off her shoes and limped past Steve's and Derek's suitcases to the oversize bathroom. She squinted beneath the flickering pinkish light over the vanity, but reveled in the feel of the cool tile against her fiery feet.

The luxurious moss green bathroom—also vaulted—featured a large vanity area, a padded stool, an electric towel warmer and a skylight over the large tub. The wall seemed curtained with thick cream-colored towels, one conspicuously missing from the long chrome rack—the one now wrapped around Derek, she presumed.

One look in the mirror brought a flood of exhausted and humiliated tears to her eyes. She looked as though she'd been—what was the saying, *rode hard and put up wet?* Her hair lay, or rather, stood, in disarray—big yellow loops out of place, and a rat's nest at the nape of her neck. Black flecks of mascara dotted her cheeks. The rest of her makeup had faded, leaving her skin streaked and blotchy. Her head hurt and her body ached and her pride smarted. And she had to get out of this unbearable costume.

She lowered herself to the stool in front of the vanity, surveying her ragged hose, frowning at her short-lived fantasy of Steve leisurely rolling them down over her knees, calves, ankles. She removed the thigh-highs with a series of frustrating yanks and tossed them into a little shell-shaped wastebasket. After much tugging and cursing, she was finally able to loosen the lacings of the bustier. Her ribs ached from their sudden release, and she inhaled deeply enough to tempt hyperventilation. Janine tossed the offending piece of lingerie onto the vanity and scrubbed her face, then contemplated dragging herself back into the bedroom to take up residence on the skimpy little rug.

Irritation at Derek Stillman welled in her chest—if it weren't for him, she wouldn't be in this mess. If he hadn't answered the phone when she called, she would've stayed at her apartment, and none of this would have happened. And if he were half a gentleman, he would've slept on the floor and given her the bed. When Steve heard about this, he'd undoubtedly find yet another best man.

Steve.

She moaned and lowered her head, shoving her fingers deep into her hair. How was she going to explain this situation to Steve? Steve, with his family's ultraconservative sensibilities? Tears of misery streamed down her cheeks.

After a good hiccuping cry, Janine sniffed and pushed herself to her feet, then buttoned her coat over the ludicrous pink panties. Everything would look better in the light of day, she told herself, then glanced in the mirror. Well, everything except her hair, maybe.

Meanwhile, she was loath to go back into the bedroom with that, that…big uncouth man-person. She lifted her head, and through bleary eyes saw the huge Jacuzzi-style bathtub and brightened. Why not?

It was certainly big enough to sleep in, and if she lined it with towels… She jumped up and spread several of the thick towels in the bottom of the tub, telling herself it would sound much better if she could tell Steve that she and Derek slept in separate rooms. And she had to admit, she hadn't discounted the possibility of acquiring Derek's illness—whatever it was—if they shared the same air. She turned off the light and closed the door, then climbed into the deep tub, feeling only slightly foolish. After the events of the past few hours, everything was relative.

The air hung damp around her, remnants of Derek's shower. The scent of soap teased her nostrils, evoking thoughts of the intriguing man lying in the next room. She wondered suddenly if he was married, or engaged, or otherwise attached. Because for some reason, the thought of her, Steve, Derek and someone else all lying awake thinking about each other seemed very funny. A split second later, she sobered.

Steve wasn't thinking about her—he was obviously still out celebrating his last few hours of freedom, while she was bunking down in a bathtub. A sliver of resentment slid up her spine, but was quickly overpowered by the onset of claustrophobia sloping in around her. Janine concentrated on the stars through the skylight above her until the panicky sensation subsided.

She snuggled farther into the pallet of towels, smoothing out a lump under her left hip, then admitted the tub was more comfortable than she'd expected. Janine sighed, trying to mine a nugget of philosophical wisdom from her predicament, concluding instead she was living an *I Love Lucy* episode.

She fell asleep with a vision of her and Steve in black and white, toothpaste smiles, hair perfectly coifed…and sleeping in twin beds.

7

WHEN DEREK STARTED AWAKE, several seconds passed before he remembered he was in Atlanta at the resort where Steve was to be married on Saturday. Other memories of the previous night were too ludicrous to believe. When he lifted his heavy, aching head to find he was alone in the room, he nearly laughed aloud with relief. Those were some strong pills he'd taken for his cold. For a while there—

Derek chuckled despite his headache. *No way.*

From the filtered light coming through the floor-to-ceiling windows to his left, he estimated the time to be around 6:00 a.m. Typically, he'd be rolling out of bed for a bike ride, weather willing, or a run on the dilapidated treadmill that sat less than five steps from his bed. Then he'd shower and arrive at the office by seven-fifteen.

But at the moment, he needed more cold medicine, hallucinogen or not. He pushed himself out of bed gingerly, tossing the still-damp towel twined around his legs to the floor. Holding his head so it wouldn't explode, and swallowing to moisten his dry throat, he stumbled through the semidarkness to the bathroom and pushed open the door. By the illumination of the skylight, he felt along the vanity for the box of cold medicine, but instead came up with a perplexing object, flat and flexible, with ties and mysterious textures.

Bewildered, he groped for the light switch and flooded the room with light. He blinked at the pink-and-black thingamajig in his hand for an entire second before a shriek sounded behind him. Derek swung around to see a person sit up in the bathtub, and when he registered the dark coat and the blond hair, he grasped the horrifying fact that he hadn't been hallucinating after all. Gripping both sides of the tub as if she were in a sinking lifeboat, Pinky looked at him and screamed.

As if he'd taken a bite from the forbidden fruit, Derek suddenly realized he was naked. He thrust the top of her costume over his privates, straining from their morning call, and backed up against the counter. "What the devil are you doing in the bathtub?" he thundered, grimacing at the pain in his temples.

She pushed a mop of hair out of her eyes. "Sleeping."

The woman was a bona fide nutcase. "I can see that," he said calmly. "But why are you sleeping *in the bathtub?*"

"Because," she mumbled, "you were in the bed." She spit hair out of her mouth. "I can see your butt in the mirror."

He clenched and opened his mouth to say something he hadn't yet thought of, but the phone rang. Backing out of the bathroom, Derek sneezed twice on his way to answer the phone. He flung the corset on the bed and managed to grab a handkerchief before he yanked up the handset. "Hello?"

"Hey, man, what's going on over there?" Steve Larsen's voice sounded concerned, but a little indistinct, as if his last drink was not in the too-distant past. "I came back to the hotel a few minutes ago and they wouldn't let me past the gate. Something about a quarantine?"

Derek stretched the phone cord to reach his jeans on the valet. He jerked them on as he answered Steve. "Yeah, several of the guests have come down with something, and the CDC put the entire facility under quarantine."

"That's nuts. For how long?"

He sat on the bed and leaned forward to cradle his head in his hands. "The top guy said at least forty-eight hours."

Steve cursed. "Which means we'll have to postpone the rehearsal and the dinner for tonight. Maybe even the wedding." He swore again, this one causing Derek to wince. "My mother is going to be irate, and I don't know how I'm going to break it to Janine."

The topic of their conversation walked into the room. With her bare legs and feet sticking out below her wrinkled black raincoat, she resembled a bag lady. A very fetching bag lady,

Derek realized with a start. "Steve," he said, loudly enough to gain her attention. "Janine already knows about the quarantine."

"What? How does Janine know?" Steve asked. "Wait a minute—how do *you* know that Janine knows?"

Derek watched her face crumble with dread as he mulled over how best to break the news to his friend. She bit her lower lip, beseeching him to…what? "She's here at the hotel," he said, nausea rolling in his stomach. Only his brother, Jack, made him feel this way: protective, yet taken advantage of. He hated it.

"At the hotel?" Steve shouted. "Where? How?"

Janine Murphy, Derek decided, was a big girl who'd gotten them both into a big mess and she and her big blue eyes could take responsibility for it. "She's…I'll have her call you when I see her," he finished lamely, ridiculously warmed at the expression of gratitude on her face. "Are you at your place?"

"I'm at a friend's," Steve said. "But I'm going to my folks' to break the news to my mom before she hears it on television."

"Television?"

"There were at least four TV crews in front of the hotel," Steve offered. "And so many uniforms we thought a bomb had gone off. By the way, what's Janine doing at the hotel?"

For a few seconds, he panicked. "Looking for you, I suppose." Derek strained to remember what she'd said when she'd crawled on top of him, but he'd been kind of distracted at the time by her roaming hands.

"So where did you run into her?"

"We…saw each other in the lobby," he hedged, looking to her for affirmation. She nodded. And it wasn't exactly a lie, though he hated covering for the minx.

"She's a sweetheart, isn't she?" Steve asked. "I know she doesn't exactly stand out when she enters a room," he continued, causing Derek to raise his eyebrows. "You probably noticed she's kind of a nature girl."

The image of Janine in that very unnatural pink getup was

seared on his brain. "Um, no, I didn't notice that," he said wryly, certain his sarcasm was lost on his hungover friend. Janine frowned and scratched her bare foot with her toe.

Steve laughed, then lowered his voice in a conspiratorial tone. "But underneath those tentlike clothes, Janine has a nice bod."

"She sure does," Derek said without thinking, then coughed and added, "She sure does seem like a nice girl, I mean."

Her eyes widened and a hint of a smile warmed her lips. He wanted to shake his head to let her know he was only talking for Steve's sake, but once again, he didn't have the heart to hurt her feelings.

"You sound horrible, man. Do you have whatever is going around at the resort?"

"Maybe," Derek admitted.

"Well, do me a favor and don't touch any of my stuff."

Steve's casual guffaw irritated him. Derek surveyed Pinky's elfin frame, tempted to inform Steve just how much of his "stuff" he'd already touched.

"And do me another favor," Steve added. "Keep an eye on Janine for me, would you?"

Derek pursed his mouth. "That should be easy."

"If you know what room she's in, I'll call her myself," Steve said. "Or I'll check with the desk."

"Um, no." Derek rushed to stop him. "She's staying with…" He rolled his hand to indicate he needed help.

She put her fingers in her ears, then pinched together the fingers of her right hand and started punching the air.

"She's staying with the operator," he said, but Janine stopped, disgusted with his guess.

He splayed his hands, at a loss. She mouthed something emphatic several times before he covered the phone. "What?"

"I'm with the doctors, Einstein," she hissed. "This—" she repeated the motion "—is using a stethoscope, not a switchboard!"

He frowned, then uncovered the phone. "I mean, she's staying with the medics…on the slim chance she can help."

His words garnered another dark look from Janine, but Steve seemed convinced. "Oh. Will you see her?"

"I'd say that's a safe bet," Derek said, his tone dry.

"Just tell her to call me." Steve said, then laughed without humor. "I'm sorry as hell you got caught in this mess, man. By all rights, it should be Jack holed up with the plague, eh?"

"Just one more reason to kick his ass when I see him," Derek grumbled, then said goodbye and hung up.

For a few seconds, neither he nor Janine spoke. Fatigue pulled at his shoulders so he stretched his arms high, then he rubbed his eyes with his fists.

"You really shouldn't do that."

He stopped. "Shouldn't do what?"

"Rub your eyes like that," she said. "You could scratch your corneas."

Derek stared at her, feeling luckier and luckier to be unencumbered by a female. "You," he said, pointing a finger, "be quiet."

She blanched, then he was horrified to see tears pool in her eyes. "Oh, no," he said, holding up his hands. "Don't cry." A big tear slid down her cheek and he groaned. "Ah, for the love of Pete," he begged, feeling like a heel. "*Please* don't cry. I shouldn't have snapped at you."

"I'm s-sorry," she whispered. "It's the wedding, and, and, and now this q-quarantine…"

"Are you feeling ill?" He'd hate to think he'd given her whatever he had. Derek bit down on the inside of his cheek—there he went again, caring.

"I don't think so," she said, her lower lip trembling.

He stood and walked over to her, then gently clasped her shoulders and turned her around to face the bathroom. "Why don't you take a nice, long bath?" he said in the voice he saved for his most neurotic clients. "I'm sure you'll feel much better."

She nodded mutely and disappeared behind the closed door. The water splashed on and, too late, he realized his cold medicine was still on the vanity. Derek blew his nose, then lowered himself to the floor for twenty-seven push-ups before he had to stop and sneeze again. He gave up and pulled an accordion file marked Phillips Honey from the bag he'd repacked, along with three pint-size clear plastic containers of Phillips's products: nearly transparent wildwood honey, pale yellow honey butter and a mahogany-colored sourwood honey with a chunk of the waxy honeycomb imbedded in its murky depths.

Derek stared at the honey, willing a brilliant idea to leap to his blank pad of paper. After a few seconds without a revelation, he numbered lines on the pad from one to twenty. He would start with trite ideas, but sometimes when he reached the end of the list, something fresh would occur to him. *A honey of a taste. How sweet it is.* He kept glancing toward the bathroom, wondering what she was doing in there. *Sweet, sweet surrender.* He tossed down his pen in disgust.

Picking up the container of light honey, he rolled it between his hands to warm and loosen the contents, then opened the flip-top lid and squeezed a tiny dollop onto his finger. He smelled the translucent stickiness, jotting down notes about the aroma—sweet but pungent and a little wild. He tasted the honey, sucking it from his finger, allowing it to dissolve in his mouth, wondering why, instead of images of warm biscuits, the nutty sweet flavor of the honey evoked images of the woman bathing in the next room. Probably because she was a nut, he reasoned, then massaged his aching temples.

A knock on the door interrupted his rambling thoughts. Derek pulled his sweatshirt over his head and ran a hand through his hair, then checked the peephole to see two sets of suited shoulders. He opened the door to Dr. Pedro and a tall blond man who introduced himself as the general manager. The doctor carried a black leather bag, and the manager sported a clipboard that held down a one-inch stack of papers. Both men appeared weary, their eyes bloodshot.

"Mr. Stillman," the doctor said. "I understand you're not

feeling well. I need to examine you, draw some blood and record your symptoms."

Derek invited them inside. The general manager hung back, then peered around warily as he entered. "Isn't Janine Murphy in this room?"

A strange sound emerged from the bathroom. The men stopped and Derek identified the low noise as the world's worst rendition of "You Light Up My Life." He looked at Mr. Oliver and nodded toward the closed door. "Janine." When she hit a particularly off-key note, he felt compelled to add, "I don't really know her."

The doctor offered him a tight smile. "She informed us of your, um, unusual circumstances." While Derek pondered *that* conversation, the shorter man pulled the straight-back chair toward the foot of the bed. "Shall we get started?"

Derek sat in the chair and allowed the doctor to take his vital signs. "What's the status of the quarantine?"

"Still on," the man muttered, while peering into Derek's ears with a lighted instrument. He made notes on a pad of yellow forms.

"Have you identified the illness?"

"Yes," the doctor replied. "But not the source. Open your mouth and say 'ah.'"

Derek obeyed, realizing he'd have to drag answers out of the man. Meanwhile, he watched Mr. Oliver pivot and take in details of the room. The man stopped, his gaze on the pink-and-black bustier lying on top of the bedcovers where Derek had tossed it after using it as a shield. With an inward groan, Derek resisted the urge to jump up and discard the misleading evidence. Mr. Oliver's perusal continued, this time stopping to stare at the stash of honey on the nightstand. One of the manager's eyebrows arched and he slid a glance toward Derek. Great, Derek thought in exasperation. He thinks I'm doing kinky things with that woman braying in the bathroom.

"Your throat is irritated," the doctor announced.

Derek gagged on the tongue depressor, then pulled away and swallowed. "I could have told you that."

"When did you arrive at the hotel?"

"Yesterday, around three o'clock."

"When did you first start exhibiting symptoms?"

"Around five o'clock, I guess."

"Describe your symptoms."

Derek shrugged. "Congestion, sore throat."

"Body aches?" the doctor prompted.

He nodded. "Some."

"Vomiting?"

"No."

"Diarrhea?"

"No."

Mr. Oliver stepped forward. "Did you eat in the hotel restaurant?"

He nodded.

"When and what did you eat?" the manager continued.

"A burger and fries, around four o'clock."

"What did you have to drink?" Dr. Pedro cut in.

"Water and coffee."

"Decaf?"

"No, I was tired and needed the boost."

"Have you eaten anything else since you arrived?" the doctor asked.

Derek shook his head.

"Honey, perhaps?" The general manager nodded toward the nightstand with an amused expression.

He frowned. "Only a taste. And just this morning."

"What else?" Dr. Pedro asked, scribbling.

"Some over-the-counter medicine I picked up in the gift shop."

"I'll need to see it."

Derek jerked his thumb toward the bathroom where Pinky continued her teeth-grating performance. "It's in there."

The doctor gestured toward the bathroom. "Is Ms. Murphy ailing?"

"Sure sounds like it, doesn't it?" Derek asked wryly, then rose. "Give me a minute or two." He walked over to the bathroom door and rapped loudly. The singing, thank goodness, stopped, although he could still hear the hum of the Jacuzzi and the gurgle of bubbling water.

"Who is it?" she called.

He rolled his eyes. "Derek. I need to get my medication."

"Just a minute." A rustling noise sounded through the door. "You can come in."

With a backward glance to their visitors, who seemed rapt, he opened the door and leaned inside, patting the vanity.

Behind the closed shower curtain, Janine held her breath as he rummaged on the vanity for what seemed like an eternity. Finally she moved the curtain aside mere inches to peer out. He was leaning inside the room, stretching his arm across the counter, but unable to reach the bright orange box at the far end.

"I said you could come in," she repeated, although grateful for his attempt at discretion.

Wordlessly, he stepped into the room to grab the box, then caught her gaze in the mirror.

For a few seconds, they were frozen in place. An erotic tingle skipped across her skin, sending chills over her shoulders and knees—the only part of her not submerged in the bubble bath. Even fully dressed, the man emitted a powerful sexual energy that spoke to her. His hands, his arms, his shoulders, his face—all of him radiated a strength and masculinity that stirred her insides in the most confounding way, which might explain why her normal levelheadedness had abandoned her, and clumsiness had taken its place.

"Found it," he said suddenly with a tight smile, holding up the box.

"Good," she said inanely, supremely aware that only a paper-thin curtain shielded her nudity from his eyes.

"Um, the doctor and the general manager of the hotel are here," he said, nodding toward the door. His grin was unexpected. "You might want to keep it down, or at least come up with a new song."

Her cheeks warmed and she returned a sheepish smile. "I didn't realize anyone could hear me."

"They want to know if you're feeling okay."

She nodded, suddenly wanting the other men to leave and wanting their conversation to continue. "Has the quarantine been lifted?"

"Nope. Looks like we're stuck here together for the day."

An unbidden thrill zipped through her. She studied Derek's face for his reaction to the news, but his expression remained unreadable, although he began to tap the box of medication against his other hand.

"Guess we'll have to make the best of it," he added lightly.

Her breasts tightened and she curled her fingers into such a tight fist, her nails bit into her palm. Could he hear her heart beating?

Suddenly he straightened. "I'd better get back to the doctor and the manager."

"I'll be out soon," she felt compelled to murmur as he headed toward the door.

He hesitated, his hand on the doorknob. "Take your time," he said, although his voice sounded hoarse.

When the door closed behind him, Janine leaned back against the smooth surface of the tub and allowed a pressing smile to emerge. Sliding deeper into the water, she ran her hands over her body. She raised her right leg and watched the suds drip from the end of her bright pink-polished toe. Without too much difficulty she could imagine Derek facing her on the other end of the tub, naked and slippery, their legs entwined. She lazily lowered her toe to the shiny chrome faucet and outlined the square opening. Feeling uncharacteristically wanton, she cupped her breasts, reveling in the textures—silky smooth and achingly hard. Long-denied sensations seized her, and she gave in to the lull of the warm bubbling water. After a moment's hesitation, she closed her eyes and slipped a washcloth to the apex of her thighs.

Holding it from corner to corner, she drew the wet nubby cloth over the folds of her flesh, sighing as tremors delivered wonderful, quivering sensations to her extremities. This was how she wanted him to touch her, with gentle, firm strokes, knowing when to take his time and…and…and…*when to speed up*. She pressed her lips together to stifle the moans of pleasure that vibrated in the back of her throat. As the waves of release diminished, she sank farther into the luxuriously warm water to enjoy the lingering hum. *Oh, Derek...*

DEREK TORE HIS GAZE from the closed bathroom door and tried to concentrate on the doctor's words. The only part of Janine he'd seen was her face, surrounded by hunks of wet blond hair, but with little imagination he could picture her slender body on the other side of that shower curtain, buoyed by the water. He ground his teeth against the image, then realized the doctor had said something and was waiting for a reply.

"Excuse me?" He put a finger to his temple to feign the distraction of a headache.

Dr. Pedro smiled as he scrutinized the box of medication Derek had handed to him. "I said I'm glad Ms. Murphy is still feeling well."

"Oh, yeah, right." With a swift mental kick, Derek reminded himself that while they were in the middle of a serious medical situation, *he* was obsessing over his unexplainable attraction to Steve's bride. With sheer determination, he pushed all thoughts of the woman from his mind.

Dr. Pedro directed Derek to keep taking the medicine for his symptoms. Afterward he quickly drew a blood sample from Derek's forearm, then stood to leave. "If your, um, friend starts exhibiting symptoms, please call the front desk and I'll be notified."

Mr. Oliver extended a sheet of green paper. "These are a few guidelines concerning movement about the property during the quarantine, how your meals will be delivered, how information will be disseminated, et cetera."

Derek exhaled noisily, then accepted the sheet. "How serious is this situation?"

Dr. Pedro's mouth turned down. "We had to transport three people to the hospital this morning, but we're optimistic they'll respond to an antibiotic IV."

Derek sobered. "How long will we be confined?"

"Until the source of the bacteria is detected, the method of contagion identified and the incubation period has passed."

"Worst-case scenario?" he asked.

The doctor shrugged. "Two weeks."

Derek felt a little rubbery in the knees. "I have to sit down." He dropped to the side of the bed, reeling. He was going to have to resist Janine for two weeks? Plus, in two weeks the Phillips Honey account would be long gone, and possibly his company's viability. *Jack, where the hell are you?*

"But that's worst-case scenario," Dr. Pedro added. The men walked toward the door, the general manager saying something about free phone calls. When the door closed, he lay back on the bed, holding his head and wondering if the situation could possibly get more bizarre.

"Derek?" Janine yelled from the bathroom. "Derek!" Her voice held a note of panic that roused him to his feet in one second flat.

He raced to the door and pressed his cheek against the smooth surface. "What's wrong?"

"I'm stuck."

Derek frowned. "What do you mean, you're stuck?"

"I mean my big toe…it's stuck in the bathtub faucet. Help me!"

8

WARM SUDSY WATER lapped at her mortified ears. Janine stared down at the end of the tub where her leg arched up out of the water—bent at the knee, dripping foam, and ending in a union with the shiny gold faucet. Trapped toe-knuckle deep into the opening of the chrome fixture, her big toe was as red as a cherry tomato from several minutes of futile tugging—a fitting end to her outrageous behavior, she decided. For fantasizing about another man, she was now trapped in this bathroom, a realization that did not sit well with her preference for open spaces. Her heartbeat thudded in her ears.

She hadn't heard the door open, but suddenly Derek's big body was silhouetted through the shower curtain.

"Janine, from the other side of the door it sounded like you said—"

"My big toe is stuck in the bathtub faucet."

He scoffed. "That's impossible."

"I beg to differ," she said miserably, then moved the curtain aside to peep out, and up. "Are you going to help me or not?"

The man looked harried. And not well. Guilt barbed through her. She should be looking after him instead of getting into scrapes. At the moment, however, she had no choice but to don the most pitiful expression she could conjure up.

It must have worked because Derek threw his hands in the air. "What do you want me to do?"

"Hand me a towel so I can cover myself, then try to get my toe unstuck."

He looked up, as if appealing to a higher power, then sighed and handed her a towel.

"Thank you." She dunked the thick towel under the water,

dissolving mounds of bubbles, and spread it over her nakedness. But her heart thumped wildly at the thought of Derek seeing her yet again in a state of near undress, especially when she was so recently sated on thoughts of him. "Okay, I'm ready."

His large fingers curled around the edge of the shower curtain, and he pushed it aside slowly. The cool air hit her bits of exposed skin and sent a chill down her neck. She shivered, an all-over body shimmy, although she conceded she couldn't blame her reaction entirely on the elements. The man was huge, especially from her angle, his proportions nearly those of a professional athlete. A memory surfaced that Steve had once told her he had a pal who had played college football. Perhaps he'd meant Derek.

He ran a hand down over his face and looked at her through his fingers. "*What* is a person thinking when she shoves her toe up a faucet?"

Janine averted her eyes. She certainly couldn't tell him what she'd been doing. "I wasn't thinking."

"Obviously," he said, his expression bewildered. He slid the curtain to the wall, then lowered himself to one knee.

She felt at a terrible disadvantage at this lower level, not to mention naked and submerged. The towel covered her, but clung to her figure in a manner that belied its purpose. Of course, it didn't matter, since the man seemed completely unfazed. He leaned close to the faucet, so close she could feel his breath on her bare leg. Thank goodness she'd shaved them earlier.

He swept a soap wrapper and an empty miniature shampoo bottle from the side of the tub into the trash to clear a spot, then picked up the dripping metal razor and gave her a pointed look. "You used my razor?"

She bit her lower lip. "To shave my legs. I thought it was Steve's."

His jaw tightened as he set aside the razor. "It isn't."

He didn't have a girlfriend, she realized suddenly. At least not a live-in. Not even a lady friend who occasionally spent the night, else he would be used to sharing his razor. Then she frowned. Not that she'd ever used Steve's.

"Would you please turn off the motor so I can think?" he asked, his voice strained.

"I can't reach the switch," she said, pointing over his shoulder.

He stabbed the button in the corner of the tub ledge and the rumbling motor died abruptly, taking the soothing bubbles with it. Suddenly the room fell so quiet, she could hear the calling of birds outside the skylight, where daybreak was well under way. The eve of her supposed wedding day. She felt light-headed and realized she hadn't eaten in hours. And Derek's imposing nearness was tripping her claustrophobic tendencies.

He gripped the side of the tub and perused her foot from all directions, then he glanced back at her. "Can't you just pull it out?"

She scratched her nose, realizing too late her hand was covered with suds. Sputtering the bubbles away from her mouth, she said, "If I could, I wouldn't have called you."

He pursed his mouth, then said, "I'm not a plumber."

"Do something," she pleaded. "The water's getting cold, and I'm shriveling up."

"Really? Gee, and you've only been in here for an hour."

She frowned at his teasing. "You were the one who suggested I take a long, hot bath."

He laughed, then turned his attention back to her foot. "Except I don't recall suggesting that you insert your toe into the metal pipe coming out of the wall."

She pressed her lips together and braced for his touch. He clasped her foot gently, but firmly, and his fingers sent arrows of tingly sensations exploding up her leg, reminiscent of her climax. She grunted and he looked over his shoulder.

"My leg is asleep," she explained.

He isolated his grip to the base of her toe, wriggling it side to side. The inside lip of the faucet dug into her tender skin.

"Ouch! Not so hard."

"I'm sorry," he said, seemingly at a loss for what to do

next. "I need something slick to lubricate your toe." He looked around. "Where's the soap?"

Janine lifted her hand and held her thumb and forefinger close together. "You mean that little bitty bar of soap the hotel provided?"

Derek nodded.

A flush warmed her cool cheeks. "I used it all."

He flicked a dubious glance over her towel-covered body. Maybe he thought she didn't look clean enough to have used an entire bar of soap. Her skin tingled, and not from her leg being asleep.

"Shampoo?" he asked.

She lifted a shaky finger to point to her hair, wet and plastered to her head. "I have a lot of hair."

A wry frown tugged at his mouth. "I can see that."

"Don't you have soap or shampoo in your toiletry bag?" she asked, pointing to the black case on the vanity she'd mistaken for Steve's.

He shook his head. "I travel light and expect hotels to have those things." Then he snapped his fingers. "But I do have shaving cream."

Janine smiled sheepishly and reached behind her to hand him the empty travel-size can of shaving cream. "You were almost out anyway," she offered in her defense.

He depressed the button to the sound of hissing emptiness. The side of his cheek bulged from his probing tongue. He rimmed the can into the trash, then pushed himself to his feet. "Maybe Steve will have something in his bag."

The bathroom seemed cavernous in his absence, and she wondered briefly how Steve would have handled this predicament. With much less good humor, she suspected, and the realization bothered her.

Derek returned with Steve's black bag, set it on the vanity and ransacked it for several minutes. "Nothing," he said, defeated. "I'll call the front desk and have something sent up."

The water had taken on a distinct chill, the last cloud of bubbles were fizzing away and her leg was beginning to throb. "Tell them to hurry," she called.

But a few minutes later, he was back in the doorway. "The line is still busy. I'll have to go downstairs."

"I thought we weren't supposed to leave our rooms."

He smirked and gestured toward her foot. "I'll leave it up to you, but I'd say this constitutes an emergency."

"Don't you have *anything* in your bag that would do? Hair gel? Lotion?"

"Nope."

"Petroleum jelly? Body oil?"

He shook his head.

"What would happen if you turned on the faucet?"

A tolerant smile curved one side of his mouth. "Believe me, you don't want to do that. But I can let out the water if you're cold."

"I think the water is helping to support my weight."

His gaze swept over her again. "What weight? I thought you southern women were supposed to have a little meat on your bones."

She scowled. "*Do* you mind? I thought you were going to help. Don't you have anything that might work?"

"I told you, I—" He stopped and his dark eyebrows drew together, then his mouth quirked.

"What?"

He shook his head, as if he'd dismissed the thought. "Never mind."

"No, what is it? Tell me!"

"It wouldn't work."

"For crissake, Derek, spit it out!"

"Honey butter."

"What?"

"I have a pint of honey butter."

Janine angled her head at him. "Are you feeling worse?"

He rubbed his eyes with thumb and forefinger. "Yes."

"You really shouldn't do that."

He stopped rubbing, gave her a silencing glance, then whirled and disappeared into the bedroom.

She stretched her neck, but he'd moved out of her line of vision. Had he said honey butter? The man was incoherent, she decided, but her worry over his deteriorating symptoms was overridden by her immediate concern of being left alone to die a slow death in this bathtub. She laid her head back and stared at the skylight. At least the view would be nice.

But Derek returned in a few seconds with a small container in his hand, reading the label. "This stuff has butter in it, so maybe it'll work."

Janine eyed the container with surprise. "Where did you get it?"

"I brought it with me."

Okay, maybe he wasn't incoherent, just strange. "And do you always travel with a stash of condiments?"

His smirk defined the laugh lines around his mouth. She guessed his age to be thirty-five or -six, a bit older than Steve. "It's a long story. Let's just hope this works."

He knelt again, and she was struck by the sheer maleness of him—the pleasing way the knobby muscle of his shoulder rose from the collar of the sweatshirt and melded into the cord of his neck, the sheen of his hair, close-cropped but as thick as a pelt, the large, well-formed features of his face. And his hands…

Janine shivered again. Square and strong and capable. Mentally she compared them to Steve's, which were slender and beautiful—a surgeon's hands—and wondered what Derek did for a living. But in the next second, she was distracted because those hands were on the verge of smearing a gob of pale yellow goo on her toe. His concentration seemed so dogged, she was overcome by a sense of being taken care of. And it occurred to her that he still hadn't questioned her about her surprise appearance last night. He probably thought she was some kind of sex-crazed kitten, when, in truth, she was a sex-*starved* kitten—er, woman.

He made a disgusted sound in his throat. "People actually eat this stuff?"

"Listen, Derek," she murmured, then cleared her throat. "About last night…*ahhhhhh.*" She couldn't help it—the combination of his hands on her foot, the slippery substance he smeared on her skin and the tingly numbness of her leg made her body twitch and surge.

He seemed not to notice and continued to slather the area around her toe.

"You're probably wondering why I showed up here wearing that, um, costume."

Derek grunted and worked her toe back and forth.

"You see, it was a little joke between me and Steve." She manufactured a laugh, but dipped her chin and accidentally swallowed a mouthful of cool soapy water, then came up sputtering.

He looked over his shoulder, then shook his head as if considering whether to hold her under until she stopped flopping. God, what about this man turned her into such a klutz? After shoving his sweatshirt sleeve up past his biceps, he plunged his hand into the water and she heard the dull thunk of the pulled plug before he returned to his greasy task.

The water level began to lower, tickling her as it drained away, and making her feel even more exposed. The towel covered her from neck to knees, but just knowing that the only thing that stood between Derek and her birthday suit was a layer of wet terry cloth left a disturbance in her stomach. When the silence became unbearable, she picked up where she'd left off. "Like I was saying, Steve and I are always joshing each other." She laughed. "Josh, josh, josh. You know how couples are," she said, hoping she didn't sound as inane as she felt.

Derek's arm moved back and forth as he worked to loosen her toe, then suddenly her foot jerked back, and she was free.

"Oh, thank you," she said, weak with both relief and immobility. "I was afraid we'd have to call the fire department."

Wiping his hands on a towel, he gave her a whisper of a smile. "Do you need a hand getting up?" She did, but she knew she'd never be able to keep herself covered in the process. He must have read her mind because he added, "Don't worry, Pinky, I'll close my eyes."

For some reason, she liked the ridiculous nickname.

"Okay." Janine raised her arms for him to clasp, then he closed his eyes and lifted her to her feet as easily as if she were a piece of fluff. Water sluiced from her hair, her body and the towel, which she tried to keep close to her with her elbows, to no avail. The towel fell to the bottom of the tub, and when she put her weight on her foot, it slipped out from under her. She shrieked and Derek responded by scooping an arm around her waist to steady her, jamming her up against his body. Desire bolted through her, although he kept his hands in innocent places. Concern rode over his features, but true to his word, his eyes remained closed.

She clung to his arms—his sleeves really, which were the first handholds she'd been able to grab. Even with her toes dangling a couple of inches off the ground, the top of her head reached only to his collarbone. The soft cotton of his sweatshirt soaked up the water from her breasts pressed against him, and the skin below her navel stung from proximity to the metal button on his jeans. His fingers curved around her waist, hot and powerfully strong, and the male scent of his skin filled her nostrils. Janine's lips parted, and in that instant, crazily, she wanted more than anything for this man to kiss her. Kiss her so she could be indignant, outraged, even insulted that he would think that she, on the verge of being married, would entertain being kissed by someone other than, um…she winced…oh, yeah—Steve.

"Are you okay?" he asked, his eyes still closed.

Other than waterlogged and adrenaline-shot? "I think so," she managed to say. "Just let me down slowly."

Derek swallowed, wondering if she could feel and hear his heart thudding like a randy fifteen-year-old's. Against screaming instincts, he kept his eyes closed. He'd been too long without a woman, he decided, if he could be so easily affected by the accident-prone wife-to-be of a friend. The same woman, he reminded himself, who was responsible for him being detained, sleep-deprived, inconvenienced and very, very wet.

Doing as he was told, he set her down slowly, although it meant her nude body slid down the length of his straining one. The ends of her wet hair tickled his hands as he lowered her, and he held her waist until she had her footing.

"I think I can stand on my own now," she murmured, but he was reluctant to let go. His thumbs rested on the firm slick skin around her navel, and his fingers brushed the small of her back. She was willowy, and lush, like a long-stemmed flower, and it was all he could do not to steal a glance of her in full bloom as he turned to exit the bathroom. She'd come to the hotel in that crazy getup to surprise Steve, and now he couldn't decide if his buddy was the luckiest man alive, or the most cursed.

Derek closed the door behind him, and exhaled mightily to regain control of his libido. He simply could *not* be physically attracted to the loony case in the bathroom, not if they were going to be in close quarters for the next several hours—possibly days—and especially since she was about to marry a friend of his.

Suddenly some of the words Janine had murmured last night when she thought he was Steve flooded back to him. *I just can't wait any longer. I need to know now if we're good together.* Thunderstruck, he repeated the words to himself. Was it possible that his buddy was about to marry a woman he hadn't yet slept with? That she had come to the hotel with the intention of seducing her groom?

Derek groaned and ran his hand through his hair. If so, that meant the hormones of the shapely woman in the next room were probably raging as high as his. And something else was bothering him. He distinctly remembered seeing Steve rummage in a gray toiletry bag yesterday before he left, but now the bag was nowhere to be found. Derek had a feeling his buddy hadn't spent the night out partying with the other groomsmen.

And while admittedly, Janine Murphy seemed like the kind of woman who attracted trouble, she also struck him as being a little naive, sweetly vulnerable and completely sincere. As a determined bachelor, he was the last man qualified to give advice about getting married, but the very least she deserved was honesty and faithfulness from her partner.

Derek cursed as those protective feelings ballooned in his chest again. What kind of fool was he even to consider protecting Janine from the man she loved? Their relationship was none of his concern. And he had to admit that his newfound attraction to the woman, not to mention his medication, was probably coloring his judgment. So the only solution was to stay as far away from her as he could, while sharing a bedroom.

The bathroom door cracked and Janine's head appeared. "Derek?"

He turned, and his gut clenched. After his best efforts to resist a glance at her while wrestling in the bathroom, her nakedness was revealed in its splendor in the mirror over the vanity, clearly visible from his vantage point. He realized she was completely oblivious to the peep show, and he saw no reason to embarrass her by voicing his admiration for the brown beauty mark on her right hip. His body hardened instantly.

Her smile, conversely, resonated abject innocence. "I found only socks and gym shoes in Steve's bag. Do you have some clothes I can borrow?"

Derek swallowed hard and managed to nod. Janine beamed and closed the door, although he knew the imprint of her slender naked body wouldn't soon be erased from his mind.

Not generally a religious man, he nonetheless recognized his limits as a mortal and muttered a silent prayer for strength.

9

JANINE ADJUSTED her borrowed clothes. Derek's gray sweat-pants—the counterpart to his University of Kentucky sweat-shirt, she assumed—swallowed her. Sans underwear, the cotton fleece nuzzled her skin, which was satiny smooth and warm from her prolonged bath. Rolled cuffs helped shorten the pants while a drawstring held the waistband just under her breasts. She was forced to go braless until Marie or her mother could drop off reinforcements. Derek's plain black T-shirt fell to her knees, so she knotted it at her waist to take up the slack. She gazed at her reflection and nodded in satis-faction. The shapeless clothes were a far cry from the cos-tume she'd shown up wearing last night, which was just the way she wanted it. After an evening of prancing around like a Frederick's of Hollywood reject, and after a morning of wrangling naked in the bathroom, big and baggy was just the look she needed to keep her body under wraps and her urges under control. She sniffed a sleeve that fell past her elbow, then pursed her lips in appreciation at the mountain-fresh scent—the man used fabric softener, so he had a sensitive side.

Either that or his mother still did his laundry.

The bathroom was equipped with a blow-dryer, but she opted to detangle her wet hair with a small comb from Derek's toiletry bag—which she rinsed and dried carefully before replacing—to allow the long strands to dry naturally. She stared at her hair for several minutes, perusing the ar-row-straight center part and waist-length style, knowing her hair was hopelessly out of date, while acknowledging it suited her. The color wasn't as blond as it used to be, but she felt no compulsion to lighten the honey-hued strands. And other than having to buy shampoo by the gallon, her long hair was low-maintenance, more often than not secured into a low ponytail with her favorite tortoiseshell clasp. For now, it would have to hang loose.

She wriggled her liberated big toe. Other than some tenderness and a few scratches in the pink nail polish—a gift pedicure from Marie—her toe seemed to have escaped permanent damage from the bathtub incident.

But her psyche, well, that was another story.

Derek Stillman had shaken her. For proof of that revelation, she needed to look no farther than her cheeks. Even in the absence of makeup or lotion, they bore an uncommon blush that marched across her nose and tingled with a fiery intensity. So she was attracted to the man. Okay, make that *wildly* attracted to the man. She had a simple explanation: Didn't it make sense that the sexual feelings she'd brought with her for Steve, she might now be projecting onto Derek?

No, came the resounding answer. It didn't make sense at all.

The body might be a fickle instrument, not caring who or what stimulated it, but the mind should be able to tell the difference between right and wrong. Carrying enough guilt on her shoulders to fill a cathedral ten minutes before Mass, she opened the bathroom door, hoping against hope that Derek would announce the quarantine had just been lifted. Or perhaps discover that her eyes had played tricks on her—her best man wasn't a great-looking, incredibly built specimen with whom she had to share four walls, but a homely, broken-down gnome who would take up residence *under* the bed if they had to spend another night together.

But Derek glanced up from his seat on the end of the bed and dispelled her hopes in one fell swoop with the concerned frown pulling at his appallingly handsome face.

"We're making headlines," he said, gesturing toward the television. Resisting the urge to sit next to him, she hovered a few steps away, riveted to the screen. The tag line on the bottom of the picture read: Quarantine Crisis, Green Stations Resort, Lake Lanier, Georgia. A grim-faced reporter wearing a yellow windbreaker, with a surgical mask dangling around his neck, stared into the camera as he delivered his report.

"A spokesperson for the Centers for Disease Control reports some form of Legionnaires' disease may have broken out among the guests at a resort near Lake Lanier, north of Atlanta, where a quarantine is in effect. An infirmary has been set up in the hotel workout facility to monitor and care for those who have fallen too ill to remain in their rooms, and other measures are being enacted to protect the many, many guests who were taken completely by surprise." The general manager appeared on-screen, holding a microphone with a gloved hand. The interview had been shot through a window.

"The resort enjoys a brisk business this time of the year," Mr. Oliver said. "So not surprisingly, we were booked solid. Including employees, we have around six hundred people inside the grounds, and we're going to do our best to make sure everyone is as comfortable as possible during the confinement period."

Dr. Pedro came on next, his setting similar to Mr. Oliver's. "As of about 5:00 a.m. this morning, approximately four dozen guests were exhibiting symptoms, with three of those cases serious enough to require hospitalization—" The clip of the doctor was cut short, obviously edited, and the reporter's dour face appeared once again.

"The resort has been inundated with calls and deliveries from relatives and well-wishers, but officials asked the media to inform the public that no objects, such as clothing, food or flowers, will be allowed inside the resort. Meals are being prepared in another facility and delivered under the supervision of the CDC." The man lowered his chin for dramatic effect. "Except for CDC personnel, *no one* is allowed to leave or enter the resort, unless, of course, a body needs to be moved to the hospital...or to the morgue." The reporter lifted the surgical mask to cover his mouth. "Reporting live from Lake Lanier. Now back to you in the studio."

Janine rolled her eyes and Derek scoffed, using the remote

to turn down the volume. "According to that guy, we should be making out our wills."

She nodded. "I would've liked to hear what the doctor had to say that didn't make it into the news segment. Did he insinuate to you this morning that the situation is worse?"

"Just what you heard on TV. Three people in the hospital, although he said he didn't think their lives were at risk."

His voice was conversational and sincere, his demeanor fatigued. What was it about this man that made her want to touch him? His boy-next-door chivalry? His all-American looks? His aloof attitude? Despite being close to Steve's age, Derek seemed decades more mature. Worry lined his serious brown eyes. Was he more concerned about his health than he let on? She felt compelled to comfort him, to ease the wrinkles from his forehead. Angling her head, she circled to stand in front of him. "How are you feeling?"

"About the same," he said with a shrug.

"Still congested?"

He nodded.

She stepped forward and placed her hand on his forehead. With him sitting and her standing, they were nearly eye to eye. More like breast to eye, although she tried not to dwell on it. His skin felt smooth and taut, and she liked the silkiness of his short bangs against the pads of her fingers. His temperature felt normal, but hers had definitely risen a couple of degrees, even higher when she realized she was standing between his open knees.

Her gaze locked with his and awareness gripped her, electrifying her limbs and warming her midsection. His brown eyes were bottomless, and she realized with a start that she'd always equated dark eyes with thoughtfulness. And sincerity. And comfort. And sensuality.

"You don't have a fever," she whispered, then wet her dry lips. Her hand fell to the muscled ledge of his shoulder, a natural resting place, it seemed.

Something was happening, she could feel it. The energy emanating from his body pulled at her, and she had to go rigid to keep from swaying into him. But his face belied none of the sexual force vibrating between them. His mouth was set in a firm line and his eyes were alert. The only indication that he was affected by her nearness was the rapid rise and fall of his chest.

She lifted her hand to probe the soft area of his neck just beneath the curve of his jaw. He stiffened, but she pretended not to notice. She could best smooth over the awkward moment by continuing to check his vital signs. "Your pulse is elevated."

He exhaled. "I guess I can chalk it up to all the, um…"

"Excitement?" she finished.

"How's your toe?" he asked, effectively changing the subject.

She looked down at her small white feet situated between his two large ones, and experienced a queer sense of intimacy. "Fine," she said. "I never thanked you for rescuing me."

He returned her smile, which made her heart lurch crazily. "Glad to pinch-hit for Steve," he said. Then his smile evaporated and he added, "In that one particular instance."

At the mention of Steve's name, she relaxed, feeling firmly back on platonic footing. "Thanks, too, for the clothes. You're a lifesaver." Impulsively, she leaned forward and dropped a kiss on his cheek. Janine realized her mistake the second she drew away. Derek's mocha-colored eyes had grown glazed and heavy-lidded. The worry lines had fled, and his lips were open in silent invitation. Blatant desire chased reason from her mind. Acting purely on instinct, she lowered her lips to his for an experimental kiss. Just one, she promised herself. One last illicit kiss for comparison.

If indeed he hesitated, it wasn't for more than a heartbeat. His lips opened to welcome hers, and the tide of longing that swept over her left her breathless. Their tongues darted, danced and dueled in a coming together that could be described as anything *but* platonic.

Her knees weakened and she became aware that his hands were at her waist, and her arms around his neck. His taste was as foreign and delicious as exotic fruit, and she wanted to draw more of him into her mouth. Derek angled his head to deepen the kiss and she moaned in gratitude. Pulling her forward, he melded her body to his, and she was conscious of his hands sliding beneath her shirt. He splayed his hands over her shoulder blades, kneading her skin with his strong fingers in long, determined caresses that gave her a glimpse into his body rhythm.

She shivered and might have buckled had he not imprisoned her legs with his knees. Janine reveled in the strength and possession of his touch. She arched her back and rolled her shoulders, then slipped her hands inside his shirt and ran her hands over the smooth expanse of his back, kneading the firm muscle. His guttural sounds propelled her excitement to the highest plateau she'd ever endured. The world fell away around them, and Janine felt completely, utterly safe. She pressed her body against his, sure in the knowledge that he could fuel the flames licking at her body to an all-consuming fire, much more satisfying than her earlier release.

When he stiffened, her first instinct was to resist, but when she heard the knock at the door, she straightened and stepped back, disentangling herself from him. The look he gave her still smoldered from their heated kiss, but he wore his remorse just as plainly.

The full extent of her shameful participation flooded over her. She backed away and clapped a hand over her traitorous mouth, sucking air against her fingers to fill her quivering lungs. If her skin hadn't still burned from his touch, she might not have believed what had just transpired. Regret nearly paralyzed her. What had she done? What had she nearly allowed Derek to do?

He was watching her. She stared at him, at the body she could now call familiar, but she didn't know what to say. Janine suspected, however, that her face reflected her horror at her own behavior.

Another knock sounded at the door. Derek panned his hand over his face, then stood, visibly trying to shake off the effects of their encounter. Her gaze flew to the telltale bulge in his pants that he didn't attempt to hide as he limped a half

circle in the room. Hair tousled, shirt askew, and hard for
her...Derek Stillman was simply the most devastatingly appealing man she'd ever met. Best man, she corrected. *Her* best
man. She might as well run headlong into a train tunnel
while the whistle sounded in her ears.

Realizing Derek was in no shape to answer the door, she
cleared her throat and murmured, "I'll see who it is."

"Thanks," he said over his shoulder, his big hands riding
his hips as he headed toward the bathroom.

Still reeling, she walked to the door and, through the peephole, saw the general manager standing in the hall. Shot with
relief without really knowing why, she swung open the door.
"Hello, Mr. Oliver."

A multishelved cart loaded with great-smelling covered
trays flanked him. He took in her ill-fitting garb with only a
blink and a smile. "Call me Manny, Ms. Murphy."

She felt warmed by the friendly tone in his voice. "Then
call me Janine."

The blond man nodded. "Glad to see you're still with us.
How are you feeling?"

Shoving a fall of hair away from her face, she pulled a
smile from nowhere to hide her shaky emotions. "F-fine."

His penetrating blue gaze seemed all-knowing, but he
didn't contradict her. "Mr., um, Stillman, isn't it?"

"Yes," she croaked.

"Mr. Stillman said this morning that you had no symptoms."

"That depends—is irrational behavior a symptom?"

He pursed his mouth, then shook his head slowly. "I don't
recall, but I can mention it to the doctor."

She sighed. "Don't bother, I'm fine."

His eyes narrowed slightly, but he didn't skip a beat.
"Good. I've brought breakfast, not a typical resort meal, I can
assure you, since our chefs didn't prepare the food, but not
bad if you're hungry."

"I am."

The door across the hall opened and Ms. Jiles stepped out,

perfectly coifed and wrapped in a coral-colored silk robe. "I heard voices."

At eight o'clock in the morning, the woman was stunning. Janine decided she must have slept in her makeup *and* sitting straight up. But she inclined her head politely. "Maureen Jiles, this is Manny Oliver, the general manager."

He smiled. "I'm delivering breakfast, ma'am."

"Something low-fat, I hope," she said in a voice reserved for lowly help.

"Yes, ma'am," Manny replied smoothly. "We have a vegetarian meal."

"That will do," she said, then turned back to Janine and smiled. "Is your friend Derek up and about?"

Is he ever. "Um, yes."

Maureen appeared to be chewing on her tongue as her face slowly erupted into a mischievous smile. "I thought about Derek all night. I love a good challenge, and I decided I'm not going to let his being gay get in the way."

Manny, setting a tray inside the Jiles woman's door, erupted into a fit of coughing.

Janine, stunned by Maureen's audacity, looked past the woman. "Are you okay, Manny?"

He nodded, facing her, and she could see he wasn't choking at all—he was laughing.

"So, Janine, do you have any suggestions for attracting a gay man?" Maureen asked, obviously warming up to her scheme.

Thrown off balance, Janine shook her head. "Since, to my knowledge, I've never dated a gay man, no, I can't say that I do."

Manny exited the woman's room. "Ms. Murphy, I'm sure Mr. Stillman will be wanting a vegetarian meal," he said, his mouth twitching. "Would you like a traditional breakfast for yourself?"

She sent him an exasperated look with her eyes. "Yes, thank you, one of each."

"And I have the magazine he requested." From a side rack

of reading material, he produced a copy of *Victorian Age Decorating*.

Janine plucked the magazine out of his hand. "He will be pleased," she said, injecting a warning note into her voice.

Oblivious to their exchange, Maureen crossed her arms. "Does Derek cut hair? Because I could use a trim."

Manny cleared his throat. "Excuse me, Ms. Jiles, but guests are not supposed to be in each other's quarters."

Maureen stepped back into her room and harrumphed at Manny. "Probably want him for yourself." Then she closed the door with a bang.

Manny looked at her, his mouth drawn back in a wry grin. "Explain."

"It's simple," Janine said in a low voice, taking a tray from him and walking it inside. She glanced at the bathroom door to make sure Derek was out of earshot. "Maureen is a sales rep who calls on the clinic. And she knows a lot of the same people I do. I had to think of something to keep the gossip down at work, so—" She glanced toward the closed bathroom door, then back to Manny. "I told her Derek is gay."

"Looks like it backfired," he observed. "She's determined to salvage the man."

One lie led to another, she realized. She set the tray on the writing desk and waited for Manny to set down the second one, her eyes tearing up. She was having a nervous breakdown, she was certain.

"Hey, come on now, it can't be that bad." Manny handed her a handkerchief, on which she blew her nose heartily.

"Manny," she whispered, "you see what a predicament I'm in here. No one can know I'm sharing a room with Derek."

"I'm sure all this will be over soon," he said in a soothing voice. "As long as you and Mr. Stillman agree to keep it quiet, who will be the wiser?"

"You're right," she said, sniffing. "It's just that I don't know how much more I can take."

"Is he hostile?" he asked, touching her arm, concern in his eyes.

"Oh, no," she said, waving off his concern. "It's not that." How could she explain her raging feelings about a man she barely knew to a man she barely knew? She gestured to her outfit. "It's the close quarters, no privacy—you know."

Manny studied her face, then gave her hand a comforting pat. "Janine, emotions run high during a crisis, and people can behave in ways that are out of character."

She hugged herself. "You think?"

He nodded. "You have a lot on your mind, with the wedding and all."

Janine sighed. "I guess we'll have to call the whole thing off."

He tipped his head to the side. "You mean postpone it, don't you?"

She straightened her shoulders. "Yes. Of course. Postpone the wedding, not call it off. Of course that's what I meant." A Freudian slip?

"Is there anything I can do to make this situation more bearable?"

"I need clothes and toiletries…and a cot would be nice."

He opened the desk drawer and removed a sheet of stationery and a pen. "We're completely out of cots, but write down whatever else you need and I'll see what I can confiscate from the gift shops."

"Thank you," she whispered, then jotted down a dozen or so items.

He gave her a brief wink before he left, and when the door closed, she felt so alone. Alone like a stone. And accident-prone.

She glanced toward the bathroom door. What was she going to say to Derek about the kiss? How was she going to explain that she was so overcome with lust that she was willing to indulge in a few hours of unfettered sex, despite her being about to exchange vows with a friend of his? What must he think of her? Probably no worse than she thought of herself, she decided, and walked to the bathroom door. Perhaps the words would come if she didn't have to talk to him face-to-face.

Janine rapped lightly on the door. "Derek? Derek, I'm so sorry for what just happened. The kiss was my fault, and I can't give you a good excuse, because I have no excuse." She sighed and leaned her cheek against the door. "Please know that I do love Steve, despite the abominable way I've behaved. If you feel compelled to tell him what happened, I'll understand and I'll accept full responsibility." She closed her eyes. "Thank goodness we stopped when we did."

When the silence on the other side of the door stretched on, she rapped again. "Derek?" No answer. "Derek?" she asked louder. Making a fist, she knocked harder. "Derek, answer me to let me know you're okay." Fingers of panic curled low in her stomach. What if he had grown more ill? What if he'd passed out and hit his head when he fell?

She turned the doorknob, relieved that it gave easily. After cracking the door open, she called his name again, but he didn't respond. Her heart pounded as she inched the door wider, but she didn't see his reflection in the mirror. Janine opened the door and stepped into the bathroom. The shower curtain was pushed back, just as she'd left it—he wasn't there. In fact, the huge mass of man was nowhere to be found.

10

THANK GOODNESS the tiny balcony was cast in the shade of the building at this early hour, because he needed to cool off. Derek leaned on the white wrought-iron railing and fought to collect himself, appreciating the view of walking paths, fountain and golf courses, and reproaching himself. He'd never acted so foolishly in his life. Women had never been high on his list of priorities—school, football, work, family and friendship had always taken precedence. Always.

At the age of fourteen, he'd lost his first girlfriend to his younger, but more debonair brother, Jack, and decided shortly thereafter that women weren't worth arguing over. He'd left the brightest flowers for both Jack and Steve, preferring to date quiet, uncomplicated girls who didn't consume him or his energy.

He still preferred the quiet ones. Which was why his infuriating attraction to Pinky—dammit—*Janine* so perplexed him. Not only was the woman the mistress of mischief, but she just happened to be engaged to a man who thought enough of Derek to ask him to be his best man.

Well, granted, he was second choice behind Jack, but still, the least he owed Steve was to keep his hands off his bride. No matter how adorably inept she was, the woman already had a protector—a rich doctor—so she certainly didn't need him, a struggling entrepreneur.

It was his near-celibate life-style of late, he decided. He'd been so caught up in trying to locate Jack, and with the goings-on at the ad agency, he hadn't indulged in much of a social life lately. Lenore, the woman he'd been seeing occasionally had moved on to greener pastures, and because he typically didn't believe in casual sex—too many crazies and too many diseases—he hadn't slept with a woman in months.

And the bizarre circumstances undoubtedly contributed to his behavior. The intimacy of the close quarters, and the highly sexual accidental encounters with Janine were enough to test any man's willpower. Plus, he had to admit, Janine was a looker with that mop of blond hair and her too-blue eyes. He grunted when the image of her body reflected in that mirror came to mind. Worse still, the silky texture of her skin was still imprinted on his hands. And that kiss...

The woman was a paradox. One minute she struck him as an innocent, the next, a tease. One minute he was running to help her, the next, he was running to escape from her. He massaged his temples and filled his lungs with morning-sweet air. Gradually, his head cleared and he was able to look at the situation logically. Even if he took Steve and the whole marriage variable out of the equation, Janine Murphy couldn't be more wrong for him or his way of life. She was messy, emotional and erratic. Fisting his hand, he pounded once on the railing with resolve, gratified by the slight echo of the iron vibrating and the dull pain that lingered in his hand. There was nothing like a little space and fresh air for perspective.

The sound of her raised voice inside the room caught his attention, and he jogged back to the sliding glass door. Apprehensive, he opened the door and pushed aside the curtain, then stepped into the room.

Janine whirled mid-yell, her eyes huge. "Oh, there you are. I was worried." Then she gestured vaguely, and added, "I mean, I was afraid you might be feeling bad. Sick, I mean. Feeling sick."

He steeled himself against the quickening in his loins at the sight of her all bundled up in his clothes. He'd have to toss them on the Goodwill pile when he returned to Kentucky. Jerking a thumb behind him, he said, "I stepped out onto the balcony."

She looked past him. "There's a balcony behind all those curtains?"

"Not much of one," he admitted, "but I needed some air." He pressed his lips together, trying to slough off the remnants of their kiss. "I'm sorry—"

"I'm sorry—" she said at the same time.

"—I had no business—"

"—I don't know what came over me—"

"—I mean, you and Steve—"

"—I'm getting married, after all—"

"—and I'm your best man—"

"—and you're my best man."

They stopped and she smiled. Begrudgingly, he returned a diluted version. He didn't know what her game was, or if she even had one, but he was *not* having fun. "We're both under a lot of stress right now," he said. "Let's try to get through this quarantine without doing something we'll regret, okay?"

She nodded. "My sentiments exactly."

Silence stretched like an elastic band between them, and she wrung her hands. "Are you hungry?" she asked, gesturing toward the desk. "Manny just delivered breakfast."

"Manny?"

"The general manager."

His stomach rumbled in response. "I could eat." Glad the initial awkwardness had passed, he crossed to the desk and lifted a lid from one of the trays, but scrutinized the assortment of fruit, yogurt and miniature bagels with distaste. "Not much here that'll stick to your ribs."

She lifted the other lid to reveal eggs, sausage, bacon and pancakes. "This one's yours."

Finally, something to smile about. "Coffee, too? Excellent."

He pulled the straight-back chair over for Janine, then scooted the desk close enough to the bed for him to sit. Faced with the task of having to make conversation over their meal, he used the remote to turn up the television news station that appeared to be giving the quarantine good coverage, replaying the clip of the general manager and doctor every few minutes, and speculating on how long the guests would be confined.

But no matter how hard he tried to concentrate on the television, he couldn't shake the almost tangible energy springing from the woman who sat across from him, eating a banana of all things. Man, was he hot for her. As soon as he finished eating, he was going to take a long, cold shower. "Do you always eat like a bird?" he asked, although the words came out a little more tersely than he'd planned.

She chewed slowly, then swallowed and licked those fabulous lips of hers. "I'm a vegetarian." Pointing a finger at his plate, she added, "You, on the other hand, are courting heart disease with all those fat grams."

"I'm a big guy," he said, frowning. "I have big arteries."

Like she hadn't noticed he was big when they were grinding against each other, Janine thought, practically choking on her last bite of banana. Personally, she liked the way he ate, not wolfishly, but with a gusto that said he was a man who appreciated food, and lots of it. It suited him, the bigness, the heartiness, and hinted of other things he probably did with barely restrained energy. She averted her eyes from his hands and cleared her throat. "I remember Steve mentioning a friend of his who was a college football star. Was that you?"

Derek scoffed good-naturedly. "I played for UK, but Steve was probably referring to Jack. He was the star receiver. I was on special teams, not nearly as flashy a position."

She knew enough about football to know Derek spoke the truth about unsung positions on the field. "If you don't mind me asking, where *is* your brother, Jack?"

He swallowed, then drank deeply of the black coffee in his cup. "I don't have any idea," he said finally, in a tone that said he was accustomed to his brother's absence.

"Did he just…disappear?"

A nod, then, "Pretty much. He tends to drop out of sight when a crisis occurs at the office."

She hadn't even asked Derek what he did for a living. "The office?"

"We own an advertising agency in Lexington, Jack and I."

Janine tried to hide her surprise, but must have failed miserably because he laughed. "Actually, my father started the company, but I went to work there after I graduated. Then when Dad up and died on me a few years ago, I persuaded Jack to help me run things."

Her heart squeezed because she detected true affection in his voice when he mentioned his father. "I'm so sorry for your loss, Derek. Is your mother still living?"

A broad smile lit his face, transforming his features to roundness and light. "Absolutely. She still lives in the home where I was raised. I built a duplex for myself and Jack a few miles away so we could keep an eye on her."

"And so you could keep an eye on Jack?"

After a brief hesitation, he nodded, then made a clicking noise with his cheek. "But he still manages to slip away."

She sensed his frustration with his brother, who sounded like a rake. Derek's few words gave her insight into his life, and she pictured two boys growing up, the older, more serious sibling burdened with the responsibility of looking out for the younger, more unpredictable one. It sounded as if the mischievous Jack had led a charmed life at his brother's expense. "How long since you've heard from him?"

Derek scooped in another forkful of eggs, then squinted at the ceiling. "Two months? Yeah, it was right around tax time."

"And he's done this before?"

He nodded. "Lots of times. But he always comes back."

Intrigued by their obviously close yet adversarial relationship, she said, "And you always welcome him back."

Contrary to the response she expected, his mouth turned down and he shook his head. "Not this time, I don't think. He's been gone too long, and I'm tired of working eighty hours a week to cover for him."

"You're going to hire someone to take his place?"

Derek balled up a paper napkin and dropped it on his empty plate. "Depending on whether or not I land the account I'm working on, I might not have to worry about hiring anyone." His voice was calm, but a crease between his dark eyebrows betrayed his concern.

Setting down her bottled water, she asked, "You might close the family firm?"

He splayed his large hands. "I might have no choice. I've always managed the accounts, the scheduling, and supervised the day-to-day operations, but my father and Jack were the creative minds, and the artists." He smiled. "A person can only do so much with computer clip art."

"Can't you simply hire another artist?"

"Not and still pay Jack."

She angled her head at him. "But why would you still pay Jack?"

"A promise to my father," he said simply, and her opinion of him catapulted. A man of his word—make that a *poor* man of his word.

"But how can Jack collect his paycheck if he's not around?"

"My mother keeps it for him and pays all his bills—his utilities, his health club membership—just as if he's going to walk back in the door tomorrow." He didn't seem bitter, just resigned.

A mother who doted on her prodigal son, Janine thought. Loath to state the obvious, but unable to help herself, Janine said, "It doesn't seem fair that you would have to sacrifice your livelihood because of your brother's selfishness."

He shrugged, moving mounds of muscle. "Life isn't fair. I'll be fine. I'm just glad I don't have a wife and family to provide for." He pointed to her left hand. "I guess Steve doesn't have to worry about those kinds of things."

She glanced down at her engagement ring, the diamonds huge and lustrous. Funny, but as beautiful as the heirloom was, she would've preferred that Steve give her something smaller, a ring he'd bought for her himself. Or one they'd purchased together. If truth be known, she was still in awe of Steve's family's money, and not entirely comfortable with the concept of being rich. Sure, Steve had worked hard to get through medical school, but a trust fund had covered his expenses, so when he completed his residency, he hadn't faced the enormous loans like most med students. And herself.

Steve lived in a nice home in Midtown, a very hip area. When they married, he would pay off her school loans, and their lives would be filled with relative luxury, as would their children's.

Assuming they actually had sex and conceived, that is.

"Steve always insisted on the very best," Derek said, pouring himself another cup of coffee.

Was he referring to the ring, she wondered, or to her? Warmth flooded her face. "I suppose I should call him and let him know what's going on," she said, then glanced up quickly. "Well, n-not *everything* that's going on."

One of his dark eyebrows arched as he sipped from the cup dwarfed by his fingers. "Nothing is going on," he said mildly, but enunciated each word.

"Right," she said, standing abruptly. "Nothing. Absolutely nothing. Which is what I'll tell him—that absolutely nothing is going on."

He pursed his mouth. "He has no reason to think otherwise."

"You're right," she said, walking to the phone. "After all, he thinks I'm staying with...what exactly did you tell him?"

"That you were staying with the medical personnel."

"Oh, right. Did Steve say he'd be at home? He took a few days off work for the wedding."

"He said he'd be at his parents'."

Janine exhaled, puffing out her cheeks. "I might as well get this over with." She dialed the number, and just as she expected, his mother answered the phone.

"Mrs. Larsen, this is Janine."

"Janine! Well, isn't this the most perfectly horrible mess? I have every television on in the house watching for news of the quarantine, and Mr. Larsen is calling a friend of his at the CDC to arrange an immediate release for you."

Janine cleared her throat. "I appreciate Mr. Larsen's efforts," she said carefully, while something deep inside her resented the Larsens' attitude that every situation could be corrected simply by pulling a string. "But in my case at least, since I've been directly exposed to the illness, I seriously doubt that they'll make an exception."

Her future mother-in-law pshawed. "You'll learn soon how many doors the name Larsen will open for you in this town, my dear. Just let Mr. Larsen handle everything, especially since you're not really in a position to argue, are you?"

Janine frowned. "Excuse me?"

"Well, dear, if you hadn't gone to the hotel, then we simply could have moved the whole kit and caboodle to the club." She tsk-tsked. "If we can get you out by noon, we might still be able to make it work. Oh, Lord, give me strength, I'll be on the phone all day. Janine," she said, her tone suspicious, "why *did* you go to the resort?"

"To, um…to talk to Steve." Her prim-and-proper future mother-in-law was the last person she'd share her marital concerns with, especially since she was certain Steve had been conceived by immaculate conception. "Is Steve there, Mrs. Larsen?"

"Yes, I'll call him to the phone."

As the woman trilled in the background, Janine's heart banged against her ribs. She heard the indistinct rumble of Steve's voice, then, "Janine?"

"Hi," she said, alarmed that his voice did not overwhelm her with the comfort she craved.

"Are you calling from the hotel?"

"Yes. The quarantine hasn't been lifted yet." A nerve rash pricked at the skin on her chest.

"I guess Derek told you I called earlier this morning."

"Um, yes." She glanced in her roommate's direction. He had risen quietly and was moving toward the bathroom, to give her privacy, no doubt. "Did you have a good time last night?"

"Sure," he said, but guilt tinged his voice. "Just guy stuff, you know."

She fought her rising anger. Had he spent all night watching strippers when he wouldn't even spend one *meaningful* night with her?

"But I know *your* party was rather spirited," he continued in a disapproving tone.

Janine frowned. "How could you know?"

He hesitated for a split second, then said, "Since Marie organized it, I don't have to stretch my imagination."

She smiled in concession. "Well, it was innocent fun. Everyone seemed to enjoy themselves."

"Janine," Steve said, lowering his voice. She could picture him turning his back to shield his voice from eavesdroppers. "What made you go to the resort in the first place?" Irritation, even anger, spiked his tone.

She chewed on her lower lip and glanced toward the bathroom. Derek had turned on the shower. The moment of truth had come, because Steve would never buy the story of her simply wanting to talk. "I thought it was time, Steve."

"Time for what?" His voice rose even higher.

Allowing the silence to speak for her, she sat on the bed and waited for realization to dawn.

"To sleep together?" he hissed.

Janine closed her eyes, since his incredulity was not a good sign. "Yes."

"Janine, we've talked about this—you know how I feel. I want to wait until we're married, and I thought you did, too."

"But Steve, if we're getting married tomorrow, why would one or two nights make a difference?"

"It does," he insisted, sounding as if he was gritting his teeth. "I thought you were a good girl, Janine. Don't disappoint me now."

Warning bells sounded in her ears. "A good girl? What's that supposed to mean?"

He sighed, clearly agitated. "You *know* what I mean. Someone who will do the family name proud."

She was stunned into silence. Panic clawed at her.

"Janine?"

He hadn't said anything about love, respect or honor. Did he simply want a virgin to take on the good family name of Larsen? A lump lodged in her throat at her own gullibility.

"Janine?" Desperation laced his voice. "Janine, honey, you know I love you. By waiting until our honeymoon, I thought I was doing the honorable thing."

But she heard his words through a haze. The honorable thing—but for an honorable reason? Nausea rolled in her stomach. "Steve, I...I have to go."

"Dad will get you out of there soon, Janine," he said. "Then we can talk."

"Yes," she murmured. "We do need to talk, Steve."

"I'll call you after Dad makes the necessary phone calls," he said, back to his congenial self, their disagreement already smoothed over in his mind. "What room are you staying in?"

"Um, the health club has been turned into an infirmary," she replied truthfully, but evasively. "But it's a madhouse. If you need to talk to me, call and ask for the general manager, Manny Oliver. He knows how to reach me."

The shower in the next room shut off, and Derek's tuneless whistle reached her ears. She closed her eyes against the sexual pull leaking through the keyhole. *Not now.*

"Oh, and Janine, check in on Derek when you can," Steve said. "I feel better just knowing the two of you are there together."

11

Dad is still working his contacts at the CDC. Don't worry, this mess will be over soon.

Love, Steve

JANINE'S SHOULDERS DROPPED in relief as she stared at the handwritten note, then she raised a smile to the messenger standing beside her in the hallway.

Manny seemed surprised at her reaction. "Gee, the message didn't sound like such great news when I took it over the phone."

"Oh, but it is," she assured him.

Looking perplexed, he said, "But not if your fiancé is trying to get you out of here."

Janine glanced guiltily over her shoulder where she'd left the room door slightly ajar. She pulled the door closed and lowered her voice. "I, um...could use some time to sort through a few things."

He nodded thoughtfully, then crossed his arms. "Since I've been away from Atlanta for a couple of years, I didn't connect with the name Larsen at first. I checked the catering records to be sure—your future father-in-law is the vice-mayor."

She nodded. "Lance Larsen."

"The champion of the Morality Movement."

"Yes." The Morality Movement was a group of conservative individuals in Atlanta who had formed to banish prostitution and crack houses in a particularly seedy part of town. But once they'd made headway, the group had moved on to more controversial practices, and in the process, had propelled Lance Larsen to one of the most recognizable personalities in the city. Steve's father had run on the platform of being a family man with solid southern values, and had won the election by a nose.

"I know the man," Manny said, reclaiming her from her muse. "Very right wing. He and I clashed a time or two during rallies in my youth." He smiled, although the mirth didn't quite reach his eyes. "Is the son anything like the senior Mr. Larsen?"

Janine shook her head. "Steve has some of his father's traditional values, but he's much more open-minded." But she stopped before the echo of her own words had died. Was Steve really more open-minded, or was it simply the persona he had perfected? "He's...a surgeon," she murmured, then caught Manny's gaze, which was crystal clear and reflected her own revelation. What did Steve being a surgeon have to do with anything that truly mattered?

But her new friend let her off the hook, his mouth softening into a smile. "A surgeon, huh? Sounds like a real catch."

She nodded slowly.

"And I understand now why you wouldn't want word of your accidental and unfortunate sleeping arrangements to get back to the Larsen family." He tilted his head and his eyes probed hers. "After all, they might jump to some crazy conclusion about you and Mr. Stillman."

Janine blinked once, twice. "Manny, I...I think I'm in over my head and I don't know what to do."

He exhaled, then smiled sadly and clasped her hand between both of his. "There's only one thing you *can* do when you're in over your head, sweetheart."

"What?" she whispered.

"You have to cut anchor." He nudged her chin up a fraction of an inch with his forefinger before giving her an encouraging wink, then turned on his heel.

"Manny," she called after him. He looked back, and she gestured to the shopping bag of goodies he'd brought her. "Thanks. For everything."

He inclined his fair head, then disappeared around the corner.

Janine hesitated long enough to scan the bright yellow tag

on the doorknob which indicated an occupant remained symptomatic. From her point of view, she could see only one additional yellow tag, on a door at the end of the hall. She frowned at Maureen Jiles's empty doorknob. Apparently the woman was still kicking.

Uneasy about returning to the tension-fraught room, she nonetheless picked up the shopping bag and elbowed open the door. Derek glanced up from the desk where he'd been sitting for the past several hours, but immediately turned his attention back to his laptop computer screen.

Setting the shopping bag on the end of the bed, Janine strove to quiet the emotions warring within her. Since she'd talked to Steve this morning, she and Derek had retreated to separate areas of the room and, except for a few words exchanged when their lunch had been delivered, they had maintained conversational silence by mutual consent.

She'd passed the time playing solitaire and performing yoga exercises, exasperated to learn that when she stood on her head he was just as handsome upside down. She pretended to watch television, when in fact she'd absorbed little of what flashed across the screen. Instead, she had replayed in her mind scenes from her relationship with Steve, from meeting him on her first P.A. job to his romantic proposal six months later at the most exclusive restaurant in Atlanta. All told, she'd known him for one year.

Had she been so swept away by Steve's charming good looks and his position and name that she'd fallen in love with the image of him? A stone of disappointment thudded to the bottom of her stomach. Not disappointment in Steve, of course, but in herself. Was she so anxious to share her life with someone that she had sacrificed the chance of finding a man who, who...*moved* her?

Involuntarily, her eyes slid to Derek, who looked cramped and uncomfortable sitting at the froufrou desk and jammed into the stiff chair. Frustration lined his face, and his dark hair looked mussed by repeated finger-combing. He winced, then ripped yet another sheet of paper from a legal pad, wadded it into a ball and tossed it toward the overflowing waste can at his knee. His face contorted, then he snagged a tissue from a box and sneezed twice, his shoulders shaking from the force. The crumpled tissue landed in the trash, displacing more yellow balls of paper. When he rubbed at his temples and groaned, a pang of sympathy zipped through her.

"You're feeling worse, aren't you?"

With head in hands, he glanced over at her, then closed his eyes and nodded.

"Have you been taking the antibiotics Dr. Pedro gave you?"

He nodded again without lifting his head.

She crossed to the desk, itching to touch him, but determined not to. "Are you running a fever?"

Straightening, Derek said, "No, my temperature is fine. It's the congestion that's so annoying." He massaged the bridge of his nose and winced.

Janine peered closer at his face, his red nose, his bloodshot eyes, and a thought struck her. "Derek, do you have allergies?"

His mouth worked side to side. "None that I know of."

She glanced around the room, at the vases of resort wildflowers on the desk, the dresser, the entertainment center. Thanks to her claustrophobia, every window was flung wide to allow a cool breeze to flow through the room. She walked to the balcony door and pushed aside the curtain, then squinted into the sun. Sure enough, tiny particles floated and zipped along on the wind. On the concrete floor of the small balcony, sticky yellow granules had accumulated in the corners. *Pollen.*

Every flower in Georgia was having sex—visitors' noses beware.

When she looked back to Derek, he was reaching for another tissue. And she was starting to think his symptoms were completely unrelated to those of the guests who were hospitalized. Circling the room, she closed and secured every window and glass door.

"I thought you said the open windows would help prevent your panic attacks," he said.

"Maybe so," she replied. "But we have to get the pollen out of this room, or you'll never feel better."

He scoffed. "I told you, I've never had allergies."

"Have you ever been to Atlanta in June?"

"No."

"Then there could be something seasonal in the air, or a combination of somethings, that might have triggered unknown allergies. Especially if your immunity is down from stress."

"Stress? What's that?"

She smirked and picked up the phone, then dialed the front desk. "Mr. Oliver, please. This is Janine Murphy." A minute or two passed, during which Derek leaned back in the chair and rubbed his eyes. "You really shouldn't do that," she admonished.

He stopped and frowned in her direction.

Manny's voice came on the line. "Janine?"

"Manny, hi. I need another favor."

"Anything within my power."

"Would you send someone up with a vacuum cleaner—I'll need all the attachments—and ask them to take away the vases of flowers that sit in the hall?"

"Sure thing. What's going on up there?"

"Well, I'm not certain, but I think Derek's symptoms are more related to our resident foliage than our resident bacteria."

"Allergies?"

"Maybe. His blood tests should be back by now, and would rule out the bacteria the other guests acquired. Would you ask Dr. Pedro to come back and reexamine him when he gets a chance?"

"Will do."

Janine thanked him and hung up the phone, then turned the air-conditioner fan on high.

Derek folded his hands behind his head and made an amused noise. "So you think I'm not afflicted with the plague after all?"

She directed a dry smile across the room. "Some people

with allergies say it's almost as bad." With a vase of flowers in either hand, she headed toward the door.

He stood and crossed to open the door. Stepping into the hall, he turned and reached for the vases, but she pulled back. "I'm trying to help you here."

A noise sounded in the hall behind him. Janine peered out over top of the flowers to see Maureen Jiles bent at the waist, her shapely rear end stuck straight up in the air as she set a food tray on the floor. The woman straightened and beamed in Derek's direction. "Well, well, well. We meet again."

Janine frowned. "Meat" was more like it. Maureen's voluptuous curves were barely contained in a silver lamé bikini top. A sheer black wrap miniskirt laughingly covered the matching bottoms. Her deeply tanned legs were so long, they appeared to extend down through the carpeted floor. Her jet hair was held back from her face with a metallic headband, and her skin was so well greased, Janine marveled that the woman hadn't congealed. Next to the sun diva, Janine felt like a...well, a boy.

Beside her, Derek had apparently been struck dumb.

"I see you haven't yet fallen ill." Janine crinkled her nose against the leaf tickling her cheek, wondering how long Maureen had been standing butt-up in the hallway hoping Derek would open the door.

Maureen finally looked her way. "Surely you're not getting rid of all those lovely flowers!"

"Derek seems to be allergic," she replied.

"Would you like them for your room?" Derek asked, rankling Janine, although she couldn't identify why. After all, the flowers would otherwise be wasted.

Maureen's smile rivaled the Cheshire cat's as she devoured Derek with her eyes. "That would be lovely. Won't you bring them inside and help me arrange them?"

"I don't think we're supposed to be in each other's rooms," Janine interjected.

"Oh, just for a minute," the woman pleaded to Derek. "I'm having trouble with a stuck window."

He looked at Janine and shrugged. "Allergies aren't contagious."

"I could be wrong about the allergies," she whispered. Besides, there was no telling what kinds of creepy-crawlies he could catch from *Maureen.*

"But I'm *so* good at getting things unstuck," he whispered back, sounding like a teenage boy making excuses to help the divorcée across the street.

Janine frowned and shoved the vases into his hands. "Take your time."

He carried the vases into the woman's room while Janine stood rooted to the spot. Maureen gave her a little wave through the opening in the door before she closed it behind them.

Absurdly miffed, she marched back into the room, gathering up two more vases of flowers, then set them in front of the woman's door. Maureen's throaty laugh sounded, and Janine harrumphed. But unable to stem her curiosity, she leaned over and pressed her ear against the door.

The low rumble of Derek's voice floated to her, then Maureen's laugh, then his own surprisingly rich laugh. The phony—he'd barely cracked a smile since she'd met him, much less out and out laughed.

"It works better if you have a juice glass."

Janine jumped, then spun around to see Manny watching her with an amused expression, holding a vacuum cleaner.

She smoothed her hands down over her hips, displacing lots of baggy fabric. "I was just, um, checking to see if Ms. Jiles is okay."

Another burst of his and her laughter sounded from behind the door.

One side of Manny's mouth drew up. "She sounds fine to me."

Janine lifted her chin. "Well…good." With cheeks burning, she crossed to her own door that she'd left propped open, and awkwardly waved him inside. "You didn't have to bring up the vacuum yourself," she murmured.

He set the vacuum in the middle of the floor. "I might have

sent someone from housekeeping, but there just isn't enough staff to go around."

A pang of regret stabbed her. "You probably haven't had a minute's peace since the quarantine was lowered."

"Not much," he admitted, then gave her a teasing grin. "But your little situation is the *most* entertaining distraction."

She shook her finger at him. "Don't be enjoying this, please."

This time he laughed, covering his mouth. "I'm sorry, Janine, I simply can't help it. This is such a feeling of déjà vu."

"Oh? You have another friend whose wedding was postponed when she was quarantined with her best man?"

"No, each of my female friends have gotten into their own little scrapes."

Untangling the hose-and-brush attachment, she gave him a wry look. "And where are they now?"

He ticked off on his long fingers. "Ellie is married with two impossibly gorgeous little girls, Pamela is married and her toddler son is a musical prodigy, and Cindy was married a couple of months ago—no kids yet."

Janine bent to the vacuum and unwound the cord, shooting him a dubious smile. "Are you saying you had something to do with all that marital bliss?"

"Well—" he splayed his hands "—I do have a perfect record to date."

"Then maybe you should rub my head," she said with a little sigh.

He laughed and helped her untangle the machinery. "May I ask if the robust Mr. Stillman has anything to do with you needing some time to sort things out?"

Fighting with the stiff cord, she broke a nail into the quick, then sucked on the end of her finger. "No."

"No? Or no, I shouldn't ask?"

Her heart galloped in her chest as she reconsidered her response. How much of her sudden uncertainty had to do with Steve's reaction to her final attempt to consummate their marriage, and how much of it had to do with her unexplainable attraction to Derek?

Misinterpreting her silence, Manny moved quietly toward the door.

"Manny."

He turned, his hand on the doorknob.

"Do you see something here that I don't?"

He pressed his lips together and his gaze floated around the perimeter of the room, then landed on her. "I see a woman who's willing to clean a room for a man who's being entertained across the hall." His smile softened his words. "You should at least consider retrieving the beast." Then he was gone.

Confounded by his words, she plugged in the vacuum and flipped the switch. She'd always enjoyed the monotonous, thought-blocking chore, but today as she decontaminated every surface within reach, her mind was far from blank. Images of Derek cavorting across the hall with Maureen kept rising to taunt her. So that was the sort of man he was, she sniffed. Common. Typical. Base. Chasing down any female within range. Their kiss had meant nothing to him, she realized. Not that it should, considering their respective relationships with Steve. But admittedly it galled her to think that what had been such a momentous lapse of character for her had left him quite unfazed.

Her naiveté didn't embarrass her—she would never be able to take sexual intimacy as lightly as most of the people in her generation seemed to, but she did recognize how her virginal perspective could put her at a slight disadvantage. After all, if any part of her decision to marry Steve was based on unrealized sexual curiosity, wasn't that just as misguided as rushing into a relationship founded purely on good sex?

Janine sighed and extended the reach on the brush she was running over the curtains. Would she even be having this bewildering conversation with herself if Steve's best man had been a chuffy married fellow instead of the "robust" Derek Stillman?

A tap on her shoulder would have sent her out of her shoes had she been wearing any. She whirled to see that Derek had returned, and he did not look happy. A flip of a switch reduced the noise of the vacuum to a fading whine.

"Gay?" he asked, arms crossed. "You told that woman I'm *gay?*"

She looked past him to the closed door. "I, um…it seemed like the prudent thing to say."

"The prudent thing to say?" His voice had risen a couple of octaves, and his face was the color of roasted tomatoes. "For whom?"

"Watch your blood pressure," she warned, bending to rewrap the cord. "I told Maureen you were gay for the sake of both our reputations—and for Steve's."

"Really?" He pursed his mouth, his body rigid. "Well, it seems to me that *your* reputation and *Steve's* reputation are safe, and now *I'm* a gay man."

She laughed at his histrionics. "I don't know what you're getting all worked up about—there's nothing wrong with being gay."

"Except," he said crisply, "I'm *not.*"

"Okay," she said, rolling the cleaner up against the wall. "So if you wanted to get it on with Maureen the Man-eater, then why didn't you just tell her you weren't gay?"

"Well, funny thing about denying you're gay after someone else has already told the person you *are* gay—" He threw his hands in the air. "They don't believe you!"

"So? The woman made it clear to me this morning that she's adopted a nondiscrimination policy. She doesn't care if you're gay."

"But I'm *not* gay!"

"But it doesn't matter to her!"

"Well, you know that's another funny thing," he said, pacing. "When a woman *thinks* you're gay, it kind of changes the dynamics."

"Well, excuse me," she said, irritated at herself for trying to make the room more comfortable for him. "If I'd known you were so hot for her, I would have gladly told her you were bisexual!"

"Whoa," he said, holding up his hand. "I am *not* bi. Okay? Repeat, I am *not* bi."

"I know that," she snapped.

"And I'm not *hot* for that, that, that…man predator. I just wanted to get away from *you* for a few minutes!"

Hurt, she stared openmouthed. "Well, it was a minivacation for me, too!"

Derek stalked across the room and dropped into the stiff chair in front of the desk, bewildered that this woman could so easily provoke him. He sighed, then pressed out his entwined fingers to the tune of ten cracking knuckles.

"You really shouldn't do that."

He pressed his lips together, then shot a weary look in her direction. "And why not?"

"It's not a natural movement for your body."

"Oh, but I suppose standing on your head *is* a natural movement."

She upended a shopping bag on the bed. "Several other species hang upside down, but none that I know of crack their knuckles."

Derek stared at her, his knuckle-cracked fingers itching to wring her tempting little neck. The woman was absolutely relentless, not to mention oblivious to how she affected him.

"I had Manny bring you some shaving cream," she said, waving a small can.

"I hope he brought *you* a razor," he said, slanting a frown across the room.

"You," she said, pointing, "are contrary."

At the sight of that little finger wagging, his blood pressure spiked again. "Well, excuse me," he said, tapping a key to bring his blank laptop screen back to life. "I'm sort of stuck in a quarantine in Atlanta, with a friend of mine's accident-prone bride, for God only knows how long, while a client in Kentucky sits patting his Flexisole wing tips." He shoved both hands into his hair, leaned his elbows on the desk and stared at the trio of bee by-products that were supposed to take his company into the millennium. "I'm a little stressed here," he croaked.

Suddenly his antagonist was behind him, her sweet breath on his neck. "You know, Derek," she murmured. "I just might be able to help."

12

JANINE COULD HELP his stress? Derek tensed for her touch. Part of him shouted he absolutely should *not* allow her to rub his shoulders, while the rest of him clamped down on his inner voice. Her right hand drifted past his ear and he fairly groaned in anticipation. But when she reached around to pluck up one of the containers of honey, he frowned and turned to face her.

She was studying the label, her lips pursing and unpursing. "Your client is Phillips Honey?"

"Potential client. You've heard of them?"

"Nope."

His shoulders fell. "Neither has anyone else."

"Bee-yoo-ti-ful honey?" she read, then made a face. "I hope that wasn't your idea."

Derek smiled and shook his head. "No. The CEO is shopping for a new ad agency."

"With a slogan like that, I can see why."

"I'm supposed to meet with him Monday. He's looking for a new label, a new slogan, a new campaign—the whole enchilada."

She shrugged. "So what's the problem?"

"Other than the fact that I might still be *here* on Monday?"

Janine nodded a little sheepishly.

"Well, excluding Winnie the Pooh, honey isn't exactly in demand these days."

"Oh?"

He gestured toward her. "Do *you* put honey on your toast in the morning?"

She shook her head. "Not typically."

"Drizzle it over homemade granola?"

"Nope."

"Dip your biscuits in a big warm pot of it?"

"Uh-uh."

"See? People our age simply aren't buying honey at the grocery store every week." His hand fell in defeat.

"You're right," she said. "I buy my honey at the health food store."

He swung back in surprise. "Really? So you do eat honey?"

"In various forms. I specialize in homeopathic medicine."

He squinted, searching for the connection.

Her smile was patient. "Treating symptoms with remedies from natural ingredients whenever possible. Honey is one of my favorites."

His interest piqued, he turned his chair around to face her. "To treat what?"

"Allergies, for one," she said, leaning forward to tap his nose with her finger.

The gesture struck him as almost domestic, and it warmed him absurdly.

"Bees make honey out of pollen," she continued, "and ingesting minute amounts of local pollen helps build immunity."

Dubious, he angled his head at her.

Janine sat on the bed facing him, still cradling the pint of honey in her hands. "It's the same concept that allergy shots are based on," she said simply.

He nodded slowly, but remained unconvinced. "So, what else is honey good for?"

Her pale eyebrows sprang up as she presumably searched her memory. "Minor arthritis pains, insomnia, superficial burns, skin irritations…among other things."

A red flag sprang up in his mind. "You mix up your own remedies and sell them to your patients?" Janine Murphy, Quack—the image wasn't much of a stretch.

A musical, appealing laugh rolled out. "No, I just encourage patients to read up on the benefits of natural foods. So instead of pushing honey as an indulgent, fattening topping for a big ol' plate of flour and lard, maybe Phillips should tap into its more healthful uses."

He held up the honey butter. "Like freeing stuck toes from bathtub faucets?"

The rosy tint on her cheeks made her look even more endearing, if possible. Derek felt an unnerving tingle of awareness that drove deep into his chest, shaking him. This mushrooming attraction to Janine was downright baffling. Certainly she was a great-looking woman, but he came into contact with attractive women on a daily basis, and he'd never before lost track of a conversation.

What *had* they been talking about?

He glanced down at the container in his hand. Oh, yeah, honey, the medicinal panacea for the new century. Derek cleared his throat, determined to focus. "Isn't it dangerous to make medical claims?"

She lifted one shoulder in a half shrug. "The medicinal uses for honey are as old as medicine itself. It should never be given to infants, and diabetics have to exercise restraint, but otherwise, it's perfectly safe. Some people swear by honey, just like some people swear by garlic or vinegar to boost general health." After averting her eyes, she added, "One male patient of mine insists that bee pollen and honey have improved his sex drive."

Derek had to swallow his guffaw. "And you?"

She nodded. "I have a teaspoon in my morning tea."

Derek swallowed. Even as his body responded to her nearness, his enthusiasm for Janine's ideas began to shrivel. He could picture himself in front of stodgy Donald Phillips, presenting his idea for a new slogan: Have Phillips Honey for Breakfast, Then Have *Your* Honey for Lunch.

Suddenly her eyes flew wide. "Not that it's improved *my* sex life," she added hastily. Her skin turned crimson as she clamped her mouth shut.

Despite his best efforts, Derek felt a smile wrap around his face. Perhaps honey was her secret. From the scant time they'd spent together, he'd learned two things about Pinky— she attracted trouble, and she oozed sex. From every tight little pore in her tight little bod. "Then I guess we're in trouble if we need a testimonial," he teased.

She pressed her lips together, eyes wide, looking as innocent as a pink bunny rabbit. Feeling like a lecherous old man, Derek shifted uncomfortably in his chair and cast about for a safer topic. "What do you think about the packaging?"

Janine smoothed a finger over the plain black-and-white label, working her mouth back and forth. "I like the simplicity, but it covers too much of the container."

He lifted an eyebrow.

"If the honey is pure, the color will sell it," she explained. "I like to see what I'm buying."

"Fine, but then where would we print all those newfangled uses, Doc?"

"On the website," she said with nonchalance, then handed him the honey. Their fingers brushed, but she must not have felt the electricity because she stood and returned to sorting through the pile of items she'd dumped out of the shopping bag, as if nothing had transpired.

On the website…of course. Not that Phillips had a website, or even a desktop computer, for that matter, but someone had to drag the man out of the Dark Ages. Derek jotted down a few notes on the legal pad.

"And what about changing the name?"

He glanced up. "Excuse me?"

"The name," she said, tearing the tag off a pair of yellow flip-flops. "Phillips. It's not very buyer friendly, at least not for honey."

He stuck his tongue in his cheek, rolling around her observation. "But it's the man's name."

"What's his first name?"

"Donald."

She made a face. "What's his wife's name?"

Derek shrugged. "I have no idea."

"Daughters?"

He started to shake his head, then remembered that Phillips had bragged about his daughter's equestrian skills.

Heather? No. Holly? No. "Hannah," he said as the name slid into place.

"Perfect," she said, dropping the brightly colored shoes to the floor and sliding her pink-tipped toes into them. Then she spread her arms as if presenting a prize. "Hannah's Honey."

Creativity flowed from her like water, and she seemed unaware of her talent. With a start, Derek realized who she reminded him of—Jack. Jack, who always needed rescuing from some scrape or another, yet somehow managed to escape unscathed. Jack, who could crank out more creative concepts in one day than Derek could eke out in a month. Jack, who was notorious for his ability to make a woman feel as if she were the most important person in the world, only to disappear before the morning paper hit the porch.

Did she know how she affected him? he wondered. Was her innocence simply a clever act? Was she the kind of woman who thrived on male attention, who flirted with danger? The kind of woman who would delight in seducing a friend of her fiancé's? His mouth tightened. Dammit, the woman probably knew just how adorable she looked swallowed up in his clothes, with clashing shoes and toenails.

Suddenly he realized she was waiting for his response. "I...I don't know how Phillips will feel about changing the name of his product line," he managed to say.

"If sales were booming, I assume he wouldn't be looking for a new agency," she said, holding a lavender Georgia on My Mind T-shirt over her chest. "A new name for the new millennium—what does he have to lose?"

He scoffed, extending his legs and crossing them at the ankles. "You make it sound so easy."

"Well, isn't it?"

"No," he insisted, a bit flustered. Leave it to someone outside the business world to overlook the nuances of wide-sweeping changes.

"I thought you said he was going to change the packaging anyway."

"It's not the same thing—"

The phone rang, and they both stared at it until the second ring had sounded.

"I could get it," she said. "But what if it's Steve?"

"I could get it," he said. "But what if it's your mother?"

Janine relented, leaned across the bed, then picked up the handset. "Hallooo," she said in her best Aunt Bea impression, fully intending to hand off the phone if Steve was on the other end.

"You *must* be sick if your voice is that distorted," Marie said, munching something fresh- and crunchy-sounding—maybe pineapple.

Mouthing to Derek that the phone was for her, she flopped onto the bed facedown. "No, I was trying to disguise my voice."

Crunch, crunch. "Why?"

She sighed. "Long story."

"Great, I just threw in a load of laundry, so I have plenty of time. I got your voice message that the wedding is off."

"Postponed," she corrected, perturbed.

"Whatever. I'm just glad to hear you're still alive. If you believe the news, everyone up there has the African flesh-eating disease."

Janine laughed. Marie could always lift her spirits. "No, it's not that bad, even though a few more guests have fallen ill. Dr. Pedro of the CDC told me the hospitalized patients are responding to antibiotics. I'm hoping we'll be out of here in another day or two."

"Speaking of we," Marie said, her voice rich with innuendo, "how's your roomie? I assume he's still there since Mother was concerned about some *bellman* in your room early this morning when she called."

"You didn't tell her, did you?"

"Of course not, and I made her promise not to call the room constantly."

Janine sighed. "Thanks."

"Well," Marie demanded. "How is Mr. Stillman?"

From beneath her lashes, Janine glanced to the desk where Derek had returned to his computer, tapping away. "Uninteresting," she said in a tone meant to stem further discussion on the subject.

"Is he still sick?"

"There's a good chance his symptoms are allergy-related instead of what the other guests have come down with."

"It has to be tough, sharing close quarters with a virtual stranger," her sister probed, crunching. "An attractive man and an attractive woman, at that."

With a last look at Derek's handsome profile, Janine pushed herself up from the bed and stretched the phone line across the room to the sliding glass door. She opened it, stepped onto the tiny balcony and closed the door to the smallest crack that would accommodate the cord. She drew in a deep breath of fresh air—pollen be damned—relieved for a few minutes of freedom from those four suffocating burgundy walls, and from those two captivating brown eyes. Slowly she exhaled, surveying the peaceful scene below her. Except for the fact that the grounds were deserted, and that two uniformed guards stood chatting at the corner of the building, one would never suspect the resort was under quarantine.

"Sis, are you there?"

Janine snapped back to attention. "Yeah, I'm here."

Marie resumed her munching. "You were about to tell me what you and your hunky best man are doing to while away the hours."

She mentally reviewed the day—getting her toe stuck in the bathtub faucet, nearly having a sexual encounter with Derek, discovering she might not be in love with Steve after all… "Not much going on. We've barely interacted, he and I."

"Ooooooooooh. Is he the big, strong, silent type?"

"No. He's the big, strong, mind-his-own-business type—hint, hint."

"So he *is* big and strong."

Janine rolled her eyes. "Marie, enough. What's going on out there?"

"Well, you know Mom—she thinks the quarantine is a bad

omen. She's been lighting candles like crazy. I took an extra fire extinguisher over there, just in case."

"Thanks for being my buffer, sis. I just can't talk to her right now."

Marie didn't respond, and she'd stopped chewing. Janine waited with dread for her sister's perceptiveness to make itself apparent.

Her sister clucked. "Are you okay, sis?"

She cleared her throat. "Other than a persistent bout of clumsiness, I'm fine."

"What does Steve think about calling off the wedding?"

"Postponing," Janine corrected her sourly.

"Whatever. He's not giving you a hard time, is he?"

Not knowingly. Misery knotted in her stomach. "No, he knows it can't be helped."

"How much longer do you think they'll have the place under quarantine?"

"I don't know. The doctor told Derek worst-case scenario, two weeks."

The announcement obviously stunned her sister into silence. After a few seconds, Marie said, "Well, you asked for something exciting, and you got it—a quarantine, mixed-up rooms, sleeping with a stranger—"

Janine yanked the phone cord tight and hissed, "I am *not* sleeping with him!"

"Easy, sis," Marie murmured, "else I might think that something *is* going on between you and your best man."

Opening her mouth to shout a denial, she realized she was only digging herself deeper into a hole.

"Speaking of which," Marie continued, "where *did* you sleep last night?"

"If you must know, I slept in the bathtub." She held the phone away from her ear until Marie's laughter petered out.

"Whew, that's a good one! So doesn't this guy have any manners?"

"He fell asleep in the bed first, while I was trying to calm down Mother."

"So? You put a pillow in the middle and lie down on the other side."

"Except he was naked."

"Okaaaaaaaay," Marie sang, ever openminded. "And that would be because…?"

"Because he wasn't wearing any clothes."

"Okeydokey," she said in an accepting tone. "Speaking of clothes, what are you doing for them?"

"He loaned me a few things."

"He being Derek?"

"Yes."

"You're wearing the man's clothes?"

"Marie, for God's sake, am I talking to myself here?"

"Is this guy on the up-and-up?"

At least once today, she thought wryly. But she recognized concern in her sister's voice when she heard it, and right now, Marie needed some peace of mind. "He's a decent guy, sis. A little uptight, but decent."

A knock on the sliding glass door spun her around. Derek slid the door open, his expression unreadable as he jerked his thumb over his shoulder. "You might want to see this," he whispered.

She covered the mouth of the phone. "What?"

"It's Steve. He's on television."

13

"WE HAD TO POSTPONE our wedding that was scheduled to take place here at the resort," Steve was saying, looking grim, but perfectly groomed in his country-club casual garb. He stood at a slight angle, the Green Stations Resort sign visible just over his left shoulder.

"So your fiancée is trapped inside the resort?" an off-camera male voice asked.

Steve crossed his arms and nodded gravely. "That's correct."

"And do you know if she's ill, Dr. Larsen?"

"The last time I spoke with her, she was feeling fine, but she's a physician's assistant and could be exposing herself to infected guests even as we speak." He was incredibly photogenic, she acknowledged, his white-blond hair cropped fashionably short on the sides, longer on top. Funny, but she'd never noticed the petulant tug at the corners of his mouth.

"Are other members of your wedding party confined at the resort?"

Steve hesitated for a split second. "My best man."

"Your bride and your best man are locked up together?" The reporter chuckled.

Clearly distressed, Steve held up a hand, as if to stop the man's train of thought. "Not *together* together, as in the same room." He laughed, a soft little snort. "That would be unthinkable."

Guilt plowed through her, leaving a wide, raw furrow. She glanced at Derek and he was looking at her, one eyebrow raised.

"I understand you actually had a room here, sir. How did *you* escape the quarantine?"

He sighed heavily. "I left the property for a medical emergency unrelated to the resort, and when I returned, the quarantine was already under way."

Janine frowned. She'd never known Steve to blatantly lie, although she understood his unwillingness to say he'd been out all night partying. Of course, she'd been lying like a rug herself lately.

The reporter made a sympathetic sound. "I assume you're going to reschedule the wedding as soon as possible."

"Absolutely," Steve said, then looked directly into the camera. "This is for the future Mrs. Steven Larsen. Sweetheart, if you're watching, remember how much I love you." He winked, and her heart scooted sideways.

The camera switched to the reporter. "So, a cruel twist of fate is keeping the fiancée of Dr. Steven Larsen confined with the doctor's best man."

Janine squinted, clutching the hastily hung-up phone.

"As a result, the vice-mayor's son's wedding has been canceled."

"Postponed," Janine muttered.

"Meanwhile, there seems to be no end in sight to the quarantine now in effect at the Green Stations Resort. This is Andy Judge. Now back to you in the studio."

The anchorwoman came on-screen. "Thank you, Andy. Keep us posted." A small smile played on her face. "Stay with us for continuing coverage of…'The Quarantine Crisis.'" A menacing bass throbbed in the background as the news faded to a commercial.

Janine gaped at the screen.

"Something tells me Steve's father is not going to like this," Derek said.

A knock sounded on the door, kicking up Janine's pulse. In two long strides, Derek reached the door and stooped to look through the keyhole. "It's Dr. Pedro," he said, then stepped back and swung open the door.

"Mr. Stillman, you requested another examination?"

Derek looked in her direction, then back to the doctor.

"Janine seems to think I might be suffering from allergies instead of an infection."

Dr. Pedro walked inside and set his bag on the foot of the bed. "Well, let's take a look, shall we?"

She knew she should stay and find out as much about the status of the quarantine as possible, but Janine swept the items Manny had brought her into the shopping bag and escaped to the bathroom to think. She closed the door and dumped the contents of the bag onto the counter, then dropped to the vanity stool, sorting toiletries from souvenir clothes. Bless Manny's heart. In addition to necessities, he'd brought her a single tube of pink lipstick, a nice quality hairbrush and a package of simple cotton underwear.

When the items had been stacked, folded and stored away, Janine sighed and stared at herself in the mirror. Her fingers jumped and twitched involuntarily. Nerves, she knew. Entwining her fingers, she stretched them out and away from her, the first time she'd ever felt compelled to crack her knuckles. One knuckle popped faintly, shooting pain up her hand, and the other fingers emitted a dull crunching sound, which made her a bit light-headed.

She'd never been so scared in her life. Nothing was more terrifying, she realized, than thinking you knew yourself, only to discover an alien had invaded your body and mind. The real Janine Murphy wouldn't be second-guessing her marriage to one of the most eligible men in Atlanta. The real Janine Murphy wouldn't be entertaining kisses from a strange man and allowing his presence to drive her to distraction. The real Janine Murphy wouldn't be lying to practically everyone she knew about her humiliating circumstances.

She squinted, hoping to find answers to her troubling questions somewhere behind her eyes, and found one.

The real Janine Murphy wouldn't be lying to herself.

When she'd seen Steve on the television screen, she'd witnessed a spoiled, polished, self-absorbed man putting on a show for the cameras. Not a single time during Steve's interview had he even mentioned her name, referring to her instead as *Mrs. Steven Larsen*. Granted, his defensive reaction on the phone to her clumsy attempt at intimacy had left a bad taste in her mouth, but she was starting to recognize a disturbing pattern in his behavior that she hadn't seen before—or rather, hadn't wanted to see.

Steve was more interested in her state of womanhood than in her as a woman. For his family name. For his father's reputation. Heck, maybe even for some kind of deep-seated territorial macho urge. None of which boded well for marital happiness.

From the other room, she heard the sound of the door closing. Dr. Pedro had left, which meant that once again she was alone with Derek. Alone for—how had he put it?—for God only knows how long. A silent groan filled her belly and chest, then lodged in her constricted throat.

She'd have to be dense not to recognize the sexual pull between them. Marie had been telling her stories about electric chemistry, tingly insides and throbbing outsides since they were teenagers, but this was the first time Janine had experienced how a physical attraction could override a person's otherwise good judgment.

A bitter laugh escaped her. Override? More like trample.

Janine's shoulders sagged with resignation because, in the midst of her general confusion, one conclusion suddenly seemed crystal clear: she simply couldn't marry Steve, at least not the way things were between them, not the way things were between her and Derek, even if it was only in her mind.

Regardless of her enigmatic feelings, she wasn't about to drag Derek into the melee. After all, he and Steve were friends long before she came into the picture. Besides, Derek would probably laugh at the notion of her putting so much stock in her physical attraction to him. It was different for men, she realized, but she couldn't help her strong, if quaint, tendency to associate sex with deep emotional feelings. Which was precisely why she found her reaction to Derek so disturbing. If she were truly in love with Steve, she wouldn't have been tempted by Derek's kisses.

Would she?

She heard the room door open and close again, and wondered briefly if Derek had gone to try to set things straight with Maureen the Machine.

A faint rap sounded at the bathroom door. "Janine, our dinner is here."

The split second of relief that he hadn't left the room was squelched by the realization that the sound of his voice had become so, so…welcome. Resolved to be cool and casual, despite her recent revelations, she pushed herself to her feet.

DEREK LEANED against the window next to the desk with one splayed hand holding open the curtain and comparing the vast, sparkling horizon to the south to the sparse, more rural skyline he'd left behind. The remnants of daylight bled pale blue into the distant violet-colored treeline, broken up with splashes of silver and light where progress encroached on the north side of the city. He sipped just-delivered coffee, then winced when the hot liquid burned his tongue.

He deserved it, he decided. For kissing an engaged woman. *Steve's* engaged woman. His pal was a bit on the uppity side, and he questioned his commitment to Janine, but seeing his face on TV, hearing him say he loved her was like a wake-up call to his snoozing sense of honor.

No matter how attracted he was to the woman, he'd simply have to keep his damn hands to himself, and pray that she did the same. She walked up behind him, flip-flops flapping, and he turned slowly, setting his jaw against the onslaught of desire that seemed to accompany every glance at her over the past few hours.

"What did Dr. Pedro have to say—*aarrrrrrrhhhhh!*"

Stumbling over the toe of one of her rubber sandals, Pinky fell forward, clutching the air. Reaching out instinctively, he grabbed her by the upper arm, managing to steady her with one hand before he felt the white sting of hot coffee on his other hand. He sucked in sharply and slammed the cup down on the desk, sending more scalding liquid over his thumb and wrist. He grunted and made a fist against the pain. Before he knew what was happening, Janine had grabbed his forearm and thrust his hand into the partially melted bucket of ice sitting next to their covered food trays.

"*Aaaah*" he moaned as the fiery sensation gave way to chilling numbness.

"I'm sorry," she gasped. "I'm so sorry!"

"It's okay," he assured her, conjuring up a smile. Truth be known, her body pressed up against his and her fingers curved around his arm were more of a threat to his well-being than the burn. "Really, it'll be fine."

Slowly he withdrew his hand, and Janine leaned in close. "No puckering and no blisters."

"Told you," he said, allowing her to turn his hand this way and that.

Clucking like a mother hen, she reached for the container of honey butter and proceeded to gently douse the reddened areas of his hand.

"That stuff will help?"

She used both her hands to sandwich his, spreading the condiment with feathery strokes that sent an ache to his groin. "The honey will soothe, and the butter will keep the skin moist," she said. "But only after the skin has cooled, else the butter will accelerate the burn, kind of like frying a piece of meat."

"Now there's an image," he said dryly.

"Good," she said, wrapping his hand loosely with a white cloth napkin from one of their trays. "Then you'll remember it the next time you burn yourself."

He bit his tongue to keep from blurting that he normally didn't toss his coffee around.

"Thank you, Derek."

Derek frowned at her bent head. She had braided her hair, and the thick blond plait fell over her shoulder, the ends skimming his arm. "For what?"

"For catching me."

He swallowed and reminded himself of his determination to keep his distance. "I would rather your 'something blue' not be a bruise."

Her hands halted briefly, but she didn't look up. "So what *did* Dr. Pedro have to say?"

"He concurred with your diagnosis," he said, nodding toward sample packets of Benedryl. "My blood tests were negative."

The whisper of a smile curved her pink mouth. "What about the quarantine?"

"Another outbreak today," he said. "Four people in this building, and a half dozen in the golf villas."

"Are the cases serious?" she asked, raising her blue eyes to meet his gaze at last.

A man could lose himself in those eyes, he decided, and he couldn't tear himself away.

"Derek?"

He blinked. "Uh, serious enough to maintain the quarantine."

"There," she said, tucking the end of the cloth into the makeshift bandage. After screwing the lid back on the honey butter, she wiped her hands on the other napkin. "I'll call down for some gauze."

She moved like a dancer, limber and graceful even in his big clothes. With an inward groan, he acknowledged his resolve to ignore her was having the opposite effect—he was more aware of her than ever. When she hung up the phone, she turned back to him, hugging herself, looking small and vulnerable. Her expression was unreadable, and the silence stretched between them. At last she looked away, her gaze landing on a stack of pillows and linens.

"I had those brought up," he said. "I'll sleep on the floor tonight and let you have the bed."

She stared at the linens as if mesmerized. What was going on in her head?

Derek's mind raced, trying to think of something to say to ease the soupy tension between them. Steve's TV interview had shaken her, that much was obvious. Was she worried he was going to tell Steve about their near lapses? That her future with the wealthy Larsen family was in jeopardy?

"I'm starved," he said with a small laugh, gesturing to their covered trays.

Janine walked over and picked up a bottle of springwater. "Go ahead, I'm going to get some air." She practically jogged across the room, escaping to the balcony. Between his company and her claustrophobia, he supposed she was doing the only thing she could under the circumstances.

Derek stared at the tray. Despite the nice aromas escaping from the lid, he discovered he wasn't starved after all. Not even hungry, if truth be known. He poured himself another cup of coffee—an awkward task with his hand wrapped—and mulled over the events of the past twenty-four hours or so. Funny, but he felt as if he'd come to know Janine almost better than he knew Steve.

Of course, he and Steve had never been quarantined in a room together.

The sexual pull between them confounded him. Was it inevitable that a man and a woman in close quarters would be drawn to each other? In a crisis, even a minor one, did age-old instincts kick in, elevating their urge to seek comfort in each other?

Perhaps, he decided with a sigh. But thankfully, humans were distinguished from other animals in the kingdom by their presumably evolved brain that gave them the ability to act counter to their instincts. He snorted in disgust. They were adults—they could talk through this situation. In the event the quarantine was drawn out for several more days, he'd prefer they at least be on speaking terms.

Setting down his coffee mug—better safe than sorry—he crossed to the sliding glass door. When he saw her standing with her back to him, leaning on the railing, he hesitated for only a second before opening the door and stepping outside.

She turned, her eyes wide in the semidarkness. "You shouldn't be out here."

"I thought we should talk."

"But your allergies—"

"Won't kill me," he cut in. Although he was beginning to

think that resisting her might. Her pale hair glowed thick and healthy in the moonlight, and he itched to loosen her braid.

"We could go back inside," she offered, her gaze darting behind him as if she were sizing up an emergency exit.

"No, I realize you're more comfortable in an open space. Besides," he said, joining her at the railing, "it's a nice night."

"Uh-huh," she said, turning back to the view, although he noticed she moved farther down the rail, away from him. Suddenly, she emitted a soft cry, reaching over the rail in futility as her plastic bottle of water fell top over end until out of sight. A couple of seconds later, a dull thud sounded as it hit something soft on the ground.

"With my luck lately, that was probably a guard," she whispered.

Derek laughed heartily, glad for the release. When she joined in, he welcomed the slight shift in atmosphere. "I hope you don't take this the wrong way, but you do seem to be a little accident-prone."

"Only recently," she said softly. "I guess I have a lot on my mind."

After a pause, he said, "Tell me about your family." He was intrigued by the upbringing that had shaped her aspirations.

She shrugged. "Not much to tell. My father is a traveling appliance repairman for Sears. My mother gardens. I have a terrific older sister who's a massage therapist. We all love each other."

Very middle-class, he acknowledged. "How did you meet Steve?"

"On the job," she replied, her voice a bit high. "I work at the clinic in the hospital where he performs surgery."

A stark reminder of his friend's career success and Derek's relative failure. At a time when most men his age were hitting their stride, he was struggling to pay the office electricity bill. He cleared his throat. "Steve certainly has a lot going for him. I can see why you're looking forward to marrying him."

She was silent for several seconds, then pointed with her

index finger out over the rail. "See those pinkish lights on top of the hill?"

He squinted. "Yeah."

"That's the gazebo where our ceremony was supposed to take place. Tomorrow."

His heart caught at the wistful tone in her voice. "So you'll reschedule. I have a feeling the hotel will bend over backward to accommodate the Larsens when this is all over."

"No."

"Sure they will," he insisted. "Steve's father will—"

"I mean, no, I'm not going to reschedule the wedding."

14

A LOW HUM OF PANIC churned in his stomach. "Wh-what did you say?"

"I said I'm not going to reschedule the wedding. I'm not going to marry Steve."

Adrenaline pumped through his body. "You're not serious," he said, his chest rising and falling hard.

"Yes, I am."

"But why?"

"That's really between me and Steve, isn't it?"

Anger sparked in his stomach. "Not if it has something to do with what happened between us." He'd messed with her mind by not keeping his hands to himself. He'd ruined not only her well-laid plans, but Steve's, too. "Those kisses didn't mean anything, Janine. We were thrown together in an intimate situation. You're a beautiful woman, I'm a red-blooded guy. People do strange things in situations like this. Things happen, but it doesn't have to change the course of our lives."

"Don't blame yourself, Derek. I'm grateful to you, really."

"Grateful?"

"For helping me realize that Steve and I wouldn't be happy."

"I n-never said that," he stammered, desperate to redirect her thinking. "In fact, you two make a great couple. If you marry Steve, you'll never want for anything."

"Except a kiss like the ones you and I shared," she said, turning to face him.

"Janine," he murmured, his heart falling to his knees. "It was just a kiss, that's all. A friendly little kiss from a best man to the bride." He tried to laugh, but a strangled sound emerged when she touched his arm. "I think you were right about me not being out here," he said, backing into the corner of the railing. "My throat is starting to tingle."

"Kiss me, Derek," she whispered, following him.

His gut clenched. "Janine, I don't think this is a good idea." But even as his mouth protested, he lowered his head to meet her. Their lips came together frantically, as if they were both afraid they might change their minds. He pulled her body against him, groaning with pleasure as her curves molded to fit his angles. She tasted so sweet, he could have bottled her and sold it. His tongue dipped into her mouth, skating over her slick teeth, teasing every surface, savoring every texture. She inhaled, taking his breath, and he lifted her to her toes to claim as much leverage as possible.

Encouraged by her soft moans, Derek slid his good hand under her baggy T-shirt, reveling in the silky texture of the tight skin on her back. He drew away long enough to loosen the tie on his old sweatpants, marveling in the erotic thrill of removing his own clothes from her lithe body. When the pants fell to her ankles, she stepped free of them. The long T-shirt hung to her knees. He pulled her back into a fierce kiss, and realized with a start that she wasn't wearing underwear. Only a skiff of cotton shirt stood between him and her nakedness.

Wild desire flooded his body, swelling his manhood against the fly of his jeans. Impatiently, he tugged on the makeshift bandage to free his hand and tossed down the napkin. He ran his hand along the cleft of her spine, cupping her rear end, rubbing the sticky-slick honey butter from his hand into her smooth skin. Lifting her against him, he slid his fingers down to the backs of her thighs, curving to the inside. His knees weakened slightly when he felt the tickle of soft curly hair against his knuckles, and the wetness of her excitement under his fingers.

He lifted his head, stunned to a moment of sanity. But she met his gaze straight on, her eyes glazed, but unwavering. When she shuddered in his arms, Derek was lost. He lifted her in his arms and somehow managed to get them back into the room, where he set Janine on the bed. She glanced around the room, uncertainty clear in her expression.

Derek ground his teeth, nearly over the edge for her, but he was determined to give her a chance to change her mind. "The lights," she murmured.

He almost buckled in relief that her concern was modesty, but he shook his head. "Lights on, Pinky, I want to see all of you." With slow deliberation, he lifted the black T-shirt over her head, then swept his gaze over her, exhaling in appreciation.

She was slender and fine-boned, as shapely as a sculpted statue, her limbs elongated to elegant proportions. Her long blond braid nestled between perfect breasts, pink-tipped and lifted in invitation. Her slim waist gave way to flaring hips, her taut skin interrupted only by the divot of her navel. A tuft of dark golden hair peeked from the vee of her thighs. Not trusting himself to speak, he gathered her in his arms and kissed the long column of her neck.

Janine arched into him, plowing her fingers through his hair, urging him lower, to her breasts. Her trembling excitement heightened his own desire, which had already spiked higher than he could ever recall. When he pulled a pearled nipple into his mouth, she gasped, a long and needful sound. As he suckled on the peaks alternately, she clawed his shirt up over his back, running her nails over his shoulder blades, making him crazy with lust. He wanted to take his time to give her pleasure, but her enthusiasm overwhelmed him. He'd intended to leave her breasts only long enough for her to remove his shirt, but she continued to tug and pull at his clothes until he was naked, too.

Janine was speechless with wanting him, her body fairly shaking in anticipation of their joining. Derek's body was covered with smooth defined muscle, lightly covered with dark hair, his shoulders breathtakingly wide, his stomach flat, his erection jutting, his thighs powerful. But his eyes were the most captivating part of him.

Softened with desire, his chocolate eyes delivered a promise of tenderness and finesse…all the things she'd dreamed of for her first time. Pushing herself back on the bed, she reclined in what she hoped was an invitation.

It was.

Derek crawled onto the bed with her, stopping short to kiss her knees, her thighs. Her stomach contracted with expectation, and her muscles tensed as his lips neared the juncture of her thighs. "Derek," she whispered, half terrified, half thrilled.

"Shh," he whispered against her mound as he eased open her legs.

She surrendered to the languid, rubbery feeling in her limbs, lying back in anticipation of...what? She wasn't sure, but only knew that if Derek was offering, she was taking. But she was unprepared for the shocking jolt of pleasure when his tongue dipped to stroke her intimate folds. Her legs fell open as she momentarily lost muscle control. An animal-like groan sounded in the room and she realized the noise had come from her lips.

She'd never known such intense indulgence, such sensual pampering. His tongue moved up and down, evoking spasms each time he stroked the little knob tucked in the midst of her slick petals. A low hum of energy swirled in her body, coming from all directions, but leading to a place deep within her womb. The loose sensations suddenly bundled together, then grew in force, as if they were trying to escape her body. Lulled into the rhythm set by his skillful mouth, she began to move with and against him. The ball of desire rolled faster and faster until she heard herself screaming for release. Then suddenly, a flash of pleasure-pain gripped her body, lifting her to a plateau of shattering ecstasy, then lowering her with numbing slowness back to earth, back to the bed, back to Derek.

Her body had barely stopped convulsing when he drew himself even with her and claimed another kiss. The musky smell of her own desire shocked her, the sharing of it so intimate. She thanked him with her kiss, pressing her sated body next to his, thrilling at the feel of his hard erection stabbing her thigh. Emboldened by his method of pleasing her, she reached down to gently grasp his arousal. His eyes fluttered closed as he groaned his approval, and she was gratified by the moisture that oozed from the tip. Stroking him with long, gentle caresses, she murmured against his neck, "Make love to me, Derek."

He lifted his head, his desire for her clear in his eyes. "Janine, I don't have protection with me."

"In my coat pocket," she said, thankful for Marie's forethought.

After a few seconds' hesitation, he lumbered to his feet, and was back in record time, ripping open a plastic packet with unrestrained vigor. She watched, riveted, as he squeezed the tip of the rubber, then quickly rolled it over his huge erection.

Weak with anticipation, Janine welcomed him back into her arms. They kissed, with fingers entwined, then he rolled her beneath him. Propped on his elbows, he held her hands on either side of her head, pressing them into the soft mattress with his strong fingers. Locking his gaze with hers, he settled between the cradle of her thighs, easily probing her still-wet entrance.

"Janine," he breathed.

A statement? A question? Heavy-lidded, his eyes glittered dark and luxurious. "Now," she whispered.

He entered her with a long, easy thrust, accompanied by their mingled moan of temporary satisfaction. The unbelievable sensation of him filling her overrode the fleeting stab of pain. He moved within her, slowly at first, and from the look of the muscle straining in his neck, with much restraint. But soon she was ready for his rhythm, urging him to a faster tempo with her hips, and clenching little-used internal muscles.

His guttural noises of pleasure banished any doubts she might have had about satisfying him. Content in the knowledge that what felt good to her also felt good to him, she rose to meet his powerful thrusts, sensing his impending release as their bodies met faster and faster. Suddenly he tensed and drove deep, burying his head in her neck, heralding his climax with a throaty growl of completion.

Holding him and holding on, she rocking with him until he quieted, until his manhood stopped pulsing.

She hadn't known, she marveled. Marie had told her. *Cosmo* had told her. Oprah had told her. But she hadn't known how wonderful intimacy could be with a man she truly cared about.

Janine stiffened at the bombshell revelation, her eyes flying open.

Derek lifted himself on one elbow. "Am I hurting you?"

"No," she murmured. But her chest was starting to tighten, and she recognized the warning signs of a panic attack. "But I need to get up."

He carefully withdrew from her body, but instead of rolling over as she'd expected, he sat up and gently pulled her into a sitting position. "Are you okay?"

She nodded, but the tug on her heart when she looked into his concerned eyes spurred her to change the subject, and fast. "I'm hungry now."

A grin climbed his face and he ran his hand through his hair. "Me too. I'll be right with you."

As he strode toward the bathroom, Janine reached for the T-shirt, then backtracked to the balcony for the sweatpants, her mind reeling.

The night air had taken on a sweeter pungency. Her senses seemed honed as she zeroed in on night birds crooning and insects chirping. Everything was louder, fresher, more vibrant. The world hadn't changed in the last hour, she acknowledged, but she certainly had.

She'd never experienced such physical and emotional intimacy with another person, and the intensity of their union frightened her. She felt vulnerable and exposed because she knew the encounter couldn't have meant as much to Derek as it had meant to her. Her heart squeezed when she thought of his face, his smile, his touch, but she quickly pushed aside her inappropriate response.

She didn't really *care* for Derek, she reasoned. She was only fond of him because, after all, she'd given him her virginity. Of course she would feel attached to him in the immediate aftermath of something so momentous in her life.

But try as she might to calm herself, to distract herself, to convince herself otherwise, the tide of emotions continued to churn in her chest. She wasn't in love with Derek, she admonished herself. That would be irrational. Illogical. And highly irregular.

Stunned, Janine forced herself to dress hastily, but could find only one flip-flop in the dark. She leaned over the railing and peered into the dark. Although she didn't see any flashes of yellow, she caught a glimpse of bright white—Derek's napkin-turned-bandage. Her flip-flop was probably down there somewhere, along with her water bottle. Glancing at her hand wrapped around the railing, Janine stifled a cry of alarm. Along with something else?

DEREK CAREFULY REMOVED the condom, dutifully checking for tears, especially since his orgasm had been so explosive. He frowned at the slight traces of blood, hoping their sex hadn't been uncomfortable for Janine. Masculine pride suddenly welled in his chest. She certainly hadn't *sounded* uncomfortable. Frankly, her eagerness had surprised him, and just remembering her spirited responses made his body twitch. He could get used to her—

He stopped, midmotion and gave himself a hard look in the mirror. He could get used to her…kind of enthusiasm. Ignoring the questions niggling at the back of his mind, he returned to the bedroom and pulled on his underwear. Janine had stepped onto the balcony, probably to fetch her clothes. He stuck his head out to check on her, and his heart lurched when her sobs reached his ears.

Remorse stabbed him. Had he hurt her? "Janine, what's wrong?" Panicked, he touched her arm, prepared to repair whatever damage he'd wrought.

"I lost it," she said tearfully.

"Lost what?" he said, then spotted the sole sandal she held. "Your flip-flop? Sweetheart, don't cry, it's just a—"

"Not my shoe," she said, her tone desperate. "I lost my engagement ring."

15

DEREK SWALLOWED. "You lost your engagement ring?"

Janine burst into tears, and leaned on the railing.

"I noticed it was missing," he said lightly, "but I just assumed you'd taken it off on purpose."

"When?" she asked, grasping his arm. "When did you notice it was missing?"

Derek cleared his throat. "When we were, um, in bed."

She tore back into the room and he followed, then stood back as she skimmed her hands across the top of the comforter, then stripped it from the bed and shook it violently.

"Do you see it?" she asked.

He shook his head, guilt galloping through his chest. "Don't worry, we'll find it. You check that side of the room, and I'll start over here."

Janine nodded, emitting a little hiccup, then fell to her knees, patting the parquet floor. Feeling absurdly responsible, he started looking in the opposite corner, patting small areas before moving on, knowing the ring would not stand out against the busy pattern of the wooden floor. Thirty minutes later, they bumped behinds in the middle, both empty-handed.

"It'll turn up somewhere," he assured her.

"Yeah," she said. "In a pawnshop." Sitting back on her heels, Janine covered her face with her hands. A bitter laugh erupted from her throat. An hour ago she was thinking that telling Steve she couldn't *marry* him would be difficult. Now she'd be able to top that tidbit by confessing she'd also lost his grandmother's heirloom ring. The only silver lining was that the ring was a distraction from her revelations concerning Derek. "Oh my God," she whispered, rocking. "Oh my God."

A knock on the door startled her so badly, she jumped. Derek yanked up his jeans and shirt and headed back to the bathroom. Janine dragged herself to the door, but her spirits rose when she saw Manny through the peephole. She swung open the door. "Oh, Manny, thank goodness you're here!"

He held up a roll of gauze. "Is someone in trouble?"

"Big time," she said. She took the gauze, then tossed it on the bed. Janine stepped into the hall, keeping the door barely cracked. She struggled to keep her voice level. "I have to go outside."

Manny sighed. "Janine, I know you're claustrophobic, but—"

"Not because I'm claustrophobic! I dropped something off the balcony, and I have to find it right away."

He held up his radio. "What is it? I'll call a guard to look for it."

"No! I can't risk someone finding it and keeping it."

"What did you drop?"

She puffed out her cheeks, then held up her left hand and wiggled her ring finger.

His eyes bulged. "Your engagement ring?"

She winced and nodded.

He touched a hand to his temple. "Oh good Lord."

"Exactly," she said. "Now you know why I'm so glad to see you."

His eyes narrowed. "I'm not getting a good feeling about this."

"You can sneak me out and I'll find my ring, then you can sneak me back in, and no one will be the wiser." She clapped her hands together under her chin, sniffing back tears.

"Janine, no one is supposed to leave the premises."

"I won't be leaving the premises, I'll just be under the balcony!"

He angled his head at her. "This isn't another pitiful attempt at escape, is it?"

"Cross my heart."

"The most sacred of vows," he noted dryly, but he was wavering.

"Manny, I'm not going to marry Steve Larsen."

His eyes bulged even wider.

"Besides the fact that I don't have enough money to pay for the ring, it's an heirloom. Irreplaceable." She adopted a pleading expression. "Please help me."

At last he sighed. "Okay, but let me do all the talking."

Hope soared in her chest. "You won't regret it."

He shot her a disbelieving look, but a half hour and a half-dozen lies later, they slipped out the side entrance. Flashlight in hand, her feet swimming in a pair of Derek's canvas lace-up tennis shoes, they made their way to the area beneath the balcony—easy to locate since her yellow flip-flop fairly glowed in the moonlight.

"What the heck were you doing up there?" Manny asked, holding up the sandal.

Instead of answering, she snatched the shoe.

"Oh," he said, the solitary word saying it all.

"We're looking for a *ring*," she reminded him, shining her flashlight over the grass.

"Is this yours, too?" He held up the half-empty bottle of water.

She nodded.

A few minutes later he asked, "And this?" The napkin she'd wrapped around Derek's hand waved in the breeze. The honey butter smelled pungent and had left some odd-looking stains on the cloth.

She gave him a tight smile, then took the napkin from him and tucked it in the waistband of her—make that *Derek's*—sweatpants.

He harrumped. "I'm not touching anything else I find unless it's fourteen-carat gold."

"The ring is platinum," she corrected him.

He let out an impressive, sad whistle. "Well, we'd better split up and cover this area systematically. I'll start here and go to the tree, then back to the wall."

With her heart thumping and her fingers crossed, Janine

started crisscrossing the area opposite Manny. Taking baby steps in her huge shoes, she stared at the beam of light until her eyeballs felt raw. After only a short while, her neck and shoulders ached. "Manny, have you found it?"

"Yeah, Janine, I found the ring ten minutes ago, but I just like walking humped over in the dark."

She smiled ruefully and shut up. A paper clip, then a foil candy wrapper raised and dashed her hopes. After an hour, she was blinking back tears. Manny came over to stand next to her, rubbing the back of his neck. "Nothing. Are you sure it fell off your finger when you were on the balcony?"

"I think it did."

He pursed his lips. "You *think* it did? I have two mosquito welts on my face the size of Stone Mountain, and you *think* it did?"

"Well, we couldn't find it in the room, so I just assumed...I mean, we dropped so many things—"

He held up one hand. "I get the picture." Manny shook his head, and chuckled. "Wow, when you mess things up, you mess them up in a big way."

"Well, it's not like I lost the ring on purpose."

"Maybe not consciously."

"What's that supposed to mean?"

"Nothing."

"*Something,*" she prompted.

"Well, it's just that the subconscious can be a powerful force." He splayed one hand. "Did you lose the ring before or after you decided you weren't going to marry Mr. Larsen?"

"After," she said miserably.

He lifted his shoulders in an exaggerated shrug. "Just a thought," he said, then steered her back toward the side entrance.

"What am I going to do?" she asked, blinking back a new wellspring of tears.

"Search the room again," he told her. "And I promise I'll come out myself first thing in the morning with a rake." He smiled, his blue eyes kind. "I might even be able to scare up a metal detector."

"You're the best," she said, giving him a hug.

"So I've heard," he said with a boyish grin. "Try to get some sleep, okay?"

FAT CHANCE, she thought hours later, staring at the bedside clock until it ticked away another thirty minutes. Her tear ducts were swollen and dry. Three o'clock in the morning on what was supposed to be her wedding day, and she lay awake, stiff and sore from the lovemaking of the man sleeping on the floor.

Who just happened *not* to be her fiancé.

But someone who'd become important to her in a shamefully short amount of time. She laughed aloud, but the velvety darkness of the room muffled the noise.

Today she would call Steve and tell him she couldn't marry him, a thought that saddened her. Even though she didn't love him, she was fond of him and his family, and she would always admire his proficiency on the job. She would miss him, along with the promise of a luxurious, if conservative, life.

She sighed. Then after breaking their engagement, she would offer Steve her car, her sole Coach purse and her right arm as a down payment on the lost ring. Now that she thought about it, a hairdresser had once told her he'd give her a hundred dollars for her hair, down to the scalp… Her mother would get used to it eventually. And she could sell her blood every six weeks at the clinic—nobody needed a full ten pints.

Derek murmured something in his sleep. She lifted her head in his direction and saw the pale sheet over him move as he rolled to face her, still sound asleep. Her stomach pitched and rolled when she replayed their passionate encounter in her head. Neither she nor Derek had broached the subject of their lovemaking when she returned from her fruitless search. He'd helped her turn the room upside down, but remained stoic as they stripped the bed and checked underneath. Obviously, the act had been little more than an enjoyable tumble for him, and now he was racked with guilt.

Janine's mouth tightened. He would never know how much their lovemaking had meant to her, not if she could help it. This little triangle she'd created had enough inherent problems without throwing love into the mix.

Love?

Suddenly, the metallic whine of the air conditioner roared in her ears, and the walls seemed to converge on her in the dark. Janine clutched at her chest and gasped for breath, succumbing to a full-fledged panic attack. And why not? she asked herself, grabbing a fistful of sheet. Never before in her life had she had so many good reasons to panic.

"Relax, Janine."

Derek's voice floated to her and she realized he was sitting on the bed, holding her hand. "Take shallow breaths and exhale through your mouth slowly. Close your eyes," he ordered gently, and she obeyed.

"Now breathe, and think about something that makes you happy," he said as if speaking to a child.

His suggestion fell flat, however, because his face kept floating behind her eyelids. She tried to focus, but his touching was so much more appealing.

"Tell me," he said. "Tell me the things that make you happy, Janine."

The concerned note in his voice sent warmth circulating through her chest, making her feel safe. "Peppermint ice cream," she whispered.

The low rumble of his laugh floated around her head. "What else?"

"Red hats...old books...polka music...cotton sheets..."

"Breathe," he reminded her. "Go on."

"Daisies...jawbreakers...bowling...brown eyes..."

Derek's own breath caught in his chest. Did she like *his* brown eyes? His chest ached with the agony of not discussing their impromptu lovemaking. On one hand, he felt compelled to tell her the sex had been a profound experience for him, but on the other hand, she was on the rebound from an engagement to a friend of his, undoubtedly consumed with guilt over sleeping with him *and* losing her priceless engagement ring. For all he knew, the flighty woman might manufacture a story about the ring being stolen and marry Steve after all. He'd be a fool to reveal any of his disturbing feelings to her now, under such volatile circumstances.

He realized her breathing had returned to normal and, eyes closed, she looked like a resting child. Her beauty seemed boundless. The more time he spent with her, the more expressions and mannerisms she revealed, each uniquely Janine, and each riveting. The woman was incredible, and he hoped Steve was smart enough to fight for her love. He hated himself for submitting to his desire for her, for taking advantage of her vulnerability during prewedding jitters. In doing so, he prayed he hadn't jeopardized her chance for happiness.

He started to withdraw his hand, but Janine's fingers closed around his, and her eyes fluttered open. "Stay with me."

Even though everything logical in him shouted not to, he stretched out beside her, careful to leave a few inches between them. Janine turned on her side away from him, then scooted back until they were touching from shoulder to knee. Instinctively, he rolled to his side and spooned her small body against his. A foreign, not completely uncomfortable heat filled his chest, and he suddenly couldn't pull her close enough. She wore a short T-shirt rucked up to her waist, revealing plain white cotton panties. His body responded immediately.

No matter, he thought. She was breathing deeply, probably already asleep and oblivious to his state. He reached up and smoothed the hair back from her face, studying her profile, wishing he knew what made her tick. Unexpectedly, she pressed her rump back against his arousal, and he bit back a groan. Was she merely moving in her sleep, or urging him to intimacy? Janine reached her hand back to hook around his thigh and pulled him so that his sex nestled against hers, settling the question.

Derek buried his face in her hair, then kissed her neck while sliding his hand beneath her shirt to caress her stomach and tuck her body even closer to his. By spreading his fingers, he stroked her breasts, gently tweaking each nipple. He cupped a handful of her firm flesh, rasping his desire for her in her ear. She responded by sliding her hand back and tugging on the waistband of his boxers. He lifted himself just enough to skim the underwear down his legs, then kicked them away. Freed, his erection sought the heat between her thighs, straining against the firm cheeks of her buttocks.

She had shed her T-shirt. With a slide of her hand and a teeth-grating wiggle, the thin panties were pushed down to her knees. Derek throbbed to be inside her, but rolled away long enough to secure a condom. Spooning her close to him again, he reached around to delve into the curls at the apex of her thighs, which were already wet. With great restraint, he inserted only the tip of his bulging erection into her slick channel from behind, and plied her nub of pleasure until she writhed in his arms, moaning his name. On the verge of climax himself, he slid into her fully, thrilling in the extra pressure of their position. Sheer concentration helped him maintain control for several long, slow strokes, then the life fluid burst from him with a force equal to that of a man who might never get to indulge in such sweetness again.

Indeed, Derek thought as his breathing returned to normal, he would never again make love to Janine. He would go back to Kentucky, immerse himself in his work and leave Janine and Steve to work through their problems. Once Steve had singled out a woman to make her his wife, Derek knew he wouldn't easily let her go. The panicky thought sprang to his mind that Janine might be using him to get back at Steve in some way. His stomach twisted. He suspected that Steve was unfaithful to Janine—did she as well?

She sighed and settled back against his chest. With his head full of troubled thoughts and his lungs full of the scent of her hair, he drifted off to sleep.

JANINE STARTED AWAKE, disoriented, but was disturbingly relieved to see Derek's face in the morning light.

"Janine," he whispered, his tone urgent. "Wake up."

"What's wrong?" she asked, looping her arms around his neck and pulling him closer.

"Shh." He pulled away her hands and flung back the covers, sending a chill over her naked body. "Janine, sweetheart, you have to get up. *Now.*"

"Why?" she asked, sitting up grudgingly, wincing at her sore muscles.

An impatient knock sounded at the door, apparently not the first.

"Because," he said, pulling on his underwear, his lowered voice tinged with warning. "Steve's here."

16

SHE SWAYED and Derek grabbed her by the shoulders to steady her. "Steve's here?" she parroted, dazed.

"Yes," he whispered, pulling her to her feet. "Keep your voice down."

Her heart threatened to burst from her chest, and her brain seemed mired in goo. "B-but what's he doing here? How?"

"I don't know," he said, fishing her panties and T-shirt from the covers. "The point is, he can't find *you* here."

Steve banged on the door. "Derek, man, are you awake? I lost my key."

At the sound of Steve's voice, her knees nearly collapsed. She bit down hard on her knuckle, terrified at what might transpire between the men if Steve found out what had happened last night. Twice.

"Give me a minute, Steve," Derek called, pivoting to scan the room. His darting eyes came full circle to rest on the bed. "Get underneath," he said, shoving her clothes into her hands.

"But I—"

"Now, Janine, under the bed!"

Dreading even the thought of being confined in such a tight space, she nonetheless relented, quickly recognizing the lesser of two evils. She shimmied the T-shirt over her head and practically vaulted into her panties. The clothes brought back a flood of erotic memories, and she felt compelled to at least acknowledge their lovemaking.

"Derek, about last night—"

"Janine," he cut in. "We definitely need to talk, but now hardly seems like the time."

Contrite, she nodded, then dropped to her belly and squeezed her way under the bed, giving thanks for her

B-cup—a C would've rendered this particular hiding place impossible. Quickly she determined the least uncomfortable position was to lie with her cheek to the dusty floor.

With her heart doing a tap dance against the parquet, she watched Derek's feet move toward the door. The foggy numbness of a panic attack encroached, but she forced herself to focus on breathing. *Please, please, please,* she begged the heavens. *Get me out of this predicament, and I'll behave myself. Really, I will.*

Inhale, exhale. *No more men until I get the ring paid off.*

Inhale, exhale. *No more engagements unless I'm certain the man is right for me.*

Inhale, exhale. *And no more sex until I'm married.*

The door opened and Steve's Cole Haan loafers came into view. Janine bit her lip, certain she was about to be discovered.

"About time, man," Steve said, walking inside.

"Sorry," Derek said, and the door closed. "I was talking to…an important client. What are you doing here?"

"Haven't you heard? The quarantine's been lifted."

She closed her eyes in relief. At least she could get out of here. Away from Derek. Her chest tightened strangely, not surprising considering her present confinement. Inhale, exhale.

"I drove up as soon as I heard," Steve continued. "Here." A paper rattled. "This was sticking half under your door. It says you're a free man." He walked over to the window and flung open the curtains, spilling light over the wooden floor. "This place is like a tomb—it's almost ten o'clock. I thought you were an early riser, man."

Derek grunted. "These damn allergies have me all messed up."

"Are you taking anything for them?"

"Yeah, some over-the-counter stuff."

Steve laughed, a harsh sound. "If Janine were here, she'd be plying you with some cockamamy tea made from crabgrass or something."

She blinked, stung by the cutting sarcasm in his voice.

"Well," Derek said with a small laugh, "she's definitely not here."

"I wonder if she knows about the quarantine being lifted."

"Um, I suspect she does," Derek hedged.

The Cole Haan loafers came closer and closer to the bed, then suddenly, the box springs bounced down, slamming into her shoulder blades and momentarily knocking the breath out of her. While gasping for air, she realized Steve had dropped onto the bed.

"What the hell are you doing?" Derek's angry voice penetrated her wheezing fog.

"What?" Steve sounded confused.

"Take it easy, you'll break the bed!"

Steve laughed. "Relax, man, I'm sure this bed has seen its share of bouncing."

Janine winced. If he only knew.

A long-suffering sigh escaped Steve. "I guess *my* bed-bouncing days are over."

Janine frowned.

"Man, am I going to miss being single. I hate like hell to grow up."

Derek's laugh sounded forced. "I'm sure married life will suit you. From what I've seen of Janine—" he cleared his throat "—she seems like a great gal."

"Yeah, she's a sweetheart. My parents love her."

But not Steve, she realized, shaken that she hadn't noticed sooner how ill-matched they were, how they never really laughed together, shared the intimate details of their everyday life or planned for the future.

"In fact, Janine is the first woman I ever brought home that my mother considered good enough to wear my grandmother's ring."

Her heart skipped a beat.

"An heirloom, eh?" Derek asked. "You probably arranged for her to wear a fake until you're actually married?"

Janine brightened considerably at the possibility.

"Oh, no," Steve said with nonchalance. "Mom insisted she

wear the real thing. Pure platinum and flawless diamonds, about forty thousand dollars' worth."

She felt faint.

Derek made a choking sound. "Wow, you must really love this woman."

"She's terrific," he responded, and Janine wondered if Derek realized how evasive his friend was being. "It's funny, though," Steve continued, his voice tinged with regret. "She's never really turned me on physically."

Mortification flowered in her chest. It was just as she'd feared. And in front of Derek, no less.

"Steve," Derek began, his voice echoing her embarrassment, but Steve seemed to be in a talkative mood.

"Oh, she's cute and all, and I have to admit, I'm looking forward to the wedding night."

"That's...great," Derek replied. "Hey, why don't we grab some breakfast?" He walked to the canvas tennis shoes she'd worn last night for her moonlight treasure hunt, and bent to pick up one. Janine grimaced. She'd left them tied so tight, the material was puckered around the eyelets. Even so, she'd still been able to walk right out of them.

The mattress moved again. Steve sat on the edge of the bed for a few seconds, then pushed himself to his feet. "I didn't tell you she's a virgin, did I?"

Janine gasped, and the shoe Derek had picked up fell back to the floor, bouncing once.

"No," Derek said in a brittle tone. "You didn't mention that little tidbit."

"Can you believe it? In this day and age... She's the perfect wife for a politician's family. No skeletons, no baggage."

"Politician, meaning your father, or politician, meaning you?" Derek still sounded a little choked.

"Of course Dad for now, although I don't rule it out for myself sometime in the future."

Another surprise, Janine noted wryly.

"How can you be sure she's a virgin?" Derek asked.

Janine gasped again, then tamped down her anger. After

all, she'd acted like a loose goose—her mother's words—around Derek.

"I mean," Derek added with a nervous little laugh, "nothing against Janine, but how's a man really to know?"

"She told me," Steve said simply.

Well, at least he'd believed her.

"And I asked her OB/GYN."

Her body clenched in fury. How *dare* he? Instinctively, she raised her head, which met solidly with a rather inflexible piece of wood. Pain exploded in her crown, and she bit back a string of curses.

"What was that?" Steve asked.

Holding her breath, Janine could feel his eyes boring through the mattress.

"Oh, it's the people in the room below," Derek said, sounding exasperated. "They can't seem to *be still.*"

She stuck her tongue out at him.

"Anyway," Steve said, shifting foot to foot, "I need to look for Janine before we eat. The wedding is back on for this evening. Mother has already worked out the details with the hotel. A small miracle, I might add."

Janine swallowed a strangled cry. She needed a miracle, but that wasn't the one she'd had in mind.

"Kind of last minute, don't you think?" Derek asked, walking toward the door.

"My folks think it would make great press, so it'll be worth it, even if things aren't picture perfect. You have to ride the media wave when it breaks, man."

The door opened and Steve exited first. Derek stepped into the hall, then said, "Oh, I almost forgot. I need to make one more phone call. Why don't you wait for me in the lobby. Maybe you'll run into Janine."

"Good idea," Steve said. "Then the two of you can get to know each other a little better."

Janine closed her eyes, guilt clawing at her chest.

"Uh, yeah," Derek replied. "Give me about fifteen minutes." He walked back inside the room, then closed the door.

Dread enveloped her, a sensation that was beginning to feel alarmingly familiar. She inhaled too deeply, filling her nostrils with dust, then sneezed violently. Before she could recover, strong hands closed around her ankles, and she was sliding across the wooden floor, being pulled out feetfirst. When her head cleared the bed, she lay still, looking up at Derek who stood over her, hands on hips. "Bless you," he said, but his expression was decidedly unsympathetic.

Inside he was seething, although he tried to maintain a certain amount of decorum. The crazy thing was that even in the midst of the frenetic situation, his mind and body paused to register her incredible natural beauty, her pink mouth and blue, blue eyes, her pale braided hair in fuzzy disarray, and long slender limbs, sprawled ridiculously on the floor. He had actually deflowered this lovely creature, destined for the bed of another man. Derek wanted to throw something, but instead he winced and rubbed his eyes with forefinger and thumb.

"You really shouldn't do that."

He opened his eyes. "You really should have told me."

She wet her lips. "Would it have made a difference?"

"Yes," he snapped. He wouldn't have touched her. He ran his hand through his hair, still unable to believe the turn of events. Okay, maybe he still would have touched her, but he would have taken his time, would have tried to make the experience more special for her, which was probably what her fiancé had been planning to do. Remorse racked his chest.

"Yes," he repeated more gently. He leaned over and extended his hand, then eased her to her feet.

"Derek, I can't imagine what you must think of me—"

He stopped her by touching his finger to her full lower lip. "I think we were both a little out of sorts—the proximity, the quarantine, the stress. What happened, happened."

Misery swam in her eyes. "But Steve..."

"Doesn't ever have to know," Derek insisted.

"You're right," she said, nodding. "Telling him would serve no purpose, and I don't want to come between your friendship."

He considered telling her they weren't as close as she might think, but doing so would only confuse the issue. "Good, then we have a pact?"

"Yes," she said with a whisper of a smile.

"And you and Steve will work things out?"

"I'm not sure that—"

"You will," he assured her, forcing cheer. He clasped her shoulders in what he'd intended to be a friendly gesture, but dropped his hands when the compulsion to kiss her became too great. "You've got a few minutes to get your things together and out of here," he said as he crossed to the door.

"Derek." She swallowed hard and looked as if she might say something, then averted her eyes and murmured, "I don't have much to get together."

He couldn't resist teasing her one last time. "A certain pink number comes to mind."

She blushed, and he decided the picture of her standing barefoot next to the bed, with disheveled hair and wearing her T-shirt inside out would remain in his mind forever.

"I guess I'll see you at the wedding," he said, then left before he could change his mind about walking away. He had problems in Kentucky that needed his full attention immediately, he reminded himself as he rode to the lobby. The sooner he got through the wedding and on a northbound plane, the better. Guilt bound his chest like a vise.

Steve was waiting for him in the lobby, jingling change in the pocket of his tailored slacks, looking every bit the part of a successful plastic surgeon.

"I haven't seen her," Steve said as he walked up, clearly perturbed. "I gave her a pager so I could keep tabs on her, but she never wears it."

Good for her, Derek thought. "Ready to get a bite to eat?"

"Let's hang around in the lobby for a little while, just in case a news camera shows." Steve craned his neck and scanned the massive lobby.

Derek frowned. "Or Janine."

"Huh? Oh, yeah."

Rankled at his seeming indifference, Derek said, "If you

don't mind me saying so, you don't seem particularly attached to your fiancée."

Steve shrugged. "What's love got to do with it, right?"

With his attitude of taking things lightly, Derek marveled how the man had made it through medical school. Then the answer hit him—Steve only took *people* lightly. "Well, it matters quite a bit when you consider you'll be spending the rest of your life with someone."

His friend turned back and presented a dismissive wave. "If you're thinking about what I said about her not putting lead in my pencil, don't worry. My surprise wedding gift to Janine is a pair of D's."

Derek frowned. "What?"

"You know—D's." Steve held his hands, palm up, wriggling his fingers in lewd squeezing motions.

Nausea rolled in Derek's stomach. What did Janine see in this guy? Hell, why did he himself call him a friend? He struggled to keep his voice calm. "That's kind of cruel, Steve. And unnecessary, from what I saw of Janine." *And felt, and tasted,* his conscience reminded him.

Steve scoffed. "You always did go for the mousy ones, didn't you, pal?"

So unexpected was Derek's fist that Steve was still smiling when he popped him in the mouth. Steve staggered back, his eyes wide and angry. An expletive rolled out of his bloody mouth, but he kept his distance. "Have you lost your freaking mind?"

"No," Derek said evenly. "But you've lost your best man."

Steve's face twisted as he swept his gaze over Derek. "Fine. I only asked you because Jack let me down."

"You and Jack," Derek said, wiping the traces of blood off his knuckles, "are two of a kind."

"You're jealous," Steve retorted. "You were always jealous of me and Jack."

Derek set his jaw and turned his back on Steve, recognizing the need to walk away. A light from a news camera blinded him, but he didn't stop. At least Steve had gotten his wish—he probably would make the local news.

Steve's spiteful words clung to Derek as he stabbed the elevator button. Jealous, ha. In his opinion, the man had only one thing worth coveting. He stepped into the elevator and leaned heavily against the back wall. A man knew his limits. He'd never competed with Steve or Jack for a woman, and he wasn't about to start now.

But at least he had his memories.

17

JANINE CLOSED the room door behind her and slung over her shoulder the pillowcase containing her ill-fated costume, her high heels and the items Manny had brought her. She'd managed a quick shower, but didn't have time to dry her hair, so she'd simply slicked it back from her face with gel. The single pair of shorts and the sole T-shirt she had left were so formfitting, she'd decided to wear the coat. Buttoned and belted, admittedly it looked a little weird with the yellow flip-flops, but she didn't care. A hysterical laugh bubbled out. With so many problems, she should be so *lucky* as to have the fashion police haul her away.

Her feet were so heavy, she could barely walk. When she reached the elevator bay, the overhead display showed one car on its way up. For a few seconds, she entertained the idea of waiting for it, then she changed her mind and headed for the stairs. Why tempt another panic attack?

Descending the stairs slowly, she tried to sort out the ugly tasks before her. Marie said she'd be there in an hour, which gave her time to find Manny, and talk to Steve.

Talk to Steve.

Her joints felt loose just thinking about it. Funny, but in her mind, breaking their engagement seemed anticlimactic compared to confessing she'd somehow misplaced a family heirloom that was worth twice as much as her education had cost. And priceless to his mother, she knew. Her stomach pitched. Oh, well, being in debt was the American way. Some people made thirty years of payments on a house, she'd simply make thirty years of payments on a ring. That she didn't have. And would never truly be able to replace.

After a few requests, and scrupulously avoiding the lobby, she found Manny at a loading dock arguing heatedly with a deliveryman trying to wheel in a cartful of red and white carnations. "Janine! Just the person I needed to see. I wanted to call you, but it's been so crazy now that we're actually back in business." He wagged his finger at the burly man. "Call your boss. She *knows* I strictly forbid carnations for our live arrangements." He clucked. "Smelly weeds." Turning back to Janine, he tugged her inside to some kind of workroom.

"I read on the sheet left in our room that the quarantine was lifted early this morning."

He rolled his eyes. "*Very* early this morning. The CDC traced the bacteria to a bad batch of barbecue *and* a peck of bad stuffed peppers served last Thursday, all from a caterer we sometimes use in a pinch. Past tense, natch."

"Is everyone going to be okay?"

Manny nodded. "All but two guests have been released from the hospital, and those two are recovering well, according to Dr. Pedro."

Starved for good news, she grinned. "Excellent."

"And now for the bad news," he said, his gaze somber.

"You didn't find the ring."

"No, I didn't." Manny pointed to the grass-stained cuffs of his white pants. "I swept the entire area with a metal detector. I found three quarters and a dime, but not what you were looking for." He stroked her hair. "I'm sorry, sweetheart, but I'll keep looking. It'll turn up somewhere, and I have an extremely trustworthy staff. If it's here and we find it, you'll get it back."

"I'm offering a reward," she said, morose. "My firstborn."

He laughed. "I'll put out the word." Then he sobered. "And what's this my catering director tells me about the wedding being back on?"

"He's misinformed," she assured him. "I am *not* marrying Steve Larsen."

"And does he know that?"

She puffed out her cheeks, then exhaled. "I'm on my way to tell him about the wedding…and the ring."

"And about Mr. Stillman?" he probed.

Her heart jerked crazily. "No. Derek and I made a pact."

"To bear children?"

A silly laugh escaped her. "To secrecy. There's nothing between us except a mistake."

He lifted one eyebrow.

"Okay, two mistakes. But that's all."

"You don't have feelings for him?"

She smirked. "Manny, don't you think I have enough problems for now?"

He nodded and relented with a shrug. "I guess I got carried away, what with my perfect record and all."

"I hope this failure isn't going to keep you from getting wings or something," she teased, thinking the silver lining of this black cloud had been making a new friend.

"Don't concern yourself about me," he said. "Now, go." He shooed her toward the door. "Put this dreadful task behind you, then burn that coat, girl."

She threw him a kiss, then made her way toward the lobby, her pulse climbing higher and higher. Every other step she reminded herself to breathe, refusing to have a panic attack now. She'd made her bed, and now she had to lie in it...alone.

Which was, all things considered, better than lying underneath it.

Steve was easy to spot pacing in a conversation area flanked with leather furniture, but she was surprised to find him alone, and apparently agitated. Pausing next to a gray marble column, she observed the man she'd thought to marry, hoping to see some kind of justification for why she had accepted his proposal in the first place.

Steve Larsen was a strikingly handsome man, no doubt. White blond hair, perpetually tanned, with breathtakingly good taste in clothing, housing and transportation. She squinted.

And an ice pack against his mouth?

At that moment he looked up and recognized her. "Janine?"

Summoning courage, she crossed the lobby. "H-hi," she said, feeling as if she were face-to-face with a stranger.

"Hi, yourself," he said with a frown. "Where the devil have you been?"

She blinked. So much for a happy reunion. Tempted to snap back, she reminded herself of the messages she had to deliver. "Collecting my things," she said, indicating her makeshift bag. "And tying up loose ends." Stepping forward, she pulled away the ice pack and gasped at the dried blood and redness beneath. "What on earth happened to your mouth?"

His scowl deepened. "I fell," he said, gesturing to the marble floor. "It's nothing."

"But you might need stitches—"

"I said it's nothing!"

Drawing back at his tone, she averted her eyes, noticing several people were staring.

Steve noticed too, instantly contrite. He bent to kiss her high on the cheek, a gesture she'd once found so romantic. Now she swallowed hard to keep from pushing him away. Her response wasn't fair, she knew. She had made a huge mistake by agreeing to marry him. He bore none of the blame for her naive acceptance.

"Let's sit," she suggested. "I need to talk to you."

Her heart skipped erratically, and her hopes of easing into the conversation were dashed when Steve asked, "Where's my ring?" He grasped her left hand with his free one.

She attempted a smile, but failed. "Um, that's one of the things I have to talk to you about." After clearing her throat, she blurted, "I lost it," and winced.

He lowered the ice pack and stared. A muscle ticked in his clenched jaw. "You...*lost* it?"

Tears sprang to her eyes and she nodded. "Steve, I'm so sorry."

"Where did you lose it?" he demanded. "How?"

She shook her head, her tears falling in earnest now. "I don't know—I've looked everywhere. I'm so, so sorry."

Steve lay his head back against the chair and moved the ice pack to his forehead. "My mother is going to kill me."

Sniffling, she said, "I'll tell Mrs. Larsen it was all my fault, Steve."

He glanced at her out of the corner of his eye. "Except you weren't the one who was supposed to get it insured—I was."

"You didn't get it insured?" she squeaked, then hiccuped.

His eyes bulged from his head, and his face turned crimson. "I didn't think you'd be careless enough to lose it!" He sat forward, his head in his hands. "Oh my God, my mother is going to kill me."

"I'll repay you," she said. "You and your family. Every dime, I promise."

He seemed less than impressed. Looking at her through his fingers, he said, "First of all, it's an heirloom, Janine. It can't be replaced. And second, I find the notion of *you* paying me or my family out of our household money, which will be primarily money *I've* earned, utterly ludicrous."

"Th-that's another thing I want to talk to you about."

"What?"

She looked around to make sure no one was within earshot. "I'm not going to marry you, Steve."

His face took on a mottled look. "You're not going to marry me?"

She nodded.

A purplish color descended over his expression, and he surprised her by laughing. "*You* are not going to marry *me?*" He slapped his knee. "Oh, that's rich. My mother spent all day Thursday calling everyone on the guest list letting them know the ceremony had been canceled, then she spent all this morning calling everyone *again* to tell them the ceremony is on again. And now you're saying she has to call everyone yet again to tell them the wedding is off again?"

Astonishment washed over her. He was more concerned about his mother being imposed upon or embarrassed than about losing her? "All I'm telling you, Steve," she said calmly, "is that I'm not marrying you." She stood and attempted to walk away, but he blocked her retreat.

"Janine, you can't just change your mind—I have plans."

What had she ever seen in him? she wondered as she studied his cold eyes. "We're too different, Steve, I should've never said yes. I'm sorry if this causes you or your parents undue embarrassment. I'd be glad to call every guest personally and accept full blame."

She tried to walk past him, but he grabbed her arm, his chest heaving. "I'm starting to think you didn't lose the ring after all."

"What?"

"Maybe you're planning to sell it."

A chill settled over her heart at the realization that she and Steve didn't know each other at all, but had still planned to marry. "I swear to you, I don't have the ring. And I swear I'll pay you the money it's worth, even if it takes a lifetime. I'm sorry it has to end this way, but we don't love each other. I'm sure we'll both be happier—"

"Will you, Janine?" he asked, still gripping her arm. "Will you be happier going back to your scruffy little old maid existence?"

His hurtful words stunned her to silence.

A little smile curled his battered lip. "Since you'll never be able to repay me for my ring, there is something you can do for me."

"What?" she whispered, frightened at the change in his demeanor.

"I still have my hotel room."

Revulsion rolled through her, and her mind reeled for something to say.

"Mr. Larsen."

They turned, and to Janine's immense relief, Manny stood a few feet away, his hands behind his back, his face completely serene.

"Yes?" Steve asked, easing his grasp on her arm a fraction.

"I'm the general manager of this hotel, and I have something for you."

He frowned. "What is it?"

Manny withdrew one hand from behind him and held up a stopwatch, which he clicked to start. "Ten minutes," he said, his voice casual. "Ten minutes to remove your personal belongings from your room and leave the premises." Then he smiled. "*Without* Ms. Murphy."

Janine suppressed a smile of her own. The general manager had succeeded in shaking Steve enough that he released her arm.

"I don't think you know who I am," Steve said, his chest visibly expanding.

"Sir, I know exactly who and what you are," Manny replied, then glanced at the stopwatch. "Oh, look, nine minutes."

Steve's bravado faded a bit. "I'd like to speak to your supervisor."

"*I* am my supervisor," Manny explained patiently, never taking his eyes off the stopwatch.

Steve looked at her, but she kept her eyes averted to avoid provoking him further.

"I'm going to sue you for the worth of the ring," he hissed.

"Why?" she asked, lifting her gaze. "I don't have anything worth taking."

His feral gaze swept her up and down. "You got that right," he said, then glared at Manny. "Forget the room. There isn't anything in my life that can't be easily replaced." After a dismissive glance in her direction, he wheeled and strode across the lobby toward the revolving door.

She stared dry-eyed until he had disappeared from sight. Then her knees started to knock and she sank onto the pale leather settee.

"Real Prince Charming," Manny muttered, patting her shoulder. "If you can wait another thirty minutes, I'll take you home."

"No, thank you, I have a ride," Janine said, although she didn't recognize her own voice.

"Janine?"

At the sound of Marie's voice, she sprang to her feet and rushed into her sister's arms. "What's going on? I just passed Steve in the parking lot and got the feeling if he'd had a gun, I would have been target practice."

"I broke our engagement."

Marie scoffed. "Is that all? Darling, men are a dime a dozen."

"And I lost my engagement ring."

Marie sucked in a sharp breath. "Oh, now *that* hurts."

Janine pulled back and looked at her sister's pained expression, then laughed in blessed relief. She turned to Manny and mouthed, "Thank you," then she and Marie strolled through the lobby arm in arm. When they passed the reservations desk where Janine had first begged her way up to room 855, she marveled at the changes in her life in a mere forty-eight hours.

She'd lost the man she thought she wanted, and met the man she knew she needed. But when Derek's face swam before her, she quickly squashed the image. She wasn't about to fall into another relationship so soon after her humbling experience with Steve. No matter what she *imagined* her feelings toward Derek to be, frankly, she simply didn't trust her own judgment right now.

On the drive home, she recounted enough details to try to satisfy Marie, while leaving out the more sordid aspects of passing time with Derek.

"So, sis, tell me about this Stillman fellow."

Janine glanced sideways at her sister. No teasing, no innuendo, no insinuation. She frowned. Marie was definitely suspicious. "Um, he's a nice enough guy."

"Nice enough to what?" Marie asked, seemingly preoccupied with a traffic light.

"Nice enough to...say hello to if I ran into him again."

Her sister nodded, presumably satisfied, then said, "I'll call Mom and the whole fam damily when we get home. Again." She grinned. "My gift to you for getting you into this mess in the first place."

"You're the greatest," Janine said.

"I know," Marie replied with a wink. "That's why I'm Mom's favorite."

Janine laughed, then told Marie all about Manny, and by the time they reached their apartment, she was feeling much better. She changed into her ugliest but most comfortable pajamas and holed up the rest of the day in the bedroom, putting her pillow over her head to shut out the sound of the phone ringing incessantly. Marie was a saint to handle it all.

She must have napped, because when she awoke, long shadows filled the room and she was thirsty. Swinging her legs over the side of the bed, she stepped on the empty box she recognized as the one that held the pink bustier and panties that Steve's receptionist, Sandy, had given her for her bachelorette party. The getup was already in the laundry, and once clean, was bound for Marie's closet. Janine would never wear it again. She scooped up the torn box to toss it in the trash on her way to the kitchen. Preoccupied with self-remorse, Janine almost missed the little note that floated out of the box.

Curious, she picked up the tiny card and opened it with her thumb.

Sandy, for Thursday, our last wicked night together.

Steve

Janine read the note again, and once again just for clarification.

Set up by his mistress. Sandy had probably thought Janine would wear the outfit sometime during her honeymoon—her revenge on Steve for marrying someone else? Perhaps. But one thing she was certain of: Steve had been with Sandy, not with the guys when she'd gone to the hotel to throw herself at him.

She should have felt betrayed. She should have felt humiliated. She should have felt manipulated. Instead, she smiled into her fingers, thinking how fitting that Steve had set events into motion that had eventually led to the breakup of his own engagement. She felt...grateful. Because Steve had inadvertently introduced her to a man she *could* love.

From afar.

18

HONEY, I'M HOME. Derek couldn't turn in any direction in the offices of Stillman & Sons without seeing the new slogan for Phillips—make that *Hannah's*—Honey. Billboard designs, print ads, product labels, website-page mock-ups. He'd outdone himself, easy to admit since he knew his own limitations as an advertising man. Phillips had been bowled over by the concept of using honey for better home health, and had signed an eighteen-month contract. Feeling good about the direction of the business for the first time in a long time, he'd placed an ad in the paper for a graphic artist. Four applicants would be stopping by this afternoon, and it would be good to have someone else in the office for company.

The direction of the business seemed to be back on course, but the direction of his life was another matter entirely.

He sighed and turned the page on his desk calendar. One month. One month was long enough to have purged nagging, accident-prone, virginal Janine Murphy from his mind. After all, she was a married woman. Married to a jerk, but married nonetheless. He had actually considered calling Steve to extend an olive branch, but changed his mind after acknowledging the ploy was a thinly veiled excuse to call on the off chance that Janine would answer the phone. Besides, despite their pact, Janine could have broken down and confessed what had transpired between them—after all, she might have had some explaining to do on her wedding night. If so, neither one of them would welcome his call.

Derek cursed his wandering mind. Jack would get such a kick out of knowing a woman had gotten under his skin.

The bell on the front door rang, breaking into his musings. The first applicant. Glad for the distraction, he stood and buttoned his suit jacket, then made his way to the front. In the hall, he froze. "Well, speak of the devil," he muttered.

"Hi, bro." Wearing a white straw Panama hat, a hideous tropical-print shirt and raggedy cut-off khaki pants, Jack Stillman walked past him, carrying only a brown paper lunch bag. He strolled to his abandoned desk, then whipped off his hat and, with a twirl of his wrist, flipped it onto the hat rack that had sat empty since his departure. After dropping into his well-worn swivel chair, Jack reared back and crossed his big sandaled feet on the corner of his desk. From a deep bottom drawer, he withdrew a can of beer and cracked it open. Then he slowly unrolled the three folds at the top of his lunch bag—their mother was famous for her three perfect folds. The bag produced a pristine white paper napkin, which he tucked into the neck of his ugly shirt, followed by a thick peanut butter and jelly sandwich.

Derek allowed him three full bites of the sandwich, chased by the room-temperature beer, before he spoke. "Care to say where you've been for the past three months?"

Jack shrugged wide, lean shoulders. "Nope, don't care at all—Florida."

"Which explains the tan," Derek noted wryly.

His brother scrutinized his brown arms as if they'd just sprouted this morning. "I suppose."

"I don't guess it would bother you to know that about three weeks ago the agency was a hairbreadth away from turning out the lights."

Jack took a long swallow of beer. "Something good must have happened."

He'd forgotten how infuriating his brother could be. "I landed the Phillips Honey account."

Nodding, Jack scanned the room. "Honey. Works for me." He polished off the rest of the sandwich, drained the beer, then laced his hands together behind his head. "So what the hell else have I missed?"

"Oh, let's see," Derek said pleasantly. "There's tax season, Easter, Mother's Day—"

"Hey, I called Mom."

"—plus Memorial Day, and Steve Larsen's wedding."

Jack frowned and snapped his fingers. "Damn. And I was supposed to be best man, wasn't I?"

"Yes."

"So did you cover for me?"

"Don't I always? When it appeared you'd dropped out of sight, Steve asked me to be best man."

Jack pursed his mouth. "But you and Steve were never that close."

Derek smirked. "I think it's safe to say we still aren't."

"So how was the wedding?"

He averted his gaze. "I have no idea."

"But I thought you said—"

"I went to Atlanta, and got caught up in a quarantine at the hotel."

"No kidding? Did anyone croak?"

Derek gritted his teeth. "Didn't you watch the news while you were gone?"

Jack grinned again. "Not a single day."

Disgusted, Derek waved him off. "Never mind."

"So what's she like?"

"Who?"

"Steve's wife." His long lost brother wadded up his napkin and banked a perfect shot into the trash can.

Derek walked over to his own desk and straightened a pile of papers that didn't need to be straightened. "She's...nice enough, I suppose."

Jack wagged his dark eyebrows. "Nice enough to do what?"

His neck suddenly felt hot. He loosened his tie a fraction, then undid the top button of his shirt. Images of Janine consumed him during the day, and at night he would take long runs to exhaust himself enough to sleep with minimum torment.

"Derek," Jack said lazily, "nice enough to do what?"

The innuendo in his brother's voice ignited a spark of anger in his stomach that he'd kept banked since his argument with Steve. "Just drop it, Jack," he said carefully.

But he'd only managed to pique Jack's interest. "Brunette? Redhead? Blonde?"

"Um, blonde." *Long and silky.*

"Tall, short?"

"Tall…ish." *And graceful.*

"Curves?"

Derek shrugged. "Not enough for Steve, but plenty for—" He stopped, mortified at what he'd been on the verge of saying.

"You?" Jack prompted. Then his jet eyebrows drew together. "You got the hots for this woman or something?"

"Of course not." He shuffled the stack of papers again, but wound up dropping several, then hitting his head on his desk when he retrieved them. Cursing under his breath, he didn't realize that Jack had moved to sit on *his* desk until he pushed himself to his feet.

"Did you sleep with her?"

Derek tossed the papers onto his desk. "What kind of question is that?"

"How many times?"

He looked into the face of the younger brother who could read him like a label, then sighed and dropped into his chair. "Twice."

"And?"

"And what?"

"And it's not the first time you bedded a woman, so there's more to this story."

"Besides the fact that she was Steve's fiancée?"

Jack scratched his head. "Wait a minute, where was Steve when you were breaking in his bride?"

Derek lunged to his feet and pulled Jack close by the collar of his shirt. "Don't say that!"

But Jack didn't even blink. "Oh, hell, she was a *virgin?*"

Stunned, he released him. "Did you pick up mind reading, too?" He wouldn't be a bit surprised.

Jack laughed, clapping him on the back. "Man, you're about as transparent as a wet, white bikini. So you dig this girl?"

"Woman," Derek felt compelled to say.

"Well, yeah, since you deflowered her."

He closed his eyes. "I think it's time to change the subject. She's a married woman, and I don't fool around with married women."

"Just fiancées," Jack said, picking up some of the honey samples sitting on Derek's desk.

"So glad to have you back," Derek said, not bothering to hide his sarcasm. "And don't eat that," he said, swiping the pint of honey butter from beneath Jack's sampling finger. "It hasn't been refrigerated and it might be bad."

"So throw it away," Jack said, moving on to a container of pure honey.

Derek nodded, staring into the container. Jack was right. Why on earth was he keeping it around? Because it reminded him of Janine, he admitted to himself. He swirled his finger on the surface of the honey butter, then flinched when the pad of his finger encountered something sharp, something unexpected. Dipping his finger, he hooked the object and lifted it free of the sticky-slick substance. With his heart in his throat, he removed most of the globs, then held Janine's engagement ring in the palm of his hand. The memories of her treating his burned hand vividly slammed home. She must have lost the bauble in the jar without realizing it.

Jack came over to take a look. "Wow, has Phillips started putting prizes in their packages?"

Already dialing directory assistance, Derek didn't answer. He had to talk to Janine right away, and he didn't want to risk calling her at home—Steve's home. But she'd mentioned she shared an apartment with her sister before, so maybe Janine's name would still be listed under the old number.

The operator gave him a number, which he punched in, his heart thrashing. Jack was holding the ring up to the light. "Put it down!" Derek barked. "That ring belonged to Steve's grandmother and is worth a *lot* of money."

Jack smirked. "No big leap how her engagement ring got into your jar of honey butter."

Derek frowned, then focused on the voice of the person who had answered the phone.

"Hello?"

"Yes, hello, may I speak with Janine Murphy's sister?"

"Speaking," the woman said, sounding wary. "This is Marie Murphy."

"Ms. Murphy, you don't know me. My name is Derek Stillman, and I—"

"I know who you are, Mr. Stillman."

He couldn't tell from her voice whether that was a good or a bad thing. "Okay. Ms. Murphy—"

"Call me Marie."

"Marie. I'd like to get a message to Janine, but it's very important that you not tell her when Steve is around."

"Steve? Steve Larsen?"

"Yes."

"Why would he be around?"

He bit the inside of his cheek. "Maybe I have the wrong number. I'm trying to locate the Janine Murphy who married Steve Larsen."

"Mr. Stillman, my sister was engaged to the jackass at one time, but she didn't marry him."

Derek felt as if every muscle in his body had suddenly atrophied. Impossible. Of course she had married him. She had said they would try to work things out. Steve wasn't the kind of guy who would simply let her walk away.

"What's wrong?" Jack asked.

Derek waved for him to be quiet. His heart was thumping so hard, he could see his own chest moving. "Uh, would you repeat that, please?"

A deep chuckle sounded across the line. "I said my sister was engaged to the jackass at one time, but she did *not* marry him. She canceled the wedding at the last minute."

His heart vaulted. "I see. How…how can I get in touch with her?"

"Well, Mr. Stillman—"

"Call me Derek."

"Derek, it's like this, Janine is juggling three jobs, and she only comes home to sleep."

He looked at his watch, estimating the time he could be in Atlanta. "Where will she be in three hours?"

"She'll be at the clinic this afternoon and evening. Got a pencil?"

Derek grabbed five.

19

JANINE JOGGED through the parking lot toward the clinic—late again. Darn the traffic, she was going to be fired for sure if she didn't find a better shortcut. The commute from the urgent-care center to the clinic was always a bit iffy, but she usually made it on time. This week, however, she'd already clocked in late twice.

By the time she reached the entrance steps, she was winded and her feet felt like anvils. She groaned under her breath—another twelve flights of concrete stairs awaited her inside. Well, at least her legs were getting stronger, not to mention her bank account. She'd be able to send Mrs. Larsen a respectable amount for the first payment on the ring.

The woman had been doubly devastated, first by the cancellation of the wedding, then by the loss of her mother's ring. Janine had paid her a visit and they had cried together. Mrs. Larsen blamed Steve to some extent because he hadn't properly insured the ring, but Janine knew exactly where the fault lay. She'd insisted on sending regular payments until the appraisal value had been met...all thirty-seven thousand, four hundred dollars of it.

This first month, she'd be paying off the four hundred. Only thirty-seven thousand to go, and at this rate, she'd have it paid off in a little less than eight years. Mrs. Stillman had graciously suspended any interest, probably because she doubted Janine would even make a dent in the principal.

But she absolutely, positively would not only make a dent, Janine promised herself, she would pay off every penny to rid herself of the psychological obligation to Steve Larsen.

If she lived that long, she thought, stopping to flex her calf muscles, stiff from standing all day, and objecting already to the next eight-hour shift ahead of her. After entering the building, she crossed the lobby, then slowed at the elevator bank, noting how quickly the cars seemed to zip through the floors. Maybe she could take the elevator just this once. Her decision was made when the doors to a car slid open. She was the only one waiting, so she stepped inside and quickly located the door-close button, lest the car fill up with big, pushing bodies.

When the door slid closed, she moved to the rear wall in the center and leaned back, grateful for a few seconds of rest, and blocking out the fact that she was in a small, moving box.

She closed her eyes, and as was customary, Derek's face popped into her mind. In the beginning, fresh from Steve's ugliness and suffering under her own guilt, she had squelched all thoughts of Derek as soon as they entered her head. But gradually, she'd come to realize that remembering their times together made her happy, and darn it, she needed a little happiness in her life. At moments like these, she especially felt like indulging.

His smiling brown eyes, his big, gentle hands, his dry sense of humor. She loved him, a feeling so intense she was embarrassed that she'd imagined herself to be in love with Steve. She wondered if she ever crossed Derek's mind.

Suddenly the car lurched to a halt. Her eyes flew open and her heart fell to her aching feet. She waited for a floor to light up and the door to slide open, but the machinery seemed strangely silent. "Oh no," she whispered, her knees going weak. "Oh, please no."

She stumbled to the control panel and stabbed the door-open button, along with several floor buttons, but none of them lit or produced any kind of movement. Hating the implication, she opened the little door on the box that held a red phone, then picked up the handset. Immediately, the operator answered and assured Janine they would have the elevator moving soon. With her chest heaving, she asked that her supervisor be contacted, and gave the man her name. After hanging up the phone, she shrank to the back wall, forcing herself to stare at the blue-carpeted floor, all too aware of the sickly sweet odor in the air that permeated most medical facilities.

She slid down the wall to sit with her legs sprawled in front of her, and bowed her head to cry—the worst thing a person could do with the onset of a panic attack imminent. But her stupidity, her broken heart and her exhaustion converged into this moment and she recognized her body's need for emotional release.

Burying her head in her folded arms, she let the tears flow and pushed at the black walls that seemed to be collapsing around her. Steel bands wrapped around her chest and began to contract, as if they were alive.

She gasped for air. Inhale, exhale. Her life certainly wasn't horrid—she met seriously ill people every day on her jobs who would gladly trade places with her. But she felt so...so cheated to have fallen in love with a man who would forever remember her as a wanton woman with a penchant for trouble. Most of her life she hadn't been overly concerned about what people thought of her. But worrying and wondering what Derek thought of her kept her awake most nights, even when her body throbbed with fatigue.

She knew Marie was worried about her. After all, she'd lost weight and rarely socialized. Most of her free time to date had been consumed with returning shower gifts with cards of apology. Steve had made one spiteful phone call to her the day after she'd talked to his mother about paying for the ring. He'd told her she'd shamed the family, and he would never forgive her for her outrageous behavior. In response, she had suggested that his receptionist, Sandy, might be a more suitable companion, then proceeded to read him the note the woman had left in the gift he'd given her. Steve hadn't called again.

Derek's connection to Steve presented yet another complication she didn't want to pursue, not in this lifetime. The friendship perplexed her—the two men seemed so different.

Her heart raced. She knew she needed to focus on her breathing, but she felt so weak, physically and mentally. Her throat constricted, forcing her to swallow convulsively for relief. A glance at her watch revealed she'd been at a standstill in the elevator for over twenty minutes. She needed to get out. Now. Struggling to her feet, she pounded on the steel doors with as much energy as she could muster. "Help! Can anyone hear me? I have to get out, please…help…me!"

The phone rang, the peal so loud in the small space that she shrieked. She knelt to pick up the handset, her hand trembling, her lungs quivering. "Please…get me…out of here."

"We're working on it, Pinky."

Her sharp inhale turned into a hiccup. "D-Derek?" she whispered.

"I'm in the lobby, and just in time, it seems. You know, this could be a full-time job, getting you out of scrapes."

"But how—"

"We'll have plenty of time to talk later. Right now, you need to relax and breathe."

Just knowing he was out there made her feel even more trapped. She had to get to him, had to explain how things had gotten so messed up. Her chest pumped up and down, like a bellows sucking the air out of her.

"Breathe, Janine, breathe. They'll have you out of there in no time. Don't think about where you are, just concentrate and breathe. Inhale through your nose, exhale through your mouth."

She did as she was told, content for the moment just to hear his voice. Inhale, exhale. Derek was here. Inhale, exhale. *Why* was Derek here? Inhale, exhale. "What…are you…doing here?"

"Keep breathing. I have some good news. I found that ring you lost."

Sheer elation shot through her. "What? Where?"

"Keep breathing. In that darned jar of honey butter. It must have fallen off when you were tending to my hand. Thank God I didn't throw it away."

Relief flooded her limbs and she tried to laugh, but it came out sounding more like a wheeze. "I can't…believe it." Her joy diminished a fraction at the realization that he'd come back on an errand—albeit a grand one—and not to see her.

But at least she'd get to talk to him, to look at him. Inhale, exhale. And she'd be able to return Mrs. Larsen's beloved ring.

"Are you feeling better?" he asked, his voice a caress.

"Yes," she whispered.

"I have more good news," he continued. "Thanks to you, I landed the Phillips Honey account. And you were right about changing the name—sales are up already."

Janine smiled. After all the trouble she'd caused him, she was glad she'd helped him in some small way. "That's wonderful. So your company is back on its feet?"

"Yeah, and my brother finally found his way home, so I'm not alone anymore."

At least she wouldn't worry so much about him.

"Hey, they're getting ready to start the elevator car."

No sooner had the words left his mouth than the car began to descend slowly, the floors ticking by until it halted at the lobby level. She hung up the phone and pushed herself to her feet just as the door opened. A small crowd had gathered and applauded when she walked out on elastic legs. She needed to sit down, but she needed to see Derek worse.

He was hard to miss, jogging toward her, the largest man in the crowd by far. He wore a dark business suit and, if possible, was more handsome than she remembered. Her heart lodged in her throat as he slowed to a walk, then stopped in front of her.

"Hi," he said, his brown eyes shining.

Oh, how she loved this man. "Hi, yourself," she croaked.

"Let's get you to a chair," he said, steering her in the direction of a furniture grouping. She realized she must look a fright—except for the elevator incident, she hadn't stopped all day. The white lab coat she wore over navy slacks and a pink blouse hung loose and rumpled, and her sensible walking shoes weren't even close to being attractive. But, she acknowledged wryly, it seemed silly to fret about her clothing when Derek was intimately acquainted with what lay beneath her clothes.

"Thank you," she murmured as she sank onto a couch. "I was going a little crazy in there."

His smile made her stomach churn with anxiety. "Good timing," he said.

"How did you know where to find me?"

"Your sister told me. I hope you don't mind me coming to your job, but I thought you might want the ring as soon as possible."

She nodded, thinking sadly that by the time she clocked out this evening, he'd be back in Kentucky. Her pulse pounded at his nearness.

"I had it cleaned," he said, withdrawing a ring box from his pocket.

She smiled. How thoughtful. He'd even bought a box.

He handed it to her and she opened the hinged lid. She blinked, then frowned. The ring was platinum all right, but instead of a gaggle of large stones, a single round diamond sparkled back at her. Lifting her gaze to his, she shook her head. "Derek, this isn't the ring that Steve gave me."

His forehead darkened for the briefest of seconds, then he exhaled, looking tentative. "I know it's not as nice as the ring Steve gave you, but I was hoping you would, um—" Derek cleared his throat noisily, then met her gaze "—accept it anyway."

Vapors of happiness fluttered on the periphery of her heart, but she wouldn't allow herself to jump to conclusions, no matter how pleasant. She wet her lips. "What do you mean?"

"I mean," Derek said, his face flushed, "I know we live a few hundred miles apart, and we didn't exactly have an auspicious beginning...but I love you, Janine, and I couldn't bear the thought of returning another man's ring without having one of my own to offer you."

Speechless, she could only stare at him. He loved her? He *loved* her.

Derek winced and scrubbed his hand down his face, then stood and walked around the couch to stare out a floor-to-ceiling window. "Forget it. It was a crazy idea." He laughed. "I let my brother convince me that things were the way I wanted them to be. I have no right to put you on the spot like this." He turned back, his face weary. "I'm sorry."

Carrying the ring, she rose and circled around to join him at the window. With her heart nearly bursting, she asked, "Do you have the other ring?"

He paused a few seconds, then he nodded and pulled a second box from another pocket.

She turned her back to him to hide her smile of jubilation. Janine opened the lid and inspected the dazzling Larsen family ring that now looked to her more like an albatross than a promise.

Derek watched her, dying a slow, agonizing death. What had he been thinking to show up unannounced with an engagement ring after a month of no contact? He could kick himself. Or better yet, Jack. The scheme had seemed like a good one when he and his brother had worked it out, but now he realized he needed Jack's flamboyance to carry it off. In addition to a woman who loved him.

Janine snapped the lid closed, then turned back to him. "Derek, did you know I'm offering a reward for the ring?"

He blinked. A reward? The last thing he wanted was her money. "Janine—" He stopped abruptly when she slid her hands up his chest and looped her arms around his neck.

His body sprang to attention and he swallowed hard. "Um, n-no, I didn't know you were offering a reward. What is it?" He was mesmerized by the love shining in her eyes.

"My firstborn," she whispered, then pulled his mouth down to hers for a long, hungry kiss.

Epilogue

MANNY OLIVER NOTICED the small brown paper package on his desk when he returned from a particularly grueling staff meeting. When he saw Janine Murphy's name on the return address, he smiled, grateful for a pleasant distraction. His pleasure turned to puzzlement, however, when he unwrapped a black jeweler's box. Intrigued, he opened a small card taped to the top.

> My Dearest Manny,
> I had these made especially for you by a talented woman I met during my blissful honeymoon. Looking forward to seeing you soon.
> > Fondly, Janine Murphy Stillman

Stillman? Manny smiled wide and murmured, "All's well that ends well." He carefully opened the hinged box, then threw his head back and laughed a deep belly laugh.

Nestled against the black velvet winked an exquisite pair of gold cuff links fashioned into two tiny sets of angel wings.

SEEKING SINGLE MALE

This book is dedicated to all the wonderful readers
who have taken the time to write letters to me
about the characters and stories that run around
in my head.Thank you, thank you, thank you.

1

Lexington, KY: SF in mid-twenties seeking SM for good times. Horse lover a plus. I'm a good cook. Coffee Girl

LEXINGTON ATTORNEY Greg Healey looked up from the ad circled in *Attitudes* magazine, his stomach twisting at the sight of his younger brother's wide smile. "You want to do *what?*"

"Meet Coffee Girl," Will said. "'SF' means single female, and 'SM' means single male—that's me."

Closing his eyes, Greg murmured, "Seeking single male."

"For good times," Will added eagerly. "Will you help me, Gregory?"

After a long morning of correcting real estate contracts, this he did *not* need. He sighed, then looked up into innocent brown eyes. Will's childlike expression seemed incongruous with his twenty-five-year-old body, which was broad and toned from grooming and riding horses at the farm that neighbored their home. Greg was tempted to dismiss his brother's request, but lately Will had been showing an elevated interest in women and dating. And in truth, considering Will's shyness and relative isolation, turning to the singles ads wasn't so far-fetched. The fact that his brother had ventured downtown to Greg's office to discuss the ad was proof that he was serious.

Still, intense protective feelings reared high. Greg gestured for his brother to sit in a plush visitor's chair, while he himself leaned against his desk and crossed his arms. "I don't think this is a good idea, buddy. You don't even know this woman—"

"But she likes horses and she likes to cook and she must like coffee." Will shrugged massive shoulders, as if he couldn't imagine what else mattered. "I love coffee, Gregory. Can I call her? There's a number at the bottom of the ad."

Greg bit down on his tongue, unable to offer an alternative for the handsome man before him who was obviously craving female companionship. The physical need, he could relate to, but Greg feared Will wouldn't be able to distinguish a physical attraction from an emotional one. And he was determined to shield Will from would-be opportunists with their sights set on his brother's half of the Healey family business.

"Will, women are…complicated creatures."

"Is that why you're not married, Gregory?"

Greg squirmed. Subtlety was not in Will's repertoire. "Er, yes." One of many reasons, the main one being he'd never met a woman who warranted the trouble of his becoming involved. Besides, most women seemed embarrassed by Will's presence, and his brother would always be his top priority.

Will scratched his temple. "But if women are complicated, then why do other men marry them?"

Greg gave him a wry grin. "Little brother, if you can answer that question, then you're a lot smarter than I am."

Will's eyes widened. "How about for sex?"

Okay, he'd asked for that one. Even after all this time, he still flew by the seat of his pants where Will was concerned. "You don't have to be married to have sex, Will."

"How often do *you* have sex, Gregory?"

He blinked. "That's a personal question." And pride barred him from answering truthfully. "Besides, how often one man has sex has nothing to do with how often another man has sex. Everyone is different. Do you understand?"

Will nodded. "Like how often you brush your teeth?"

"Er, something like that, yes."

Scooting to the edge of the chair, Will said, "I want to have sex, Gregory, but I want to be married first. Don't you think that's best?"

And how could he answer *that* question without being hypocritical? If he said yes and believed it, he would be sentencing himself to a life of celibacy, since marriage was nowhere in his plan. He inhaled deeply, then exhaled slowly.

"Let's take it one step at a time, okay? First you need to meet a nice girl."

Excitement lit Will's entire face. "So I can call Coffee Girl?"

Greg massaged the bridge of his nose. His brother was a late bloomer with raging hormones. When mixed with Will's trusting nature, it was a recipe for trouble. The woman who placed the ad could be a hooker, for all they knew. On the other hand, a hooker would be preferable to a gold digger, or to a woman who would make fun of Will's mental disability. None of the scenarios that played out in his head had a good ending.

"Please, Gregory?"

This had to be what parenting felt like, Greg decided as he looked at his brother's hopeful expression. Being torn between good judgment and giving in. At last a compromise struck him. "How about if I check out this…Coffee Girl first?"

Will bit on his lower lip. "I don't know…"

"Will, don't I always take care of you?"

"Yes, Gregory." Will gestured toward the phone. "But will you call her right now?"

Greg hesitated, noting with alarm that his brother seemed fixated on the idea that this woman in the ad was somehow his soul mate. But the sooner Greg called, the sooner Will would realize that women were a disappointing lot.

"Sure, buddy, I'll call." Consulting the voice mailbox at the bottom of the ad, Greg dialed the number and, after the mechanical voice identified the mailbox, said, "Yes…I'm calling about your ad. My name is…Greg, and I'd like to meet you for…a cup of coffee." Feeling like a colossal fool, he left the number for his private office line and banged down the receiver.

"She wasn't home?" Will asked, his eyebrows knit.

"It doesn't work like that. The number is for a voice mailbox, where I left the message. The lady will call in to pick up the message, then she'll return my call. It's safer that way."

Will jumped to his feet. "But what if she doesn't call back?"

"She'll call."

"But what if she meets you for a cup of coffee and she likes *you*, Gregory?"

Greg draped his arm around his brother's shoulders. "You're the one looking for a woman, aren't you?"

"Yeah."

"And you're the horseman of the family, aren't you?"

"Yeah."

"Then don't worry."

Will frowned, obviously trying to follow the reasoning. "But when will *I* get to have coffee with her?"

"If she's a nice lady, then I'll introduce the two of you." But not until she passed every test he planned to throw at the woman.

A grin transformed Will's face again. "Okay, Gregory." He gave Greg a giant bear hug. "Maybe we'll find a lady for you, too. One that's not so complicated."

With effort, Greg maintained a smile while Will waved goodbye, but as soon as his brother was out of sight, he leaned heavily on his desk. Gentle, big-hearted Will was always full of surprises, but this one had topped them all. Greg glanced at his desk piled high with papers, and heaved a sigh. *And now back to our tedious, mind-numbing program, already in progress.*

Moving in slow motion, he settled into his father's worn leather chair and tried to remember where he'd left off. Increasingly intricate real estate transactions had quadrupled the Healey Land Group's paperwork over the past year. At times he felt more like a pencil-pushing clerk than president and chief legal counsel. Rewriting mountains of contracts wasn't what he'd had in mind when he passed the bar exam a decade ago.

His phone bleeped, and he pushed a button with one hand while massaging a pain needling his temple with the other. "Yes, Peg?"

"I need your sign-off on plans for the company Christmas party on the twenty-second, sir."

He rolled his eyes. Was it his imagination, or had it only

been six months since the last agonizing company Christmas party? "Are you within budget?"

"Yes, sir."

"Then go ahead with it."

"It's only two weeks away, and you haven't yet RSVPed, sir."

Greg sighed. "Will and I both are coming."

"Shall I put you down for two or four?"

Peg's polite way of asking if they were bringing dates, although they never had before. "Two, Peg. And I can't be interrupted right now." He knew he sounded like a grinch, but he couldn't help it—as far as he was concerned, Christmas simply heralded the end of another year of being trapped in this corner office. "Hold my calls."

"Yes, sir."

He stabbed the disconnect button, then walked to the window that consumed two entire walls of his office. The glass transferred the outside chill to his splayed hand, providing the most pleasurable experience of the prolonged morning. Downtown Lexington, Kentucky was all dressed up for the holidays with giant white plastic garlands and shiny blue bulbs twined around street lamps, the colors a tribute to the university.

Regardless of the season, his eyes were always drawn to the same building—the city courthouse. Indulging in a favorite daydream, he imagined how his life would be different if he'd gone into criminal law, instead of taking over the legal responsibilities for his father's real estate company when he'd graduated law school. Now, as the sole heir capable of running the business, he had no choice.

Greg reached up to loosen his tie in an attempt to assuage his sudden claustrophobia. Lately he'd had the pressing feeling that he was missing out on something, that life was passing him by. God, he hated the holidays. So damn lonely.

And now Will was wanting to leave him—or so it seemed.

Unable to face the paperwork that loomed large on his desk, Greg grabbed his gym bag and strode out the door. Without much success, he tried to push the singles ad business from his mind during his lunch-hour run, which he extended by a mile. For a reason that now escaped him, he'd never considered the day when his brother might marry and strike out on his own.

When their father had died seven years ago, Greg had sold his plush condo and moved back home, partly so Will could remain in familiar surroundings, partly to put the proceeds from his condo toward the mountain of debt their father had amassed. The bond the brothers had shared when they were children was forged even stronger, and Greg had simply assumed they would always live together, two happy bachelors.

Except, Will obviously wasn't completely happy. Later, as Greg toweled his neck, he admitted that some small part of him was grateful that his cynicism where women were concerned hadn't rubbed off on Will. But then again, it hadn't been an issue for a while; he hadn't dated anyone seriously since moving back home—the work required to get the family business headed back toward profitability had been enormous.

Oh, he'd had a few dinner dates here and there, but all the women had made their intentions rather clear—marriage. And their interest in his family's money had been equally apparent. He couldn't blame a woman for wanting financial security, but even a token interest in him, in his hobbies, in his dreams—was it too much to ask?

Of course, the real kicker was that, thanks to the string of bad investments their father had made before anyone realized his mind was slipping, the Healey brothers weren't worth nearly as much money as most people believed. He groaned as he stepped under the club shower, regretting more and more the call he'd made on Will's behalf. They had each other now—a woman would change everything, and not for the better.

When he returned to the office with a boxed lunch, he was cranky and favoring a pulled calf muscle. At the sight of a silver garland strung across his windows, he frowned. "Peg!"

The owlish woman appeared at his door. "Yes, sir?"

"I thought I said I didn't want my office decorated."

Her eyes bugged wider. "Do you want me to have it taken down, sir?"

He dragged a hand down his face and sighed. "No, never mind." He gestured to the slips of paper in her hand. "Do I have messages?"

"Yes, sir. Mr. Payton wants you to call him as soon as possible, sir. And a woman called about an ad, sir. Someone named...Coffee Girl?"

Heat flooded his face. "In the future, please don't answer my personal phone line."

"It rings so rarely—I thought it might be an emergency."

A nice way of saying he had no social life. "Did you say you took a message?"

"Yes, sir. Here it is, sir."

"Thank you," he chirped, then took the note and stuffed it into his pants pocket without looking at it. "That will be all."

Peg trotted out and closed the door.

Greg closed his eyes and counted to ten, willing away this restless, frustrated feeling that seemed to have escalated recently. He knew he needed to reduce the stress in his life, to simplify his obligations, but for the time being, things were what they were.

Glad for a reason to postpone contacting the woman from the singles ad, he phoned his general manager, Art Payton, convinced another problem was afoot. "Art, this is Greg. What's up?"

"Great news, Greg. The interest from developers is snowballing on the Hyde Parkland parcels." Art's hearty laugh rumbled over the line. "If the rezoning goes through, you could be sitting on the most valuable property in central Kentucky."

Greg refrained from reminding Art of his opposition to the acquisition of Regal Properties that Greg had targeted two years ago specifically *for* the Hyde Parkland property under its ownership. "Cut to the chase, Art. How valuable?"

"I'm talking about *serious* money. You could retire."

He managed a small laugh. "You're exaggerating." But he

paced in front of the window to expend a burst of nervous energy.

"No, I'm not. If the rezoning goes through, you'll be set for life. Will, too, of course."

His feet stopped moving. Will was the sole reason he hadn't left the company when their father died. When he discovered the financial disaster they'd inherited, Greg had been thrust nearer to panic than he'd ever been in his life. He had to be certain that if something happened to him, Will would always be taken care of. If what Art was saying was true, the Hyde Parkland project would be the parachute he'd been hoping for.

"I'm telling you, Greg, this time next year you could be doing anything your heart desires."

Greg walked to the tinsel bedecked window, zeroed in on the courthouse roof, and smiled—actually smiled. Maybe this Christmas wouldn't be so bad, after all. Still, anything that sounded too good to be true… "I need more details, Art. Can we get together this afternoon?"

"How about three-thirty?"

"I'll see you then."

He slowly returned the handset, while hope thrashed in his chest. Was this deal the light at the end of a long tunnel? Greg shoved a fidgety hand into his pocket, and his fingers brushed the note Peg had given him. A groan welled in his chest, but a promise made to Will was a promise kept, so he pulled out the piece of paper.

Meet me at The Best Cuppa Joe tomorrow morning at eleven. Coffee Girl

Greg scowled and wadded the note into a ball. Romance—bah! As if he didn't have enough on his mind.

2

The next morning

LANA MARTINA CONJURED UP a beaming smile for Miss Half-Caf-Nonfat-Whip-Extra-Mocha. Secretly Lana thought that without the fat, why bother with whipped cream at all. But then again, she didn't even drink coffee—an admitted peculiarity for the owner of a coffee shop—so she offered no comment. Especially since her customers were usually a bit testy before they had their first jolt of caffeine.

Ringing up the three hundred and fifty-sixth sale of the morning, she instead thanked her lucky stars for the large number of Lexington, Kentucky downtowners who relied on the ritual of sucking down coffee before facing their respective daily grinds. Addictions were profitable for the supplier, and Lana prided herself on supplying the best cup of Joe in the city. Ergo, the name of her shop: The Best Cuppa Joe. Okay, she couldn't take credit for the name since the shop had been located at 145 Hunt Street for thirty years—as long as she'd been alive—but she was proud to carry on the tradition as owner and manager for going on six months now.

The woman exited, and with the morning rush officially over, Lana slumped into the counter and willed away the anxiety roiling in her stomach. She'd promised herself she wouldn't turn into a workaholic entrepreneur, but lately one circumstance after another had made long hours unavoidable. Her pastry chef Annette had arrived at four-thirty a.m. with her regular supply of decadent muffins, bagels and baklava, but had sprained her ankle in the parking lot. Lana had sent her home, knowing she'd be shorthanded until Wesley clocked in before lunch.

Oh well, at least she'd be spared Annette's monologue about her ongoing manhunt. The girl was convinced her life was incomplete without the perfect man, and she never ran out of inventive ways to extend her search. Lana, on the other hand, had already found the perfect man. His name was Harry and his maintenance consisted of an occasional puff of air into the valve on the top of his rubber head. Harry never questioned her decisions, never wrestled for the remote, never criticized her hairstyle or clothing.

On the other hand, the only release Harry's anatomically correct body offered her was an occasional burst of laughter.

The bell on the door rang, and Lana straightened automatically until she recognized her friend Alexandria Stillman. "Oh, it's only you."

Alexandria glided toward the counter, sleek and catlike in a cobalt designer suit from her family's upscale department store across town. "Nice to see you, too."

Lana waved off Alex's comment and rubbed her aching pouring arm. "You know what I mean."

"Business is good, huh?"

Lana surveyed the space she'd come to love so fiercely, from the ancient brick walls to the whorled wood floors, to the slightly sagging stage where talented and not-so-talented hopefuls put their pride on the line during open-mike nights. A far cry from the claustrophobic accounting office where she'd spent seven years of her life after college—holy humdrum.

"I can't complain," Lana said with a satisfied sigh, pouring a mug of the almond-flavored coffee Alex liked. "Do you have time to visit for a while?"

"That's why I came." Alex took the proffered cup.

Lana quirked an eyebrow. "Is Jack out of town?"

A blush stained Alex's cheeks. "Have I been neglecting you? I'm sorry."

"Since you've never looked better, *Mrs. Stillman*, I'll let you off the hook this time."

"Marriage does seem to agree with me," her friend gushed uncharacteristically. At least, the gushing had been uncharacteristic *before* she'd been swept off her feet by "Jack the Attack" Stillman.

"Yeah, yeah," Lana said with a grin. "Just don't turn into one of those marriage evangelists, okay?"

"I can't promise anything. Hey, do you have plans for Christmas Eve?"

A smile claimed her lips that for once, Alex didn't have to share her family for yet another holiday. "As a matter of fact, Janet is coming up."

"Great. I'm sure you and your mother will have a good time. If your plans change, though, you're welcome to come to Dad's."

Lana didn't respond. Maybe Janet had been a little unreliable in the past, but she'd come. She *would*.

Alex sipped the coffee and murmured her approval. "Nice hat, by the way."

Lana flicked the fuzzy ball at the end of the floppy red Santa hat. "Thanks. I wanted to go for the elf shoes, too, but my crew threatened to quit."

"Speaking of crew, where's Annette?"

"She sprained her ankle this morning, and I didn't want her to have to stand on it all day."

Alex tilted her head. "You look exhausted. Maybe you should sell yourself a cup of your energy blend."

"I'm not that desperate yet," Lana said, laughing. She pulled a bag of Earl Grey tea from beneath the counter and dropped it into a mug, then added steaming water from a dispenser. Janet, a bona fide Anglophile, had introduced her to tea as a youngster, and to tea she remained loyal.

"I guess I'm just stressed out over this roommate situation," Lana said. "I'm glad to be rid of Vile Vicki, but I can't afford to keep paying the entire rent much longer." Not and cover the lease on the coffee shop space, and the short-term note for new equipment, and the payments for the additional cash registers, refrigerator and pastry case.

"If you need a loan—"

Lana cut off her friend with a look. "I appreciate the offer, but no thanks." If she could squeak by for another year, she'd be able to pocket some of the profits instead of sinking all the money back into the business.

Alex relented with a nod. "Any responses from your roommate ads?"

They claimed a small square table painted with a red-and-black gameboard. Lana sat back in a padded chair and shook her head. "A couple dozen oddballs I wouldn't even consider."

"Oh, that's rich—you calling someone an oddball."

Lana pulled a face, then reached behind her to retrieve the magazine that lay discarded on a table. "I let Annette talk me into placing an ad, so maybe I'll hear something before Christmas, although it's a lousy time of the year to be looking for a roommate."

Alex leaned forward when Lana pointed out her ad:

Lexington, KY: SF seeking roommate, F or GM, nonsmoker, preferably sane and willing to share kitchen duties.

"GM?" her friend asked.

"Gay male," Lana said matter-of-factly. "I don't want some straight guy getting the wrong idea about the sleeping arrangements."

"Oh, I don't know," Alex teased, tapping her finger on the singles ads on the next page. "Maybe you should've placed a combination ad and killed two birds with one stone."

"Oh, please. Don't start."

"You were the one hounding me to get a man before I met Jack."

"That was before I bought the coffee shop. Now I don't have time for scratch-off lottery tickets, much less a man."

"Are the ads national?"

"Yep."

"Well, you should be able to find a roommate over the entire country," Alex agreed, grinning over the brim of her cup.

Lana frowned. "Are you saying that I'm too picky?"

"Absolutely."

"Well, do you blame me, after living with that witch for so long?"

Alex blew onto the surface of her drink. "I'm just wondering how much of the animosity for your former roommate had to do with the fact that she went out with the only man you ever cared about."

Ignoring the flash of pain that the memory of Bill Friar conjured up, Lana wagged her finger. "*Thought* I cared about. Bill Friar is a low-life cheat who was threatened by a woman smarter than he is." She'd trusted him, the cad. Lately she'd been pondering whether the problem was that she was too trusting of the people she cared about, or perversely drawn to untrustworthy people—excluding Alex, of course.

"Lana, you're smarter than anyone I know. Maybe you should start accepting invitations to those Mensa meetings to find a date."

"What? Holy hallucinogen, Alex, you know the only reason I maintain my membership in that uppity organization is for the insurance."

"Afraid of hooking up with a thinking man?"

She frowned at her friend. "No. I'd love to find a man with a big brain. But most eggheads are just that—eggheads. No life, no *passion*. Now, finding a man with a big brain *and* a big—"

The phone rang, cutting off her tirade, and spurring Alex's laughter. Lana sprang for the receiver. "Best Cuppa Joe, this is Lana. Merry Christmas, Happy Hanukkah, and a Cheery Kwanza."

"Lana, this is Marshall Ballou."

Of Ballou's Antique Clothing Boutique at the end of the block. "Hey, Marsh. What's up?"

"I just picked up my mail. Did you know there's a rezoning meeting this Friday?"

Black dread ballooned in her stomach—so the rumor was true. "I hadn't heard yet, but of course I'll be there."

"I was hoping you'd say that, hon, because I was just talking to Vic and Paige and Maxie, and we'd like for you to be our spokeswoman."

She lifted her eyebrows. "Me?"

"What do you say?"

"I say you must be desperate."

"Quite the contrary, my dear, you're perfect. And we need you. The company that owns the property thinks they can rail-

road this rezoning plan through because it's our busy season
and we won't notice."

Lana swallowed to force down the bad taste in her mouth.
When she'd gone headfirst into debt to buy the coffee shop,
she'd bought a virtual landmark. Everyone in Lexington knew
there was a coffee shop at 145 Hunt Street. Parking was decent,
the atmosphere was good. She'd never be able to build this kind
of traffic at a new location—not enough to pay back her loans.
"S-sure, Marsh, whatever I can do."

"Great. Call me after closing tonight. Gotta run."

Lana returned the receiver gingerly, telling herself not to
panic. Yet.

"Bad news?" Alex asked.

"Potentially. There's a council meeting Friday night to introduce a rezoning plan for the blocks between here and Hyde. The
local shop owners want me to be their mouthpiece."

"Good choice, since some of the council members already
know who you are."

"Yeah, from *protest rallies*." She dropped into the chair. "I so
do *not* need this right now. Besides, without the landlord's support, I don't believe it'll do much good."

"So get the landlord's support."

"We've tried, but the property is in the hands of so many
holding companies, we haven't even been able to reach a real
live person."

"I can have Daddy talk to his friend on the council and at least
make them aware of the way the merchants have been ignored."

Her friend had offered help many times before—usually financial—but this was the first time Lana was desperate enough
to take advantage of the clout the Tremont name commanded in
the city. She touched Alex's hand and nodded. "Thanks. I know
all of the shop owners will be grateful."

"Consider it done. If there's going to be a fight, at least it'll be
a fair fight."

Lana puffed out her cheeks in a weary sigh. "So much for
sleeping the rest of the week."

"Don't worry—you'll knock 'em dead." Alex stood and lifted
her mug, but her obviously forced smile did not put Lana at

ease. "I'd better get back to work. Thanks for the coffee." She walked to the door, then turned back with a little frown. "Cheery Kwanza?"

Lana shrugged.

Alex laughed. "Keep me posted on the roommate search."

Lana relinquished a smile as she watched the woman she'd known since junior high leave the shop with a sexy bounce to her step. Alex, it seemed, had nabbed the last gorgeous, independent, thinking man walking the face of the earth, or at least walking in the vicinity of the Bluegrass. Lana was happy for her friend, and sad for the rest of the female population, primarily herself. In times like these, it would have been nice to have a big, dependable shoulder to lean on. But since she'd bought the shop, she no longer had time to entertain her fantasies about a stranger arriving to sweep her off her feet. Now she'd settle for someone willing to sweep the floor.

With great effort, she pushed the upcoming council meeting from her mind while she tidied up the tables and plugged in the lights of the four Christmas trees on the stage. The liquid bubble lights on the smallest tree cheered her immensely. She loved this time of year—people were in a generous spirit during the holidays, if at no other time. It served a little glimpse into how things were supposed to be.

She worked around a college-age couple reading from a shared book and holding hands. A pang of envy cut through her chest. Young love was so sweet, so powerful. But she looked at the young woman and willed her to remain her own person, to follow her own interests, to make her own way. Not to marry out of sheer infatuation, then someday wake up dissatisfied with the life she'd built around another person's needs and wants.

Like her mother. The divorce had taken all of thirty days—and Lana hadn't even known until she'd dropped by her parents' apartment during a college class break and found her old room stacked with moving boxes. Janet now lived in Florida, selling tour packages and dating men that were wrong for her. Lana's father had bought a secondhand RV and hit the road with a chick named Mia. She hadn't seen him in years. The sordid clichés had broken Lana's heart. She'd thrown herself into her studies, determined to make something of herself that had nothing to do with a man.

About that time she had discovered The Best Cuppa Joe as a hangout. Old Mr. Haffner had given her grief about not liking coffee—but kept tea bags beneath the counter just for her. She loved the artsy feel of the place, the way musicians and poets and would-be philosophers gathered to try to solve the world's problems. Who would've thought that she would someday own the place?

She knocked over a mug and chastised herself for wasting precious time before the lunch rush. Picking up her pace, she carried table scraps to the back door and fed the two stray cats that magically appeared each morning. The day-old pastries went into a box to be delivered to a soup kitchen a few blocks away. Sorting the trash between serving customers took a while, with each recyclable going into its proper bin. When the morning chores were finished, Lana straightened the magazine she and Alex had been reading and decided to check the voice mailbox for the ad she'd placed. Juggling the receiver, she punched buttons while reaching for a pad of paper.

Eight calls—five men and three women. For one reason or another, none of them sounded exactly right. Then, remembering what Alex had said about her being too choosy, Lana replayed the messages and jotted down names, then just numbers when the pen threatened to run out of ink. Okay, so one of the women had a voice so annoying Lana struck her from the list, but she did return the rest of the calls, inviting the applicants to stop by the coffee shop for a chat as soon as possible—the first to make the grade would sign the lease.

She hung up the phone and turned to the mirror that ran along one wall to adjust her Santa hat. Her unruly pale hair stuck out from under it, hair that she'd finally whacked off in deference to the widow's peak and wavy texture. Her father had once said she was a hairbreadth from being albino, but instead of pinkish eyes, hers were violet. People thought she wore contact lenses, and when she told them different, they dubbed her eyes "spooky."

Funny thing, but when a person looked different, their behavior sometimes rose to the occasion. Even as a child, she'd stepped to the beat of a different drummer. Friends were hard to come by, doubly so since she was teased for living in a low-income apartment tenement. Teachers dismissed her as an oddity. A fluke pop quiz by a school administrator had led to IQ testing in the seventh grade. It was amazing how a "159" changed her in the eyes of her instructors. She was moved into private school on a scholarship, where she'd met Alexandria Tremont, heiress to a local department store chain. Their backgrounds couldn't have been more different, and their friendship couldn't have been more strong.

The warbling of the blue jay from the Birds of North America clock dragged her from her nostalgic musings. Ten o'clock—the lunch rush would start in an hour, and without Annette, it would be nuts. Thank goodness Wesley, a bespectacled college student, arrived a few minutes early.

But by eleven, customers were standing at the counter three-and four-deep. Lana deftly doled out coffee and bagels and biscotti until she was sure her arms would fall off. The rezoning meeting nagged at the back of her mind, although she tried to concentrate on each customer.

She glanced toward the door to gauge how long the rush would last, and did a double take when a seriously good-looking man walked in—tall, dark hair, wide features, great tie. On the heels of her initial assessment, disappointment set in. Such an interesting face for a working stiff. And holy houndstooth, hadn't she met enough shallow yuppie guys on her old job?

Yet she couldn't pull away her gaze, and to her surprise, the man stared back with such intensity that she wondered if she knew him from somewhere. He wasn't a regular customer, she was sure. In fact, he seemed more interested in her than in the menu. A second later, Lana laughed at herself—the man was probably there about the ad. When he claimed an empty booth without ordering, she was almost certain. It made perfect sense—all the best-looking specimens were gay. Although from the permanent wrinkle in his brow, this man appeared to be gay and depressed at the same time.

Oh well, if the man could cook and didn't steal, she'd be content. And just because he was gay didn't mean she couldn't enjoy the scenery. The crowd thinned in thirty minutes, and the man still loitered in the booth, occasionally glancing her way. Jeez, he might smile once in a while. When Wesley signaled he could handle the orders, Lana wiped her hands on her red apron and approached the man.

Upon closer inspection, the man was even better looking than she'd thought. His dark hair was closely shorn, his black eyebrows thick and expressive. His brown eyes were framed with heavy lashes and his skin glowed with health. Unusually affected, Lana overcompensated with a broad grin. "Hi! Would you happen to be here about the ad in *Attitudes*?"

He studied her for so long that she started to feel foolish. Then the man gave her a conservative smile and nodded his well-shaped head. "Yes. As a matter of fact, I am."

3

GREG STARED at the unusual-looking woman, tamping down his surprise. He had assumed that most women who placed singles ads were...desperate, shy or even homely. This woman appeared to be none of those things—the fuzzy Santa hat notwithstanding. In fact, her beauty slammed into him like a sucker punch. The white-blond hair that framed her perky face, and those violet-colored eyes—well, surely she was wearing contact lenses, but the color suited her enormously. His initial thought was that a woman this beautiful wouldn't be sincerely interested in Will, no matter how sweet his temperament.

A purely selfish reaction, he conceded a split second later. Because while he'd never denied his brother anything, he had to admit he wouldn't mind spending time with this woman himself.

"You must be Coffee Girl," he said stupidly, standing.

Her laugh was musical. "Well, my friends call me Lana. Lana Martina."

He luxuriated in her voice—smooth and full-bodied, like heavily creamed coffee. His vision tilted slightly, and he felt off balance. Suddenly remembering his manners, he extended his hand. "Greg Healey." Her handshake was firm and surprisingly strong.

"Nice to meet you, Greg. Would you like something to drink?"

"No, thank you." Only because his swallowing reflex was behaving strangely.

She gestured for him to sit, and they claimed opposite sides of the booth. Lana Martina was lean and long-limbed, and moved like a dancer. She also seemed completely at ease, so much so that he wondered how long she'd been placing singles ads. In his mind, he filled in the blanks: She worked a minimum-wage job at a coffee shop, and was hoping to snag a vulnerable, wealthy man. Like Will.

"Have you had a lot of responses to your ad?" he asked, at a loss for protocol.

"Several," she admitted, then smiled. "But you're the first person I've met face-to-face, so you'll have the best shot."

He blinked. First come, first served?

She looked around, then dipped her chin conspiratorially. "Look, this is a little awkward, but I have to ask—do you meet all the, um...requirements?"

"Requirements?" Those eyes of hers were mesmerizing, and so incredibly large. With a start he realized she was referring to the items in her ad—being a horse lover and someone who appreciates good cooking. Well, he wasn't a horseman like Will, but he could hold his own at the dinner table. "Uh, sure. And I make a pretty mean omelette myself." Had he *said* that?

She pursed her mouth as if impressed. "So, Greg, when were you looking to make a move?"

The woman was nothing if not to the point. Wiping his palms on his slacks, he said, "Well, I thought I might find out a little more about you first, like...where you live."

She laughed, nodding. "Sorry, I was getting a little ahead of myself. My apartment is on Wisteria, walking distance from here."

"I'm familiar with this area." He should be—he and Art had discussed it in depth yesterday afternoon. In fact, the hazing of this building and the one next door were critical to their plans. Coffee Girl would be out of a job—but those were the breaks.

"Listen," she said. "I can step out for a moment. Why don't we go over to my apartment right now?"

Her words obliterated all real-estate-related thoughts. "Right now?"

She shrugged. "Sure. You seem like a nice guy."

He wasn't a nice guy—everyone said so. But his neglected sex stirred. He could be a nice guy for an hour or so.

"That is, if *you* like *me*," she added.

So...while he was cooped up in his corner office, this kind of stuff was going on all over the city. Men and women hooking up through singles ads for hot rendezvouses. Greg tingled with naiveté. No wonder he felt as if life were passing him by. He swallowed hard. "Wh-what's not to like?"

Her smile lit up the room. "Great. Give me a sec to grab my coat and purse."

The mention of her purse rang a bell. He needed to know if this was a *business* transaction. "Um, speaking of money..."

She dismissed his worry with a flip of her wrist. "If you like it, we'll talk about money later."

Greg's stomach and mind churned with indecision as she walked away. She removed her red apron, revealing a stunning silhouette. *Seeking single male for good times.* His collar felt moist. He ran his hand over his mouth. He'd never done anything remotely like this in his thirty-five years.

But when Lana turned her smile in his direction, Greg discarded rational thought. Why not? Why the hell not? He'd spent his life looking after his brother, his family's business—satisfying external obligations. Because he had no desire for a messy emotional relationship, his physical needs had gone unfulfilled. And here was Lady Luck, standing before him in a snug Christmas sweater. He was going for it, damn it. *Merry Christmas to me.*

She rejoined him, now hatless and pulling on a black-and-white spotted, fake fur coat more befitting of a ten-year-old. But he supposed most women with her, er, *hobby* were a tad on the flamboyant side.

"Are you ready?" she asked, hooking her arm through his in a familiar way that both startled and pleased him.

Greg's thoughts turned to the pocket in his wallet where he kept protection. If memory served, he had two condoms stashed there. Male satisfaction swelled in his chest. "I'm ready."

LANA SLID HER GAZE sideways at the handsome man walking next to her. The day was definitely looking up. The first person to respond to her ad seemed like a pretty cool guy, even if he was a little stiff. Greg Healey was certainly one of the most masculine gay men she'd ever met. She was a tall woman, and he was a full head taller. His profile was strong, his shoulders wide, his stride assertive. A bizarre thrill raced through her at his proximity, causing Lana to chastise herself. She wasn't the type of woman who would try to "convert" a gay man, but if she found out that he was intelligent on top of looking good, she was going to be supremely irritated.

Meanwhile, she liked him. There was something… undiscovered about him. In fact, she'd bet her tea bag that he was very recently out of the closet.

"So, Greg, what do you do for a living?" she asked, a few steps down the block.

"I'm an attorney," he said. From the tone of his voice, he wasn't in love with his job. Little wonder, if he didn't make enough money to afford his own apartment. When he glanced at his watch, she said, "Don't worry—this shouldn't take long, so you can get right back to work."

He coughed, and Lana hoped he didn't have any kind of weird allergies, such as to rubber. Choosing between this guy and Harry, her blow-up doll, would be tough. "Any hobbies?"

"Hmm?" He looked as if she'd spoken in a foreign language.

"Hobbies?" she repeated with a laugh. "If we're going to be spending so much time together, I'd just like to know if you have any strange pastimes."

"I have a telescope," he said, then his cheeks reddened. "I mean, I used to enjoy astronomy."

Ah, a Science Club guy—how sweet. "Used to?"

"My job is rather demanding. I don't have a lot of free time."

"I can relate. What else should I know about you?"

He shrugged. "What do you want to know?"

Lana laughed. "Well, do you sleepwalk?"

At last he cracked a smile, an extraordinary smile that transformed his grave features. "No, I don't sleepwalk."

"Good, because I live on the third floor."

He suddenly looked uncertain, and his step slowed.

She winked. "You're not afraid of heights, are you?"

He ran his hand over his dark hair. The movement revealed the barest glints of silver. Suddenly he stopped, and a bemused expression came over his face. "Listen, um, Lana, this is pretty new to me."

Poor guy, he *was* still wrestling with coming out. "Don't worry," she said, laying a comforting hand on his arm. "I'll help you as much as I can. I want us to be friends, you know."

In fact, until this moment, she hadn't realized how much she missed having someone with whom she could share little things. Oh sure, Alex lived just down the hall—but Jack was there now, too, and they were building a home on Versailles Road, where the rich of Lexington migrated to live among endangered horse farms. She sensed an uncommon connection with Greg and hoped he would feel comfortable with her, too.

He shook his head. "But the money—"

"Hey, I'm fairly flexible. My rent is due on the first of the month, so as long as you pay me the day before, we're square."

He pursed his mouth. "Exactly how much money are we talking about?"

Ah—he was broke. A man who lived above his means, by the looks of his suit, and who probably hated the thought of having to share an apartment. Well, at least the man had good taste in clothing, even if he erred a bit on the Republican side. She smiled. "Four hundred a month."

He studied her, as if sizing up what kind of a roommate she'd make. "In return for?"

She gestured ahead of them to an ivy-covered brick structure. "There's my building up ahead. Why don't I just show you?"

More studying—Greg Healey was a studier. Suddenly, she

very much wanted the chance to get to know him better. *Say yes,* she urged him silently.

His chest rose as he inhaled deeply, then he lifted his hands in a gesture of submission. "Okay, let's go."

GREG'S HEART POUNDED as he climbed the stairs behind Lana. He suspected, however, that his elevated pulse had more to do with the side-to-side motion of Lana's curvy behind than the exertion of ascending two flights of stairs.

"The elevator works most of the time," she offered over her shoulder. "But to be honest, it's so slow, I always take the stairs, anyway."

She talked as if he'd be spending a lot of time in the building, Greg noted. He had to admit he admired the woman's chutzpah. He followed her mutely through the door at the top of the stairs, into a corridor, then wound around two corners before stopping behind her in front of number thirty-six.

"This is it," she said, swinging open the wooden door.

As Greg stood rooted at the threshold, a tiny voice he recognized as his conscience whispered, *Don't do it. This woman is complicated.* Greg's nerve endings danced with indecision. He could still turn back. He *should* turn back.

But when she beamed a glorious smile his way, her eyes flashing an invitation, anticipation waxed over caution. A powerful surge of attraction hardened his sex. At this moment, he would have followed this beauty into a pit of tar. His feet must have moved, because suddenly he was standing in an eccentric, if slightly bare, loft. He barely took his eyes off Lana, whose sexual appeal now bordered on hazardous. His body strained for fulfillment. Greg wet his lips, feeling like a teenager in his haste to touch her.

"This is the living room," she said, practically bouncing on the heels of her thick-soled pink tennis shoes.

The "living room" was defined by a large red area rug in the shape of an apple. In contrast, the couch facing them was yellow; the chair, an oversize beanbag chair in University-of-Kentucky-blue. An enormous live Christmas tree stood against the wall, its branches bowed from the dozens of ornaments and dangling crystals. The scent of fresh evergreen stirred his senses even more. Sitting on a wooden stool was a small antique television sporting a rabbit-ear antenna contraption that extended into the air at least four feet.

"You're welcome to bring a bigger set if you want," she offered.

Did she plan on them watching that much TV? Scratching his head, Greg turned to the left and came up short, his heart skipping a beat at the sight of the man standing mere inches in front of him. He felt foolish when he realized the "man" was a blow-up doll dressed in striped pajamas.

"Oh, meet Harry," Lana said with a grin. "He's my sidekick."

"Okay," Greg murmured. Even with the pajamas, it was clear that the doll was anatomically correct. A prop of Lana's?

She hung her coat on Harry's shoulder, then pivoted and swept an arm toward a galley-style kitchen decorated with…cows. Everywhere. Black-and-white, pink-nosed Jersey cows with fat udders. "Not much counter space," she said cheerfully. "But I'm willing to make room for your omelette pan."

Greg stared across the arm's length of space between them, and something…*unfamiliar* happened. Her gaze locked with his, and the static electricity in the air stung his skin. A weird humming noise sounded in his ears, like a frequency interrupted. God, she was lovely—her violet eyes, her pink mouth, her creamy skin. And with her leaning back against the gray-speckled counter, all he could think was how perfect the height would be for…good times.

She glanced away, and the moment was gone, perhaps a figment of his imagination to ease his guilt, a delusion that he shared some sort of connection with this stranger he was about to bed.

"And here—" she said, brushing by him to stand in a vacant area in front of two tall windows, "is where the table and chairs used to sit. I don't suppose you could fill up the space with something interesting?"

He swallowed at the picture she presented, her lush, willowy figure silhouetted by the midday sun slanting in through the windows, her hair a white halo. A piano. He'd buy her a baby grand piano if she'd only stand there a few moments longer.

Her eyes went wide. "Did you say a piano?"

Damn, had he spoken? A thermometer on his neck at this moment would have registered at least one hundred degrees Fahrenheit.

She clasped her hands together, her face lit up like a child's. "You're right, this would be the perfect spot for a piano! I haven't played in years, but it would be so fun!" Then her white teeth appeared on her lower lip, and she looked almost embarrassed. She grabbed both his hands in hers. "Greg, I don't mean to get all girly on you, but I just have a very good feeling about this situation."

He had the same feeling, and it made his pants tighter.

"I have this strange vibe that we were supposed to meet. Weird, huh?"

Her smile revealed a dimple in her chin. Greg might have thought it adorable, but he wasn't the kind of man who used the word *adorable*.

"Well—" she blushed "—I'm sure you'd like to see the bedroom."

If they didn't get down to it soon, he thought, limping slightly as he followed her, he might embarrass himself. On the far side of the loft, opposite the door they'd entered, a narrow hallway ran between two rooms partitioned off with permanent walls, but open to the vaulted ceiling. The bathroom is at the end of the hall," she said, pointing. "And this is the bedroom."

She pushed open the door to the room on the right and walked in a few steps ahead of him. He had the vague impression of a bed with white linens in the otherwise empty and modest room. The room where she…entertained?

Lana was talking, but he only caught a few words. "…great lighting…comfy mattress." Frankly, he couldn't concentrate on anything she was saying for watching her move. She was fine-boned, her arms long and lithe, her wrists small, her neck and collarbone well defined.

"So," she said, stopping in front of him and spreading her arms, "what do you think?"

Overcome with longing, Greg swallowed hard. The woman, his need, the circumstances—the combination overwhelmed him. His control was slipping, badly. "I think," he murmured, "that you are the most desirable woman I've ever met."

She stared at him and her lips parted. She blinked, but she couldn't hide the desire that flared in her eyes. Before he could change his mind, he reached up, curled his fingers around the back of her neck, and pulled her lips against his.

Their meeting was electric. Her mouth moved under his. Her sweet fragrance swirled in his nostrils, her tongue was as smooth as cream. She opened her lips, inviting him inside, where he foraged like a starved man. It was the perfect kiss, fueled by the tide of raw passion pulsing through his body. He'd never felt so in tune with a woman—they both wanted it. Wrapping his arms around her, he pulled her against him, reveling in the way her slim figure melded to him. His erection sought warm resistance, and found it against her thigh. He—

—was suddenly spun around and his arm yanked up between his shoulder blades. Greg grunted at the pain exploding in his rotator cuff. Before he could form a question, a knee in his back propelled him into the hall between the rooms. The wall stopped him. With his head smarting and his mind reeling, Greg straightened and turned around, but at the sight of the fuming blonde advancing on him, he backed into the living room. "Wh-what's wrong?"

"What's wrong?" she shouted. "What was that, that, that...*kiss* all about?"

"I thought you brought me here to..." He gestured helplessly toward the bedroom. "You know, for a good time."

Her eyes bugged. "*What?* How dare you!" She reached into the purse she'd set on the floor and withdrew a bottle of hair spray. "Get out before I call the police!"

Incredulous, Greg shook his head. "But your ad—
arrgghhh!" He clawed at his eyes, which were suddenly filled
with burning, clotting hair spray. "You're insane!" he
gasped, blinded and feeling for the door. He found it, with
the help of her foot on his backside. Greg tumbled through
the opening and landed facedown on musty, smelly carpet.
The door slammed shut behind him.

Greg lay there a few seconds before groaning and rolling to
his back. Cursing under his breath, he rubbed his burning,
watery eyes and tried to sort out what had just happened.
The woman was obviously an unstable individual who set
up men, teased them unmercifully, and then…what? Black-
mailed them? Deciding he didn't want to wait to find out,
Greg pushed himself to his feet, fished his handkerchief from
his back pocket, and escaped the building while mopping his
stricken eyes.

This was the reason he was single, and the reason Will
would be better off as a bachelor, too. Women were like pet
snakes—damn unpredictable. If he never saw the statuesque
blonde again, it would be too soon.

4

LANA OPENED HER DOOR and peeked out into the empty hall-way, hair spray poised. It looked as if Greg Healey—assuming that was his real name—was long gone, the baboon. He obviously hadn't expected her to object to his pilfered kiss.

And in truth, the kiss had been quite remarkable, but it was where the kiss was leading that she had a problem with. Lana pressed her fingers to her mouth, dizzy and a little perplexed as to why a guy who looked that good and kissed that well would resort to answering a lousy roommate ad on the remote chance of getting lucky. Strange. Very strange.

Heavy footsteps sounded in the opposite direction, and for a second she thought he'd come back, or had lost his way since his eyes were full of Aqua-Net. But instead, Jack Stillman loped around the corner, barefoot and wearing only jeans, his wet hair and torso evidence that he'd just stepped out of the shower. Holy he-man—Alex was one lucky woman.

"What's all the commotion?" he asked, his eyebrows drawn together. "Are you all right, Lana?"

She nodded, then waved in the direction of the exit. "Some guy answered my ad for a roommate, told me he was gay, and agreed to see the place." A wry frown pulled one side of her mouth back. "Then he tried to cop a feel in the bedroom."

Jack was trying not to smile. "Are you converting gay men now?"

"You're such a comedian, Jack."

"Seriously, did the guy hurt you?"

"No."

"Then what was that loud thump?"

"I threw him out, and he sort of, um, bounced off the wall."

He shook his head. "Alex assures me you can take care of yourself, but *why* would you invite a stranger to your apartment?"

"He looked trustworthy. And like I said, he said he was gay." Then she frowned. "Or rather, he let me *think* he was gay."

Jack scratched his temple. "Couldn't you tell?"

"What a completely homophobic thing to say."

He sighed. "Forget it. Should I go after the guy?"

Lana thought about it, then shook her head. "Nah. I don't think he's dangerous."

"You also thought he was gay."

"Yeah, but I don't think he meant to harm me. In fact, I had the strangest feeling he was…*scared* of me when I resisted."

"*I'm* scared of you," Jack said. "So, did you hurt him?"

"He has a few bruises, I suppose. And I sprayed him in the face with this—" She held up the pump spray bottle. "Extra hold."

Jack winced. "Do you know his name, just in case he shows up again?"

"He *said* his name was Greg Healey."

Her neighbor's eyes widened. "Greg Healey?"

She nodded. "He said he was an attorney. Do you know him?"

A laugh exploded from Jack's mouth. "I used to know *a* Greg Healey. But it can't be the same guy."

"Mid-thirties, dark hair, stuffed shirt."

Jack pursed his mouth. "Sounds right, but the Greg Healey I knew was a wealthy SOB—he wouldn't have been looking for a roommate. Damn unlikable. And for that matter, he wouldn't have been looking for a woman."

"Let me guess—he's gay?" she asked with an arched brow.

"No. But he was a seriously confirmed bachelor."

"Like you?" she teased, nodding toward the gleaming wedding band on his finger.

"More so," he assured her.

"Must be a different guy," she said with a shrug, wanting

to erase the disturbing incident from her mind. "I guess I should chalk it up to experience and get back to the coffee shop."

Jack shook his finger. "Don't invite strange men back to your apartment until you know what you're dealing with."

She stood erect and saluted. "Sir, yes, sir." Lana pretended to click her tennis shoe heels together, then returned to her apartment for her purse and coat. But she was immensely troubled by the fact that equal to the relief for her safety, she felt a curious sense of loss. She had sensed a connection between herself and Greg Healey, darn it, and had been looking forward to a new friendship. Before he'd gone and ruined it all with that kiss of his.

Lana slipped her coat off Harry's shoulder, then angled her head at him. "I think we should make a pact, Harry old boy. If I haven't found a decent man by the time I'm ninety-five, and you still have air left in you, what say we tie the knot?"

He stared at her with a big permanent grin.

"Oh, good grief, don't tell me *you're* gay." She sighed, tracing her finger around the lock of brown hair printed on his wide forehead. "I don't blame you—the man was rather extraordinary looking, wasn't he?"

Harry's big vacant eyes looked at her pityingly.

"I know, I'm getting desperate." She laughed ruefully. "It must be the holidays. Just don't tell anyone, okay?" Lana planted a kiss on his plastic cheek and walked out the door, trying to salvage her attitude. She wasn't about to give Greg Healey the satisfaction of ruining her day—not when so many other things were vying for that special honor.

GREG'S LINGERING INCREDULITY over his encounter with Lana Martina weighted his foot on the accelerator. The black Porsche coupe responded well to his frustration, gripping the curves of the winding driveway leading to the three-story house where he'd spent the majority of his life. His father had ordered that the sprawling structure on Versailles Road be constructed from genuine limestone mined from fertile Kentucky ground. The Healey homestead was a virtual fortress, and would be standing long after the family name died out.

And that would, quite possibly, happen fairly soon, since perpetuating the Healey name depended on his or Will's producing offspring. His parents had intended that the rooms be filled with grandchildren and great-grandchildren, but they hadn't counted on Greg's opposition to marriage, or on Will's special problems.

Flanked by towering hardwoods standing leafless but proud, the house never failed to lift his spirits. Until now. Now all he wanted was to take a shower, rinse his stinging eyes, and change his clothing that reeked of musty carpet.

The woman could certainly defend herself, he conceded. Almost as well as she could kiss. Not that it mattered, since she was a tease *and* a nut. He couldn't imagine how much that woman would have messed with Will's mind.

Spotting a large package by the front door, he parked in front of the four-car garage and made his way around the sweeping sidewalk to the main entrance. He caught a glimpse of his disheveled self in the glass of the doors and was glad their housekeeper, Yvonne, was away visiting her brother for a couple of days, or else she'd give him the third degree about his appearance and his impromptu trip home in the middle of the day.

But when he realized that the carton contained the saddle he'd ordered for Will for Christmas, he was almost glad for the incident; otherwise Will might have seen the box. *Almost* being the operative word, considering the bruises Coffee Girl had inflicted upon his person and his pride. Still, Greg admitted with a wry smile as he wrestled the box inside the door, it would be nice to surprise his brother for once.

"Whatcha got, Gregory?"

His brother's voice startled him so badly he nearly dropped the carton in the foyer. "Jesus, Will, I wasn't expecting you to be here."

Will held up a thick sandwich. "I forgot to pack my lunch this morning. Want some help?"

"No, that's okay—"

With his free arm, Will took the box from him as if it were a bale of goose down. "Is it a new telescope?"

Greg blinked. He hadn't thought of his broken telescope in months, and it had come up twice today, once with Miss Looney Tunes, and now with Will. "Er, yeah, it is," he lied, glad the return address label of Cloak's Saddlery had gone unnoticed.

"Good. I'll take it upstairs for you," Will said, hoisting the box to his shoulder while nonchalantly taking a bite out of the sandwich.

Greg followed, shaking his head. He himself was a big man, but Will's stocky frame was solid muscle from his strenuous job on Kelty's stud farm that bordered their property. The gentle giant carried the carton to Greg's suite and deposited it in a closet, none the wiser that he'd just stowed his own gift.

Greg envied his brother sometimes—working outdoors, doing what he loved—and today was one of those times. Tugging on his tie, he suddenly dreaded returning to that damnable corner office. As far as he was concerned, the Hyde Parkland rezoning proposal couldn't be approved soon enough. He entertained a moment of vindictive pleasure at the knowledge that Lana Martina would be out of a job— she'd regret she hadn't earned that four hundred dollars when she'd had the chance.

"Gregory, your eye is bruised. Did someone hit you?" Will leaned close for a better look.

He sighed and ran a hand over his eye, wishing he could think of a good lie. But Will had to know how risky the singles scene could be. "I met Coffee Girl this morning."

His brother's eyes lit up. "You did?"

He hadn't told Will for this very reason—he hadn't wanted to give him false hope.

"Yes," Greg said, unbuttoning his sleeves. "She attacked me and sprayed hair spray in my eyes."

Will's head jutted forward. "Why?"

"Because she's—" At the wide-eyed innocence on his

brother's face, he stopped and nodded toward a leather club chair. "Have a seat while I wash up, huh, buddy?"

"Okay."

Greg walked into the adjoining bathroom, stripped his shirt and flushed his eyes with handfuls of cool, soothing water. Sure enough, he'd gotten a shiner when he'd hit a wall—which wall, he wasn't sure. Pressing a towel against his tender eyelids, he nearly groaned in blessed relief. Meanwhile his mind raced as he tried to decide how many details about the encounter he should divulge to Will. Guilt churned in his stomach when he realized that his promise to help Will meet a girl had fled his mind as soon as he set eyes on Lana Martina. In hindsight, he'd gotten exactly what he deserved for being so pettily distracted from his goal.

"Are you okay, Gregory?"

He walked back into the bedroom, drying his face with the towel. "Yeah, I'm okay."

"So why did Coffee Girl attack you?" Will sat on the edge of his seat, wringing his big hands.

Greg dropped onto the side of his bed and slipped off his shoes. "Will, Coffee Girl isn't the woman for you."

His face fell. "Why not?"

"She's a…" *A lovely, bubbly, bright light whose medication wore off mid-kiss.* "She's a…um…" The only woman who'd ever managed to kick up his libido *and* kick his ass. He sighed, fidgeting.

His brother stood abruptly. "You told her I was s-slow, and she doesn't want to meet me."

Feeling morose, Greg stood and held out his hand. "No, Will, that's not it. In fact, I didn't even get to the point of mentioning your name."

He frowned. "Why not?"

"Trust me, buddy, this woman is…weird."

"Most people think *I'm* weird, Gregory."

Greg smiled. "No, I mean this lady is…" He floundered for words that would nip this whole singles ad business in the bud. "She's mentally unstable."

Will's expression was one of near fright. "Coffee Girl is crazy?"

"As a bat."

"That's too bad."

"Yeah, but I'm afraid that's the kind of desperate person who places those ads."

Will bit into his lip. "But I'm desperate, too."

"You're not desperate," Greg said, putting his arm around Will. "You're just impatient. Relax, okay?"

"Okay, Gregory. I know you'll help me find the right girl."

Greg pasted on a smile and bit his tongue to keep from saying such a girl didn't exist—for either one of them.

Will jerked his thumb toward the door. "I have to go back to the farm. They're bringing in Miner's Nephew today."

At last, something to really smile about. His brother loved his job, and the Keltys were good people to have given him the chance to prove himself.

"Can I look through your new telescope tonight, Gregory?"

He nodded, thinking now he had no choice but to buy a new telescope. And he gave quiet thanks that Will hadn't dwelled on Coffee Girl. After Will left, Greg showered quickly and changed into more casual clothes. He only wished *he* were able to dismiss Lana Martina so easily. The bizarre encounter plagued him as he jogged downstairs, and as he drove toward the science museum gift shop.

One minute she'd been enjoying the kiss as much as he, then she'd gone completely berserk. Maybe he'd simply been too assertive, or maybe—oh, hell, he'd probably never know what had caused the woman to snap.

Finally, the idea of buying a new telescope pushed troubling thoughts of Lana Martina from his mind. He called Peg to let her know he'd be late returning from lunch. "Any messages?"

"Just two, sir. The closing on the Toler building has been moved to the twenty-third. And Art Payton called about the Friday rezoning meeting for the Hyde Parkland area. He can't attend because of a family emergency, and his key managers are committed elsewhere. Wanted you to know so you could send someone else, perhaps Ms. Hughs or Mr. Weber, sir?"

He hadn't been to a rezoning meeting in ages—usually they were routine and uncontested. But his future and Will's rested on the outcome of this particular meeting, so he wanted to ensure their interests were represented. Vigorously.

"Add the meeting to my schedule, Peg. I'll go." He hung up the phone and tried on a smile. Finally, something to look forward to.

5

"THE DOCTOR WHO WRAPPED my ankle was dreamy," Annette said as she slid the tray of cranberry Danishes into place. "But he was married, darn it, with four kids."

Lana rolled her eyes at yet another chapter in Annette's manhunt. The woman was a grown-up version of Little Orphan Annie, her petite figure overwhelmed by a helmet of wild red curls. Lana typically endured the woman's nonstop chatter good-naturedly, but her own usual good mood had been compromised by an unexplainable preoccupation with the man who'd called himself Greg Healey. All last evening she'd been restless, fidgety and irritated. Even a formidable amount of cake icing eaten straight from the carton hadn't helped.

Annette sighed dramatically. "I'll never get to wear my wedding gown."

Lana bit her tongue. Everyone who knew Annette had seen the wedding gown she'd been working on for going on ten years, because she carried it around in the back of her van on a mannequin.

"Mr. Right is out there somewhere, Lana, I just know it," Annette continued. "And he's looking for me, too."

"Well, if he's looking for you, I hope he likes coffee."

"From your mouth to God's ear. Hey, speaking of looking, have you found a roommate?"

Lana's laugh was as dry as yesterday's biscotti. "No, but I found a certified weirdo."

The pastry chef's eyes lit up curiously. "What happened?"

"A guy came in yesterday and said he was here about the ad. I asked him if he met all the requirements, meaning was he gay, and he said yes. He seemed all right, maybe a little stuffy, but definitely good-looking. But when I took him to see the apartment, he made a pass at me, right in the bed-room!"

Annette's face had gone totally white.

Lana laughed. "Oh, don't worry—I shot his eyes full of hair spray. But it was all very bizarre."

"Was his name Greg something-or-other?"

A tiny alarm went off in Lana's brain. "Do you *know* him?"

Annette touched a hand to her forehead. "Lana…oh my goodness, I completely forgot. A guy called about the singles ad I put in the paper, and I told him to meet me here yester-day at eleven a.m."

Lana's throat tightened—the timing was right. "You're running singles ads now?"

Annette nodded, her face red.

She gripped the counter. "What did your ad say, exactly?"

While Annette scrambled to find the magazine, Lana's mind swirled with the implication of a missed connection.

"Here it is," Annette said, smoothing the page on the counter. "'Lexington, Kentucky: Single female in mid-twenties seeking single male for good times. Horse lover a plus. I'm a good cook. Coffee Girl.'"

"Coffee Girl?" Lana murmured, remembering the man's puzzling enquiry.

"I thought it fit," Annette said with a sheepish shrug. "And I thought meeting in a public place was a good idea."

She had to sit down to sort through it all—while ignoring the tiny thrill that he'd mistaken her for someone in her mid-twenties. "You mean this guy I thought was answering my roommate ad was actually answering your singles ad?"

"I'm sorry, Lana. With going to the doctor and all, I forgot that I asked him to meet me here." She leaned in close. "But you said he was cute?"

Lana barely heard Annette as snatches of her conversation with Greg Healy came back to her and she realized how in-criminating her words had been. She closed her eyes and managed a small hysterical laugh. He must have thought she was propositioning him. And being a red-blooded male, he'd accepted.

Then Lana froze as his other comments floated back to her. She swallowed a lump of mortification that lodged in her throat. Holy hooker! The man thought she was proposition- ing him, all right—for *money*.

"Lana," Annette said loudly, yanking her back to the pres- ent.

"Huh?"

The redhead's eyes glowed with hope. "You said he was cute?"

"I...guess so. But he made a pass at me, remember?"

"Well, you took him back to your apartment!"

"Yeah, but...if he were a decent guy, he wouldn't have gone!"

Annette's mouth was grim. "You're absolutely right. Any guy who would be that forward wouldn't be willing to wait until the wedding night, would he?"

Another one of Annette's romantic fantasies—that her gentleman prince would be willing to wait until their wed- ding night before consummating their relationship. Lana re- membered Greg Healey's hot kiss, the split-second hardness of his sex against her thigh. "Er, no, he didn't strike me as the waiting type."

"Oh well, I'm just relieved that nothing bad happened. Thanks, Lana, for weeding out another loser."

Lana smirked. "That's me, the jerk strainer."

Annette grinned. "I'll bet he got more than he bargained for when he made that pass."

Lana returned a weak smile.

"Well, I'd better unload the rest of the doughnuts before the doors open."

When Annette exited to the back room, Lana rubbed her breastbone. Her internal organs had begun behaving strangely at the news that Greg Healey might not be the per- vert she had originally thought. She swallowed hard, realiz- ing that maybe Mr. Healey wasn't the only one who'd gotten more than he bargained for when he'd made that pass.

The alien sensation stayed with her throughout the day. Business was good due to a college sports conference going on downtown, and she found herself watching the door for the appearance of Greg Healey's tall, broad figure. It was silly, she knew, because the only reason the guy would come back would be to sue her for blinding him.

Her neighbor Jack's comments came back to her, and she idly wondered if this Greg Healey was the same rich SOB bachelor Jack used to know, after all. But if what Jack said was true, the Greg Healey he knew would be even less prone to answer a singles ad than an ad for a roommate.

She frowned. Unless the man simply shopped the singles ads for sex.

Her opinion of him continued to flip-flop. Lana even debated whether she should try to contact him and explain the misunderstanding. But she suspected he wouldn't find the situation quite so humorous.

No, better to let sleeping dogs lie. She'd lived in Lexington most of her adult life and had crossed paths with Greg Healey once. The chances of it happening again were astronomical.

Of course, when she arrived home that night, it occurred to her that he knew where she lived. She would certainly feel better if she'd found a roommate, but she'd had no luck.

"You're too picky," Alex chided her when she came over that night to bring a velvet footstool she said she didn't want to haul to the new house. "And you should be careful about who you let in your apartment."

Lana sighed. "I suppose Jack told you what happened yesterday?"

"We have no secrets."

"Are you interested in hearing the rest of the story?"

Alex sat down on the yellow couch. "Absolutely."

Lana dropped onto the blue beanbag chair and watched as little foam balls went flying out of the tired seams. "The guy actually thought he was meeting someone who placed a singles ad."

Alex squinted. "Hmm?"

"My pastry chef, Annette, placed a singles ad and asked the guy to meet her at the coffee shop."

Her friend's eyes widened. "And he thought you were—"

"—looking for more than a roommate when I invited him up to see the apartment."

"Oh, that's hysterical."

"Oh, yeah, I'm still laughing about it," she said, rolling her eyes.

Alex tilted her head. "Wait a minute—why *aren't* you laughing? Did this guy scare you more than you're letting on?"

"Oh, no. He backed off as soon as I put up resistance."

"What is it, then?"

She laid her head back, wishing she could put her finger on this elusive unease. "It's nothing."

Alex gasped. "I don't believe it. You actually *liked* this guy, didn't you."

Lana lifted her head. "Are you insane?"

But her friend wore the most infuriatingly triumphant expression.

"That's it! You dig this Greg Healey." She clasped her hands together. "I'll have Jack call him up and—"

"Oh, no, you won't," Lana warned, shaking her finger. "I do not like this guy. I just…don't like the idea of him thinking I'm…loose."

"But he doesn't even know you."

"He knows my name and where I work and where I live. God only knows how many people he could tell."

Alex arched an eyebrow. "You practically beat him up. I'd say the man has as much incentive to keep it quiet as you do."

She frowned. "I guess you're right."

"Besides, if you're so worried about it, why don't you call him and set the record straight?" Alex suggested with a sly smile.

Lana frowned harder. "No, thanks."

"Okay," Alex said with a shrug. "If you change your mind—"

"I won't."

Alex relented with a nod, then gestured toward the ornament-laden evergreen. "I think it's leaning. Shall I warn the people in the apartment beneath you?"

Lana grinned, but her friend's awkward small talk alerted her to something more serious. "What's wrong, Alex? Wait a minute—you didn't come down to bring me a footstool, did you."

Sighing, her friend shook her head. "No. I came to show you this." From her jacket pocket she removed a folded sheet of paper and handed it to Lana.

Alex's father owned Tremont's, an upscale department store chain based in Lexington. Their downtown location occupied a city block, and they rented most of the first floor to eateries and service businesses. The space was expensive and in high demand, and overseeing the signing of the best mix of businesses was only part of Alex's job as the new president. The letter in Lana's hand was an enquiry about space from Buckhead Coffee. Dread flooded her chest. Buckhead was only the biggest, most commercial coffee chain in the country. The company had two locations in Louisville, but hadn't yet entered the Lexington market.

"We probably don't have the kind of space they're looking for," Alex said quickly.

"But they'll find it somewhere," Lana finished.

"But you already have lots of competition, and you're going strong."

Lana sighed. "But that's primarily due to my location, which is subject to change, depending on the outcome of the rezoning proposal before the council."

"Don't worry about this before you have to," Alex urged, standing. "I just wanted you to be forearmed."

Lana thanked her and walked her to the door. "This is good timing, at least. I have two days to come up with a brilliant speech for the council meeting."

"Do you know if the owner will be there?"

She nodded. "I called Regal Properties myself, and they guaranteed that a representative who had decision authority would be present. The shop owners are spoiling for a fight."

"I'll be there to cheer you on." Alex gave her a smile of encouragement. "But you might want to leave the hair spray at home."

Lana laughed. "I will. Besides, I daresay a lady-killer like Greg Healey won't be anywhere in the vicinity of a city council meeting on a Friday night."

6

"YOU'RE STILL WEARING your suit, Gregory. Do you have a date tonight?"

Greg smiled wryly over the dinner table. "A date with the city council."

Will's eyebrows came together. "The people who make decisions for the city?"

"That's right."

"Why do you have a date with them?"

"I want them to change the zoning for some property so we can sell it to developers who want to build homes."

"What's on the property now?"

"Some of the buildings are abandoned, some have small businesses in them."

His brother set down his fork. "What will happen to the small businesses?"

Greg saw where the conversation was headed. He glanced to their housekeeper Yvonne for help, but she gave him a look over the Parmesan chicken that said, "You're on your own, sonny."

He cleared his throat. "They'll relocate."

"You mean they'll have to move?"

"Yes."

"Do they want to move?"

Greg took a sip from his water glass. "Some of them probably don't want to move, no."

"Then I don't think you should make them."

"Will, we own the property. These people only rent space, like having an apartment. If you were renting an apartment, would you expect the owner to operate at a loss just so you wouldn't have to move?"

"No."

"This is the same principle. Besides, the business owners will have the opportunity to present their side to the council meeting tonight, too."

Will leaned forward. "Will there be girls at the council meeting, Gregory?"

Yvonne arched a gray eyebrow in Greg's direction. He shifted in his seat. "A few, I suppose."

"Maybe I could go with you."

"Er, you'd probably be bored, Will."

"I don't mind, Gregory."

He exchanged another glance with their housekeeper, then shrugged. "Sure, if you'd like to go."

Will's grin was so wide, Greg was sorry he hadn't suggested it himself. Will gestured to his own jeans and khaki shirt. "Should I wear a suit, too?"

The sweet innocence of Will wanting to impress a woman he hadn't even met pulled at Greg's heart. In his mind, there wasn't a female breathing who was good enough for Will. "No, buddy, you look just fine."

WET FROM THE DRIZZLING RAIN, Lana jogged into the community center where garland and paper snowflakes abounded, and glanced at the doors she passed, searching for the right room number. A minor emergency with the alarm system at the coffee shop had her running late. She had hoped to go home and change into something more impressive than hip-hugger jeans and a coffee-stained yellow smiley-face sweatshirt, but it couldn't be helped now. At last, she found the door to the room and slipped inside.

She was thankful the meeting hadn't yet started. Voices of what looked to be about one hundred people mingled in a low roar. Rows of folding chairs had been erected for participants, facing a long table at the front of the room where six council members sat talking among themselves. Margaret Wheeler—the president of the city council, if Lana's memory served—was giving an interview to a local news reporter. Lana's mouth went dry with nervousness.

From across the room, an arm waved. Marshall Ballou and

some of the other merchants were sitting together. Alex was there, too, wearing a supportive smile. Lana made her way toward them, hoping they wouldn't be sorry they'd asked her to speak on their behalf. But she'd tried to do her homework, and her canvas tote was full of facts and figures.

"Are you nervous?" Marsh asked.

"A little."

"Just be yourself and let them know we're taking a stand."

In the front, the president pounded a gavel on a wooden block several times. "Everyone, please take your seats. If you're planning to speak on the issue of Rezoning Proposal 642, please sit near the front so you can access the standing microphone more easily."

Alex gave her arm a squeeze. "We'll be right here cheering you on."

Lana took a deep breath and moved through the settling crowd, searching for a seat. The gathering was much larger than she'd imagined. Her pulse kicked up at the thought that her life savings and livelihood could be swept away by a single decision from the six people sitting at the table, people who might remember her as a rabble-rouser on previous issues.

"You can sit here, ma'am," a man's kind voice said.

Lana turned and looked up at one of the largest men she'd ever seen. He was pleasingly handsome, and in command of a hulking muscular body. But there was something infinitely gentle in his eyes and his shy smile. He gestured to a seat in the second row that he had obviously just vacated.

"I don't want to take your seat," she protested.

"I'm glad to give up my seat for a lady," he said, enunciating very deliberately.

Lana suddenly realized the man had a slight mental deficiency or neurological disorder. She flashed him a grateful smile. "And I thought chivalry had died. Thank you very much."

The large man pointed to a black briefcase on the seat next to the one he was giving up. "My brother had to make a phone call, but he's coming back."

"I'll let him know how kind you were when he returns." Suddenly cheered by the stranger's thoughtfulness, Lana inhaled deeply and claimed the seat with an optimistic smile. Maybe this night wouldn't turn out so badly, after all.

"Excuse me." The kind man's brother had returned. She moved her knees sideways and shifted her bag in her lap to allow him to pass. The councilwoman banged again for the crowd to settle down. The man picked up his briefcase and dropped into the seat.

Lana turned her head. "Your brother gave me his—" She felt her jaw drop at the sight of Greg Healey. "You!"

His eyes flew wide, and he recoiled as if she'd hit him—again. "You!"

They vaulted to their feet and sprang away from each other, trampling toes of the people around them. Lana could not find her voice. A hot flush swept over her body. What the devil was *he* doing here?

"We need to get started," the woman in the front repeated loudly, and Lana realized that everyone was staring at them. "Please take your seats."

Lana eyed him warily, and he looked equally cautious. But when the silent stares around them became uncomfortable, they slowly reclaimed their seats. Lana sat rigid with shock. Every inch of her skin burned. Her mind spun with the coincidence of seeing him again and the inevitable embarrassment of explaining the mix-up. How would he react? Keenly distracted by his appearance and his proximity, Lana could barely concentrate on what was being said.

"...Margaret Wheeler, council president. Proceed to the microphone when your name is called. First, we'll hear from a representative from the city planner's office, who will read the proposal and define the specific area involved in the rezoning plan."

The lights were dimmed, plunging her into forced intimacy with the man next to her. The negative energy rolled off him in waves. An overhead projector kicked on, and a blurry map of the Hyde Parkland area appeared. A small man named Peterson droned on and on about the formal process

of enacting a zoning change. She had contacted the city planner's office countless times to share her ideas about community conservation projects; Peterson thought she was a royal
pest.

Suddenly Lana wanted to be anywhere but this blasted
council meeting.

"Where is the man who was sitting there?" Greg Healey
demanded close to her ear.

She jumped. "Your brother? I don't know," she whispered
back. "He gave me his seat."

His soft snort could be translated to mean lots of things—
none of them complimentary. She pulled away even farther,
until she was practically in the lap of the woman sitting on
the other side of her.

Lana faded in and out of the speaker's thirty-minute
speech because she had already researched the tedious details he was providing. Instead, her mind zeroed in on Greg
Healey, although she dared not look in his direction, not
even with her peripheral vision. He was irritated, as evi-
denced by his frequent sighs and constant fidgeting. His
chair creaked incessantly and the fabric of his suit slid back
and forth, back and forth.

Her mind drifted as she recalled her first impression of
him. Darkly handsome, friendly, even appealing. Holy hood-
wink, looks could be *so* deceiving. Too late, she felt the heavy
canvas bag slipping out of her lap. All twenty pounds of it hit
the ground with a crash, punctuated nicely by Greg Healey's
grunt of pain. She surmised his foot was underneath. Lana
lunged forward to retrieve her bag, and promptly banged
heads with him—hard. Pain exploded in her forehead. Their
subsequent groans were audible enough to make people turn
in their seats.

"Christ," he whispered hoarsely. "Are you some kind of
lethal weapon?"

His breath was sweet, and just that easily she remembered
how he'd tasted when he'd kissed her—like citrus and mint.
"Keep your distance and you won't have to worry about it,"

she whispered back, ridiculously wondering if her own breath was as agreeable.

The lights came on suddenly, blinding her. The contents of her bag—binders, folders, papers of all kinds—lay all around their feet. She scraped the pages together, trying to return them to some semblance of order. At this rate, she was going to blow her entire presentation. He handed her a few items that had rolled out of reach, but he was wearing an inconvenienced frown.

"Why are you even here?" she asked, yanking the pages from his hands.

"Next on the agenda is Mr. Greg Healey," the councilwoman announced. Mr. Peterson had finished while they were arguing at knee level. "Mr. Healey will address us as the owner of Regal Properties, the company proposing the zone change."

He gave her a flat smile. "That's why I'm here."

Lana gaped. "You? You're…my *landlord?*"

"Landlord?" he asked, squinting.

"Following Mr. Healey, we'll hear from Ms. Lana Martina, who owns a coffee shop in Hyde Parkland. She'll be speaking on behalf of the business owners in the area."

She gave him a flat smile. "That's why *I'm* here."

He stared. "You *own* that coffee shop?"

"Gee, you're quick."

His frown was as black as Cuban coffee. "Then, yes, I'm your landlord. Do you mind letting me pass?"

Even under the artificial lighting she could see the fading bruises around his right eyebrow—bruises *she'd* inflicted. Numb, she straightened in her seat and shifted sideways so he could exit to the aisle. His pants leg brushed her knees, sending unreasonable tremors of awareness to her thighs. She caught Alex's wide-eyed gaze across the room. Her friend mouthed, *Is that the same guy?*

Lana nodded miserably. What had a few minutes ago seemed like an embarrassing encounter was now a bona fide disaster. She was going to have to debate the man she'd attacked? While he was still under the impression that she had taken him to her apartment to—

Holy Toledo, she was sunk.

7

GREG STEPPED UP to the microphone, forcing his mind away from the fact that the woman who had dominated his thoughts since their bizarre encounter a few days ago was not only sitting in this room, but planned to oppose him on the matter before the council. The coincidence was mind-boggling. He removed a folder from his briefcase with a hand that was somewhat less steady than he would have liked.

"Members of the City Council," he began, then turned to nod to the audience, "and concerned citizens." He scrupulously avoided looking in her direction, but he could feel those violet eyes boring into him. "The proposal before you would resurrect the once vital district of downtown known as the Hyde Parkland area." He directed that the lights be lowered, and recalled the sensation of sitting next to Lana Martina in the dark. The woman's tension practically glowed. Would she accuse him of trying to take advantage of her in front of everyone?

He cleared his throat and refocused. "This district is riddled with large, vacant buildings that once housed small factories. They've been vandalized and are beginning to pose a pest problem. None of the buildings, sewers or utilities are up to code, or suitable to attract the kinds of businesses necessary to revitalize the area." The words tumbled out more rapidly than he wanted, but he couldn't seem to slow down.

"Rezoning for residential development would mean hundreds of construction jobs for demolition and rebuilding. It would beautify the area, and attract home owners to Hyde Parkland. Property taxes would increase, as would business for the downtown merchants." Any second, he expected her to bolt from her seat and start shouting damning words.

"Is that all, Mr. Healey?" president Wheeler prompted.

"Er, no," he said, then inhaled deeply. Good grief, he had to keep his mind on the matter at hand. He fumbled with an acetate overlay for the map, upon which he drew black Xs over the buildings that were falling to ruin.

"My company has attempted to sell these properties for more than two years, but has found it impossible to interest business owners in making the investment that would be required for renovations. They can lease or buy ready-made real estate in the malls for less money, and so the dollars continue to be siphoned away from downtown Lexington."

He replaced the overlay with another one. "This drawing represents a restoration plan my company has worked out with the input of developers and the city planner's office. Single-family dwellings are in red, apartments in blue, condos in green."

"And the yellow?" president Wheeler asked.

The yellow area overlaid the buildings at 145 and 150 Hunt Street, where Lana Martina's shop was housed. He cleared his voice. "The yellow represents a parking garage."

He heard her gasp, even from across the room—and tensed for a blade in his back. "If the area were optimally developed, it could provide housing for more than twelve thousand people. And if we could increase the population within the city limits by a mere ten thousand, Lexington would qualify for an additional two million dollars in the form of government grants to upgrade utilities, to build more schools and to improve roads."

When the lights came up, the room remained quiet, which was a good sign.

"Once you read the detailed economic forecast for this rezoning proposal, I'm certain you'll see, the sooner the measure is approved, the sooner the city will begin to reap the benefits."

Wheeler nodded. "Thank you, Mr. Healey."

"Yea, Gregory," came Will's voice from the back, accompanied by his enthusiastic applause, to which a few people contributed.

Greg conjured up a smile and waved to Will without encouraging him. Leave it to his big-hearted brother to applaud regardless of the occasion. And leave it to his big-hearted brother to offer his seat to the very woman Greg least wanted to meet again.

"Next, we'll hear from Ms. Martina," the president said.

Greg swallowed hard and returned his presentation to his briefcase. He wasn't worried about what the woman might say regarding the rezoning project—hell, if her behavior ran true to form, she might *help* his case. But he had a feeling that he and Ms. Martina had at least one more confrontation in the cards.

When he turned and met her gaze, the feeling increased tenfold. Loathing emanated from those violet depths, reminding him yet again why he was single. With her chin lifted, she passed him, carrying the overloaded bag she'd dropped on his foot.

He returned to his seat, then pulled on his chin, waiting, wondering what the volatile woman might reveal. If he had to defend himself, what would he say? That he went back to her apartment thinking she wanted to have sex? That he thought a quickie with a beautiful stranger would lift him from the holiday doldrums?

Greg removed his handkerchief and mopped at the perspiration on his brow. Jesus, why hadn't he simply walked away?

"My name is Lana Martina," she said, her voice strong, her projection good. "I run a coffee shop in the proposed zoning area. In fact, I just discovered that I'm the parking garage."

The crowd tittered.

"I lease the building from Mr. Healey," she continued, then turned and gestured in his direction. "Although I didn't realize my landlord was an actual person until this evening."

The crowd laughed outright, and his face burned.

She turned back to the council members. "I'm speaking on behalf of thirteen Hyde Parkland shop owners. Part of the reason we're here tonight is that the ownership of the property is so deftly hidden in holding companies and leasing agents, we simply couldn't *find* the owner." She bestowed a magnanimous smile upon the council and the audience. "I'd like to believe that our being shuffled around like a deck of cards was simply an oversight, but I doubt it."

She knew how to work the crowd. A couple of the council members shot a disapproving glance in Greg's direction. He bit down on the inside of his cheek—he'd had no idea any of the shop owners had been misled or ignored.

Lana Martina plunked her own transparency on top of the rezoning map. "What Mr. Healey didn't tell you was that around the vacant buildings here, here, and here, are over a dozen viable businesses whose owners have a considerable investment in their locations and who will lose their livelihood if they're forced to move."

He frowned.

She whipped out another transparency, this one with statistics. "This graph shows that similar downtown rezoning projects in Dukeville and Franklin resulted in a *decrease* in city taxes because the residential buildings could not be filled and eventually were turned into low-income housing. The *reason* the residential buildings could not be filled to capacity was that the retail area, the character of the city, had been decimated, and there weren't enough attractions left to draw potential buyers downtown."

He blinked.

Forty minutes later, he'd lost count of the pie charts and bar graphs, not to mention handouts of the possible negative economical effects of his plan if 1) interest rates rose, 2) unemployment increased, or 3) property taxes jumped. She had projected housing costs, population growth and the effect on the city's declining sewer system, which was currently costing the city such-and-such in fines every day because untreated water was being dumped into a nearby lake.

"So as you can see," Lana said with a flourish, "the proposal before the council is far more than a simple rezoning project. You, ladies and gentlemen, might be held accountable for passing a proposal that would lead to the decline of the entire downtown economy simply to line the coffers of

Regal Properties and—" she shot him a pointed look "—the pockets of Mr. Greg Healey."

The shop owners burst into applause, and Greg shifted in his chair. Despite the woman's emotional argument, however, he felt confident the city council would side with him. After all, leaving the zoning as is would only lead to more decline.

"Is that all, Ms. Martina?" the council president asked.

"Just one more thing," she said in a charming voice.

Greg's heartbeat thrashed in his ears. *She was going to spill her guts about their encounter.*

Leaning closer to the microphone, she said, "I'd like to go on record, saying that even the timing of the proposal is suspect, considering this is the busiest time of the year for those of us who run our own retail businesses." She sent a stinging look in his direction. "One might conclude the owner was trying to sneak this rezoning project by the shop owners and the city council."

A decidedly suspicious mood descended over the audience, and it was all directed toward Greg.

"Thank you for listening," she closed in a solemn tone typically reserved for eulogies.

Greg closed his eyes briefly, as the crowd once again erupted in applause. Christ, she was good. Everyone in the room either wanted to hire her or sleep with her. Except him, of course. And she'd as good as painted a bull's-eye on his back.

LANA GATHERED UP her papers, her heart beating a relieved tattoo that she'd gotten through the presentation. Actually, she felt an incredible rush of satisfaction, a sensation that lasted until she made eye contact with Greg Healey as she returned to her seat. The man's jaw was clenched, and his eyes were dark. Gone was the carefree Science Club guy she'd shot the breeze with on the way to her apartment. Here was the real Greg Healey, and he was the kind of person she loathed—powerful and greedy. She lowered herself into the chair, positioning herself on the edge farthest from him. The meeting couldn't end soon enough as far as she was concerned.

But there were more speakers: a few private citizens who wanted to voice their opinions, and two politicians who simply wanted to get their name and face in front of potential voters. At the end, the president called for a fifteen-minute recess so the members might confer. Lana's nerves jumped with the knowledge that her life as she knew it could be over in mere minutes. Oh sure, she might have six months to clear out. But the loans—holy Chapter 11, she'd have to return to the corporate world just to make a dent in her debts.

Before she could worry about what, if anything, to say to Greg Healey during the recess, Alex and her other friends gathered around, showering her with accolades while shooting barbed glances over her shoulder at the enemy. His energy prickled the skin on her back.

"I have to leave," Alex murmured, her eyes brimming with questions. "But call me tomorrow and tell me what the devil is going on."

"If I figure it out myself," she whispered back. As Alex slipped away, the council members filed back in, and the president banged for quiet.

"The members have considered the arguments presented this evening. A formal vote will take place the second week of January, but the council is not convinced that this proposal has been properly investigated. We will reconvene two days before the vote for final arguments on both sides. In the meantime, the council charges Mr. Healey and Ms. Martina to work together to come up with a compromise that will benefit both parties."

"But—" Lana said.

"But—" Greg said.

The banging gavel interrupted their protests. "Meeting adjourned."

8

LANA WAS STRUCK SPEECHLESS. Work with Greg Healey to come up with a compromise? Her mind reeled with the new development, her consolation being that he looked as displeased as she, his handsome face caught somewhere between bewilderment and mortification.

A week ago she hadn't known this man existed, yet in the space of a few days their paths had intersected at rather bizarre crosshairs. She'd read about these kinds of coincidences, something about the inevitability of two souls crossing that were destined to meet from the beginning of time. Her fingertips tingled. Did he feel it, this…*mystique* that reverberated between them?

He leaned in close, and she held her breath.

"Did you set me up?" he demanded.

She gaped. "Excuse me?"

"I don't believe in coincidence."

So this was the real Greg Healey—condescending, arrogant. suspicious. Lana crossed her arms over her stained sweatshirt. "Haven't you heard, Mr. Healey—it's a small, small world. Or are you always this paranoid?"

The man's ears twitched.

She smirked. "Listen, about the other day—"

"Stop," he cut in, causing her to blink. "If you mention what happened the other day to anyone, I'll slap a civil suit on you for assault."

Maybe it was the fact that she knew he cooked a mean omelette, or that she knew he liked astronomy, or that he'd told her she was the most desirable woman he'd ever met—but this man did not scare her. In fact, she realized she had this puffed-up Richie Rich right where she wanted him: off balance. A warm, fuzzy feeling of feminine power infused her chest.

"Oh, *please* sue me. Then I can tell the court how I had to defend myself with a bottle of hair spray from an unwelcome advance."

His expression was incredulous. "You invited me back to your apartment! You even talked about money, for heaven's sake."

"The only thing I charge for, Mr. Healey, is coffee."

"Really? Does 'four hundred a month' ring a bell?"

She shook her head and snorted softly. "Like I was *trying* to tell you earlier, there was a mix-up in the ads."

"Mix-up?"

"There were two ads, Mr. Healey, and I realized later that our wires got crossed. I thought you were answering my ad for a roommate."

He balked, and she actually enjoyed watching the color leave his face. "Room…mate?"

"Which was why I was giving you a tour of my apartment."

He shook his head. "I'm supposed to believe you were running *two* ads—one for a roommate and one for a… playmate?"

Lana hesitated. If she told him that her employee Annette had run the ad, would he arrange to meet Annette again? Annette didn't need this man trampling on the fairy-tale image of Mr. Right she had conjured up in her head. And despite Lana's warning, Annette might throw caution to the wind and agree to meet him, just because Lana had told her he was good-looking. And a smooth talker like Greg Healey might even talk Annette into giving up her fiercely guarded virginity, to no good end.

"Yes," she lied. "I ran two ads."

He looked dubious. "I think you made up this cockamamy story about two ads to save your pride."

Her laugh of outrage was genuine. "Deposit? Pay by the end of the month? If I *were* a prostitute, Mr. Healey, I'd be charging more than four hundred a month, and I *wouldn't* be offering term payments."

His ears moved again—*how did he do that?* She could tell he was starting to believe her. She almost felt sorry for him. Almost.

"But don't worry," she added, lowering her voice to a whisper. "I won't tell anyone that you shop the singles ads for sex."

His face turned a mottled crimson. "You—"

"Mr. Healey and Ms. Martina?"

She turned to see council president Wheeler walking toward them.

The older woman lifted an eyebrow. "I'm going to take the fact that the two of you are already talking as a good sign."

Greg cleared his throat and Lana extended a forced smile. Talking, yes, but the woman would probably faint if she knew what they'd been talking *about.*

"I'd like to check in with you both before we meet again, just to make sure everyone is working toward a resolution." The woman maintained a pleasant expression, but her eyes glittered a warning at Greg. Lana realized that president Wheeler was the friend of Alex's father who had been informed of the owner's lack of communication with the tenants. Not enough to sway the woman's vote, much less the entire council, but at least she was putting Greg Healey on notice.

"Of course," Greg said cordially, then removed a business card from an expensive-looking holder. As if as an afterthought, he extended one to Lana, as well.

She took it, her fingers carefully avoiding contact with his. His intense gaze skimmed over her, and she wished she could read his mind. Was he contrite? Shamed? Angry? Lana glanced away to rummage through her bag for her own business card and wound up dumping the contents on the floor before coming up with a handful. Greg Healey glanced at the neon-orange card cut in the shape of a coffee cup before he dropped it into his jacket pocket.

"Very original," president Wheeler said of the card. "And

may I congratulate you on an impressive presentation, Ms. Martina.''

''Thank you.''

''I'm aware that you've taken a leadership role in many community issues, and I applaud your involvement. How do you feel about working directly with Mr. Healey on this matter?''

Caught off guard, Lana chanced a glance in his direction. His thick eyebrows came together and he shook his head ever so slightly.

''I—''

''Ms. Wheeler,'' Greg cut in with a disarming smile, ''I've been thinking that my manager, Ms. Hughs, would be a more appropriate person to handle this project.''

The woman shot Greg a stern look. ''Mr. Healey, I think *you* are the appropriate person to handle this project. If that's agreeable to you, Ms. Martina?''

Lana pursed her lips and shrugged. ''I'm nothing if not agreeable.'' She added a broad smile for emphasis.

A muscle ticked in his jaw. ''In that case, I'm certain that Ms. Martina and I will be able to reach a *friendly* compromise for the good of the city.''

Lana swallowed at the unfriendly way the man said ''friendly.''

''I'm betting on it,'' the president said, her tone bordering on parental. ''Now if you'll excuse me…''

And the next thing Lana knew, she was alone with Greg and a big, fat, awkward silence.

''Well,'' she said, clasping her hands and rocking back on her heels.

''Well.'' The muscle in his jaw ticked again.

She sighed. ''Look, what happened was pretty darn embarrassing for both of us, so why don't we just forget about it?''

Tic. ''Fine with me.''

The firm set of his mouth conjured up memories of the ill-fated kiss, pricking her senses. The roar of voices around them swelled, insulating them in a cocoon of awareness. In his black suit and ultraconservative tie, dark-headed, dark-eyed Greg Healey was quite possibly the best-looking man she'd ever seen. She wet her lips. Pity he had so many issues.

"Gregory?"

She turned to see the big man who'd given her his seat approaching. Her heart squeezed when she remembered he had clapped for his brother.

"Gregory, you were great."

And right before her eyes, Greg Healey transformed back into Science Club guy. "Thanks, pal."

"You were good, too," the brother said to Lana.

"Thank you." She extended her hand. "I'm Lana Martina."

He grinned. "I'm William Healey. But you can call me Will."

His good mood was like·a breath of fresh air in the stifling atmosphere. "It's very nice to meet you, Will. Thank you again for giving up your seat. Are you interested in city politics?"

He shook his head. "I came because Gregory said there would be girls here."

She shot an amused expression toward "Gregory," who seemed less amused, but more tolerant of his brother than of…anyone else.

"Will, I'm sure Ms. Martina isn't interested in our *private* conversations."

"I'm riveted," she assured them with a little laugh, "but I really must get back to work. Good night, gentlemen."

"Do you need a ride?" Will offered.

She hadn't driven her moped because of the rain, and, in truth, she was dreading trying to find a taxi, but she wasn't about to test that look of warning on Greg Healey's face. "Thanks, anyway."

"But we have the big car," Will continued. "And plenty of room, don't we, Gregory?"

Greg poked his tongue into his cheek and nodded.

Suddenly gripped with a wicked urge to provoke the man, Lana brightened. "Well, since you have the *big* car…"

GREG WATCHED AS Will tucked Lana into the front passenger seat, holding an umbrella over her so she wouldn't melt. Greg slung water from the sleeves of his all-weather coat, then swung behind the wheel. His mind still reeled from her pronouncement that when she'd taken him back to her apartment, the only thing she'd been offering was a room to rent. Damn, she must think him a pervert. No wonder she'd gone on the attack.

Embarrassment coursed through him at their proximity. For such a slender woman, she seemed to fill up the roomy cab.

But in his own defense, damn it, she'd *heard* him call her Coffee Girl—she should have known which one of her ads he'd been responding to. Jeez. Looking for love in one ad, and looking for a roommate in another. Complicated.

She sighed musically, as if he needed to be reminded that she was within arm's reach. He kept his gaze straight ahead, wondering what about this woman had made him forget himself that day to the point of considering *paying* her to sleep with him. Good God. On hindsight, the idea seemed so ludicrous, he should have known something was wrong. He'd never before allowed his lust for a woman to override his good sense.

For some reason Greg couldn't yet pinpoint, this woman was hazardous to his judgment, and right now all he wanted to do was put as much distance between himself and Lana Martina as possible. He'd sort things out at home. Alone. He latched on to the steering wheel with a grip meant to drain some of his frustration. His brother, on the other hand, was grinning like a fool as he closed the door and climbed into the back seat.

"This certainly is a big car," Lana said, surveying the interior of the four-door Mercedes.

"It was our dad's," Will said, leaning forward to stick his head between their seats. "He died seven years ago."

"I'm so sorry."

"Will," Greg chided as he turned over the engine. "I doubt

that Ms. Martina wants the history of the Healey brothers." He'd never seen his brother so talkative around a stranger.

Her white teeth flashed in the dark. "Since we're going to be working together, why don't you call me 'Lana'?"

She smelled sweet, but then so did rat poison. "Okay," he murmured through gritted teeth. *"Lana."*

"Since you own a coffee shop, Lana, you must like coffee, huh?" Will asked.

Concerned about the potential direction of the conversation, Greg cleared his throat noisily as he set the car in motion. "Will, why don't you sit back?" The last thing he needed was for his brother to find out she was Coffee Girl— his "intended."

But Lana's pleasing laugh filled the car. "Actually, Will, I have a confession to make."

Will's eyes bugged. "What is it?"

Greg pulled out into the traffic, mentally mapping the shortest route to The Best Cuppa Joe. "Will, sit back, please."

He did, for which Greg was thankful, although he remained riveted on their passenger. "What's your confession, Lana?"

"I don't like coffee."

"Really?"

Greg scoffed. "You're kidding."

"Nope. I drink tea."

"Don't you think it's a little hypocritical not to consume what you sell?"

"It's not just coffee that I sell," she protested. "I sell an experience—the aroma, the crowd, the gaming tables, the music. That's what my customers pay for when they buy a cup of coffee."

He tried not to frown, but the woman placed a tad too much importance on a product that was little more than a commodity you could buy at any fast-food drive-thru.

"Yvonne says Gregory drinks too much coffee," Will informed her.

"Yvonne?"

"She lives with us," his brother said happily.

"Will," Greg admonished, shooting him a warning look. He felt Lana's gaze piercing him with questions. "Can we talk about something else?"

"Gregory bought a new telescope," Will said.

He rolled his eyes. His brother seemed determined to share the details of their life.

"Did he?" Lana asked. "Do you like to look at the stars, too, Will?"

He had to hand it to her, she didn't use the singsongy voice that most women used with Will, as if they were talking to a child.

"Oh, yeah. Gregory shows me how to connect the dots and come up with a picture in the sky."

"What kinds of pictures?" She actually sounded interested.

"The big water dipper, and the little one. And people, and animals. Maybe you can come to Gregory's bedroom sometime and see his telescope."

Greg closed his eyes briefly. "Will, allow someone else to talk, please."

"Thank you for the invitation, Will," Lana said, her voice breezy. "So the two of you live together?"

"And Yvonne," his brother reminded her.

"Of course," she said, nodding. "Where do you live?"

"On Versailles Road," Greg piped in before Will could answer and veer off on another tangent.

"I have a friend who's building a new home on Versailles Road. Alexandria Tremont?"

He sighed. She seemed bent on engaging him in conversation. "Is she associated with Tremont's department stores?"

"Her father founded the company, but Alex is the new president. And she recently married someone you might know—Jack Stillman?"

He frowned as the name tickled his memory. "Jack the Attack Stillman?"

"One and the same."

"I was a couple years ahead of him at UK."

"He remembered you, too. Let's see, how did he put it? That you were a 'seriously confirmed bachelor.'"

"What does that mean, Gregory?"

He swallowed and tightened his grip on the wheel. "It means, er…"

"It means that your brother wishes never to marry," Lana supplied.

If he didn't know better, he'd think she was laughing at him. And it sounded as though she must have told her friends about the "incident" and that was when Jack Stillman had remembered him. Were they laughing at him, too?

"Gregory thinks women are too complicated to marry."

"Really?" Lana asked.

"Here we are," Greg said in relief, pulling up in front of the coffee shop ablaze with Christmas lights. Even from the street he could see the place was alive with activity.

Will immediately bounded from the car into the rain to open her door, leaving Greg chagrined. Perhaps he'd forgotten how to behave around a woman. Did that explain why he'd jumped to the conclusion that Lana had wanted to—?

"I'm sorry," he blurted.

She glanced at him, her eyes wide in the lighted cab.

"For…what happened the other day," he said, speaking quickly. "I have no excuse for my behavior." A deprived libido didn't count.

Her smile cheered him ridiculously.

"I share some of the blame for the misunderstanding," she said. "We both were looking for…something else."

Her eyes were mesmerizing.

She straightened. "So, when can we get together to talk about business?"

He blinked. Business? Yes, business. "Why don't you call me," he said, more brusquely than he'd intended, "when you get your thoughts together."

"Sure," she murmured. "Thanks for the ride." She wet her lips, and he watched until the moisture disappeared. "I guess we'll be seeing a lot of each other over the next few weeks."

Rub it in, rub it in.

Suddenly she laughed. "Don't worry, I'll leave my hair spray holstered."

He bit down on his cheek. Was she going to throw salt on his wounded ego at every opportunity?

She slid one leg out the door, then turned back suddenly. "Oh, and one more thing."

He sighed. "What?"

"I really like your brother."

He watched her swing out, her curvy behind swaying as she stepped up onto the curb. He heard her laugh and guessed she'd said something clever to poor, unsuspecting Will, who walked with her to the door of the shop, holding the umbrella over her blond head. She smiled up at Will, and a foreign sensation bolted through Greg's chest. Jealousy? Impossible. He scoffed silently and focused on the swishing windshield wipers.

When Will slid into the passenger seat and banged the door closed, a grin split his face. "I like Lana. Don't you, Gregory?"

He pulled away, watching the rearview mirror until the lights of the coffee shop disappeared. "Er, well, I hardly know her."

"Are you going to ask her out on a date?"

He frowned. "Absolutely not. Lana Martina is not my type."

"Can I have her?"

Greg nearly swerved off the road. "What?"

"If you don't want to ask her out, can I have her, Gregory?"

"She's not a horse—you can't just 'claim' her. When it comes to dating, the woman sort of has to agree." He scratched his head. "What if…she already has a boyfriend?"

"She doesn't." Will grinned. "I asked her."

Well, of course he had. Greg tucked away the nugget of information, then shifted in his seat. "Will, sometimes women prefer it if you're a little aloof, not so assertive."

"What do you mean?"

His mind raced for a suitable answer. "I don't think you

should rush into anything with Lana Martina. Trust me on this, okay, pal?"

"Okay," Will said happily. "Lana is worth waiting for."

Greg hunched down in his seat, miserable in his wet coat, wishing very much that he'd never heard the name Lana Martina.

9

"I CAN'T BELIEVE IT," Alex said. "I simply can't believe it's the same guy!"

"Believe it," Lana said, lifting her cup of tea.

"And now the two of you have to work together. Oh, this is *good*."

"Good? Alex, we'd just as soon set fire to each other."

"But you explained the mix-up, didn't you?"

She was still harboring the teensiest amount of guilt over allowing Greg to believe she had placed both ads. But it was for Annette's own good, after all. "Um, yeah."

"And?"

"Let's just say that things are still a little…strained."

"Well, no man likes to be turned down, no matter the circumstances."

Lana grunted her agreement. "Plus, I think it bothers him that I know he gets his kicks from the singles ads." A wicked smile curled her mouth. "Then it occurred to me that I might be able to use that little tidbit to my advantage."

Alex's eyes widened over her mug of coffee. "You're going to blackmail him?"

"No." Lana wagged her eyebrows. "But *he* doesn't know that."

Her friend laughed, then shook her head. "I don't know, it sounds dangerous."

"I'm not afraid of the man's law degree."

"That's not what I meant." Alex took a slow sip, then set down her cup. "I think there's something between you and Greg Healey."

Lana's mouth fell open. "What? You saw the man—Greg Healey is a poster boy for corporate greed."

"He's powerful, yes."

"Then there's that little sticking point about him leveling my coffee shop to build a parking garage. Alex, I can't stand him!"

Alex looked dubious. "There's a thin line between love and hate."

"But I'm indifferent!"

"People who are indifferent don't use exclamation points when they talk."

Lana rolled her eyes.

"And I find it curious that you failed to mention how handsome he is."

"Is he?" Lana asked, studying the way the milk swirled in her cup. "I hadn't noticed."

"Probably too many other things on your mind," Alex agreed solemnly, "which would account for those circles under your eyes."

She sipped from her cup carefully. "I stayed up late working on the ideas I want to discuss with Greg—I mean, with Mr. Healey." She didn't add that the reason she stayed up late was that the coincidental encounters with the aloof real estate guru had left her big-eyed and restless at two in the morning. She kept remembering the way they had walked arm-in-arm to her apartment. Their exchange had been casual and comfortable when she'd thought him harmless and of no threat to…what? Her livelihood? The little pocket of relationships she'd built around the coffee shop? Her self-imposed celibacy?

"Earth to Lana."

She blinked. "Hmm?"

"I said, did you come up with any good ideas?"

"Well, I'm no architect." She sighed and dragged the papers she'd been working on toward them. "But I tried to come up with different ways to combine commercial and residential dwellings."

They looked through the stack of plans, pencil drawings and scribbled notes.

Alex shook her head. "I'm sorry. I just don't see a painless solution."

"And I don't expect to find one," Lana admitted. "But I do hope that the pain can be borne by more than a small group of people."

"Greg Healey's shoulders looked like they could carry quite a load," Alex said with a sly smile.

Lana shook her pencil. "This is strictly a working relationship."

"It doesn't have to be."

She frowned even as the heat rose in her cheeks. "Alex, doesn't it strike you as a bit bizarre that a rich, good-looking bachelor has to resort to the personal ads?"

"Ah, so you *do* think he's good-looking."

"Don't change the subject."

"Maybe he's shy."

"Oh, yeah, he was a regular shrinking violet at the council meeting. The man's an ogre."

"Maybe he's shy with *women.*"

"He made an unsolicited pass at me in my bedroom."

"Which means he finds you irresistible."

"Which means he thought I was easy."

Alex sighed. "Okay, you're right. If you think this guy's a jerk, then I believe you. Just remember, I thought Jack was a jerk when we first met."

"Jack *was* a jerk when you first met."

A seductive grin lit her friend's face. "A man can change."

Lana's shoulders drooped in exasperation. "Alex, if I had time for a man in my life, he wouldn't be Greg Healey, whose only redeeming quality seems to be his brother."

"Yeah, his brother sounds like a sweetheart. But Greg can't be all bad if he lives with his brother."

"And a woman named Yvonne."

"Oh. The plot thickens."

"Well, *something* is getting thicker, all right."

"When will you see the infamous Mr. Healey again?"

"I'm supposed to call him to set up a meeting as soon as I get my thoughts together." Lana tapped the pencil harder. Of course, no one had to know she was referring to her thoughts concerning Greg. She knew her plan to tease the man could backfire. But when a woman had her back to a wall, she did what she had to do with everything she had to do it with. For now, she'd let him stew.

"HAVE YOU TALKED to Lana, Gregory?"

"No." And if Will asked him one more time, he would surely have an aneurysm. "The meeting was only last night," he reminded him gently.

"I've been practicing how her name would sound. *Lana Healey*. Doesn't that sound great, Gregory?"

He cut into a sausage link with more energy than was required. "Beautiful, pal, just beautiful."

"Who is this Lana person?" Yvonne asked, glancing back and forth between them.

"Nobody," Greg said.

"A really pretty girl with white hair and purple eyes."

Yvonne lifted an eyebrow in Greg's direction.

He sighed. "She represented a group of business owners in the council meeting last night," he said. "I'll be working with her to tweak a rezoning proposal. It's just a formality."

"Gregory wants to shut down her coffee shop," added Will.

Greg put down his fork and rubbed his scratchy eyes. "It's not that I want to shut down her business, Will. But *we* own the property, and it'll be worth a lot of money once the rezoning goes through."

"You sound confident that the proposal will be approved," Yvonne said.

"I believe it will, but thanks to Lana Martina, it'll be at least another month before we can get things moving."

"Ah, she's a rabble-rouser," Yvonne said with a hint of admiration. "Well, not much would have happened over the holidays, anyway."

"Whose side are you on?" he asked with a frown.

But he couldn't ruffle the woman who was more like a family member than an employee. "Yours, *grouch*, but Ms. Martina sounds like a person fighting for what she believes in."

"I want to marry her," Will announced.

Greg closed his eyes.

"Really?" Yvonne asked mildly.

"She has a nice smile."

"I see."

"Gregory, can I call Lana and ask her out on a date?"

Greg wiped his mouth. "I don't think that's a good idea."

"Why not?"

Greg tossed his napkin on his plate. *"Because, I just don't."*

Will pulled back, his expression wounded.

Remorse pushed the air out of his lungs in a noisy exhale. "I'm sorry, pal. I didn't mean to yell. I've got a lot on my mind right now."

"Will," Yvonne said quietly, "would you mind refilling the juice pitcher?"

His brother nodded, picking up the empty pitcher and exiting through the swinging door to the kitchen.

"Would you like to talk about it?" Yvonne asked.

"What?"

Her laugh was soft, abbreviated. "Greg, you've been in a disagreeable mood for fifteen years—and not without good reason. But when you snap at Will, I know something's wrong."

He sighed. "It's this obsession he has with finding a girl-friend."

"Seems perfectly natural to me."

"But he'll get hurt."

"Maybe. But that's between him and the woman, isn't it?"

"Will's welfare is *my* business."

She gave him a pointed look. "And one of these days, you might not be around. Don't you think Will deserves to build a life with someone?"

Gripped with a mounting frustration he couldn't identify, he silently chewed on the inside of his cheek.

"And while we're on the subject, Greg, you deserve the same."

He looked away. "I like my own company."

"And if you'd salvage what's left of your personality, someone else might like your company, too."

"This isn't about me."

"Isn't it?" she pressed.

He looked back to the middle-aged woman. "No. And I'm not going to stand by and watch Will have his hopes dashed by someone like Lana Martina."

"How do you know she'll dash his hopes?"

"Because she's—" he shot a glance toward the kitchen and lowered his voice "—out of his league."

"Oh. And would she happen to be in *your* league?"

He scowled. "What's that supposed to mean?"

She gave him a smile that only a woman who had bounced the brothers on her knee could get away with. He ground his teeth.

Will burst back into the room. "We were out of juice, so I brought milk. Want some, Gregory?"

Greg looked up at his brother's happy face and lifted his empty glass. "Sure."

"Gregory, I think I know why you don't want me to ask Lana Martina out on a date."

He choked on the milk he'd just swallowed. "Why?"

"Because she's against you on the rezoning proposal, and I should be on your side. I'm sorry, Gregory."

One hurt expression from Will was like a thousand knives in the heart. "You don't have to apologize, buddy. We're square, okay?"

"Okay." Will poured himself a huge glass of milk. "But I was thinking—if you have to win Lana Martina over to your side, shouldn't you try to be nice to her, Gregory?"

Flustered at Will's simple but unerring logic, he glanced to Yvonne, who lifted her glass of milk to silently second the suggestion.

Faced with two people with whom arguing was nearly impossible, Greg counted to ten silently, then resumed eating. "Yes, Will, I suppose I should try even harder to be nice to her."

Will grinned.

"But do me a favor—no more of that 'Lana Healey' stuff, okay?"

"Okay, Gregory."

LANA WAS WIPING TABLES, her mind rearranging the bits of property in question like a jigsaw puzzle that seemed to have no matching pieces, when the bell on the door rang. She'd grown accustomed to the bizarre jerk of her heart each time she looked up with the notion that Greg Healey would stride in bearing an olive branch.

But while the man who walked in was about the same age and pleasing to look at, he was no Greg Healey. His hair was auburn, his eyes bright blue, plus he was generous with his smile.

"I'm looking for Lana Martina."

She wiped her hands on a coffee-stained apron, and smiled in return. "You found her."

Another smile. "I'm Rich Enderling. I called about the ad for a roommate."

Lana brightened, and gestured for him to sit. She harbored hope that he would be the answer to one of her immediate problems, but she was wary. "Are you from around here?"

"No. I've been living in a small town in Mississippi for the past few years." His smile was sheepish. "I'm supposed to start a new job Monday, but the apartment I arranged for over the Internet is unlivable, so I'm driving around with a U-Haul and the *Attitude*'s want ads."

"What kind of job?" she asked warily. The last thing she needed was a live-in deadbeat.

"Product development with Phillips Foods. Are you familiar with the company?"

"Vaguely. My best friend's husband runs an advertising agency, and I think Phillips is one of his clients. They process honey or something?"

"Right."

"You don't look like a beekeeper."

He laughed. "I'm a food scientist, and Phillips is expanding into other product lines."

Lana perked up. "You cook?"

"Yes, some."

She bit back her excitement. This guy would be perfect…if he was of the requisite, um, *orientation*. Recalling Jack's comment about not inviting strange men back to her apartment until she knew what she was dealing with, she squinted, surveying Rich Enderling for…what? Color coordination? Good taste? The man looked great in chinos, T-shirt and a denim jacket. He smelled nice and…masculine. She sighed—if this man was gay, she couldn't tell. After all, she'd thought Greg Healey was gay, and look where *that* mistake had gotten her.

Leaning close, she lowered her voice conspiratorially. "Just one more thing before I show you the apartment."

Rich leaned forward, as well. "Yes?"

Lana grabbed him by the jacket collar and pulled his lips against hers for an experimental kiss. From her point of view, the kiss was pleasant—nice moisture, good firmness, with a full bouquet. But no zing, no electricity, no promise. Distantly she heard the bell on the door.

When Lana pulled back, Rich was wearing an amused smile. "I was under the impression you were looking for a *gay* roommate."

Satisfied, she grinned. "Don't move. I'll be right back." She stood and turned a bright smile in the direction of her customer, but faltered when she met Greg Healey's smirking gaze.

10

WHEN GREG WALKED into the coffee shop, a strange gnawing attacked his stomach. It could have been hunger pains triggered by the wonderful aromas inside the shop, but he had a sneaking suspicion the sensation had something to do with seeing Lana Martina engaged in a kiss with the man seated at the table. A "boyfriend" probably, from her ad. After all, Coffee Girl was nationwide.

"Hi, Greg," she said, offering him a sunny smile. "This is a surprise."

Obviously. He steeled himself against her powerful allure, but she was radiant in a violet-colored sweater that complemented her eyes. She didn't appear to be armed—the guy at the table must be a better kisser.

Unreasonable anger sparked in him. "I was on my way in to the office," he said in his boardroom voice, "and thought I'd see if we could set up a time to meet."

"You're working on a Saturday?"

He wasn't in the mood for conversation—not with her boyfriend watching from five feet away. Besides, he had to bite his tongue to keep from telling her that her filibuster of the rezoning proposal meant extra work for him. "Yes, I'm working today. How about lunch?"

She looked regretful. "Lunch is one of my busiest times. How about dinner, instead?"

"Dinner?" He tried to mask his surprise—and the unexpected flutter of pleasure.

"Oh, you probably already have plans."

"No," he said quickly, then recovered. "I mean, I'd like to get the ball rolling as soon as possible."

"Super—"

Her smile made his heart jump.

"Give me a minute to make sure someone can cover for me this evening."

Greg watched her disappear into the back room, hips swaying. Lust clutched his stomach—the woman had a fabulous rear view. When he made himself look away, the Kissing Man at the table gave him a knowing smile. Warmth crept up his neck. He acknowledged the man with a curt nod, then busied himself studying the large room.

The tables were surprisingly crowded. A funky, upbeat station played over the speakers on the drooping stage at the far end of the room. Students lounged on couches and in overstuffed chairs, pretending to study for upcoming final exams. They looked so young and carefree, he experienced a pang of envy. His own college years seemed like a lifetime ago, and not nearly so happy-go-lucky. In hindsight, his father's pressure to perform had chafed him like a saddle—

"Good news," Lana said behind him.

He dragged his mind back to the present.

"I can get away around eight for a couple of hours."

"Great," he said, almost smiling before he realized what he was doing. "How about Brady's?"

"I'll meet you there."

"I'll pick you up."

"No," she said sweetly. "I'll meet you there. Can I offer you a cappuccino—on the house?"

"I'll...I'll take a raincheck," he said, mesmerized by her eyes. "And I'll let you get back to—" he gestured toward Kissing Man "—work."

"Okay. Later," she said with a little wave.

Her smile stayed with him until he drove right past the parking garage for his office building. Since he'd already missed his turn, he somehow found his way down to the courthouse. The place would be relatively quiet on a Saturday.

He entered the echoing halls of the building, staring at the pictures of great judges who'd come before, dredging up memories of his collegiate aspirations. When the rumble of raised voices reached him, he followed the noise down a corridor where a trial was taking place. With his heart pounding in anticipation, Greg slipped inside the half-empty courtroom and took a seat on the back bench. Quickly he was transported from the world of contracts and hours-long conference calls into the cogs of the legal machine he had revered for as long as he could remember.

When the judge's gavel came down to adjourn court, Greg realized with a start that the entire afternoon had slipped away. The To Do list in his office seemed even more unappealing than it had this morning. With regret, he left the courtroom, but was infused with a powerful energy he hadn't experienced in ages. What a curious turn his life had taken in the past few days—Will's unexpected quest for a girlfriend, the prospect of financial freedom, and Lana Martina's peculiar intersection with both issues.

Somehow over the next few weeks he would win her over to his side. Perhaps he could appeal to the woman's sense of community obligation, or maybe…Greg pursed his mouth as Will's words over breakfast came back to him. *Be nice to her.* Maybe he could win her over the old-fashioned way. He puffed out his cheeks in a noisy exhale. And that meant he had to be charming. Damn.

Regardless, the sooner the rezoning proposal passed, the sooner contracts with developers would be signed, and the closer he would be to spending his days in the courtroom.

When a brother's security and a person's own lifelong dreams were at stake, a man had to do what a man had to do.

"YOU'VE GOT YOURSELF a deal," Rich Enderling said.

Lana accepted his hand in a friendly shake and squealed. "You can't imagine how happy I am that this worked out."

Her new roommate gave her a teasing grin. "Isn't going from kissing to a handshake considered a step backward?"

A blush warmed her cheeks. "Sorry about that. I had to make sure that—well, you know."

"That I'm gay?"

She nodded.

"Hey, I was fine with the kiss, but I got the feeling that the guy in the coffee shop wasn't."

She frowned. "What guy?"

"Dark hair, Brooks Brothers clothes."

"Greg Healey?"

He smiled. "I didn't catch his name, and when I saw he only had eyes for you, I didn't bother."

Lana held up her hands. "Hold on. Greg Healey is the man trying to shut down my coffee shop by rezoning the property. The only thing he has eyes for is my unemployment."

He shrugged. "I guess I was wrong. I thought I saw some sort of history between you two. Listen, I need to take care of some things before I start unloading my stuff."

She was still pondering his observation. "Um, sure."

"Great. See you," he said on the way out the door.

Lana sighed in relief. At least one of her problems seemed resolved. Of course, there was that little matter left of saving her business.

FROM HIS SEAT AT A TABLE inside the bar at Brady's, Greg glanced out the window for the fiftieth time to catch sight of Lana Martina coming down the sidewalk. His finger tapped against his glass. The unplanned sojourn into the courtroom today had fueled his fever to practice law, and this rezoning project was his escape hatch from a lifetime of obligation. He did sympathize with the business owners who leased the property he owned, but this was, after all, the United States of America, where the person who owned the land was typically given a voice on what to do with it. He simply needed to neutralize—

He blinked as a red scooter zipped by, the helmeted driver wearing a telltale black-and-white spotted coat. Lana Martina pulled up to valet parking, put down the kickstand, hopped off, then removed her helmet. She said something to the suited valet before bounding toward the entrance. Greg shook his head in wonder, as the man climbed on gingerly and drove the cycle away.

She created a bit of a scene, walking into the upscale restaurant wearing that ridiculous coat, carrying a blue helmet and fluffing her pale hair. Desire, thick and heavy, pooled in his stomach.

"Hi," she said breathlessly. "Sorry I'm late."

With some effort, he dragged his tongue from the roof of his mouth. "Nothing serious, I hope."

"No, just a minor glitch at the shop."

Her cheeks glowed, her eyes shone—and his body reacted accordingly. Greg jerked his thumb toward the window. "Don't tell me that souped-up bicycle is your primary mode of transportation."

"It's a moped," she corrected him. "And if more people drove mopeds instead of gas-guzzling luxury cars, the city wouldn't have to worry about high auto emissions."

One corner of his mouth lifted. "Touché." He stared at her, desire still throbbing inside him and wondered what about this woman spurred him to unusual behavior, then decided he didn't want to delve too deeply. "Our table is ready." Following her to the hostess station, Greg silently repeated his goal: to secure her cooperation.

"Check your coat?" he asked, then helped her out of the dalmatian look-alike garment.

"I'm afraid I'm underdressed," she said, looking around at the elegantly clad patrons. She smoothed a hand down the sleeve of the pink ruffled poet's blouse with a neckline so plunging that it stole the moisture from his mouth.

"You look great," he managed to say. Surely she was wearing a bra. With much effort, he tore his gaze from her cleavage. The rest of her slender body was clad in black jeans with embroidery running down one leg. Jingle-bell earrings with tiny green ribbons swung from her delicate earlobes. Her hair was arranged in that messy style that women were paying a lot of money for these days, although he suspected that Lana Martina might have been the person who started the look because it seemed so...*right* on her.

The sleek hostess apparently disagreed, based on the dubious glance she bestowed on Lana when Lana wasn't looking. At the woman's snub, protective feelings bloomed in his chest, much like when Will was slighted by others. Greg stepped closer to Lana, and his hand involuntarily snaked to her back. She stiffened, but he simply pressed her forward, the warm skin between her shoulder blades burning through the thin layer of fabric into his palm.

Greg summoned strength. The woman was playing dirty. She was definitely not wearing a bra.

11

HE MAINTAINED steady pressure against her back, while they threaded between round tables adorned with candles and flowers, and spaced for privacy. He liked touching her, but he suspected the feeling wasn't mutual.

"I knew this was a nice place," she said, as he pulled out her seat. "I just didn't realize *how* nice."

He acknowledged with a nod the white tablecloth, the fine crystal, the gleaming china. Orchestral holiday tunes floated around them. "Your first time here?"

She nodded, opening the menu. "This kind of place really isn't my bag. A little pricey for my budget."

"Dinner is my treat, of course," he said quickly.

"No, thank you. I'm not out of a job *yet*."

Greg frowned. "I'm not trying to put you out of a job."

She set aside her menu. "But that's exactly what will happen if the rezoning proposal passes as is. For me and a lot of other people."

He looked at her over the top of the wine list. "I was hoping we could have a nice meal before we got down to business."

She looked as if she were about to argue, then her expression changed. "You're right."

Her relenting smile coincided with the arrival of the waiter. "Something from the wine list, sir?"

"Split a bottle of pinot noir with me?" Greg asked her.

"Wine goes straight to my head," she said, then turned to the waiter. "Do you have cranberry juice?"

The man seemed surprised, then nodded.

Greg bit back a smile. "Then make that a carafe of pinot and a carafe of cranberry juice."

"Very good, sir. Would you like appetizers?"

Lana pressed her lips together, then shook her head.

Suspecting she was calculating the check in her head, Greg had the urge to order one of everything for her, but he swallowed words he knew she would resent and told the waiter he would pass, as well.

She sneaked a look at her watch, which had some kind of cartoon character on its face. "Would it be all right if we placed our entrée orders now?"

A tiny frown flitted across the waiter's face, but he acquiesced. Greg was vaguely disappointed that she was already anticipating the end of their date—er, meeting. Maybe she had something planned with the Kissing Man. She ordered pasta and roasted tomatoes; Greg opted for steak and asparagus.

"Are you a vegetarian?" he asked, when the waiter left.

"Reformed," she said.

"Meaning?"

"Meaning I don't eat red meat, but I don't like to wear plastic shoes, either."

He laughed in spite of himself. "And do you champion other causes?"

She gave him a self-deprecating smile. "Recycling, fuel conservation, water management, and a few others."

"Let me guess. You were in the Peace Corps?"

"No, as a matter of fact, I graduated from UK a few years behind you. Accounting and French."

Another surprise. "And how did accounting and French lead to owning a coffee shop?"

"I did my time at Ladd-Markham, then moved on to better things."

"Ladd-Markham?" He drew back. "Somehow I can't see you in a navy suit and starched white shirt."

"The seven longest years of my life. When the company offered severance packages a year ago, I jumped on it. Best Cuppa Joe had been a favorite hangout of mine since college, so when I found out it was for sale..." She shrugged. "It probably sounds crazy to you, leaving a high-powered corporate job to pursue something so esoteric."

A slow wonder crept over him, and his mouth went curiously dry. "You might be surprised."

Their drinks arrived, and Greg did the pouring honors while his head swam with new revelations. "A toast," he said, raising his glass. "To noble motivation."

He clinked his wineglass to her glass of cranberry juice.

Greg savored the dry wine on his tongue before swallowing. His senses seemed heightened, poised for stimulation. Lana unwittingly obliged with her intense eye contact.

"Speaking of motivation," she said, "what's yours regarding the rezoning project?"

Determined not to reveal how squarely she'd hit a nerve, he shrugged. "I want what's best for the city."

"And your bank account?" Her fingers slid up and down her glass in a caress.

"My *family's* bank account. And in this case, what's good for one is also good for the other. I'm running a business, the same as you."

"I wonder if it's the only thing we have in common," she said lightly.

Again their gazes connected, and the sight of her glowing in the candlelight stole the breath from Greg's lungs. The cranberry juice had stained her lips crimson. Her earrings tinkled when she moved. The memory of their kiss hit him again, and he was overwhelmed with the urge to touch her.

From inside his jacket pocket, his phone emitted a muted ring, breaking the moment. "Excuse me," he murmured, then withdrew the phone and glanced at the tiny display screen. "It's Will," he said. "Otherwise, I wouldn't bother."

"Would you like some privacy?"

He shook his head as he flipped open the mouthpiece. "Hey, buddy, what's up?"

"I'm sorry to bother you, Gregory. Are you busy?"

"As a matter of fact, I'm having a meeting with Ms. Martina."

"Really? I bet she looks pretty, doesn't she?"

He glanced across the table where Lana was buttering a

roll. She discreetly licked the tip of her index finger, then blushed when she realized he'd caught her.

"Gregory, did you hear me?"

He cleared his throat. "Er, yes, Will. Yes, you're right. Did you need something?"

"Yvonne and I are decorating the Christmas tree, and I can't find the angel for the top. Do you know where it is?"

Greg smiled into the phone—Will and that angel. "When I was in the storage closet this summer, I believe it was on the top shelf, behind the ski equipment."

"Thanks, Gregory, I'll go look. But I'll wait until you get home before we put the angel on top."

"Sure, pal."

"Tell Lana hello for me. And don't forget—you're supposed to be nice to her."

"I will be. Goodbye."

"Goodbye, Gregory."

He hung up the phone, and accepted the bread basket Lana handed him.

"And how is Will?" she asked.

Her sincerity loosened his tongue. "He has a crush on you."

She grinned. "Ah, that's why he asked me the other evening if I had a boyfriend. He's a real gem."

"Yes," he said carefully. "I'd hate for him to be hurt by…anyone."

She tilted her head. "I could never hurt Will."

He could lose himself in her eyes. Did she realize the power she wielded with a flutter of those sooty lashes? "Maybe not intentionally, but he's more sensitive than most people."

"I could see that," she murmured. "There's quite an age difference between you, isn't there?"

"Ten years."

She smiled. "I suppose you've always looked out for him."

Sediment swirled in the bottom of his wineglass. "Except for the time he followed me up a tree and fell twenty feet to the ground—" As soon as the words were out of his mouth, he wanted them back. He never talked about the accident. When he lifted his gaze to see the sympathy in her eyes, he considered leaving.

"When was that?" she asked softly.

In for a penny, in for a pound. "I was fourteen, he was four." In the silence that followed, he drained his glass and refilled it.

"It wasn't your fault, Greg."

He manufactured a dry smile. "Will has said that a thousand times."

She smiled so deeply, that elusive dimple emerged. "He knows when you're hurting. You're very lucky to have Will for a brother."

Funny, but everyone had always said that Will was lucky to have *him*. Lana's words resounded in his heart. "Yes, I am." He squared his shoulders, grateful for the graceful exit she'd given him. "Do you have brothers and sisters?"

"No."

The one word reverberated with a sadness that surprised him. "Are your parents living?"

She nodded. "But they're divorced. My father moves around a lot, and Janet lives in Florida."

"Janet?"

Her laugh was self-conscious. "My mother looks young for her age, so she doesn't like to be called 'Mom.'"

So she had one of *those* mothers. Maybe that explained why Lana was so…complicated.

"But she's coming to spend an old-fashioned Christmas Eve with me." Her voice was childlike in her mother's defense. "How will you spend Christmas?"

He shrugged. "At home with Will and Yvonne." It was a quiet ritual he took for granted. If Will found a woman, all their routines would change—holidays, vacations, perhaps even living arrangements.

"Yvonne?" She seemed intent on removing a spot from the side of her glass.

"Our housekeeper. She was also a friend of my mother's."

"Oh. Your mother is deceased, too?"

He nodded.

"I'm so sorry," she murmured, her voice catching in such a way that he wished they hadn't ventured into personal territory. "You're very young to be alone."

"Well...I'm not alone," he said, flustered. "I mean, like you said, I have Will."

"And he has you."

"Yes."

"That's nice," she said, nodding. "Brothers should stick together. Have either of you ever been married?"

"No." He hadn't meant to sound so vehement. "You?"

A small smile lifted the corners of her mouth. "No. The single life suits me. I love my business, and I spend most of my free time on causes I believe in. I don't see marriage in my future."

One of those bald-faced lies that women told, he noted sardonically. Designed to trick a man into thinking he wasn't being silently measured for a tux. He decided to call her bluff. "If that's the case, then why would an attractive, successful woman like you place a singles ad?"

She stared at him for the longest time, her mouth pursing and unpursing, then she leaned her elbows on the table. "And why, Mr. Seriously Confirmed Bachelor, would an attractive, successful man like you answer one?"

Now he'd painted himself into a corner. Once again he considered telling her the truth—that he'd been checking her out for Will. Now that she'd met Will, surely she would understand his motives. But if he admitted he'd gone on Will's behalf, wouldn't he also have to admit that he'd chucked his brotherly concern in the face of his raging libido? Debating the lesser of two evils, Greg chose silence.

And by some miracle, their food arrived to relieve the awkward lapse.

She was either just as hungry as he, or just as reluctant to revisit the subject of their first meeting, because she ate in relative silence, dividing the black olives from her pasta into a forlorn little pile on the side of her plate.

"I take it you don't like olives?"

She blushed like a schoolgirl. "Well, I don't lie awake thinking about them, no."

He leaned one elbow on the table. "What *do* you lie awake thinking about?"

She played with the stem of her glass. "Oh, the usual—world peace and clean air."

"Seriously?"

She nodded. "Sometimes." She smiled into her drink. "And sometimes I lie awake thinking about people I care about, wondering what they're doing."

He held his breath, wondering who belonged in that privileged circle.

She turned a pointed look in his direction. "And sometimes I lie awake thinking about meeting my business loan payments."

Greg lifted his glass. "Then it's safe to say we lie awake thinking about the same things. Sometimes." Of course, for the past couple of nights he'd lain awake thinking about her.

Lana pushed aside her half-empty plate and withdrew a notepad from her purse, the pages crammed with handwriting. "I have to relieve an employee in an hour, so if you don't mind…" She leaned forward, inadvertently giving him a gut-clutching glimpse inside her pink blouse.

He dropped his napkin in his plate. "I'm looking—er, listening."

Her smile was conciliatory. "First of all, I don't deny that I'm trying to save my business," she said. "But I also don't want to see the character of the downtown area sacrificed for cookie-cutter condos and town homes."

He refilled both of their glasses. "The residential area doesn't have to be cookie-cutter. And I don't think you're looking at the proposal objectively."

"Well, if that isn't the pot calling the kettle black."

He attributed her seductive laugh to the fact that he'd drunk too much wine. Greg's frustration climbed, partly because they were getting nowhere, and partly because it was the first time in months he'd had dinner with a beautiful woman, and they were talking business. "You'd prefer that I let my investment decay?"

"Of course not. The timing is lousy, but I'm glad the subject has been raised. You see, *I* live in the city, so I have a vested interest in what happens to it."

"Yes, but *I* own property in the city, so I have more of a vested interest."

She cocked her head at him. "Is that so? Do you shop in Hyde Parkland?"

He shifted in his seat. "Occasionally."

Her laugh was dubious. "The day we met was the first time you'd even been inside my shop, wasn't it."

"Yes."

"And can you tell me what is on either side of my shop?"

He squinted, trying to remember, but it was so hard to concentrate when she was looking at him like that, her eyes on fire, her color heightened. And that blouse—good grief, he was only human. "I don't remember."

She leaned back in her chair, shaking her head. "I don't believe this. You're not even familiar with your own property?"

"The company owns dozens of parcels of property. I can't be expected to know about each one in detail."

"Oh, really?" Wearing a conspiratorial smile, Lana waved her hand and called, "Waiter, our checks, please."

"But we're not finished," Greg said, gesturing to his wineglass. In truth, he wasn't ready for the evening to end. Not even close.

"We're finished here," she assured him. "Drink up. I'm taking you on a little tour."

12

"I DON'T BELIEVE I'm doing this," Greg said near her ear.

Lana laughed at his self-consciousness. "Just try to blend. If the police see that you're not wearing a helmet, you'll get a ticket."

"Oh, great. Why can't we just go in my car?"

"The gas-guzzler?"

"Dad left the Mercedes to Will. I drive a..."

"A what?"

"A Porsche," he muttered. "But it gets decent gas mileage," he added, as if the car's fuel economy made up for its obscene price tag.

Lana threw a smirk over her shoulder. "Slumming will be good for you."

"I feel ridiculous."

"Relax," she said. "You *look* ridiculous, too. Hang on."

Not that the moped had an engine that would tear a person's head off, but balancing could be a bit tricky riding double. She goosed the gas, and after an initial protest at the unaccustomed load, the cycle chugged forward. Carefully, she pulled from the parking lot onto the quiet, dark side street, and soon they were humming along at top speed—around thirty miles an hour—with a nippy wind blowing over them. Her cheeks stung and her eyes watered, but the night riding exhilarated her. At least she *thought* it was the night riding that had her blood pumping so efficiently.

"This is as fast as the thing goes?"

"What do you expect?"

"Somebody could practically run up beside you and have a conversation."

"Another plus," she agreed.

He was hanging on to the bar behind the seat, but his body

was tucked up close around hers, emanating warmth she consciously had to avoid sinking back into. At the first light she stopped for, he put his feet down to help her steady the bike. But when the light turned, their push-off was so uncoordinated, Greg lost a shoe. Turning the moped around was difficult because her arms were weak from laughing. He, on the other hand, had an expression that would have rivaled the Grinch's.

"Careful, your face will get stuck that way," she chided, as he leaned over to scoop up his shoe.

If possible, his scowl deepened.

"Of course, in your case," she continued dryly, "it might save you time in future." She zoomed off the minute he slid the shoe onto his foot, gratified at the yelp he gave before he got a handhold.

Laughter bubbled in her stomach. The dour man was so easy to provoke, and doing so gave her the most wicked sense of delight. But even as she smiled to herself, mixed feelings coursed through her—a faint pang of disappointment that this man seemed too stiff and unwieldy to enjoy simple pleasures, and relief that if not for The Best Cuppa Joe, she might still be rooted in a job she hated, with the same narrow view of the world: cynical and clinical. Holy high heels.

But even though she carried a reluctant passenger tonight, the streets were beautiful, awash with twinkling lights and strung with banners heralding the holiday season. The air was as cool as peppermint in her throat and lungs. People moved along the sidewalks in clusters, leaving restaurants and visiting shops that had extended their hours for Christmas. On impulse, she detoured a few blocks to buzz by Tremont's department store and take in the lit window displays—looping trains and animated dolls and spinning tricycles. Pure magic.

"My father brought me here every year to look in the windows when I was little," Lana said, slowing at the corner to relive the memories.

"Mine, too," he said, his voice thick.

Surprised at his admission, she tried to imagine Greg as a

child. Solemn, brooding, temperamental. "And afterward, we'd have hot cider from a street cart," she added.

"With cinnamon sticks to stir."

His words triggered a smile. "Yes!" How extraordinary that they shared a memory. But when she turned her head to say so, his face was closer than she'd expected. The wind had whipped his dark hair over his forehead, concealing the furrows there. Her pulse picked up at the glimpse of a more carefree Greg Healey. A faint smile licked at the corners of his strong mouth. Then his eyes went wide.

"Watch out!"

She jerked her attention back to the road and swerved to avoid a metal trash can that had rolled into the street. They nearly wiped out, but Greg saved the day by assuming their weight, first on one foot then the other, as she fought for control. Finally Lana yanked the cycle toward the curb and braked to a stop. They promptly fell over, bike and all, spilling onto the sidewalk, a knot of arms and legs and handlebars. She lay still for a few seconds, taking stock of her limbs and joints. Actually, the impact hadn't been that bad.

A grunt sounded beneath her, explaining *why* the impact hadn't been that bad. "Are you all right?" she asked.

"I will be when you get off me," he muttered, his voice menacingly calm.

She was suddenly very aware of his big, firm body beneath hers, warm and accommodating. The sensation wasn't wholly unpleasant, but she couldn't very well lie there enjoying it when the man obviously didn't share her opinion. She flailed her arms, but her efforts were futile in the bulky coat. Beneath her, his body jerked, and she realized she heard laughter. The shocking sound started her laughing, too, and their voices blended in the clear air.

"You folks need a hand?"

She sobered and looked up into the face of a middle-aged stranger. "Uh, no. No, thank you."

The man shook his head and moved on.

She burst into giggles and tried again to get up, but succeeded only in grinding her body against his—to noticeable effect. Finally, Greg grabbed her arms and rolled her off his body.

She stopped laughing when she realized he was practically on top of her now. His head was bent close, and his torso covered hers. His labored breath puffed out in little white clouds. Hers might have, if it hadn't been trapped in her chest. Lust stabbed her low and hard. Shadows swathed his face, but his eyes glinted with…desire? Her lips parted, and she realized that she wanted him to kiss her again. He swallowed audibly. The absurdity of the situation was overridden by the unmistakable chemistry that resonated between them, even when heavily clothed, helmeted and lying on freezing pavement.

"Are you okay?" he finally asked, his voice a bit unsteady.

"I think so." If she could think. "You?"

"I think so." He pushed himself up, rubbed his shoulder, then extended his hand to help her. His fingers were long and strong and warm, even through her thin driving gloves. The passionate moment lingered between them. Confusion clogged her mind because she couldn't reconcile her dislike of the person with her attraction to the man.

"I—I'm sorry about, um, crashing." She thought it wise not to mention the source of her distraction. "I'm not used to having another person along."

But if possible, his eyes grew even more serious. "That makes two of us."

She realized with a start that His Uptightness was being philosophical on a cold night standing in the middle of a sidewalk. She didn't like this side of him because it…messed up her plans.

Averting her gaze, Lana noticed a tear in the sleeve of his suit jacket. "Oh, no, your jacket is ripped." She fingered the expensive fabric, seized by a curiously domestic urge to fix it.

He glanced down and brushed his hand over the tear, then grinned. "Do you realize that I've walked away from every encounter with you bearing a battle wound? I can't decide if you're bad luck or if you're trying to get rid of the competition."

She managed a grin as she tightened the strap on her helmet. "I think I'll keep you guessing. I am sorry about the jacket, though. I'll have it repaired."

"That's not necessary," he said, righting her moped with one hand.

"No, really," she said as she straddled the bike. "I have this employee who's a whiz with a needle and thread." It was Annette's fault that she and Greg had gotten off to such a rotten start in the first place. "Believe me, she owes me one."

He was standing with his arms crossed.

"Aren't you going to get on?"

"I don't think so."

"Oh, come on, I'll be extra careful."

He shook his head. "Not unless I can drive."

"What? No way."

"Yes way. I'm driving, or I take a taxi back to the restaurant."

Lana frowned and looked around. They were only about four blocks away from her shop. "Okay," she said, climbing off to give him access to the handlebars. "But if you demolish my bike, you have to provide me with another mode of transportation."

"I'm sure Will would loan you his horse," he said, his voice almost teasing, except the man didn't tease. He threw one long leg over the moped, turned the key and wrapped his big hands around the grips.

"I'm afraid of horses," she said with a little laugh. He looked preposterous, twice as big as the bike, dressed in suit and tie, his legs winged out to the sides. She climbed on behind him, her mood lighter than in recent memory. "But I might take that little Porsche until my bike got out of the shop."

"Hypocrite," he said over his shoulder.

"Bully."

"Hang on."

He accelerated so quickly, she grabbed his waist, and when he didn't resist, she leaned into his warmth to give him directions. "Turn here. Okay, go straight." He had a few problems changing gears, and he was heavy on the brakes, but they moved along at a fairly consistent pace and finally reached the Hyde Parkland section.

"Slow down," she urged, and he slowed until the bike was barely moving. "There's Marshall Ballou's place. He was at the council meeting. Marsh has built quite a following."

"Used clothing?" he asked, his voice dubious.

"Vintage clothing," she corrected. "Just another way to re-cycle. Over there is Vic's Barber Shop. He's been in that lo-cation for longer than you and I have been alive."

He grunted acknowledgment. They wound around a cou-ple more streets, dodging cars illegally parked.

"And over there is Paige Hollander's gift shop—she has a herb garden in the back where she serves sandwiches and tea. And two doors up is Maxie Dodd's bakery—she makes the best sourdough in town. I'll bet the restaurant where we ate tonight buys their dinner rolls from Maxie."

She pointed out another half-dozen mom-and-pop shops before they turned onto Hunt Street and headed toward her own business. "There's a rare-books store on one side of my shop, and a T-shirt business on the other side. Do you mind if I stop by my shop to check on things before taking you back to your car? It'll give us a chance to talk, too."

"Fine with me. I could use a hot cup of coffee."

Too late, she realized she'd have to let Annette in on her plan to butter up Greg Healey. Otherwise, the woman might take one look at him and decide that he wasn't a loser, after all, then spill the beans that *she* was Coffee Girl and *they* were destined to be together.

He wheeled into a tight spot and came to a too-abrupt stop, jamming her up against his shoulder blades. "Sorry," she murmured, tingling with awareness.

He turned his head. "I'm not."

They were still for an agonizing few seconds. To her dis-may, she didn't want to let go, didn't want their intimate ride to end. In that split second, she wished she and Greg weren't embroiled in a sticky business fray—but things were what they were. Besides, the complications forced her to maintain a respectable distance from a man who was completely wrong for her. He'd seemed duly unimpressed with the causes she thought were important.

Lana eased back and dismounted, then quickly secured the cycle, her heart still pounding over his provocative statement. *I'm not.* Hadn't Alex warned her about letting her lust lead her astray?

While walking inside, she chided herself—she couldn't afford to become emotionally involved; she just needed him to ease up on the rezoning issue. Just a little flirting. *Maybe* a kiss or two.

He held open the door the way her father used to—so she'd have to pass under his arm. The gesture made her feel strangely protected, but she didn't have long to savor it. Her jaw dropped to see her friend Alex working behind the counter, her mussed hair and flushed face indicative of her frazzled state. "Alex, what are you doing here?"

Alex put a hand to her chest. "Thank goodness, you're back."

"Where's Annette?" Lana asked as she automatically grabbed an apron and slid behind the counter.

"Her ankle swelled up like a balloon. She called me, thinking I might know where you'd gone, and I told her I'd fill in." She blew her bangs straight up. "I hope I didn't scare away any customers."

"Don't be silly. Thanks, Alex. I should've told Annette where I'd be."

"And where were you?" her friend asked, her voice low and laced with innuendo as she glanced toward Greg, then back. "Working the man into a lather?"

"Shh. Here he comes." She smiled at him, struck anew by his dark good looks. "Greg Healey, meet my best friend, Alex Stillman."

"Nice to meet you," he said smoothly. "Weren't you at the council meeting last night?"

"Yes," Alex said, then smacked Lana on the back. "Wasn't

Lana great? She's very smart, you know. She's a member of Mensa—*ow!*"

Lana patted the skin where she'd just inflicted a pinch on her friend's arm. "Thanks, Alex. I'm sure Jack is wondering where you are."

The corners of Greg's mouth twitched. "You're the one who married Jack the Attack Stillman. I remember him from UK."

"He remembers you, too," Alex said in a saccharine-sweet tone. "Except he used other letters when he talked about you—*ow!*"

Lana pasted on a smile and jerked her head toward the door. "Say *good-night*, Alex."

Her friend smirked and removed her apron. "Good night. Call me when you get a chance?" Alex's voice was high and unnatural.

She shot her an exasperated look. "Yes. Don't worry about me."

"Oh, I won't," Alex said loudly as she walked from behind the counter. "Because I know you have a black belt and you can take care of yourself."

Lana could only stare at her lying friend until Alex had walked out the door.

Greg walked to the counter and lifted an eyebrow. "Mensa?"

"Don't listen to her," she said with a laugh. "Alex must have drunk too much caffeine while she was here."

One corner of his mouth went back, and he jerked his thumb toward the door. "Listen, you're busy. I'll just take a taxi back to my car."

Her heart quickened as Greg took a tentative step backward. She realized with awful clarity that she didn't want him to leave, and that while saving her business should have been uppermost in her mind, it wasn't. "Wait!"

He stopped.

She conjured up a shaky smile. "I close in less than an hour, if you want to stick around. Maybe we'll get a quiet moment to…talk."

He looked back at the door, hesitating. Lana's heart thumped in her chest. Maybe he didn't feel the same push-pull sensation when their bodies came within ten feet of each other. Maybe he thought she was a kook, and wanted to return to his own kind. Heck, maybe she *was* a kook.

"Okay," he said with a shrug. "I'll stay."

Her friend Alex probably would have declared the little jolt of happiness Lana experienced at his response, which was casual at best, a sign of desperate loneliness. Thank goodness, Alex wasn't around.

13

GREG TOOK IN THE BUSTLING SHOP—customers sitting and standing, laughing and talking over the music of two acoustic guitarists flanked by no fewer than four Christmas trees on the cramped little stage. Miles of lights twinkled from the rafters. Aromas of coffee and chocolate and sugar filled his lungs. The place had charm, all right. Then he looked back to Lana Martina, tousled and red-cheeked and electric.

She was the charm. People gravitated toward her. *He* gravitated toward her. The realization hit him hard, and he tried to rationalize his irrational feelings. He wasn't completely immune to the sappiness of the holidays. And her wild sense of adventure was simply a passing intrigue. Still, this... *attraction* would make his task of winning her over to his side a bit easier, and much more pleasurable.

So why did he have the feeling that when he'd said "I'll stay," he was committing to something much larger?

Her smile erased his concern. "Good. What can I get you to drink?"

"Decaf, black."

"What kind?"

"What kind what?"

"What kind of decaf?" She pointed to the menu behind her that listed as least thirty different types of bean blends, several of them decaf.

He shrugged. "Pick one."

She plunked a fuzzy Santa hat on her head, the same one she'd been wearing when he first met her. "How about our special holiday blend?"

"As long as it's hot."

The drink appeared in front of him within thirty seconds, then she returned to her customers. He sipped his coffee, which was surprisingly good, and took advantage of the time to study her. She moved efficiently behind the bar, taking orders and dispensing beverages while bantering with patrons. Her profile was exquisite, both above and below the neck. She was finely boned, richly curved and eminently appealing. Gripped by a strong urge to have her, he was reminded that the woman already had a man in her life. There was the Kissing Man, and possibly others. He didn't relish being one in a long line of her classified-ad lovers.

Yet he knew if the opportunity presented itself, he'd dive headfirst into her bed.

In an attempt to distract himself from his unexplainable fixation with the woman, he left the bar to read the items posted on the enormous bulletin board along the wall leading to the rest rooms. Flyers were posted for typing services, cars for sale, and dog-sitting. Plus a half-dozen petitions were posted for saving the rain forest, preventing animal abuse and other causes.

Greg shook his head because the people who had signed the petitions were fooling themselves if they thought a mere signature would change the shape of things. If they really wanted to make a difference, they'd do something concrete. In his experience, only money—the incentive to make it, or not to lose it—had the power to influence change. Couldn't Lana see that the best chance for solving the world's problems lay in commerce, not in caring?

No, which demonstrated how fundamentally oppositely he and she were wired.

"Lana!"

At the sound of her name over the microphone, Greg turned to see the two young male singers beckoning her toward the stage.

"Come and lead us in a song."

Despite the chorus of encouragement, she shook her head and held up her hands to decline. "I can't sing!"

But the cheers grew louder, and Greg joined in. She glanced at him, her cheeks bright red, and he realized with a start that she cared what he thought. He jerked his head toward the stage and mouthed, *Chicken.*

The correct word choice, judging by the sudden lift of her chin. She marched up to the stage, conferred with the musicians, then led the room in a rousing rendition of "I Wanna Hippopotamus for Christmas." Her voice was horrifically off-key, but loud and enthusiastic as she conducted a crowd that was on a cumulative caffeine buzz. Greg found himself smiling into his hand. Despite his dare, he marveled at her nerve. No amount of money, much less plain goading, would have gotten him on that stage. But she was a sport, bouncing around like a child, acting out the song like a vaudeville entertainer.

The applause was thunderous, and he joined in good-naturedly. She glanced his way and delivered a little salute, then reminded everyone that one of the trees on the stage was decorated with tags bearing the name of a needy boy or girl and his or her Christmas wish list. "Help make this year special for one child who might not otherwise have any gifts at all."

Greg drained his coffee cup. Good grief, she'd turned the place into her own little do-good center. Still, guilt stirred in his stomach at the sight of the tree she indicated, covered with name tags, each representing a child. Others must have felt the same guilt, because as she left the stage, the tree was surrounded by customers. The guitarists extended the spirited mood with more holiday songs.

And for a moment, Greg *almost* bought into the whole Christmas spirit thing. But a more sensible part of him stubbornly resisted. What good did it do to be kind to your fellow man a couple of weeks out of the year? To participate in hand-out programs that made the giver feel good, and the recipient feel pitied? Lana Martina was a comely ambassador, perky and persuasive. But one woman wouldn't change his entire mode of thinking. Even if she was compelling. And braless.

Still, he conceded a proprietary thrill when she left the stage and made her way toward him, as if they were together. The woman was certainly more interesting than most of the women he'd dated. But interesting translated to one thing: complicated.

"You're multitalented," he observed, when she stopped in front of him.

"If I didn't know better, I'd think that was a compliment."

He lifted his coffee cup. "But you know better."

"Yes, I do. Need a refill?"

"Sure." He followed her to the bar, confounded by his urge to be near her. She yanked on a red cord, which rang a bell he was sure could be heard all the way to Louisville.

"Last call!" she bellowed.

Greg blinked. Last call in a coffee shop?

One by one, the customers unfolded themselves from their comfortable seats, most of them sauntering to the counter for half-cup refills, although a few collected their coats from the long row of hooks along one wall. Those leaving called good-night to Lana, and she knew each person by name. A half hour later, the two musicians, who were the last to leave, waved and carried their acoustic guitars out the front door. Lana locked the door behind them, and pulled down the blinds. She flipped knobs on an old metal switch plate to extinguish the lights over the door and windows, then turned an ancient sign from *Come on in* to *Sorry, we're closed.* At long last, they were alone. His vital signs increased, and longing pooled in his belly.

She began to clear the tables. "This shouldn't take long, then we can talk."

Greg remained glued to the padded stool, turning to watch her as unobtrusively as possible. She bussed the tables with remarkable energy, humming as she dumped trash into a compartmentalized bin she wheeled around. The woman had a fabulous figure.

"Was the crowd typical for a Saturday night?" he asked. It was more difficult to ogle while talking.

"Most evenings are decent when classes are in session. Otherwise, night business is dead. I'd love to see something open downtown to draw people out of the suburbs after five o'clock."

"Like what?"

She stopped and shrugged. "Like a planetarium."

He pursed his mouth. "Not a bad idea."

"I have others."

Be nice to her. "So let's hear them."

She dragged a canvas bag from beneath the counter and extracted the notebook he recognized from the restaurant. "Okay, but first a question. Why not just zone some of the buildings in question commercial and some residential?"

A legitimate question—from a layperson. "Property values will be more stable if the areas are blocked off separately rather than intermixed. Who wants to live next to a bar, for instance?"

She sighed. "And who wants to operate a business where customers have to fight for parking spaces?"

"Exactly."

"But it's pretty common in downtown areas to see storefronts on the first floor of a building, and condos or apartments above." She pointed to her ceiling. "There's an enormous attic in this building large enough for two apartments."

He smiled patiently. "*After* retrofitted plumbing and wiring. And adding handicapped access. And don't forget about the parking problems around here. To support all-day, permanent parking needed for employees and customers and residents, you're looking at a parking garage."

She smirked. "So why does the parking garage have to go *here*?"

"Because the architects and engineers said so." At her frustrated sigh, he plunged on. "Listen, Lana, contrary to popular belief, this rezoning plan is not some kind of whimsical conspiracy to evict the shop owners of Hyde Parkland. My company has been working on this project for months, even years on some aspects. This is a huge undertaking that will, whether you want to believe it or not, give a much-needed boost to the downtown economy." He splayed his hands and lowered his voice to reflect his sympathy. "Unfortunately, there are always casualties of progress."

She shook her head stubbornly. "But this business has been here for thirty years! Doesn't that count for something?"

He pressed his lips together, then chose his words carefully. "Yes. It means something to you and to your customers. But if you'll be honest with yourself, you'll realize this area needs a parking garage more than it needs a coffee shop."

She averted her eyes and bit into her lower lip. She didn't seem like the crying type, but a man never knew. He watched her nervously, poised to whip out a clean hanky if she erupted. She didn't. He realized as he had before that the only other person in the world who evoked these protective feelings in him was Will. Not a good realization, considering that protecting Lana Martina's interests ran counter to protecting his own interests. And Will's.

Still, he felt compelled to say something healing. "Um, about that planetarium—maybe I'll look for a suitable piece of land and try to interest a developer."

She lifted her gaze. Sure enough, her violet eyes were falsely bright. "A lot of good a planetarium will do me when my coffee shop is a parking garage."

"Why don't you simply move your shop?"

"There isn't a location in town that would bring me the same amount of traffic."

Had he imagined that her voice broke on the last word? "How about your friend Alex's property, beneath Tremont's department store?"

"It's not *Alex's* property, and I can't afford the space."

"Surely she has enough pull to cut you slack on the rent."

From the set of her mouth, he'd hit a nerve.

"Alex offered. But I have this little hang-up about doing things on my own."

They were nearly eye to eye, and he was mesmerized by her beauty—her flawless skin, her unusual eyes, her plump mouth. Her work perfume of coffee beans and sugar and cinnamon tickled his nose. The woman had spunk, and sex appeal in spades.

"Funny," he said, reaching out to clasp her wrist, "so do I." He tested her resistance, pulling gently. She blinked, then came into his arms.

"What about the other shop owners?" she asked quietly. "Can you help them?"

"For you," he murmured, "I will certainly try."

Greg drew her into the cradle between his knees for a slow, thorough kiss, while alarms sounded in his head. What had he promised? What was this woman doing to him? She seemed tentative at first, but he beckoned her tongue with his and drew her into his intensity. Overwhelmed with the urge to devour her, his sex hardened to the point of pleasure-pain. He pressed his legs together, capturing her, drawing her heat closer to his. He wrapped his arms around her narrow waist, splaying his hands across her back. A whisper of fabric lay between his fingers and her warm skin. Her unbound breasts bore into his chest, and he groaned against the tide of desire that flooded his limbs.

He wanted her. Badly.

14

LANA WAS GLAD for his strength—her own had vanished. She was emotionally wrung, and Greg's arms gave her a place to escape the pressures weighing on her head. Just one kiss, she promised herself. They were finally talking, and he seemed somewhat sympathetic to the shop owners. He would help them, he would help her.

But thoughts of rezoning plans and parking garages and loan payments dissolved as the kiss matured into uncontrollable desire. She matched his parlaying tongue, stroke for stroke. When he slipped his hands beneath her blouse and skimmed the indention of her spine, she shuddered and moaned into his mouth. His lips slid to her neck, licking and kissing her throat. She leaned her head back and drove her fingers into his dark hair. He slid his hands forward and thumbed the undersides of her breasts, sending moisture to the juncture of her thighs. She cried out, and the shock of hearing her own voice echo off the brick walls restored a small measure of sanity.

"Greg," she said, her voice thick.

He mumbled an incoherent response against her collarbone.

"Greg, someone might see us."

He lifted his head, but maintained his hold on her. "Then let's go somewhere. To your place."

She opened her mouth to say yes, then remembered that Rich Enderling was still moving his things in and shook her head. "No. It's…complicated."

"Lana, I want you." And he upped the ante by brushing his thumbs over the stiff peaks of her breasts.

Her shoulders rolled involuntarily as pleasure coursed through her chest and arms. She was powerless to speak. In one movement, he lifted her and spun on the stool, setting her on the cool wooden bar. His eyes were level with her tingling breasts, his arms encircling her and his hands cupping her bottom as if he were afraid she would try to pull away.

She didn't. The blinds were pulled and the lights were low. Anyone nosy enough to peek inside deserved the eyeful they got. His eyes were glazed with passion—passion for her. The knowledge that she was able to move this staid man filled her with an incredible surge of feminine power. Was there anything more sexy than pure enthusiasm?

"I want you, too," she whispered, and pulled his face to her breasts. He nipped at the aching tips, suckling through the gauzy cloth, wetting the pink fabric. She strained into him, luxuriating in the feel of his warm tongue against her sensitive zones. Kneading his shoulders through his starched shirt, she hungered to feel his bare skin.

Lana tugged at his loosened tie, then rapidly undid as many buttons as she could reach. Springy black hair met her fingers above a white ribbed undershirt that clung to smooth chest muscles. She fumbled with the buttons on his cuffs and helped him shrug out of the shirt, while he feasted on her breasts. When his dress shirt, undershirt and tie hit the floor, he stood and lifted her blouse over her head.

Perched on the edge of the bar and bare to the waist, she allowed him to look at her, and she looked back, wetting her lips at the sight of superbly defined shoulders, biceps, pectorals. When she'd had her fill, she lifted her gaze to his hooded one, and trembled at the promise she saw there. Intensity. Endurance. Satisfaction.

"You are exquisite," he murmured, his eyes shining.

Lana wrapped her legs around his waist and looped her arms around his neck before lowering her mouth to his. Something pulled at the back of her mind, a vague uneasiness that she shouldn't be doing what she was doing—but at the moment she couldn't fathom why. His body had been speaking to hers all evening.

With a groan, he pulled her off the bar and carried her across the darkened room. Her Santa hat fell off somewhere along the way. She wasn't certain of his destination until his lips left hers and she felt velour upholstery at her back. She smiled up at him and sank into the soft worn cushions of one of the vintage couches, anticipating the weight of him, the breadth of him, the length of him. Everything was perfect at the moment. Tomorrow would take care of itself.

A loud chiming sounded, startling her because she had to pull herself so far out of her real-life fantasy to decipher its source.

Greg's brow lowered. "What is it?"

She sat up and crossed her arms over her breasts. "The bell on the back door. I'm supposed to meet someone." She suddenly remembered.

"They'll leave," Greg said, reaching for her.

"No. He'll come around the front and see my moped. And he's liable to call the police if I don't answer the door."

"He?" Greg asked, his voice suspicious. "A boyfriend?"

Shame enveloped her as she stared at him. *A* boyfriend, as in one of many? Is that what he thought of her—that she had many men? Lana stood and brushed by him to scoop up her blouse. And why wouldn't he think the worst? Hadn't she allowed him to believe she'd placed that singles ad? Hadn't she planned to lead him on, to cajole him into seeing her side of the rezoning matter? Of course, she'd never meant for things to go so far. A kiss, maybe two…

Lana jerked the blouse over her head to the tune of more insistent chiming from the back door. "He's a friend," she said through clenched teeth. "An artist who comes by every week to pick up colored glass I save."

He scoffed. "You've got to be kidding."

At the condescending look on his face, she swallowed the lump of disappointment that formed in her throat. She bent to retrieve his clothes so he wouldn't notice that what had almost happened had almost meant something to her, or that his opinion of her mattered. "Get dressed," she said.

GREG PULLED HIS UNDERSHIRT over his head and watched her walk away, feeling more empty and powerless than in recent memory. The interruption had frustrated him beyond logic. And reminded him that Lana dated lots of men. Plus, the woman had so damn many projects. He dragged his hand down over his face and exhaled noisily. Cripes, the woman was so…complicated.

Muttering to himself, he yanked on his dress shirt, then hastily buttoned the front and rolled up the cuffs. He looked for his jacket, then remembered she'd absconded with it to have it repaired, and sighed noisily. He hadn't planned for things to go so far, but he'd given in to the incredible attraction to her that ratcheted higher every time they were together. Now he was in worse shape than before. Greg unzipped his pants, adjusted his still rigid erection and tucked in his shirt. God, he'd never wanted a woman so much. The image of her sitting on the counter, bare-breasted, would forever be burned in his brain. They were both grown, consenting adults—what was the harm?

He sighed, massaging his neck. The rezoning plan was the harm. The rezoning plan that was supposed to breeze through the council and save downtown Lexington and set him free, all in one fell swoop. And now one little woman stood in his way. Lana Martina tripped his conscience not because she was right, but because she *thought* she was right. God save him from a hot-blooded do-gooder.

The murmur of voices floated to him from the back; then he heard a terrific clattering of glass as several boxes must have changed hands. He shook his head, then his gaze drifted to the Christmas tree with tags bearing the names of the children Lana had talked about earlier. Idly, he turned over one of the tags.

Joey, age 5, would like tennis shoes, size eleven.

Greg frowned. Shoes? Kids were supposed to get trucks and dolls and bikes for Christmas, not shoes. He turned over another tag. *Warm coat.* And another. *Books.*

He swore softly under his breath, stole a glance toward the back door, then yanked off the remaining tags and stuffed them into his pants pockets. Straightening self-consciously, he strode to the phone to call a taxi—a return trip on the moped would probably be somewhat less enjoyable than the one here. Besides, he didn't want Lana to ride back from the restaurant alone since it was getting late. He was just returning the receiver when he heard her call goodbye and the back door close.

She barely glanced at him when she returned, walking straight to a pan of dirty ceramic mugs sitting on one of the tables. "Give me a couple of minutes to clean up, then I'll take you back to your car."

"I called a taxi."

"Suit yourself." Her movements were rapid and jerky. "Tomorrow I'll call Ms. Wheeler and let her know that you and I can't work together on this plan, after all. Didn't you say you had a manager who would be more—"

"Lana." He walked up behind her, catching a whiff of her womanly scent, itching to touch her again. He knew instantly that despite the danger of becoming involved with her, he didn't want to turn the project over to someone else. "What just happened...it won't happen again."

She stopped working, but she didn't turn around. "Greg, 'what just happened' aside, you don't really care about me or any of the other business owners down here. You've lost touch with the community you're supposed to be helping. This situation is going nowhere."

He hated the droop of her shoulders, and the muted tone of her voice. He longed for the good-natured banter they'd shared earlier in the evening. "What would it take to convince you that I do care about...the business owners?"

Lana turned to face him and crossed her arms. "I don't know. Spend some time with them, talk to them. Maybe you'll come to realize how important they are to the downtown economy." Then she dismissed him with a wave of her hand. "Forget it, you won't get that close to real people."

"*Real* people? What's that supposed to mean?"

Her laugh mocked him. "You figure it out."

Greg straightened, irritated by her words. "I'm not afraid of getting close to...any kind of people."

She bent down to scoop up the Santa hat that had fallen off

when he carried her to the couch, then she tossed it into the pan of dirty dishes. "Prove it."

He stared at the hat. Had she so casually dismissed what had almost happened? "How?"

"Tomorrow afternoon. Come down, tie on an apron, and walk a day in my shoes. Then we'll go around and meet the other shop owners."

An emphatic "no" hovered in the back of his throat, but he swallowed it when he looked into her violet eyes. After all, subsequent to that embarrassing display of physical weakness, he needed to initiate damage control. He still needed to win her over—if she told councilwoman Wheeler *why* they couldn't work together, who knew what kind of obstacles Wheeler could put in his way?

"I'll be here," he said.

15

"DID YOU SLEEP WELL?" Lana asked Rich, when he emerged from his bedroom looking scrubbed and spiffy in slacks and a turtleneck. She lay on her back beneath the Christmas tree, adjusting the tree stand to compensate for the substantial lean that had developed overnight. She knew exactly how the tree felt. Her world had certainly been knocked off-kilter these past few days.

"As a matter of fact, I did sleep well," her new roommate said, crouching near her. "Need some help?"

"Nope. I've got it." She gave the pliers one last turn, then wriggled out. "There."

Rich appraised the tree by tilting his head. "Is it supposed to be straight?"

"You mean it isn't?"

"My mistake—the tree's perfect." He stood. "And huge."

She smiled from her sitting position on the floor, gesturing to the mound of packages. "My mom is coming up from Florida Christmas Eve, and I want everything to be nice." Her bank account was precariously low, but she'd found so many things she knew her mother would like.

"How long is your mom staying?"

Lana bit her lip and studied the bent pliers. "I'm not sure. Mom is sort of…flexible. A couple of days, I'm guessing." Unless she was in a hurry to get back to Gary or Larry or whatever his name was…this week.

"She's welcome to my room. I'll be in Houston visiting my sister and her family for a few days."

She stood and dusted her backside. "Thanks, but she'll probably stay in my room, and I'll take the pullout."

"Well, at least I won't be underfoot." He smiled sheepishly

and splayed his hands. "I don't normally sleep this late, but I guess I was exhausted from unpacking yesterday."

She gestured to the new furniture, stylishly situated amongst her own. "I'm sorry I didn't have a chance to help you."

"You're a lifesaver just to take me in on such short notice."

"That goes both ways."

"So—" he wagged his eyebrows "—how was your date last night? Or am I being too nosy?"

"You're not being too nosy," she said, her voice high and innocent. "But it wasn't a date. It was a business meeting." At the end of which, she and Greg had gotten half-naked on the bar. Business meetings at Ladd-Markham had been somewhat less…revealing. "Would you like some tea?"

He nodded and sat on one of the two red stools she'd dragged out of a Dumpster and repainted years ago. She poured them both a cup of tea with cream, then joined him at the counter.

"So, Lana, what's your story?"

She blew on the surface of her tea. "What do you mean?"

"You're a great-looking gal who owns her own business and, from what I can see, is pretty darn smart. Why hasn't some Kentucky stud tied you to his hitching post?"

She laughed. "Because this filly rather likes her freedom."

"You're not lonely?"

"No," she lied breezily.

"Says the woman who lives with a blow-up doll," he teased.

Lana glanced over at her plastic, grinning sidekick. "Harry's a gem, isn't he?"

"Where on earth did you find him?"

Her memories rewound, sliding past her. "I met Harry at a bachelorette party in college. The bride-to-be brought him and passed him off to a single friend, and the tradition continued. One day I got this box in the mail, and Harry was inside. Now he's mine."

"Until you're married?"

She grinned. "Well, that's the idea. But I think I've had him longer than anyone. Going on three years now."

"Is there anyone else left in the group who's single?"

Lana pursed her mouth and nodded. "A few, I think. There were these two sisters from Chicago. Seems like they're still single." She brightened. "But no matter—I plan to keep him around for quite a while. The shop requires so much attention, I don't have time for a man."

"Uh-oh."

"Uh-oh, what?"

"Uh-oh, that's when love always knocks you down—when it's least convenient."

She scoffed. "I'm firmly on my feet." Okay, Greg had had her on her back for a few seconds last night, but everyone was allowed one mistake. "So, Rich, what's *your* story?"

He shook his head. "It's not a bestseller."

"Try me."

After a gulp of tea, he shrugged. "Lots of failed relationships with women. I admitted about a year ago that I'm gay."

"And how's that going?" she asked mildly.

"Admitting I'm gay is one thing, but entering into a relationship is something else. I'm not ready."

But she recognized the longing in his voice. Loneliness had the same address regardless of a person's reasons for being there. She sighed. Was that why she'd clicked on a primal level with Greg Healey—was he also lonely?

Rich stood and walked to the window, then turned back with a broad smile. "But I have a good feeling about Lexington, Lana, like something significant is going to happen for me here."

She returned his smile. "Then it will." The man truly was handsome, she acknowledged. Handsome and…comfortable. She sighed. Why couldn't all relationships be like this? Sexual tension ruined everything by tying tongues, quickening tempers, sensitizing erogenous zones.

Lana sipped her tea. She wasn't looking forward to seeing Greg Healey again today. Really, she wasn't.

"What's his name?"

"Greg," she blurted, then realized her gaffe. "I mean, who?"

"The man you're not thinking about."

She frowned miserably. "Greg Healey."

"Nice name."

"*Not* a nice guy."

"So why bother?"

She could have said she'd been forced to work with him on the rezoning project, but councilwoman Wheeler had given her a choice. There was something about the man… She shook her head, at a loss. "I honestly don't know."

"Can I hazard a guess?"

Lana shrugged.

"You think that, deep down, everyone is good, and you like trying to tap into that goodness."

"What makes you think that?"

"From talking to you, from looking around your shop and seeing the causes you care about. It's refreshing," he added quickly. "But it also sets you up for disappointment when people turn out to be…themselves. What does this guy do for a living?"

Her frown deepened. "He's an attorney."

Rich gasped and covered his mouth. "How dare he?"

She laughed. "I don't have anything against attorneys in general. It's just that *this* attorney seems to only want to use his power and money to get more power and more money."

"Sounds personal. You're not the least bit attracted to this guy?"

In the short time she'd known him, she'd observed Rich Enderling display uncanny insight into the people around him. The man missed nothing. The creamed tea curdled in her throat as it went down. "I think what I feel for Greg Healey is the morbid fascination one has with a person who can destroy one's life as one knows it. And for the record, I do take my livelihood personally."

"Maybe he truly believes the rezoning plan will be good for the city."

"Whose side are you on?"

He grinned. "Yours—because if you lose your job, you might lose this great apartment, and then where would I be?"

"At the Y."

"So all I'm saying is that I think you're right—that there's good in everybody. For some people, though, it takes a special person or the right circumstances to bring that goodness to the surface." He shrugged. "Who knows? You might be the person who brings out the best in Greg Healey."

She winced. "I haven't told you how he and I really met."

"Now I'm intrigued."

She glanced at her watch. "It's a long story, and I have to open the shop. How about lunch on me?"

"I never pass up a free meal or a good story. But then I have to drop off the U-Haul trailer."

"Okay. Just one more thing."

"Yeah?"

"Um, Greg Healey is working in the shop today."

He lifted an eyebrow.

"*Only* because I challenged him to get to know the business owners better before he rezones us all out of a job. So if he drops by while you're there, ip zay your ip lay."

Rich walked over to Harry and put his arm around the doll's shoulder. "Harry, man, it's been nice knowing you. But don't worry, the food's great in Chicago."

GREG DROVE AROUND the coffee shop three times looking for a parking place. Regret for his hasty response to Lana's challenge last night had built in his stomach since the minute he awoke this morning from a fitful sleep. He chewed on the inside of his cheek—he'd simply go in, dispense a few cups of coffee, and get out. Quick and painless; one hour, tops. And no way was he going to wear an apron.

The worst part had been trying to explain to Will why he was going to "work for Lana" today. He'd been tempted to lie, but lying to Will was difficult any day of the week, and impossible on Sunday while hanging outside Christmas lights. Watching his brother's childlike reaction to the twinkling decorations when they'd finished had reminded him that it was a good thing he'd fielded Lana's ad for his brother, or else Will would have fallen head over heels for the woman.

Greg pulled into a cramped parking spot and squeezed out the door. Blaming his accelerated heartbeat on the extra cup of coffee he'd needed to get going this morning, Greg pushed open the door to the shop.

His gaze went first to Lana, who looked long and lush in a straight, blue velvet jumper that fell to her ankles, and a white turtleneck. Nearly every inch of her was covered, but the image of her naked to the waist overrode the present. With much effort, his gaze next went to the man seated on a stool in front of her. Kissing Man.

Greg set his jaw. What the devil was *he* doing here?

They both turned in his direction, and Lana didn't even have the good grace to look sheepish. Instead, she offered up a guileless smile. "Hello there. I figured you'd changed your mind."

"No. Although I can't stay more than an hour or so."

She glanced at the clock, one of those bird clocks that were annoying as hell. "It'll get busy soon. Come on around, and I'll show you how things work."

He walked behind the bar, supremely self-conscious. Kissing Man watched him carefully.

"Rich Enderling," the guy said, thrusting his hand over the bar.

"Greg Healey," he said, returning a firm handshake.

"Rich is a friend of mine," Lana interjected, but she was talking fast and her voice was artificially high. "He was just leaving, weren't you, Rich?"

Rich seemed amused when he looked back to her. "Yeah. I'll see you tonight?"

She seemed exasperated. "Yes. Goodbye."

"Thanks for lunch." He glanced back to Greg. "Nice to meet you."

Greg gave him a curt nod.

Lana's gaze followed the man until he left, her movements

suspended until the door closed behind him. Then her body relaxed, as if she'd just escaped some near miss. A chime sounded—the same noise that had interrupted them last night, seconds shy of making love. His body warmed, and from the color that bloomed in her cheeks, he assumed she was remembering, as well. "Excuse me," she said. "That'll be Andy from the soup kitchen."

"Soup kitchen?"

"I give them my day-old pastries."

Of course she did. "Let me give you a hand."

"No, the boxes are stacked by the door. I just need to let him in. If you get any customers, dazzle them for a few minutes with brilliant conversation."

The swing of her hips as she hurried away sent a spasm of lust surging to his midsection. Greg gripped the counter, cursing his curious weakness where she was concerned. Thankfully, the bell on the front door rang, announcing a customer. Feeling a little foolish, Greg prepared to stall the person, until he realized it was Rich Enderling returning.

"Lana's in the back," Greg said with a jerk of his head.

"Would you let her know that I'll cook dinner this evening when I get home?"

Greg blinked. "Home?"

The man nodded.

His stomach knotted. "You two *live* together?"

He nodded again. "I moved in last night. She's a real catch, isn't she? See you around, Craig."

The man gave him a triumphant little salute, then exited with a spring in his step. Greg scowled after him and muttered, "That's *Greg*."

16

LANA WAVED GOODBYE to Andy, then paused a moment to calm the beating of her heart. Good grief, after his humiliating near accusation last night that she had men all over the place, she had hoped to be appropriately irritated with him this morning, or at least indifferent. Instead she had a weird tingling, breathless sensation that she didn't want him to leave the room.

Holy hormones, what was wrong with her?

She inhaled and exhaled deeply, then reminded herself that this little "shadow" exercise today was to make Greg feel invested in the area. Too many people were counting on her for her to let herself be distracted by last night's misguided encounter. So she pasted on a professional smile and returned to the front of the shop, steeling herself against him.

Greg was standing with his back to her, leaning one hand on the bar, looking out the window as if he wanted to be anywhere but here. Dark slacks hugged slim, muscular hips she recognized as part of a runner's physique. A sparkling white collarless dress shirt spanned his broad shoulders—shoulders that bowed slightly as though under the pressure of something. Was it this rezoning project? Personal demons? She couldn't guess because the man was so unreachable. Last night she'd thought he'd relaxed a tiny bit on the ride over from the restaurant. She might even have ventured to say they had fun. But today…well, after last night…

Perfectly creased and starched—indeed, Greg looked as if he belonged anywhere but here. The differences in their lifestyles and their futures couldn't have been more apparent.

"I have an apron with your name on it," she said with forced cheer.

He turned, and she blinked at the dark look on his face. "I'll pass on the apron if it's all the same to you."

She shrugged, wondering why the man didn't have whiplash from his sudden mood swings. "Then I guess the Santa hat is out of the question."

He frowned more deeply.

She tried to laugh. "That sour face of yours will scare off my customers."

"I'm not much of a people person."

"Really? I wouldn't have guessed."

"Your roommate came back."

She couldn't hide her surprise or her alarm. Rich suspected she was developing feelings for Greg. Had he said something? "Wh-what did Rich want?"

"He said he'd fix dinner this evening."

"Is that all?"

He nodded, then gestured to the bar and laughed awkwardly. "Look, this was a bad idea."

"Then why did you agree to do it?"

His mouth tightened and his gaze pierced her. "I wasn't thinking straight last night."

She swallowed. "That makes two of us."

He ran his hand down over his face. "The sooner we hash through this rezoning plan, the sooner we can get back to our own lives."

"You mean the sooner we can forget we ever met?"

He shrugged, and his nonchalance squeezed her heart painfully. She hadn't realized how much she had hoped... That rich and powerful Greg Healey would fall so hopelessly in love with her that he would change his whole outlook on life? For a woman with an above-average IQ, she could be so dim.

"You're right," she managed to say. "Why don't I see if someone can cover for me today, so you and I can take a walk around the Parkland area and meet some of the other shop owners?"

"Whatever speeds things along," he said in an uninterested voice.

Fighting an ache of frustration, Lana called Wesley first, then Annette. Annette's ankle was better, and she agreed to come in as soon as possible. In the meantime, Lana showed Greg how to work the coffee dispensers. Supremely out of his element, he moved stiffly with a frown pulling at his face. Last night's encounter hung in the air around him, like a song she couldn't put out of her head, compromising her focus.

He seemed as cagey as she, reluctant to draw closer than an arm's length lest whatever had come over them last night strike again. But the space behind the bar was tight, and, truthfully, he was in the way more than he helped. She was constantly brushing past him, reaching behind him, or stepping around him, every movement bolstering her throbbing awareness of his body in close proximity to hers.

In her rush to wait on an impatient customer, Lana tripped over Greg's feet and fell into him. He steadied her, but not before hot coffee sloshed over the cup she was holding and down the front of his pristine white shirt. He gasped and held the fabric away from him, leaving her with the bad feeling he'd have a third-degree burn in the shape of his undershirt.

"I'm so sorry," she murmured, dabbing at the runaway stain halfheartedly. The shirt was ruined—and she doubted that he'd bought it on a clearance table.

"You burned your hand," he said, then pulled her to the sink and ran cold water over the pink tingling flesh.

"It's nothing," she protested, but admitted the water felt good on her scorched palm. Or was it his fingers on her hand, brown skin against white, that felt good? He stood just behind her, his head bent close to hers. Perhaps the hot coffee had stirred up his cologne, because the musky scent enveloped her, teasing her senses, dredging up a flood of forgotten sensations from last night. She was grateful he couldn't see that her face was as pink as her injured hand. Had the oxygen in the air suddenly decreased?

"Thanks, it's better," she said, then pulled her shaky hand from his and dried it on her apron.

He unbuttoned the top couple of buttons on his stained shirt to expose his throat and collarbone to the air, and her cheeks burned with the realization that she knew the planes of the rest of his torso in intimate detail.

"The first rule of working in a coffee shop," she said with a rueful laugh, "is not to wear white."

"I guess I should've taken the apron," he said, then one side of his mouth pulled back. "But at least now my shirt matches my torn jacket."

Lana winced. "I haven't had a chance to get your jacket repaired yet."

"Can I get some service here?" a man asked loudly from the other side of the bar.

She opened her mouth to apologize, but Greg spoke first. "Take it easy, man. Can't you see the lady burned her hand?"

"All I see is you making moon eyes at her," the customer said dryly. "Can I have my coffee, or what?"

Greg's face was a thundercloud, so Lana cut in and handled the man's order, her mind humming like a teenager's at the offhand comment. Had Greg been making moon eyes at her? Nah. More likely, his eyes had been dilated in pain from his scalding hot coffee bath. She busied herself filling orders, until, as was the way of retail, the customers were gone and a lull ensued. Lana glanced at her watch. Where the devil was Annette?

Greg wore a closed expression, and he, too, checked the time. He had better things to do, of course. But at least business had been good for the short time he'd been there. Maybe he would realize that she provided a service that people wanted. That he couldn't just go around uprooting people's lives, like he'd uprooted hers.

At a loss for conversation, she gestured to a nearby table with a game board. "Do you play chess?"

He shrugged. "It's been a while."

"Come on, I'll go easy on you."

But he snorted softly as he sat down. "I'm a pretty good player."

So he'd belonged to the science club *and* the chess club. "Well, I'm not so bad myself."

He cracked his knuckles in a sweeping motion. "Give it your best shot."

She looked into his dark eyes, and for a split second she wondered if he were talking about the game, or about trying to breach his stony exterior. He looked away and gravely set up the game pieces. The tiniest of smug smiles played on his lips, and Lana shook her head. *The bigger they are, the harder they fall.*

Six moves later she announced, "Checkmate."

"Huh?" Greg jammed his hand into his hair as he stared down at the chessboard. "That's impossible. We've barely moved any pieces."

Instead of scoffing at his disbelief, she swallowed hard at the sudden realization that his large, handsome features were becoming too familiar, and too appealing. She pushed back her chair—she needed some distance. "While you're second-guessing me, I'm going to sort the recyclables." She grabbed a couple of paper cups from a table as she walked by, then slipped behind the bar, trying to keep her gaze from straying to him. She needed to get a grip.

"How did you do that?" he asked, gesturing to the game board.

"Diversion," she said. "While you were pursuing my queen, you left your king at risk."

His head was still bent, and his index finger moved, re-creating plays in his head.

"Can you handle refills for about five minutes?" she asked.

He waved and frowned, which she interpreted as yes.

Fighting a smile, Lana wheeled the garbage down the hall to where the recycle bins were stacked behind a folding door. She separated paper, glass, plastic.

Undoubtedly, no one had ever beat Greg Healey at chess, and certainly not a complicated female-type. *Paper, glass, plastic.* Most likely, the women he met through the singles ads had more lively pursuits. *Paper, glass, plastic.* She closed the folding door with a sigh and headed back to the front.

Lana froze at the sight of her smiling pastry chef Annette coming through the front door. Good grief, she'd forgotten. The last thing she needed was for Annette to reveal that *she* was Coffee Girl and fall head over heels in love with Greg Healey. He'd trample the woman's heart for sure. And Lana should know.

Lana blinked with the revelation, then shouted "Annette!" before the girl's hand left the doorknob. Lana glided past Greg, who had moved behind the bar. "Thanks for coming in."

Annette cast a quizzical glance toward Greg, who was, amazingly, wiping up the counter. "Who's that?"

Lana lowered her voice conspiratorially. "Um, he's the owner of the building, the one who's trying to rezone the area and close me down."

Annette pursed her lips. "Close you down? Looks to me like he's cleaning up."

Lana rolled her eyes for effect. "He's only here to prove to the city council that he's concerned about the merchants."

"He's gorgeous. What's his name?"

She took in Annette's perky face and voluptuous figure, and suddenly realized that keeping Annette and Greg apart had little to do with her concern for Annette's fragile heart. Was it possible that she wanted to keep him all to herself? Preposterous, considering the man probably answered singles ads every week. Still…

Her heart skipped a beat in relief when she remembered that Annette didn't know the last name of the man who had answered her ad. "It's, um, Mr. Healey. Listen, Annette, while you're here, I wondered if you could do me a little favor." Lana led a craning Annette past the bar out of sight to a coat closet in the back. She withdrew Greg's torn jacket. "Is it possible to repair this tear so that it doesn't show?"

Annette studied the rip. "Nice fabric. Whose jacket?"

"Um, the guy out front."

She grinned. "What did you do? Tear his clothes off in a fight?"

"Can you fix it or not?"

Annette nodded. "To the point that it won't be noticeable."

Lana sighed with relief. At least she wouldn't have to replace an expensive suit on her already strained budget. "Great. Write me up a bill when you're finished."

"No charge. It's the least I can do for accidentally setting you up with that creepy Greg What's-his-name last week."

"Shh!"

"What?"

"I thought I heard something."

"I didn't hear anything."

Lana waved off the imaginary noise. "Thanks for watching the shop for me."

"With that hunky guy? No problem."

Lana frowned. "Actually, I was planning to take Hunky Guy around to meet some of the other shop owners that he wants to put out of business."

Annette's face fell. "Oh."

Lana untied her apron and handed it to Annette. "I'll be back soon."

"Take your time," Annette said, winking. "Maybe you can sweet-talk Mr. Healey into not going through with his plan." She laughed. "And if he doesn't cooperate, you can always spray his eyes full of hair spray like you did that other guy."

LANA DROVE HER HANDS deeper into her coat pockets and glanced sideways at Greg. "Now that you've met some of the shop owners, what do you think?" Her shop was in sight, up ahead and on the opposite side of the street. The weather had taken a sudden turn toward raw, spitting ice crystals and blowing up sudden blasts of Arctic wind. She could no longer feel her toes or her nose, but, curiously, she hated for the tour to end.

"Not the friendliest bunch," he said wryly.

"You're trying to shut down their businesses."

"How many times do I have to tell you that this isn't personal—it's business?"

She stopped and turned to face him. "It's personal to me."

He stopped, too, and a muscle ticked in his jaw. He'd

turned up the collar of his sleek black leather coat to ward off the biting wind. "You shouldn't allow personal entanglements to cloud your business judgment."

"I can't make decisions without considering the people who will be affected," she said softly. "I'm not wired that way."

He looked away, jammed his hands into this pockets, then looked back. "I'm not responsible for those people. If their livelihoods are tied up in their businesses, why haven't any of them offered to buy their buildings?"

"Because they can't afford them?" She knew *she* couldn't afford a mortgage on the building her shop was in.

"That's right," he said. "They can't afford to carry a mortgage and pay the property taxes and maintain the rotten plumbing. They want to have a say-so in how the property is developed, but none of them are rushing to assume the risk."

He was right, of course. At least in her case. "Last night you said you would help."

"Last night I was…distracted." Regret laced his words.

Her heart shivered with disappointment. "Meaning, you would have said anything to get in my pants?"

He shook his head and rubbed his jaw. "Don't put words in my mouth. I said I would *try* to help, and I will, but there's more at stake here than a few miscellaneous shops. Look, I have to go. I've wasted—" He stopped and scratched his temple to cover his gaffe, but she'd heard him loud and clear. He'd wasted enough time on her.

"I have to go," he said simply.

She struggled to keep the hurt from her voice, angry at herself because she had no right to feel hurt. Greg Healey meant nothing to her. She reached into her shoulder bag and withdrew a folder of photocopied notes—all her scribbled thoughts for regenerating the Hyde Parkland area. "For what it's worth, these are my ideas," she said, thrusting the folder into his hand. "I'll see you around."

Lana crossed the street and walked toward the shop. It was a good thing she knew the route by heart, or else she'd never have found the place through the blur of tears—caused by the stinging wind, of course.

17

"GREGORY?"

Greg snapped out of another Lana-induced reverie. "What?"

"Do you think that Eddie Age Seven would like the red bike helmet or the blue?"

"The blue."

Will grinned. "I think so, too." He added the box to a toy-laden buggy. "That's the last one on the list. This is fun."

"Thanks for coming to help me, pal." The past week had been a blur of disjointed events. He'd left things badly with Lana, and his regret had escalated each day. Her folder of notes had become his bedtime reading, which dovetailed perfectly into dreaming about the woman. Greg dragged his hand down his face. He was feeling a little stressed.

"How do we get the gifts to the boys and girls?"

"We'll take them back to the coffee shop, and Lana will make sure they go to the right person." Of course, his dilemma was how to get the gifts to Lana's coffee shop without running into her. He'd considered posting them, but with only five more mailing days until Christmas, he was afraid the packages would be waylaid.

"I'm sorry that you and Lana had an argument."

He frowned. "How did you know we had an argument?"

"I heard you telling Yvonne."

"Oh. Well, it wasn't an argument—it was a disagreement."

"But Yvonne said you were the disagreeable one."

"It's not nice to eavesdrop on other people's conversations."

"But I thought you were trying to be nice to Lana to win her over to your side."

He sighed. "It's complicated."

"I know you said that women are complicated, Gregory, but I still want one."

Oh, no, not that again. "You're not looking in the singles ads again, are you?"

"Nope. Coffee Girl was the only one I liked, but she turned out to be complicated, too, didn't she."

Greg's head was spinning, but he managed a nod.

"I guess I'll just have to wait until the right girl comes along." Will lifted a fire truck from the buggy and moved the ladder up and down. "Lana's a good person, isn't she, Gregory?"

"Do we have to talk about Lana?"

"Well, she is a nice person, isn't she?"

He swallowed hard. "I suppose." He could always have the gifts couriered over.

"So why are you shutting down her coffee shop?"

"Will, we've been over this a dozen times." But what the heck was he so afraid of? He would just drive over there and drop them off. Period.

"I know, Gregory, but I don't understand why everybody can't be happy."

He massaged the bridge of his nose. "It's impossible for everybody to be happy at the same time." He would simply park, and let Will take the packages inside.

"I want to buy Yvonne a suitcase for Christmas."

He sighed in relief at Will's sudden diversion. "I think that's a very good idea. Why don't you go to the luggage department, and I'll—"

"Mr. Healey?"

Greg turned to see Lana's friend Alex walking toward him. He wasn't sure how to respond. The woman hadn't exactly been friendly when he'd met her, although now she looked cordial enough. "Hello," he said. "I know Tremont's is your family's store, but I didn't expect you to be here all the time."

"Christmas shopping with a friend, same as you," she said, then glanced over his shoulder. "Here's my friend now."

Greg turned his head and stemmed a groan as councilwoman Wheeler walked up with a smug smile. "Mr. Healey, what a surprise."

"Ms. Wheeler." He looked back and forth between the women. "Somehow I'm not quite as surprised as you are." He introduced Will to both women.

"I saw you at the council meeting," Alex said to Will.

"You mean the meeting where Gregory was trying to shut down Lana's coffee shop?"

"*Will.*" Greg forced a laugh and clapped his brother on the back. "We've been over this."

The councilwoman offered up a little smile. "I've tried to reach you every day this week."

He'd played hooky every day this week, taking up residence in the back row of the city courthouse, even renewing old acquaintanceships with law buddies he ran into in the halls. His secretary was ready to quit. "I was going to return your call first thing in the morning." A lie.

She nodded. "And how are things going between you and Ms. Martina?"

"Fine," he said with as much enthusiasm as he could summon.

"They had a big argument," Will supplied.

"A little disagreement." Greg shot Will a warning look.

"Oh? Do I need to intervene?" the councilwoman asked, her tone a subtle threat.

"No," he assured her. "In fact, I'll be seeing Ms. Martina today." Two lies in two minutes.

"Gregory bought all these toys for Lana's children."

"For needy children that Lana sponsors," Greg clarified.

Both women arched an eyebrow, and he wondered if his face was as red as it felt.

"That's generous of you, Mr. Healey," the councilwoman said.

"*Very* generous," Alex seconded.

He shifted uncomfortably. No one had ever called him *generous.* "Well, it was nice seeing both of you."

"I look forward to that call in the morning, Mr. Healey, with an update on the progress you've made."

He managed a shaky smile. "Absolutely."

LANA SLIPPED THE BUSINESS CARD Greg had given her the night of the council meeting out of her apron pocket and studied it again, as if somewhere between the lines of formal raised script announcing, "Gregory K. Healey, President and Chief Legal Counsel, Healey Land Group," she would find some encrypted code to reinforce her suspicion that Greg Healey, Science Club guy, lurked just beneath the surface and was someone worth knowing.

The edges of the card were rounded from her constant fingering over the past week. She regretted walking away from him in anger last Sunday because no matter how the man affected her, the shop owners were counting on her to work out a compromise. She had to find a way to overcome their personal...difficulties, and break through his mind-set that newer was better.

She'd called him at work every day the past week, but hadn't identified herself or left a message when his secretary said he was out of the office. Out of the office for an entire week? Greg didn't strike her as the kind of man who vacationed frivolously, so perhaps he'd been traveling. Regardless, after a week of no contact, she was starting to panic because the days before the final council vote were slipping away.

Calling him at home was out of the question if they were going to maintain a professional relationship. She would phone him again in the morning and leave her name if he wasn't available. And if he hadn't returned her call by midweek, she would be forced to call councilwoman Wheeler and ask her to intervene—a thought that made Lana ill. If Greg told Wheeler why they couldn't work together, her credibility would be ruined.

And with good reason, she noted miserably. The merchants had trusted her when they'd asked her to be their spokesperson, and she might have compromised their position by succumbing to the physical attraction she felt for Greg. She groaned aloud and dropped her head into her hands. How had her life gone downhill so quickly? The respite of her mother's Christmas Eve visit loomed like an emotional gift. Janet was nothing if not entertaining.

The bell on the back door rang, and Lana dragged herself up to answer it, surprised to find Annette holding a covered tray emitting a wonderful aroma.

"I hope it's chocolate," Lana said.

Annette cringed. "Bad day?"

"Crummy."

"It's a new recipe—chocolate pound cake."

"I love you." She held the door open for Annette to squeeze by. "Not that I'm not glad to see you, but what are you doing here?"

"You seemed kind of blue this week, so I thought I'd drop off these goodies and try to cheer you up."

She smiled and followed Annette to the pastry case. "You're a dear. Have you had any more responses to your ad?"

"One extremely humiliating fraternity prank, one guy who just got out of Attica, and one guy who was about a hundred years old."

"Ouch."

"I know. So as appalling as Greg What's-his-face was to you, he's still the best thing that came out of that stupid ad."

Lana squirmed. "Well, the holidays are the worst time to start a new relationship. You'll probably get some takers after the first of the year."

"I hope so." They crouched behind the pastry case and used tongs to arrange the slices of dark moist cake that smelled like heaven.

"You'll meet Mr. Right soon," Lana said, although she was feeling a little down on love these days.

Not that she was in love with Greg. Or anything like that.

Annette laughed ruefully. "I hope so. But I have to admit I'm getting a little discouraged. Why can't the man of my dreams just walk through the door?"

The bell on the front door rang, sending them into a fit of giggles. But when Lana straightened to see Greg and Will, their arms laden with Christmas packages, she sobered with a hiccup.

"Hi, Lana," Will said with a grin. "Gregory and I bought presents for your kids."

She frowned. "My kids?" Then she remembered the needy-children Christmas tree, picked clean of name tags. "My kids!" Her gaze flew to Greg. "*You* took all the tags?" Slow wonder crept into her heart.

"It's no big deal," he said casually. "I wouldn't want to start a rumor that I'm a nice guy." But his faint blush belied his nonchalance.

Telling herself not to overreact, Lana pressed her lips together to suppress her happiness at seeing him again and to hide how much his gesture had touched her. "No, we wouldn't want to start a nasty rumor like that."

He shifted the load in his arms. "We put the gifts in bags so you can double-check everything."

She nodded, unable to tear her gaze from his. "You can put the gifts under the tree if you like."

He stared back, and once again she caught a glimpse of the man beneath the stoic facade before he looked away. "Come on, Will, we still have more packages to unload from the car—Will?"

Will's eyes were wide and riveted on some point behind her shoulder. Lana turned to see a similar expression on Annette's face as she peeked over the top of the pastry case. A slow smile crept up Lana's face. "Will, this is my pastry chef, Annette Bowman. Annette, this is William Healey."

"You can call me Will," he blurted.

"Hello, Will," she murmured.

Time stood still as the unmistakable instant attraction reverberated between them. Lana had the distinct feeling that she was witnessing the birth of something special, and for a split second, she was envious of Annette's good fortune. She sighed, then chanced a glance at Greg, who seemed less sure of what was happening.

"Will? Are you going to help me with the packages?"

"I'll help," Annette announced, then moved in slow motion from behind the counter to stand in front of Will.

"Do you have a boyfriend?" he asked.

Lana bit back a smile at his forthrightness.

Annette shook her head no, sending her red curls bouncing.

"Will you go to a Christmas party with me Friday night?"

She nodded yes, sending her curls bouncing in the other direction, then took the packages from Greg's arms and led Will toward the stage where the Christmas trees sat with packages scattered beneath.

Greg stared after them, then looked at Lana. "What just happened?"

"I think your brother just asked my friend out on a date."

He frowned suspiciously. "What sort of girl is she?"

Lana crossed her arms. "The sort of girl your brother likes, apparently."

"He doesn't know about these things."

"And you do?"

Greg's first impulse was to say that yes, he did. He knew that women were high-maintenance, emotional creatures who complicated the simplest of issues. He knew a woman would drive a wedge between him and his brother. He knew a woman said one thing when she meant something else entirely. But as always, Lana's eyes derailed his thoughts. "Huh?"

"And you do know about these things?"

He dragged his gaze and thoughts back to Will. "This isn't about me."

"They're only going to a party, for heaven's sake."

At least he would be able to keep an eye on them. And beforehand he would sit down with Will and make sure he understood how risky it was to have unprotected sex. His brother had good intentions about waiting until he was married, but in the heat of the moment, sometimes good intentions went out the window. Greg frowned. No one knew that better than he.

This Annette person was cute, no doubt. Oh, not *his* type at all—he definitely preferred tall women, and a more slender build. And the eyes…well, the eyes were important.

"Greg?"

Jarred from his thoughts by the voice he could not evict from his brain, he looked at Lana. "What?"

Her little frown told him she'd been trying to get his attention.

"I was saying that I feel bad about the way we left things last week. I was unprofessional, and I apologize—"

God, she had the most incredible eyes. And a slender figure. And she was tall.

"—And I was hoping," she continued, "that we could pick up where we left off."

And now he was confused about which came first—the definition of what kind of woman was his type or Lana Martina?

"Where we left off on the rezoning project," she added quickly.

He'd be able to keep an eye on Will most of the time Friday night, but if he had a date, they could double. Then he could check out this girl who had captured his brother's fancy. "Are you busy Friday night?" he asked Lana.

"I can get away."

"Then come to a party with me."

"A party?"

"Company function," he explained. "You can meet some of the folks who've been involved in the rezoning project from the beginning."

"It's business?" she asked, her voice wary.

"Strictly," he assured her.

"Okay. What time and where?"

"We'll pick you up."

"We?"

He gestured across the room. "Will and Annette and I. We'll all go together."

18

LANA'S LINGERING QUESTIONS about why she had agreed to go to the party with Greg were banished when she opened the door to her apartment. Frustrating or not, she missed his company. His eyes widened at the sight of her in the long black sheath with spaghetti straps that dated back to Ladd-Markham cocktail parties.

"Wow," he murmured.

Ridiculously pleased, she said, "Wow yourself," surveying his immaculate charcoal-gray suit, blinding white shirt and deep red tie. The colors suited him immensely. "Come in while I get my wrap."

He strolled in warily, and she suspected he was remembering the last time he'd visited her apartment. The man's eyes were probably watering.

"Is your roomie home?" he asked.

"No," she called over her shoulder. "Rich is working late." In her bedroom, she checked her carefully applied makeup one more time, then adjusted the rhinestone barrettes scattered through the layers of her hair. Satisfied that she looked festive, she retrieved her shoulder wrap from the foot of the bed, breathed deeply to slow her pulse, then returned to the living room.

"I see you still have Harry," he said with a wry smile.

"Oh, I'll always have Harry." As fond as she was of Harry, the past few days she'd begun to see him as a symbol of always being alone. She liked her own company, but she also held out hope that someday she'd meet someone to share her life with.

Such as it was. If her life could so easily be set on end, maybe she wasn't living the existence of substance she had haughtily assumed. Pressing her lips together in thought, she draped the wrap over one shoulder, then twisted to reach behind her.

"Allow me," Greg murmured near her ear, then he lifted the other end of the wrap and placed it around her shoulders.

Her breath caught in her chest as his hand lingered longer than necessary upon the sensitive hollow of her collarbone. Their date was strictly business, he'd said—and she needed to keep her wits about her. But her body had its own agenda, established when his warm breath tickled the nape of her neck. She closed her eyes against the onslaught of desire, holding herself rigid to suppress the urge to lean back into his body.

"Please, Greg."

His breath grew warmer and more rapid upon her neck, although he fell short of lowering his lips to her skin.

"Please, what?" he whispered, his voice heavy with the promise of fulfillment.

Her breasts tightened, the peaks hardening at the memory of his silky mouth, but she turned her head away from him. "Please...let's go."

"Right," he said, clearing his voice. "Sorry."

She turned to face him, drawing the wrap over her tingling breasts. "Greg, I'd be a fool not to notice this...attraction between us, but things are already complicated enough."

"Complicated," he said, shoving his hands into his pockets. "That they are."

"If only..." Lana bit her tongue. If only they'd met at a bar somewhere instead of through a missed connection in the classified ads. If only he didn't own the building where her shop was located... "Never mind, let's go." Quashing the memory of his touch, she retrieved her evening purse and door key.

He held open the door for her, but his strained expression indicated he was still struggling with the effects of their brush with intimacy.

"I would say that Will and Annette are wondering what's keeping us, but they don't seem to realize that anything else is going on in the world."

She locked the door and smiled. "That's sweet. Annette told me they've talked on the phone every night this week. She adores him."

"Maybe for now," Greg said. "But how long will that last?"

Lana glanced up sharply as they descended the stairs. "You're not giving your brother much credit."

"I didn't mean it that way," he said. "I just know…"

"You just know what?"

"I just know how women are."

She lifted an eyebrow. "Oh? And how are we?"

One side of his mouth drew back. "I don't want Will to get hurt."

"You don't know Annette—she's a good person. She would never lead Will on."

"Will wouldn't need much encouragement. He's still, um, innocent in some areas."

She laughed softly as they approached the big Mercedes. "You have nothing to worry about where Annette is concerned. She's the original little Miss Innocent."

Greg frowned toward the car. "If she's the original little Miss Innocent, then why are the windows fogged up?"

She followed his gaze, then winced and picked up her pace to match his. "It's cold, they're probably running the heater."

"That's one way to put it," he said dryly. He strode to the car and rapped on the front passenger window before opening the door for her.

The inside light came on, illuminating the couple in the back seat tangled in an embrace. They pulled apart and turned wide eyes toward the intruders. Lana swallowed a smile at the sight of Annette's red lipstick transferred to Will's face.

"Hi, Gregory. Hi, Lana."

Lana looked at Greg and discreetly covered her mouth to keep from bursting out laughing. He, on the other hand, did not look amused. "Hello, Will." Lana allowed Greg to help her into the seat, then flinched when he banged the door shut. Through the condensation on the window, she watched him stalk around the front of the car. Lana chuckled to herself. The man would be a force to reckon with if he ever had a daughter.

The unbidden thought sent an odd sensation to her stomach. What on earth made her picture him in a domestic situation? Of all the men she'd met, Greg Healey was probably the man least likely to make a trip down the aisle. He wore his bachelorhood like a sign on his sleeve: Do Not Enter.

He opened the driver's door and swung inside. A sigh passed over his lips, then he removed a snowy handkerchief and handed it over his shoulder. "Wipe your face, man," he said quietly.

"Okay, Gregory."

The gentle exchange brought unexpected tears to her eyes, and for the first time she had a glimpse into why Greg seemed old for his years. Did his responsibility for Will fuel his ambition and explain why he was such a seriously confirmed bachelor? In that moment his stoic personality seemed endearing, and his pursuits, noble. While he facilitated large real estate transactions every day, she was selling half-caf-nonfat-whip-extra-mochas. In the scheme of things, her contribution to society seemed pretty darn trivial, a concept she'd given a lot of thought to this week. Greg's secretary had called her several times to clarify Lana's notes as she was typing them up, so at least he hadn't discarded the ideas she'd given him.

But as they drove through the Hyde Parkland area, Lana saw every empty building, every overgrown lot, every graffitied bus stop, as if she were seeing it all for the first time. What had a week ago seemed like vintage charm, now smacked of urban neglect. Maybe Greg was right. Maybe the area needed renovation and a parking garage more than it needed a coffee shop.

She studied Greg's profile with grudging respect. She'd been little more than a thorn in his side since they met, yet he had taken the step to repair the lines of communication last Sunday when he and Will had come into the shop. A curious little quiver of revelation bloomed in her breast, stealing her breath. She was overwhelmed with the urge to touch him, to spend time with him, even if they were arguing. As crazy as her life had been the past couple of weeks, she'd never felt more alive. Was it possible to be in love with someone she barely knew?

Kissing noises sounded from the back seat. Maybe *so*, she conceded wryly. With Will and Annette, it had been love at first sight—ironic since it was Greg who had answered Annette's ad. Considering the way things had turned out, though, she was planning to keep that tidbit to herself.

Lana shook her head. Falling in love with Greg Healey— how dumb could she be? Not only was he one of the most unavailable men in the city, but their goals were so different. Even if the man were looking for a significant other—which he wasn't—a relationship between them would never work. Had she inherited her mother's knack for gravitating to men who were wrong for her? Lana chanced a glance sideways, wondering how hard Greg Healey would laugh if he could read her mind right now.

GREG WOULD HAVE GIVEN anything to be able to read Lana's mind. She'd been uncharacteristically quiet during their ride, forcing Greg to turn up the stereo to drown out the enthusiastic kissing in the back seat. And while his concern for Will remained uppermost in his mind, another concern had been gaining momentum over the past few days: his overwhelming attraction to Lana Martina. He didn't know what to make of this woman who had walked away from a lucrative field to become a struggling entrepreneur. Who sold coffee but drank tea, and played chess like a genius. Who volunteered time, space and resources to causes he merely read about in the Sunday paper. He glanced at her profile with new respect. Despite her quirks, Lana seemed to be a person of principle.

Greg pulled at his too-tight collar. Between their near miss at her apartment, and Will making out in the back seat like a teenager, Greg was no longer in the mood to go to the Christmas party.

Two weeks ago Art had called with what had seemed like the best news of his life. How had things deteriorated so rapidly?

When they walked into the small ballroom of the hotel, every person in the room craned for a look at Lana. Unreasonable pride swelled in Greg's chest. She *was* magnificent in that long, clingy black dress, and tonight she was on his arm. He'd always felt out of place at the company get-togethers because he'd always felt out of place at the helm of his father's company. But while he retrieved a glass of wine for each of them, he watched as Lana made the rounds, shaking hands and charming his employees, and was struck by the difference one person could make in a roomful of people…or in an organization.

Art Payton walked up to him, holding a hefty drink. "Who's the filly?"

Greg frowned. "Her name is Lana Martina. She owns a coffee shop in the building we have designated as a parking garage in the Hyde Parkland parcel."

Art nodded. "Best Cuppa Joe."

"You know the place?"

"Used to hang out there when I was single, about a hundred years ago."

He sighed. "Art, I've been thinking that maybe we should try to save some of the buildings down there, after all—you know, in the spirit of preservation."

Art's eyes narrowed. "You're not serious."

"Just thinking about it. Can you run some numbers for me?"

"I don't have to. If you start changing that parcel now, you're liable to spook all the developers, which means a big goose egg." Art elbowed him in the ribs and nodded to Lana. "And the spirit that's moving you, son, has nothing to do with preservation."

Greg frowned. "Just run the numbers."

He carried their wineglasses across the room and stopped where Lana was chatting with a knot of employees that included Peg. "They were out of cranberry juice. Is chardonnay okay?"

She gave him a heart-stalling smile. "Sure. Thank you."

He was vaguely aware that his employees were staring at him—especially his secretary. "Is something wrong, Peg?"

"Um, no, sir. The time off you took last week agrees with you, sir. You look...different."

Her words registered, but Greg couldn't take his eyes off Lana. She was a good conversationalist, and a natural people person. She was telling a humorous story that had everyone riveted, him included. When she finished, she launched into another topic of conversation. She held court for nearly an hour. Greg watched her unobtrusively while he walked the perimeter of the ballroom, shaking hands. His mood was buoyant tonight and he felt pretty certain it was because of Lana.

"I thought you weren't bringing a date, sir," Peg whispered at one point in the evening.

"She isn't a date," he murmured back. "We're working together on a project—you know that."

"Ms. Martina is beautiful, sir."

He looked at the owlish woman, noticing for the first time that she was wearing makeup. And did she always wear her hair like that? "Peg, why do you punctuate almost every sentence with 'sir'?"

She blinked. "Because, sir—I mean, because, um...it just seems right."

"But you called my father by his first name."

She fidgeted with her purse. "But your father, sir—I mean, your father, well, he was...friendly."

"Friendly?"

"You know, a nice man. Sir."

Her words knifed through him. "Nice?"

"Yes, sir. Nice."

Greg glanced around the room at the faces of the people who worked for him. He knew very few of them by their first names, and he knew nothing about their families, their hobbies, their concerns. They stood more than an arm's length

from him when they spoke, and looked downright uncomfortable when he approached. The truth of Peg's comparison
hit him hard. He wasn't a nice guy. Not like his father, not
like Will.

Will.

His immediate concerns were put on hold when he realized he hadn't seen Will and his date for some time. "Peg,
have you seen Will?"

"He left, sir."

Greg swallowed hard. "What?"

"I heard him tell Ms. Martina that he was taking a taxi
home, sir."

To have sex, he thought instantly. Right now, Will and that
Annette person were having sex in Will's bed. She'd be pregnant, and Will would insist on marrying her. Greg strode to
Lana's side and pulled her away from the crowd. "We have
to go."

"What's wrong?"

"Why didn't you tell me that Will and Annette left?"

She shrugged. "They were bored, so they went to your
house."

"To do what?"

She frowned. "Probably to be alone."

He took her empty wineglass and handed it to a passing
waiter. "Let's go."

"Where?"

"To my house. Yvonne is away visiting, and they can't be
alone."

"Greg, they're consenting adults. Besides, I don't think
they're going to do anything."

"You saw them in the car!"

"They were *kissing,* for heaven's sake."

"I'm going home to check on them. Are you coming with
me or not?"

She sighed. "Only to keep you from doing something
you'll regret."

19

"IT'S BEAUTIFUL," Lana murmured, as they made their way up a lighted stone walkway. Actually, "beautiful" was an understated adjective for the limestone mansion. Holy hotel. "Did you grow up here?"

He nodded absently, scanning the lighted windows, oblivious to her awe. "They've definitely been here." He unlocked the door and swung it open, then gestured for her to precede him.

"Just for the record, I don't think this is a good idea," she said as she walked into a foyer large enough to host a dinner party.

He closed the door, his head cocked for sound—but only silence greeted them. Thank goodness. She had visions of him crashing in on Will and Annette in an intimate embrace.

"Will?" he called, but there was no answer. He dropped his keys on a table in the hall and walked straight ahead, past a sweeping staircase and toward a lighted room. Lana followed, ogling the gray-and-pink marble tile laid down in a checkerboard pattern. She glimpsed a monstrous living room on one side, a gigantic dining room on the other. She felt like Alice in Wonderland, shrunk to miniature.

Their footsteps clicked against the smooth tile as they entered a gargantuan kitchen with *two* refrigerators, commercial grade. Enough storage for a couple of hundred cartons of Betty Crocker cake icing, at least.

"He left a note," he said, his voice tense as he snatched the piece of paper propped up on a cherry sideboard.

She turned in place, taking in the elegant glass-fronted cabinets, the solid-surface counters. Not a beanbag chair or a refurbished stool from the Dumpster in sight. "What does the note say?"

"They went to the stables where he works, to see the horses." Relief threaded his voice, and he sagged against the counter.

"This late?"

"It's like a resort over there," he said, wadding up the note. "The horses are treated like pampered guests—lighted stalls, music, the works."

She crossed her arms. "So Will and Annette didn't come back to do what you thought they came back to do."

His expression turned wry. "But that doesn't mean they won't."

"He's a grown man. You can't keep tabs on him all the time."

Greg rubbed his eyes. "I can try."

"Annette is a little immature, but she's a great girl."

"I'd like to believe you."

Lana looked around at the opulence Greg obviously took for granted, and a slow burn of disappointment gnawed at her stomach. He dated women from the classifieds, but he looked down on her friend? What must he think of *her?* She pressed her lips together, biting down painfully. She and Greg were worlds apart—the chances of them becoming involved were nil. In hindsight, her reason for keeping the truth from him about the ad seemed laughable.

"Annette is Coffee Girl," she blurted.

He squinted. "What?"

"Annette is Coffee Girl. I only placed the ad for a roommate. *She* placed the ad that you answered, so I'd appreciate it if you didn't talk about her—"

"Wait a minute." He put his hand to his forehead. "You're telling me that I was supposed to meet Annette that day instead of you?"

She nodded.

"And you didn't place a singles ad?"

"Uh-uh. No offense, but it's not my bag. I didn't tell you because I was afraid you'd try to meet her again, and after what happened at my apartment…"

"You were trying to protect your friend from me?"

"Sort of."

He started laughing, a tired I-don't-believe-this laugh.

Lana straightened. "I don't think it's so funny."

He laughed harder, a long half moan.

"Are you going to let me in on the punch line?"

"Lana, I was answering the singles ad for *Will*."

She blinked. "For Will?"

He gestured wildly. "He brought me an ad he found in a magazine and was fixated on meeting this Coffee Girl. I didn't want him to meet a stranger, so I told him I would check her out first, and if she was nice, I would introduce the two of them."

It was her turn to think. "So you don't answer singles ads?"

He shook his head. "It's, um, not my bag, either."

Lana narrowed her eyes. "Since you never mentioned Will's name to me that day, should I assume you didn't think I was nice?"

His expression changed, the light in his eye shifting from humor to something more primitive. Her pulse quickened. He leaned forward to capture her wrist and gently pulled her toward him.

"That was the problem," he said softly. "Once I saw you, my thoughts turned purely selfish."

She scoffed. "You thought I was a hooker." Then she angled her head. "Of course, I thought you were gay."

His eyebrows dove. *"What?"*

"My ad for a roommate specified females or gay males."

Realization dawned. "So when you asked me if I met all the requirements, you meant…?"

She nodded.

"Does that mean that your roommate is gay?"

She nodded.

He looked dubious. "But I saw you kiss him that day in the shop."

She reached up to trace the outline of his mouth. "Because you spooked me so badly, I had to be sure before I took him back to my apartment."

"And?"

"And," she said, moistening her lips slowly, "I'd rather kiss you."

He lowered his head, his eyes hooded with desire. Their mouths met in a slow, needy kiss that drained her. He moved from her mouth to her jaw, then to her neck, then he slid the spaghetti strap off her shoulder and kissed the pale bare slope. "You are so gorgeous tonight," he murmured against her skin.

"Mmm. Hadn't we better get back to the party?" she whispered, trying to control the waves of shudders his mouth triggered. "I still have some shmoozing to do."

"Relax," he whispered, then slid the other strap from its home. "I already asked my general manager to rerun the project numbers to reflect some of the buildings being preserved."

Lana's heart swelled with relief and happiness. "You did?"

He nodded while he nuzzled her neck. "Mmm-hmm."

"Thank you!" She showered his face with kisses. "Oh, thank you, Greg."

He pulled her face to his, so they were forehead to forehead. "You're welcome. Let's go upstairs."

Her heart thudded in her chest, and she felt herself wavering. God help her, she wanted to experience this man. "What's upstairs?" she asked with a little smile, stalling.

A wicked grin crinkled the corners of his eyes. "My telescope."

She liked him like this. Teasing. Sexy. Science Club guy. Was it possible that here was the real Greg Healey, and the blustery corporate image was just that—an image? A girl could hope. But trust? Lana swallowed hard and studied his chocolate-brown eyes at close range. Could she trust Greg Healey not to break her heart?

Take a chance, her heart whispered. *Maybe he's worth it.*

Reluctant to speak because she wasn't sure what would come out of her mouth, she simply smiled.

WHEN GREG CLOSED his bedroom door and watched Lana pivot slowly, taking in the masculine furnishings, her gaze lingering on the king-size bed, he realized with a start that she was the only woman he'd ever invited to his bedroom. When he'd moved back home seven years ago, he'd been supremely conscious of sharing living space with Will and Yvonne. Frankly, none of the few passable dates he'd been on had warranted an awkward breakfast table scene. Sex had taken place at the home of his dates, and once or twice at a nice hotel. So why now, and why Lana?

As he scrutinized the length of her shapely figure wrapped in the simple black gown, longing stabbed deep in his loins. He'd invited her because she was irresistibly gorgeous, and his desire for her was blurring the edges of his judgment. He had the pressing feeling that if he could only get her out of his system, he could get back to business, back to his life.

She dropped her evening bag and her wrap on the foot of his bed, then walked away from him, climbing two steps to the raised landing. A wall of windows surrounded his telescope where it sat on a tripod. "Nice setup," she murmured, then leaned over to peer into the lens. The unobstructed view of her derriere sent the blood pulsing through his body.

Greg set his jaw, then reached to the wall and extinguished the room's light with the flip of a switch. In the moon-glow streaming through the window, she straightened slightly. "You can see the constellations better in the dark," he explained.

"Oh." Her voice was barely above a whisper.

Greg walked up behind her, his heart thrashing in his ears. He cursed himself for feeling like a jumpy teenager. They were adults, and she knew he'd invited her upstairs to do more than gaze at the stars.

"You have a lovely view of downtown," she said, gesturing to the lights that were even more numerous in celebration of the holidays.

"Sometimes I take the telescope up on the roof," he said. "But the sky is so clear this time of year, I can usually get a good view from here." He swung open the window in front of the telescope, ushering in creaky night sounds and a rush of brisk air. She shivered, and he shrugged out of his jacket, then settled it across her slender shoulders. The fruity scent of her shampoo filled his lungs, and he was struck by an unfamiliar urge to protect her from more than the cold. A ludicrous thought, because Lana Martina could certainly take care of herself. Hadn't he learned that the first day they met?

"What should I be looking for?" she asked, her blond head bent to the lens. "Oh, wow, I can see…*wait a minute.*"

When Greg realized where the telescope was directed, the bottom seemed to fall out of his stomach. His mouth opened and closed, but no sound emerged.

"You've been looking at my apartment building?" Her voice was incredulous and suspicious as she stared at him in the dark.

He swallowed hard. "I've been reviewing your notes and looking over the Hyde Parkland area for traffic patterns. You make it sound as if I've been spying."

Her silence wasn't a comforting reply.

He sighed, exasperated. "You can see for yourself that the scope isn't powerful enough to look into windows or anything."

"I can see my balcony," she said, her voice partly accusing, partly amused.

"I don't even know which balcony is yours." Technically true—he wasn't certain which one was hers, and when he'd realized he could see her building fairly clearly, guilt had kept him from trying to figure it out.

"It's the one with the big wreath on the sliding glass door."

He'd figured as much. "I *wasn't* spying."

"Well, you'd be wasting your time, since I rarely go out on the balcony," she chirped, then bent back to the lens. "So, what can *I* look for? In the sky, that is."

He ignored her barb and tore his gaze from her to take in the dark wintry sky, so black it was nearly purple. He searched for a simple sky mark. "There's the Milky Way galaxy," he said, pointing to the west.

She swung the telescope and looked again. "I see it! It's like a blanket of glitter."

Not an analogy he would have used, but he couldn't help smiling at her childlike enthusiasm. "At the mouth of the Milky Way is the constellation Aquila, then it becomes most dense at Cygnus, then begins to peter out at the Charioteer."

Lana swung the scope slowly, following the galaxy that was millions of miles long. And he studied her, the lines of her lithe arms, the slope of her shoulder, the curve of her hip. Her hair and skin glowed luminous in the low light. Mere inches separated their bodies, and the distance shrank as he succumbed to the pull emanating from her—

"Greg?"

He started. "What?"

"I asked if you wanted to be an astronaut when you were little."

A tiny laugh escaped him. "For about a month. The summer I was ten my career aspirations ran the gamut from professional baseball pitcher to race car driver."

"When did you become interested in astronomy?"

"It was my mother's passion," he admitted.

She straightened and turned to look at him. "Your mother must have been a fascinating woman."

He nodded, the memories still bittersweet. "She was. We all miss her, especially Will."

"I can imagine," she murmured, her voice wistful. "I miss my mother, and she lives only a day's drive away."

"Do you see her often?"

"Well, Janet sells real estate, so it's hard for her to take time off, and now I have the shop…"

Her voice trailed off, and he had the strangest feeling she was making excuses for her mother, not for herself.

"Anyway, I can't wait until Christmas Eve. We're going to make a gingerbread house and—I'm sorry, I'm rambling."

His ego swelled a tiny bit at the idea that her nervousness stemmed from being in his bedroom.

"Greg," she said, turning toward him. "I don't think coming up here was such a good idea."

He hadn't realized how much he wanted her in his bed until faced with the prospect of her walking out. A murmur of protest emerged from his tight throat. "Why don't we double-check?" he asked, then pulled her against him for a long, breathless kiss.

Two seconds into the kiss, it was clear that despite her misgivings about the wisdom of their actions, she was where she wanted to be. Their mouths and bodies melded perfectly. Greg planted his feet on either side of her, creating an intimate cradle for her to lean into. Adrenaline and desire pumped through his body at the knowledge that they would soon be intimately entwined.

He broke their kiss long enough to lean over and scoop her into his arms. Romantic gesture aside, carrying her to the bed simply seemed…expeditious. He carried her down the two steps, then crossed to the massive bed in two strides. His control already precarious, stretching out next to her on the cool comforter sent a wave of longing barbing through his body. Her soft moan of acquiescence had him setting his jaw in restraint.

His eyes had adjusted to the dark. Moonlight streamed in through the open window, casting a sheen upon the floor and the bed. She lay slightly diagonally, her chin tipped up expectantly, her chest rising and falling rapidly. So lovely. So beguiling. Greg feasted upon the sight of her, overcome by the enormous swell of passion that surged through him. "Have I told you that you're the most desirable woman I've ever met?" he murmured, then lowered a kiss to her jawline.

"Yes, but I bet you say that to all the women." Her voice was the sexy rasp of a woman who knew she had a man by the hormones.

He moaned denial, relieved that she hadn't bolted from his room. Anticipation coursed through him. He held an exquisite gift, which he intended to unwrap with infinite care. He eased his suit jacket from her shoulders, lowering one strap, then the other to make way for his tongue. Gathering her into his arms, he lowered his mouth to nuzzle just above the low neckline of her gown, gratified when she arched into him, and that her movement tugged the dress down so far that the hard peaks of her breasts popped into view. Greg accepted her subtle invitation with fervor, laving the pearled tips while a delicate citrus scent lurking in the valley between her breasts teased his senses higher.

His control was slipping badly. He buried his face against her skin, marveling how he could feel so safe and so anxious at the same time. As alarms sounded in his brain, another sensation registered. A distant noise—a voice. He stiffened at the sound of his name being called from the first floor.

"Gregory?"

Greg hesitated, then lifted his head. "It's Will." Remorse knifed through him. How could he make sure his brother wasn't...doing *this* if he was in his bedroom with Lana... doing *this?* He heaved a sigh and sat up, ignoring the ache in his loins. "I'm sorry. I can't do this while Will is around. I feel like I need to set an example."

She pushed into a sitting position with her back to him, adjusting the bodice of her dress. "I understand."

Her voice was strained and shaky. Was she upset at being interrupted, or relieved?

"Gregory?"

Frustration clawed at him as he stood and shrugged into his jacket. "Let's go back to your place," he suggested, reaching out but stopping short of touching her shoulder, "or get a room."

"No," she said quietly, then stood abruptly, smoothing her hand over the skirt of her gown as she retrieved her purse. "I'd better be leaving."

"Gregory? Are you here?"

Greg pulled his hand down over his face. He wanted to throw caution and responsibilities to the wind, then throw Lana on the bed and ravish her. Instead, he inhaled deeply and did what he always did—the right thing. "I'll take you home," he conceded. He'd probably be thanking Will tomorrow for the timely interruption, but he still had tonight to get through.

Her wrap had fallen to the floor at the corner of the bed.

Greg bent to pick up the silky length of fabric, and extended it to her in the semidarkness. She reached for it, her eyes averted, but he held on, engaging in a slight tug-of-war until she looked up. "I'm sorry. My life isn't always my own. I have responsibilities." Even as the words left his mouth, he recognized their meaning in a larger context. *If things were different…*

But things weren't different. Lana's eyes were luminous in the low lighting. Her pale hair glowed, the ends curling around her slender neck. "You don't owe me anything, Greg."

At her detached tone, he released the wrap. She draped it over her arm carefully, then walked to the door, just as if nothing had transpired between them.

He clenched his jaw to the point of pain. Then again, in her opinion, maybe nothing had.

20

LANA WAS IN THE THROES of a full-body yawn when the tell-tale sound of Annette's double ring at the back door reverberated through the empty shop. Thanks to last night's encounter with Greg, Lana had become acquainted with every square inch of her lumpy mattress after she'd gotten home and crawled into bed.

She walked toward the back door, steeling for Annette's certain barrage. When they had emerged from Greg's room last night, Annette's eyes had been full of questions. Will had been more direct.

"What were you all doing, Gregory?"

"Looking at the stars, pal."

"Gregory has a big telescope," Will had informed Annette, whose eyebrows seemed to have frozen high on her forehead as she studied Lana. Thank goodness Will had then announced that Annette was Coffee Girl, and the four had laughed over the mix-up.

Annette didn't get the chance to drill Lana afterward because Greg drove and Will rode along to take them both home. Lana's apartment was closer, and after a tense ride during which she and Greg exchanged only a dozen words, she'd practically vaulted from the car.

Now, forcing a cheerful smile, she undid the latch. "Good morning."

"Yes, it is," Annette sang, blowing in on an early morning chill, carrying warm delicacies covered with fogged-up wax paper.

Lana ignored the obvious invitation to discussion. "Smells de-lish."

"I was inspired." More singing.

She sighed and took the tray, conceding defeat. "Let's see…you're in love?"

"How can you tell?"

"Wild guess."

Annette grinned. "Isn't Will the kindest, handsomest man you've ever seen?"

"Yes." At least the "handsome" part ran in the family.

"He's all I think about, Lana. It's like we were meant to be. Imagine, if you and Greg weren't working together on this rezoning thing, Will and I would never have met."

"You would have met sooner if Greg hadn't interfered," Lana pointed out.

The redhead shrugged. "Things happen for a reason."

Did they? Lana wondered. She had always thought so, but what good could possibly come of meeting Greg Healey? Even if he decided to spare her business, what about her heart?

"You like him, don't you?"

Lana snapped back to the present. "Will? I think he's a great guy."

"No, I mean Greg."

"Oh. Greg and I are…opposites," she said lamely.

"I think he likes you, too."

"But I don't—"

"Lana, did Will and I interrupt something last night?"

"Don't you have more trays to carry in? I suspect today will be hopping with all the last-minute shoppers."

Annette angled her head, but finally nodded. "You're right—I'll get the rest. Oh, are you definitely going to be closed tomorrow?"

She nodded. "I'm going to deliver the gifts for the children in the morning, then do some last-minute decorating, and make a big Christmas Eve dinner before my mother arrives."

"Will invited me to have dinner with him and Greg and Yvonne."

If she hadn't had her own plans, Lana might have been envious. But the Healey brothers couldn't be more different. Will was looking for someone to include in his life. Greg was looking for someone to include in his bed… But only when no one else was in the house, she thought wryly.

"That's nice," she said. "But are you sure you aren't moving too fast, Annette?"

Astonishment widened her friend's features. "Lana, life is short. When love finds you, you shouldn't waste time. I'll be back with the cranberry truffles."

Such a simple concept, Lana thought as she watched her friend walk away, her every step punctuated with a happy bounce. When love finds you, you shouldn't waste time. But did love find everyone? And what if your every waking thought was occupied by a person who you knew didn't feel the same? And what if that person held your future in their hands?

Holy heartbreak.

"ALL NEXT WEEK OFF, sir—I mean, Mr. Healey? For everyone in the company?"

Greg nodded his approval at Peg's more casual address. "Yes. Do you think you can contact everyone at home?" It was, after all, Saturday morning. He and Peg were the only two in the office. He'd showered, but hadn't bothered to shave since the party last night. Hadn't bothered to sleep, either.

"Sure, Mr. Healey. I'll use the calling tree we have in place in case we close due to bad weather."

"Then I'll leave the matter in your capable hands. Merry Christmas."

She blinked, then smiled. "Merry Christmas, Mr. Healey."

At a rap on the door, they both looked up. Art Payton stood in the doorway.

"Got a minute?"

"Sure," Greg said, waving him in. Peg slipped out and closed the door behind her.

Art dropped his considerable bulk into a chair. "I got a call this morning from Mitch Ryder, the largest developer who's shown interest in the Hyde Parkland project."

Dread curled in his stomach, but Greg nodded. "Go on."

"Well, seems as though a couple of big apartment buildings are available in Frankfort. Ryder thinks he can convert them to condos. Trouble is, he can't handle both jobs at once, so it's either the Hyde parcel or the Frankfort parcel."

"And he needs to know right away," Greg said.

"As soon as possible. He'd rather do business here."

"And if we make changes to the plans at this point?"

"We'll lose Ryder."

"But we can find another developer."

"In time. But why risk it? You can have a home run when this rezoning goes through by sticking to your original plan. Or you can give in to the merchants, and settle for a lot less money coming in over a longer period of time."

"Either way we won't go bankrupt."

"But with Ryder, you can retire. Buy a sailboat. Cruise the South Seas."

Greg respected Art's candor—the man worked on salary, so he was speaking from an unbiased viewpoint. "The rezoning vote will take place the second week of January."

"I can hold Ryder off until then," Art promised, "but no longer." He pushed himself to his feet and headed for the door. "Greg?"

Greg looked up.

"This is no time to start being Mr. Nice Guy." Art lifted his hand in a wave, then swaggered out the door.

Greg tossed down his pen, then scooted his chair back with a frustrated sigh. Hell, if he could convince Lana to go along with the rezoning, they'd have enough money to do whatever they wanted. She'd never miss the coffee shop. He frowned. *They?*

A dry laugh escaped him. He knew Lana Martina well enough to know that the way to her heart was not through money derived at the expense of things she held dear. His frown deepened. *The way to her heart.* Where had that come from? Besides, Lana had told him she wasn't interested in a relationship. How could he possibly walk away from the chance of a lifetime in return for—what? A few weeks of torrid lovemaking? And who's to say she even wanted to have an affair?

The phone rang, and he answered since Peg was probably busy spreading Christmas cheer to the employees. "Greg Healey."

"Greg, it's Charlie Andrews."

Greg grinned when he heard the voice of a buddy from law school he'd run into last week while playing hooky at the courthouse. "Hey, Charlie."

"Only you would be working on the Saturday before Christmas."

Greg laughed. "What about you?"

"And me. Listen, I've been thinking about our conversation last week, and you hinting at making a move into the courtroom."

His pulse picked up. "And?"

"And I have a proposition for you. The DA's office is recovering from some political infighting. To make a long story short, they're looking for a few good men."

Greg sat forward in his chair, barely able to contain his excitement. "But Charlie, I have no courtroom experience."

"I know, but the money is barely enough to live on, so it evens out. In fact, I'm sure you'll be up to speed long before your salary is. The office has some big cases coming up in the next six months. Could be career makers for a guy with the right stuff who's willing to work on the cheap."

"I don't know what to say, Charlie." Every muscle in his body screamed yes.

"Say you'll think about it over the holidays. I'll catch up with you after the New Year."

"Great. And thanks."

"Merry Christmas, man."

"To you, too."

Greg returned the receiver slowly, pleasure pooling in his stomach. A chance to work in the DA's office, doing what he'd always wanted to do.

But for pauper's pay. He sighed, then pushed himself to his feet and walked over to the garland-decorated window to stare at the courthouse roof. If the rezoning proposal went through, he'd be a rich man. A rich man who could prosecute landmark cases without worrying about providing for himself and for Will—and, now with a girlfriend in the picture, perhaps Will's offspring. His brother couldn't raise a family on the minimum wage he earned.

And then there was Lana. And her violet eyes. And her bleeding heart.

He groaned as Art's parting words came back to him. After all these years, what a bad time to have grown a conscience.

21

LANA WOKE ON Christmas Eve morning with little-girl anticipation at seeing her mother again. She smiled wide as she
stretched, then jumped into the shower, humming Christmas
tunes under her breath. Janet already would have left for the
eight-hour trip north. She'd told Lana the last time they'd
spoken on the phone to expect her around four in the afternoon, which gave Lana plenty of time to deliver the gifts to
the children's center where a breakfast for the kids was being
held.

She still marveled at Greg's generosity. Alex had teased
her that he was simply trying to butter her up, but she liked
to think that his heart had truly gone out to the children.

She had to make two trips with a huge bag of gifts
strapped to her moped, but it was more than worth it to see
the looks on the faces of the children. Her own problems—
real and perceived—seemed petty next to the trials that other
people experienced day in and day out.

Even though the Christmas card she'd mailed to her father
a month ago had been returned yesterday with no forward-
ing address, at least she still had Janet. Even if her business
were shut down in the next few months, she'd still find a way
to make a living and eventually repay her debt. Even if Greg
Healey didn't care for her, she had her health and good
friends around her. Everything was relative.

So with much effort, she quashed the emotions that
seemed to have careened out of control since the episode in
his room two nights ago. Her left brain told her there was no
future with Greg Healey. But her right brain had wrapped its
synapses around the words Annette had spoken yesterday.
When love finds you, you shouldn't waste time.

She hadn't shared her burgeoning feelings for Greg with

anyone, although Annette suspected something was going on. Alex had asked a few vague questions about the rezoning proposal the last time they'd talked on the phone, but was preoccupied with overseeing the Christmas rush at Tremont's and with moving into her new home. Rich had left Friday and wouldn't return until the thirtieth. Harry was no help whatsoever.

But she planned to tell Janet about Greg, another reason she was looking forward to their time together. Her mother would want all the details, would want to sit up until two in the morning in their pj's, talking about life and love and men. And maybe in the course of trying to express her thoughts about Greg, some unforgivable wart on his character would be revealed, some defect that would neutralize these... stirrings of her heart. Janet would tease her mercilessly because Lana had never before been in...deep like this. She'd scattered candles around the kitchen and living room. Her mother loved candles, and Elvis's "Blue Christmas" album, which Lana had found on CD, along with Jim Reeves and Lou Rawls, two more of her mother's faves. She loaded the CDs into the stereo, smiling as the strains of the old recordings came over her speakers. She'd be tired of them by the time Janet arrived, but it put her in the mood to finish decorating.

Harry wore a tolerant smile as she dressed him in a Santa suit. "Behave while Mom's here, okay?" She stuffed his hard plastic doll manhood into the red pants and pulled the hem of the coat down for more camouflage. By two o'clock she had hung garlands from every surface, set luminaries in her windows, removed the turkey from the oven, and had begun baking the walls for the gingerbread house they would build together. Just looking over the ingredients sent a little tremor of happiness through her chest—gumdrops and sugar cubes and squeeze tubes of colored icing. Nothing said Christmas like the gingerbread houses she and her mother used to make when Lana was little.

While the gingerbread baked, she showered and changed into a black velvet jumpsuit, then dabbed perfume behind her ears. Janet had sent her a rhinestone candy-cane pin for Christmas last year from the Bahamas, and it showed up well against the dark fabric. The gingerbread came out more perfectly than she'd ever seen it. A good omen, she thought, smiling to herself while keeping one eye on the clock. One more hour. She let the slabs cool on the breakfast bar while she put together the rest of their feast.

The phone rang, and she picked it up while sliding the asparagus into the oven. "Hello?"

"Hey, it's Alex. Merry Christmas."

"Merry Christmas to you, too."

"I just called to check in. I hear Elvis in the background, so your mom must be there."

She glanced at the clock—3:45. "Not yet, but she should be here any minute."

"Okay." Her friend was trying hard to sound casual, bless her. "Jack and I are spending the night at Dad's, if you need anything."

"I won't, but thanks."

"Sure. And don't forget about our New Year's Eve party next Sunday."

"Are you sure you want to have a party in your new house after you've just moved in?"

"It'll be fun. And it's shaping up to be a good-size crowd. Jack's brother will be there, and his wife. You'll like them."

"If it's all couples, maybe I should pass."

"Don't be silly. Derek's wife has a friend in from Atlanta, and some of the people I work with are coming. Don't forget to invite your roommate. Oh, and Annette and her new beau, of course."

Lana waited as two seconds passed, then three, four, five.

"And you can invite a date if you like."

She smiled into the phone. "Really? Whoever would I ask?"

"Anyone," Alex said in her most innocent voice. "Hey, since Greg Healey's brother is coming with Annette, why don't you ask him? I know Jack would like to see him again."

A smirk pulled back one side of Lana's mouth. "Hmm. I'll

probably just ride with Rich, if he can come. But thanks for offering."

"Okay. Well, have a good time with your mother," Alex said.

"I will," Lana said. "I'll call you later in the week."

She hung up and snacked on a celery stick dipped in peanut butter while she put the finishing touches on the decorations. She lit all the candles and lowered the lights to show off the masterpiece of a Christmas tree that was leaning ever so slightly. And she rearranged her mother's gifts so that the bows were perky. At the last minute she remembered the two disposable cameras she'd bought and put them on the counter so she could take pictures as soon as Janet arrived.

And she tried not to check the clock too often. Four-ten. Four-seventeen. Four-twenty-four. At four-thirty she considered blowing out some of the wilting candles, and turned off all the warming burners for the food.

At five-fifteen the phone rang again. Lana snapped it up. "Hello?"

The crackly noise of a cellular phone with bad reception sounded over the line. "Lana, darling, it's Mother."

Her heart raced. Janet only called herself "Mother" under dire circumstances. "Mom? Is something wrong?" Her father's Christmas card had been returned. Was he okay?

"No, nothing's wrong. You're such a worrywart."

A by-product of growing up fast. "Are you held up in traffic?"

"Darling, I'm afraid I'm not going to be able to make it this year."

Lana swallowed hard and blinked back sudden hot tears. "Oh?" was all she could manage to say.

"Yes, dear. At the last minute, Larry got this fabulous deal on a cruise to Cancún, and we're getting ready to set sail."

"Set sail?" She cleared her throat of the emotion that lodged there. "I wish you had called. I...wish you had called."

"I'm sorry, darling. We had to leave in a rush, and this is

the first chance I've had to ring you. I hope you didn't go to any trouble."

Lana looked around the sparkly, glittery apartment, awash with holiday magic, with Elvis crooning in the background, and savory scents coming from the kitchen. "No. No trouble."

"Oh, there's our boarding call, dear. I have to go. I'll send you a nice blanket or something from Mexico."

Or something.

"Lana, are you there?"

"I'm here," she croaked. "Have a good time."

"We will—"

The line went dead. Lana stared at the phone until a piercing tone sounded and a voice informed her that if she would like to make a call, please hang up and try again. She dropped the phone on the love seat, then slowly walked around the room. The cooling gingerbread house walls had developed half-inch wide cracks. How fitting.

She tore off the chimney and chewed on it as she wandered around, blowing out candles. She attributed the haze and the smoky odor to the extinguished candles, until she realized the asparagus was burning. When she opened the oven, the green spears were black—and on fire. Lana shrieked, then yanked a mitt from the counter, pulled out the flaming dish and carried it to the sliding glass door. The balcony was antique wrought iron—fireproof. She set the casserole dish on the floor and jerked her hand away, sucking on a burned thumb.

Then the tears came. She hugged the oven mitt to her aching chest and wept as she looked out over a glittery Lexington, where normal people were tucked in their warm houses having dinner and exchanging gifts with loved ones. How big a loser was she if even her parents didn't want to be with her on Christmas Eve?

In the light of day, she could nonchalantly announce she was happy living alone. But at this forlorn moment, she felt as if she were being paid a courtesy visit from the Ghost of

Christmas Future: a vision of her at eighty-five, living alone save for Harry and seventeen cats.

She'd trained herself to believe, especially over the past few years, that she could only truly rely on herself. But her tears were tangible proof that she needed someone else to share her life, to fill the void in her heart that in rare moments of despair seemed bottomless.

She wasn't sure how long she stood there in the cold. It could have been ten minutes or an hour. The next stimulus she was aware of was a buzzing noise inside her apartment. Afraid she might have set something else on fire and triggered an alarm, Lana rushed back inside to the tune of her doorbell ringing. Puzzled, she pressed a watery eye to the peephole.

Greg stood in the hallway. Her breath froze in her chest. What was he doing here?

He knocked on the door sharply. "Lana? It's Greg. Are you okay? Lana?"

She swung open the door.

Greg had his hand raised, poised to knock again. He looked out of place in the musty hallway, tall and broad and sexy, wearing dark slacks and a white shirt and a black leather jacket, smelling like a man and sporting a tentative smile. He was the most welcome sight imaginable.

"Wh-what are you doing here?"

His brown eyes narrowed. "You've been crying."

She swiped at her eyes. "I, uh, burned something in the oven and the smoke got in my eyes. What are you doing here?"

He shrugged, and shifted foot to foot. "Did your mother arrive?"

"Um, no, she had a change in plans—" Lana stopped, then looked to the sliding glass door and back to Greg. "You saw me on the balcony, didn't you."

"By accident."

"Your eye fell against your telescope that just happened to be trained on my balcony?"

A flush climbed his face. "You were standing outside in

the cold for over an hour. I called, but your phone is off the hook."

She glanced to her couch where the phone lay, emitting a fast busy signal.

"Is anything wrong?" he asked.

A hysterical little laugh bubbled out. At the moment there was more wrong in her life than was right, and this man was responsible for at least half of it. Suddenly bombarded with the concern in his eyes, the disappointment of her mother's call, and the melancholy strains of Jim Reeves crooning "Silver Bells" in the background, Lana burst into tears.

22

GREG STOOD STOCK-STILL, watching the sudden display of waterworks, at a complete loss. How did women *do* that? He fumbled in his back pocket for a handkerchief and offered it to her. She was really boo-hooing now, and at least two neighbors stuck their heads into the hall to stare at him. "May I come in?" he asked.

She nodded and stepped aside, her shoulders heaving with the great mouthfuls of air she gulped.

Greg walked in and carefully closed the door, his pupils dilating in response to the wonderland of decorations. The air was hazy, probably from all the half-burned candles sitting around the room. His nostrils flared at the aroma of food—burned and otherwise—emanating from the kitchen. From the surroundings and Lana's dressy outfit and her tears, it was clear that she had been stood up. Stood up by her mother on Christmas Eve. His heart squeezed for her, and he resisted the urge to fold her into his arms.

Just a little while ago he'd been pacing in his room, agonizing over how to tell Lana that his response to the council would be uncompromising—pass the rezoning proposal as is, or he would be forced to hike the shop owners' rents to offset his company's losses. Higher rents would force some merchants out of business—a no-win situation. The city council would pass the rezoning plan, but he'd be painted as the bad guy. Still, it would be worth the intense unpopularity if the deal put him one step closer to that job Charlie had promised him.

Lana, of course, would hate him.

He'd been drawn to the window, to the telescope. Absurdly, looking at her apartment building made him feel closer to her. He'd even practiced telling her, trying to put a good spin on his words: *You're an accountant, Lana. You know this is a simple case of sacrificing the needs of a few to satisfy the needs of many.*

Yes, she would say. *You're right, Greg. Now make love to me.*

He'd laughed at his own foolishness. And when she'd emerged from the sliding glass door, he'd nearly knocked over the telescope. Then she'd remained on the balcony, in the cold and without that ridiculous dalmation coat, and he'd known something was wrong.

But he hadn't counted on an emotional dilemma. Now, powerless to stem her tears, Greg bit down on the inside of his cheek and waited for her to take a breath. "If you don't have other plans, come back to the house with me for Christmas Eve dinner."

She stopped crying and hiccuped, then blew her nose heartily into his handkerchief. She was considering his question—knowing her, spinning through the ramifications, looking for an ulterior motive.

"Annette is already there," he cajoled. "And you can meet Yvonne and her brother."

She dabbed at her eyes and sniffed mightily.

"And besides," he added. "I'd like it very much if you'd come."

At the widening of her tear-streaked eyes, he thought he'd gone too far, almost admitted something he didn't even want to admit to himself—that he had grown attached to her violet eyes and her quick wit and her funky clothes.

"Otherwise, I'm going to feel like a fifth wheel at the table," he continued with a little laugh.

"Oh," she croaked, then blew her nose again. "Well, it's nice of you to include me, but—" she gestured vaguely toward the kitchen "—I have so much food here, and I don't think I'd be very good company."

"No one should be alone on Christmas Eve."

She laughed, a strained, high-pitched sound. "I don't suppose you'd consider staying and having dinner with me? Overcooked turkey and asparagus flambé?"

He blinked. Dining together *alone* on Christmas Eve

smacked of...intimacy. "Well, I'm expected back at home. Will and Annette—"

"I forgot," she cut in with a little wave. "You're chaperoning."

He smirked at her teasing tone, but was glad beyond comprehension that her mood had lightened. "I'm not chaperoning. I'm just...keeping an eye on them."

She leaned toward him, her eyes dancing with mischief. "Do you know how much sex they could be having right now?"

His body leapt to rapt attention at her words and her proximity. Every muscle strained toward her, pulled by some invisible force that baffled him. "How much?" he murmured, no longer able to resist touching her.

He opened his arms, and she came into them with a little groan. Greg wrapped his arms around her, closed his eyes and inhaled the scent of her—fruit and...smoke? The burned food, of course. He smiled into her hair while his chest swelled with a firestorm of emotion, including sympathy for her. How could a mother not appreciate having this beautiful, intelligent creature for a daughter? Overcome with the urge to protect her, he kissed her hard and kneaded her back. The fuzzy nap of her jumpsuit felt luxurious under his fingers, smooth and sexy and inviting. His sex hardened and ached for release.

Days of pent-up desire and near misses hurried their movements. He didn't know how they made it to her bedroom, but he knew he would forever remember the way they'd tumbled onto her bed, tugging at clothes, wordless in their need and urgency to have each other. Within seconds, they were stripped to their underwear—Lana hadn't been wearing a bra.

He pulled away long enough to take in the sight of her, lying on her side, the curve of her hip rising above the dip of her waist, the fullness of her breasts rising and falling in her breathlessness. Black bikini panties were a perfect contrast to the pale, flat plane of her stomach. Her legs extended long and lean and limber. Greg's erection, already straining painfully, surged anew, prompting him to shed his boxers. Speechless with need, he turned his mind and body over to automatic, kissing and massaging her exposed skin. He acknowledged on a subconscious level that one of the emotions driving him to please her was regret—regret that he would be the next person who would disappoint her. He poured all his energy into lavishing on her body the attention she deserved. An advance apology, of sorts. With a groan, he slipped his hand inside the scrap of black fabric between her legs.

Already near the point of sensory overload, Lana cried out in response to his gentle probing and opened her legs to accommodate one, then two long fingers. Moving with his slow rhythm, she felt an intense orgasm flowering, blooming deep in her womb. Part of her wanted him to prolong the deft exploration, but part of her wanted him to take her quickly to end the sensual torture. Then without warning, her muscles contracted around his muscular fingers, unleashing a tide of pleasure so fierce, she dug her fingernails into his shoulders. "Greg...Greg...oh, Greg." Bright spots of light swirled behind her eyes, and her body convulsed as the orgasm claimed her, wave by wave.

When the world righted itself, she was primed for his remarkable body to join hers. He was the personification of Adam—tall, broad, lean and equipped. Every movement displaced toned muscle. Lana watched, fascinated, engrossed, thrilled.

While he rolled a condom onto his raging erection, she lifted her hips and shimmied out of the panties, her inhibitions long gone. She reached for him, pulling at his shoulders, levering her hips beneath his.

His back was moist with perspiration, as was his brow. His breath escaped in staccato bursts as he gathered her beneath him, vying for the best angle. His erection, hard and thick with want, prodded her folds. She waited for his sensual invasion, her breath caught in her thudding chest. Then he entered her with one deliberate thrust.

She sucked in a sharp breath at the incredible fullness his

body added to hers. Strange, but in those few seconds of intense physical union, Lana was struck by her participation in this ritual that had made the world go around since the dawn of mankind. Never had she felt such a connection with nature and with her base emotions. She kneaded his back, adopting his slow, thorough rhythm, meeting his hip thrusts with her own.

"Amazing," he whispered, his breathing compromised. "So...good."

Age-old female satisfaction curled in her chest. "Love me, Greg...*harder*."

He slid his hands under her hips, cradling her bottom with his large hands, and obliged, plunging in and out like a piston, faster and harder, until his body went rigid and a sharp guttural moan tore from his mouth. Triumph flooded her limbs as the ragged sighs of his release filled her ears. At last he quieted, sagging against her, raining exhausted kisses on her throat before he rolled away to lie beside her on the rumpled comforter.

Amazing, she seconded silently, sinking deeper into the softness at her back. Her body hummed with fulfillment and discovery, and other sensations too complicated to delve into. Their lovemaking was a result of unrealized chemistry and loneliness—no need to overanalyze the obvious. *Keep it casual*, she told herself. He was probably already regretting what had happened.

"Are you hungry?" she whispered to the ceiling, then braced for his excuse to leave as soon as possible.

"Starved."

She rolled over on her side to study his profile—strong brow, jutting nose, square jaw. How easy it would be to fall for this man.

"Greg, do you have plans for New Year's Eve?" she asked.

He turned his head, and for a few seconds she was afraid she'd pushed too far, assumed too much.

"Lana," he said, his voice raspy. "I..."

Her heart withdrew, preparing for rejection. He wasn't looking for a relationship, he would remind her. He had more important obligations—his business, his brother. He stared at her, and she tried to banish the thought that he was the most handsome man she'd ever known. And their chemistry—holy high voltage! She could barely keep from touching him. But common sense told her that their raging passion would soon burn itself out.

Now that the conquest was over, had his interest in her already been extinguished?

"What?" she asked, then closed her eyes. The sooner he put his feelings—or lack thereof—on the table, the sooner she could dispel the fairy tales that had infiltrated her holiday-weakened mind.

"I, um…" He cleared his throat. "No, as a matter of fact, I don't have plans for New Year's Eve."

Her heart lurched crazily. "How about Christmas morning?" she murmured, braver now. She slid her hand over his rock-hard stomach.

The flash of his white teeth coincided with his surrendering groan. "This is going to be hard to explain to Will."

She laughed, a little afraid of how much his words buoyed her. "You'll think of something."

23

EVEN IN THE CROWDED great room of the Stillmans' new home, Greg knew the precise moment that Lana arrived at the New Year's Eve party. The energy in the air increased markedly, ratcheting up the temperature. Her voice reached him before he saw her—a lyrical, uplifting sound that elicited involuntary responses from his nether regions.

They'd decided after spending Christmas Eve together that it would be prudent to put their relationship on hold until after the conflict of interest passed. No good would come of the shop owners finding out she was sleeping with the enemy. But Lana had asked Greg to attend the New Year's Eve party, anyway, promising to flirt with him from across the room.

The week since he'd left her bed had seemed like an eternity. The past few days he'd been plagued by the potentially life-changing decisions he had to make that would have been straightforward just a few weeks ago. If he remained firm on the rezoning plan, he'd pocket a small fortune. The money would allow him to accept a low-paying entry-level position in the DA's office. And a neglected area of downtown Lexington would receive an economic boost.

So why couldn't he find the nerve to tell Lana? And why did the faces of the Hyde Parkland shop owners haunt him— the dubious smirk on Marshall Ballou's face, the wrinkled concern on Vic the Barber's ugly mug, the nervous twitch on Maxie Dodd's flour-covered features.

Lana came into view, stealing his breath. He couldn't fail to notice the trusting optimism on her sweet face.

What should be a slam-dunk decision was being blocked by a pair of violet-colored eyes. She smiled at him from across the room, a private I-know-what-you-look-like-naked smile that made breathing more difficult. Greg swallowed hard and tried to ignore the stab of disappointment when she turned to greet someone else.

"Greg Healey?" a man's voice asked behind him.

Greg turned to see his host, Alex's husband, striding up.

"Jack Stillman."

Dressed in jeans and an untucked shirt, the big man looked more like the UK football icon he'd been in college than a partner in a successful advertising firm. Greg extended his hand. "I remember you from the university."

"I remember you, too," Jack said with a lifted eyebrow. "We've both changed a little, eh?"

Greg nodded, wondering if Jack, like everyone else, had thought he was a jerk in college, and if the man knew about his disastrous first meeting with Lana.

"Lana explained the mix-up about the classified ads," Jack said, as if he'd read Greg's mind.

Heat suffused his face. "Damn embarrassing."

Jack laughed heartily. "Reminds me of when I met Alex. I thought she was an IRS agent coming to audit the advertising agency, so I laid it on pretty thick about how we were barely able to pay the light bill, etcetera. Then I found out that she was from Tremont's and she'd come by early to scout me and the agency before I pitched the account."

Greg grinned and pulled on his chin. "Ouch."

"Yeah. And she's been a thorn in my side ever since," he said good-naturedly, then indicated his striking wife with a nod. "But it's worth every minute of the pain."

Greg's gaze involuntarily strayed to Lana. She was stunning in snug pink jeans and an oversize white shirt cinched with a silver belt.

"Lana's a great gal, man. Tread lightly, if you know what's good for you."

He frowned. "I'm not going to do anything to hurt Lana."

Jack laughed. "Lana can take care of herself. I was talking about saving yourself." He clapped Greg on the back. "Enjoy the party, man."

Greg didn't have time to ponder Jack's words, because a

redhead with harsh makeup slinked up to him, smiling wide. Her lipstick was drawn outside of her mouth, making her look as if she were all gums. "Hello," she said silkily, batting tarantula-like eyelashes.

"Hello," he said with a tight smile, his mind so…elsewhere.

"THIS IS DEREK STILLMAN, Jack's brother," Alex said, making introductions. "And his wife, Janine."

A very *pregnant* Janine, Lana noted with a smile. "It's nice to meet you." They made a fabulous-looking couple—she the blond flower-child, he the brawny businessman. Newlyweds, she remembered Alex saying. Something about Derek standing in for his brother Jack as best man at a wedding and falling in love with the bride.

"And this is my friend Manny Oliver from Atlanta," Janine said, gesturing to a tall blond man, impeccably dressed.

Lana shook hands all around, immediately liking Manny's friendly demeanor. He worked in the hospitality industry, he said. Hotel management. He seemed impressed that she owned her own business—for how long, though, was another story.

"Everyone, this is my friend and roommate, Rich Enderling," she said, repeating the introductions.

Rich and Derek exchanged a few humorous observations about Rich's employer, Phillips Foods, which was also a client of Jack and Derek's advertising agency. Then Rich extended his hand to Manny.

Lana noticed the slightest pause when the men's hands met, and the split second of awareness that ricocheted between them. Was it possible that Manny was gay?

Yes, she realized a few seconds later when the men extricated themselves unobtrusively from the little knot of people and moved in the direction of the chilled buffet on a granite-topped sideboard. Lana angled her head, recalling Rich's wistful words as he stood in front of her kitchen window. *I have a good feeling about Lexington, Lana, like something significant is going to happen for me here.* And perhaps it just had, she acknowledged, as Rich laughed in response to something Manny had said.

"So what do you think about the house?" Alex whispered near her ear.

Lana lifted her hand to indicate...everything. The high ceilings, the elaborate fixtures, the sumptuous natural materials. Her friend had exquisite taste, and the money to indulge her knack. "The house is spectacular, as you well know."

Alex's smile was mischievous. "I was just curious, seeing as you've barely taken your eyes off Greg Healey since you arrived."

Lana blushed, resisting the urge to seek him out. "I didn't even ride with Greg, Alex. Don't make a big deal out of the fact that I invited him."

"So what's really going on with the two of you?" Alex asked, sipping from a mixed drink.

If Lana knew herself, she'd be tempted to tell her best friend. Christmas Eve night had been magical, not to mention exhausting. Greg had left the next morning after daybreak, limping slightly. Lana had drifted through the day in an endorphin-induced haze. He had called twice during the week, both times when she'd been out, but had left brief messages of no consequence. Still, the sound of his voice had sent her pulse racing. And every night after she'd closed the shop, she'd invented a reason to step out onto the balcony for a few minutes, reveling in the remote but delicious possibility that his eyes were on her.

"Lana?"

She jerked back to the present. "What?"

Alex tsk-tsked. "You've fallen for him, haven't you."

After looking around to make sure they were out of earshot of everyone else, she smiled sheepishly. "That depends. What was it like when you fell for Jack?"

A dreamy look came over her friend's face. "Oh, I merely thought about him every waking second, and the sight of him made me forget my name."

Lana winced. "I was afraid you were going to say that."

"I knew it! It's about time you fell in love."

"Shh! Keep your voice down!"

Alex grinned and did a little dance that Lana attributed to the rum in her cola. Then her friend stopped, mid-jig. "But what does this mean for the rezoning proposal?"

Lana studied her coffee-stained fingernails. "We agreed not to see each other until after the vote on the rezoning proposal, to avoid any appearance of impropriety. We're meeting with Ms. Wheeler the day after tomorrow to review all angles of the proposal and to submit our final arguments." Then she sighed. "But to be honest, Alex, I've been thinking for some time that Greg's plan is the best chance the Hyde Parkland area has for resurrection."

Alex's eyes widened. "But your arguments against the development were so convincing."

She shook her head. "My arguments were based on historical factors with a dozen variables that differ from this situation. My projections could be wrong. I think I was more fired up by the way the proposal was being railroaded through than by the proposal itself."

"Are you sure Greg hasn't influenced you to change your mind?"

She nodded. Not directly, anyway. But how could she explain that she'd begun to see him in another light, not just as a money-hungry landowner trying to take advantage of his tenants? She admired the quiet wisdom he exuded. And any man who had made love to her as tenderly as he had... Well, in a word, she trusted him. Incredible, but true. "Greg and I haven't talked about the project since—for a while. In fact, the couple of times I tried to bring it up, he changed the subject. He has no idea I'm leaning in favor of his proposal."

"So have you told the other shop owners?"

She nodded. "We met twice this week to talk about the state of the neighborhood, which is rapidly declining. The truth is, I don't know if Greg's plan will work, but like it or not, his is the only plan that's being funded. If the shop owners negotiate a delay or a compromise, I'm afraid we're simply postponing the inevitable."

"So just like that, you're going to give in?"

"Alex, I know when to surrender."

"Then is now a good time to tell you that I agree with your new stance completely?"

Lana gaped. "But all along you've been saying—"

"That I would be there for moral support. Personally, I think Greg Healey is the best chance the Hyde Parkland area has to survive."

She put a hand to her temple. "But you enlisted Ms. Wheeler's help for the shop owners."

Alex nodded. "She and I both believe that even the best ideas need to be challenged in case something better evolves."

Lana swallowed. "So you think Greg's plan is best."

"I'd prefer that some of the retail landscape be left intact, but the residential zoning is badly needed."

Jack was headed their way, looking as if he wanted to talk to his wife about something. Alex's hand was warm when she gave Lana's arm an affectionate squeeze. "We'll talk about this more later, okay?"

Lana nodded, feeling powerless. Her best friend, the council president, Greg—they'd all been humoring her? Pretending to consider her concerns when the decision had already been made? Her skin tingled with embarrassment and hurt. She realized Greg had no intention of their picking up where they'd left off after the rezoning project was decided. The rezoning project had *already* been decided.

Across the room, Greg was talking to a sleek redhead, an employee of Alex's who tossed her hair to effect. The cat-and-mouse game that Lana and Greg had been playing since she'd arrived had seemed playful and proprietary at first, but now seemed immature and manipulative. She took a deep drink of cranberry juice and grenadine, pursing her mouth and swallowing tightly. She glanced over again at Greg and the redhead—it looked like the cat had found the catnip.

"Lana!"

She conjured up a smile at the sound of Will's happy voice. He and Annette walked toward her, Annette clinging to his arm possessively. They looked adorable. "Hi, you two. Having a good time?" If nothing else good came out of this fiasco, at least *they* had found each other—a small miracle, really.

Will nodded and Annette squealed. "Isn't this a gorgeous house?"

"Absolutely," she agreed, taking another drink.

"Why aren't you with Gregory?" Will asked with a little frown.

Her pride smarting, Lana pointed. "Gregory is occupied."

The couple turned to look at Greg and the she-cat.

Will's frown deepened. "But he's supposed to be nice to *you*, Lana. We talked about it."

She frowned. Greg had talked to Will about their relationship? "What do you mean, Will?"

The big man was agitated now. "Gregory said he was going to be nice to you to win you over. Now he's messing things up."

A tiny alarm sounded in the back of her mind, but Lana laid a hand on his arm. "Calm down, Will. What do you mean 'win me over'?"

But Will looked confused, his eyes wide and troubled. Greg must have noticed Will's body language because he broke away from the woman and moved in their direction, his face a mask of concern. "Is something wrong, Will?"

"You're not being nice to Lana," he accused loudly.

From the shocked looked on Greg's face, she gathered Will rarely raised his voice.

"What are you talking about?" Greg asked, clearly puzzled.

Will shook his finger. "Shame on you, Gregory. You said you were going to be nice to Lana to win her over to your side—"

Her heart shivered and shrank. She took one, two steps backward.

"—but you're over there being nice to someone else. Are you shutting down that other lady's business, too?"

The expression on Greg's face when his gaze met hers

could have best been described as guilt, pure and unadulterated guilt.

The picture was suddenly so clear. He'd slept with her to neutralize her opposition to the project. The outcome had already been decided, but he must have wanted to be certain she wouldn't pose a problem. Or maybe he saw the conquest as a bonus. Through the metallic hum in her ears, Lana heard a *thump* and felt moisture on her leg. She looked down and stared at the growing stain of cranberry juice on the expensive handwoven sisal. Alex would kill her for ruining her brand-new carpet.

In the midst of the small commotion that ensued, Lana slipped through the crowd toward the door. She didn't look back.

24

"MESSAGE ONE…Lana, it's Alex. Why did you leave in such a hurry last night? Call me."

"Message two…Lana, it's Greg. I need to explain about the things Will said last night. Call me."

"Message three…Lana, it's Mother. I'm back from the cruise. Call me so I can tell you all about it, dear."

"Message four…Lana, it's Greg. I went by the shop today thinking I'd find you there, but saw you were closed for New Year's. Please call me when you get this message."

"Message five…Lana, it's Alex. I went by the shop today thinking you might be open, then swung by your apartment, but you must have been out. I wanted to let you know that Buckhead Coffee has decided against renting space in Tremont's. And I want to find out how you're doing. Call me when you get in."

Lana set down her blue helmet, ruffled her hair and pushed a button to delete all the messages.

"Where have you been all day?" Rich asked, strolling into the living room.

"Oh, just riding around, looking for a new location for the coffee shop."

"Find anything?"

She shook her head. It had seemed like a good idea, but her heart wasn't in it—like looking for a new home when you truly loved the one you were already living in.

"Your phone has been ringing off the hook," he said. "Sorry we got separated last night at the party. I didn't even realize you'd left."

"I should have told you. Did you have a good time?"

The smile on his face was answer enough, but he nodded.

"I met some interesting people. Did you and Greg cut out early?"

"No," she said with a shaky smile. "Just me. I spilled my drink all over myself, and decided to leave before the night got any worse."

He angled his head at her. "Lovers' quarrel?"

"We're not lovers," she amended, then shrugged nonchalantly. "He was only being nice to me to win me over to his side of the rezoning project." She couldn't even say his name.

Rich made a rueful sound with his cheek. "How do you know that?"

"His brother told me."

"Is his brother trustworthy?"

"The man couldn't tell a lie if he wanted to."

"So you were under the impression that Greg was looking for a relationship when you slept with him?"

Lana shucked off her black-and-white spotted coat and hung it on Harry's obliging shoulder. "No. But I thought...I mean, I was hoping..."

"That he would fall in love with you and change his mind?" he asked softly.

She bit into her lip and blinked back hot tears. "Ridiculous, isn't it?"

"Not really. Like I said, you want to believe that people have good motivations. It's kind of refreshing."

Lana walked to the kitchen and filled her teakettle with water. "But it hurts," she murmured.

"So, you love this guy?"

She studied the water rushing into the kettle. Making tea was such a soothing process. "I think I must, or else I wouldn't feel so lousy." Her laugh was humorless. "I've been alone most of my life and liked it that way. But now..."

"Everything's different?" He sat on a stool and leaned in to the counter. "When do you see him again?"

"Tomorrow morning we're meeting with the president of the city council to talk about the rezoning proposal for the last time before the council takes a vote."

"Sounds tense."

She shook her head. "I'm tired, Rich. I don't have the money, or the influence, or the energy. It's easier just to give people who have money what they want and get out of the way. I'd have been better off if I'd never fought Greg Healey. He's going to win, anyway, and all I'll have to show for it is a bankrupt business and a broken heart."

He cracked a tiny smile. "There's a country-western song in there somewhere."

She smiled in spite of herself, grateful that Rich had come into her life. "Will you watch the water while I change?" But her feet dragged during the short walk to her bedroom. She kept reliving the scene last night at the party, the look on Greg's face. She felt so…foolish. She'd been falling in love with the man, and he'd probably been laughing at her the entire time. Her face burned when she thought of her research and the notebook of ideas that he'd probably found laughably simplistic.

She'd obviously set her life goals too high—a good relationship with her parents, her own business…Greg. Time to regroup. Tomorrow she would find out how long she'd have to transfer out of business, and would start hitting the Help Wanted ads.

A wry frown curved her mouth. Back to the classifieds, where this whole miserable mess had started.

"ARE YOU MAD AT ME, Gregory?"

Greg lifted his eye from his telescope. He'd hoped to catch a glimpse of Lana today—maybe smiling or giving some indication that she didn't hate him as much as he thought she did—but he'd given up and turned his attention to Orion, the Hunter, featuring the red star of Betelgeuse. He sighed at the anguished look on his brother's face. "Of course I'm not mad at you."

"Annette said I stuck my foot in your mouth."

"I'm starting to like Annette," Greg murmured.

"Did I ruin things between you and Lana?"

"Nope," Greg said, dropping into an overstuffed chair. "I did that all by myself."

"Don't you like Lana?"

He pressed his lips together, then nodded. "Yeah, I like her a lot."

"Do you love her?"

Greg swung his head around in surprise. "I, uh…it doesn't matter. She doesn't feel that way about me."

"How do you know?"

"How could she, after what I'm about to do?"

"Close her shop?"

He nodded.

"But do you have to close her shop?"

"We've been through this, Will, and the money—"

"Isn't Lana more important than money?"

Greg blinked. Will had never interrupted him before. *Never.* "I—"

"Gregory, I'm not always going to be around to take care of you, you know."

Greg's eyebrows lifted.

"So if you love Lana, you'd better find a way to get her to love you back."

Greg felt his jaw loosen. Will was giving *him* relationship advice?

"And as far as the business goes," Will continued, "Daddy left me half, didn't he?"

Incredulity gripped him. Will had never shown an ounce of interest in the company. Was he threatening to *veto* Greg's decision?

"Look into your heart, Gregory, and do the right thing."

"LET'S TRY TO KEEP this brief," councilwoman Wheeler said with a smile as she closed her office door. "A few weeks ago I charged the two of you to come up with a compromise on the Hyde Parkland revitalization project—a plan that would please the landowner and the existing merchants. Were you able to reach a compromise?"

"No," Lana said without looking in Greg's direction. Her skin tingled at his proximity. She had a death grip on the bag that held his repaired jacket, which she intended to throw in his face at an appropriate time. Hopefully soon. She wanted to get this over with, quickly. "But the merchants—"

"Yes," Greg cut in. "I'll be presenting a compromise to the city council next week which I think will please all parties."

Lana swung her head to narrow her eyes at him. "Is this another trick?" she murmured, breaking her vow not to speak to him.

"No. Just hear me out."

"We're listening, Mr. Healey."

He opened his briefcase and withdrew a foldout poster. "These drawings are a little crude, but basically the modified proposal details the development of a village in the Hyde Parkland area."

"A village?" Lana parroted.

He nodded. "Structures that would house a store on the first floor, and living quarters for the business owner above."

"Like an old-time village," Wheeler said, obviously warming to the idea.

"Exactly," Greg said, nodding enthusiastically. "If two blocks of Hyde Parkland were developed in this fashion, then most of the retail landscape could be retained, and more businesses would be attracted. Food shops, hair salons, service businesses—we would cater to the small business owner who wants the convenience of being close to his or her shop. When everything is renovated, it'll be the best of the old and the new—sidewalks, parks, lampposts, awnings."

Lana could only gape.

The councilwoman hummed her approval. "Well done, Mr. Healey, Ms. Martina. Much better than leveling blocks and starting over. I knew you could come up with something if the two of you worked together. I assume you have a developer who's interested in executing the plan?"

"The primary developer pulled out when I presented this idea, but I have two smaller companies who are interested. The time line will be longer than we previously discussed— maybe as long as three years."

"What's three years?" Wheeler asked. "We're talking about the future of downtown Lexington."

"My feelings exactly," Greg said.

Lana's head was spinning. She certainly couldn't deny the attractiveness of the idea—a village atmosphere would be the perfect solution for the neighborhood. But why the sudden change of heart?

She met his gaze, knowing her confusion was clear. He stared back, his eyes shining with what seemed like regret, or guilt.

There was a knock on the door, and someone who needed to speak with the councilwoman appeared. "I'll be right back," Ms. Wheeler promised, then left them in an awkward silence.

Lana squirmed on the hard chair, afraid to look at him, afraid to get drawn in again by what she wanted to see.

"I'm sorry about the other night," Greg said softly. "I can imagine what you must think of me."

"Good," she said. "Then I don't have to tell you."

"I want to see you again."

Her breath froze in her chest. A blip of happiness at his request was overridden by the memory of the past couple of days. Greg was too easy to love, and he'd never feel the same way about her. "No," she said, shaking her head. "We're too different, Greg, and—"

"I love you."

She gripped the edges of the chair to steady herself, and her pulse. "What?" she croaked.

"I love you. I want us to be together."

Lana stood abruptly, making a chopping motion with her hand. "I'm not having this conversation." She blinked furious tears. "You get me down here, knowing I'm expecting the worst, then spring this idea on me, which is pretty good, but you could have had the decency to share it earlier, and now you've decided that you love me and that we should be together, and you think you can just snap your fingers, and I'll come running?"

A little frown marred his brow. "Is that a question?"

"I'm out of here."

"Lana—"

"Don't," she said, raising her hand like a crossing guard. Her tears were falling freely now. "You've put me through a lot the past few weeks. Excuse me if I don't want to be manipulated anymore." Remembering the jacket, she flung it at him, then walked to the door, wiping her eyes. "Give my apologies to Ms. Wheeler."

LANA LAY on the beanbag chair, looking up at the ceiling, enjoying the floating sensation. She hadn't been able to go back to the shop after the meeting, so she'd called Alex and apologized for ruining the rug, which led to a crying jag, then had spent the afternoon in the beanbag, replaying what Greg had said during the meeting. *I love you. I want us to be together. I love you. I want us to be together. I love you. I want us to be together.*

Together, how? Together, dating? Together, live together? Together, married?

"What am I going to do, Harry?" she asked her sidekick, who was dressed again in his striped pajamas. "The man scares me. I've known him for a few weeks, and he completely wrecked my life."

Harry grinned.

"I was willing to let him bulldoze my coffee shop because I trusted him so much to do what was right."

Harry grinned.

"Do you think if he were in a similar situation, he'd be willing to make such a big sacrifice for me?"

Harry grinned.

"But if I give up now, I'll never know."

Harry grinned.

"You're right!" she cried, and grabbed the doll to give him a smooch on the cheek. Then she picked up the phone with a shaky hand. She'd dialed three numbers when she glanced toward the balcony and an idea took root. With a sudden burst of energy, she slammed down the phone and went to the bedroom for supplies.

GREG DROPPED onto the foot of his bed to remove his shoes. What a day. What a disconcerting, chaotic day. The meeting with Wheeler, the phone call to turn down the job offer, the hours-long staff meeting to outline the new, more relaxed, company policies.

It had been a big decision to give up the chance at criminal law, but Greg had taken Will's words to heart. Not only was Lana more important to him than money, but she meant more to him than a job in the courthouse.

But the satisfaction of making decisions and setting the wheels in motion was tempered by his disappointment over Lana's reaction to his proclamation. He was a proud man. Words like *I love you* did not spill out of his mouth easily. Call him vain, but he'd expected a better response.

He closed his eyes. Complicated. He'd fallen in love with a complicated woman. He didn't know how, but he was going to wear her down. He was going to, as Will said, find a way to get her to love him back.

Will. He laughed. What a surprise his brother could be.

Greg pushed himself to his tired feet, peeled off his shirt, then splashed his face with cold water. Moving slowly— damn, he was feeling old—he spun the telescope around, pointing it northwest in the falling dusk, hoping for a good view of Cassiopeia, the Queen. The constellation was dim but visible, and promised a brighter show later in the month. Whistling tunelessly, he spun the telescope toward the sky-line, more out of habit than out of hope. When he focused on her apartment building, he lifted his head, squinted, then looked again. Something was draped across her balcony. A sheet. A sheet with lettering.

He adjusted the power of the lens, then refocused. Yes, it was a sheet with...a message. His heart beat faster as he linked the large, black letters into words. He read them out loud. "'Complicated...woman...seeking...single...male.'"

Greg's heart vaulted in his chest.

Epilogue

"WHAT ARE YOU going to do with Harry?" Greg asked, draping his arm around the grinning doll's shoulders.

Lana straightened from packing a box and smiled. "Alex is getting me the address of the Valentine sisters. We knew them in college, and Alex thinks they're both still single. One of them will be the lucky recipient of Harry."

Greg scratched his head. "What happens when everyone is eventually married?"

She frowned. "Well, if statistics bear out, someone's bound to be single again sometime."

He walked over and gathered her in his arms. "Not you, Mrs. Healey."

She laughed. "*Lana Healey.* It still sounds so strange."

"But good," he murmured, nuzzling her cheek. "Will and I had a discussion about that very thing right after he met you." He laughed. "Of course, at the time he thought *he* would marry you."

"I can't imagine him with anyone but Annette."

"And I can't imagine me with anyone but you."

A little thrill raced through her at the sight of the love in his dark eyes. Lately he looked years younger, his features more relaxed, his mouth more apt to smile. Lana sighed. "I love our life. You, husband, were brilliant on TV last night. Alex says your company is bound to win all kinds of awards for engineering such an innovative revitalization plan."

"We still have a long way to go."

"You're off to an impressive start." She angled her head at him. "You're so…persuasive when you want to be. You would've made a great criminal lawyer."

A tiny smile softened his mouth.

"Did you ever think about it?"

"Oh, once or twice," he said, then shrugged. "But it just wasn't my cuppa...Joe."

He pulled her into his embrace and she buried her nose in his soft sweatshirt. Holy happily-ever-after. Here was the male she'd been seeking all along.

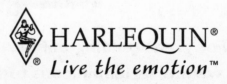